Available in July 2010
from Mills & Boon® Blaze®

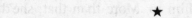

TWIN TEMPTATION

"Who are you and what are you doing in my bed?"

The note of command in Jase's voice snapped Maddie out of the trance she'd fallen into ever since he'd pulled back and she'd looked into those mesmerising blue-green eyes. A moment ago, she'd been sure he was going to kiss her again. And she'd wanted him to. More than that, she'd willed him to. But he hadn't. And now he seemed to be focused on getting answers. OK, maybe he had a right. But so did she.

She squirmed backwards, intending to get out of bed. But she was naked. Sweeping her hand beneath the covers, she searched for her tank top. Without success.

"I'm still waiting for an answer."

TWIN SEDUCTION

She wanted to taste him. She had to taste him.

As if he'd read her mind, he turned his head until his lips were just brushing hers. For a moment, she hesitated and she sensed that he was hesitating too. She was tempted to open her eyes, to try to see what he was thinking. But she knew, didn't she? And if she opened her eyes, he might disappear.

She couldn't let that happen. She had to keep him here. Tightening her fingers on his face, she drew him closer and whispered, "It's all right. I want you to kiss me."

First published in Great Britain 2010
Harlequin Mills & Boon Limited,
Eton House, 18-24 Paradise Road, Richmond, Surrey TW9 1SR

Twin Temptation © Carolyn Hanlon 2009
Twin Seduction © Carolyn Hanlon 2009

ISBN: 978 0 263 88136 3

14-0710

Harlequin Mills & Boon policy is to use papers that are natural, renewable and recyclable products and made from wood grown in sustainable forests. The logging and manufacturing processes conform to the legal environmental regulations of the country of origin.

Printed and bound in Spain
by Litografia Rosés S.A., Barcelona

TWIN TEMPTATION
BY
CARA SUMMERS

TWIN SEDUCTION
BY
CARA SUMMERS

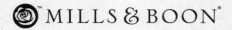

MILLS & BOON

Cara Summers has written more than thirty books. She has won several awards, including an Award of Excellence, two Golden Quills and two Golden Leaf Awards. Last year she was also honoured with a Lifetime Achievement Award for Series Storyteller of the Year from *Romantic Times BOOKreviews*. She loves writing for the Blaze® line because it allows her to write so many different kinds of stories – from Gothic romances and mystery adventures to romantic comedies. When Cara isn't creating new stories, she teaches in the writing programme at Syracuse University.

TWIN TEMPTATION

BY
CARA SUMMERS

To my daughter-in-law Mary Plante Hanlon –
who just happens to be a twin!

You're also an amazing mother and a good friend.
I love you!

Prologue

IT WAS a mansion right out of the books she'd read as a child—*Jane Eyre, Rebecca, Wuthering Heights.*

Those were Maddie's first fanciful thoughts when she stepped out of the limousine and got a good look at the massive stone structure. Gray and solitary, Ware House soared up three stories and boasted three turrets and a roof edged in carved stone. *A man could have tucked away a crazy wife in any of those turrets,* she thought a bit giddily. And the fact that the sky was lead colored and cast the front of the house in shadows only added to the illusion.

But this wasn't some English gentleman's mysterious country home. It was the Long Island residence of the Ware family. And she was about to meet them for the first time.

A tall man who reminded her a bit of Michael Caine answered the door. He had to be a butler. His posture was ramrod-straight and his face totally expressionless. But Maddie thought she saw a flicker of surprise in his eyes before he stepped aside and said, "Come in, Ms. Farrell. Let me take your bag." Just as if she were a regular visitor.

Still hesitating on the threshold, Maddie firmly reined in her imagination. It had rocketed into overdrive from the moment she'd received the phone call from that attorney, Edward Fitzwalter III. Gripping the strap of her purse more tightly, she stepped into the dark-paneled foyer. Since she wasn't at all sure of her welcome, she'd asked the limo driver to wait for her. She had an escape plan in place.

"This way." The man turned and started down a wide hallway. "The family has already gathered in the library."

Family.

The knot of anxiety in Maddie's stomach tightened. She was about to meet a family she hadn't known existed until two days ago. Up until that time, she'd believed that she was the only daughter of Mike Farrell, a successful cattleman whose ranch was located about an hour north of Santa Fe. Mike had been an only child, the last of a line of ranchers, and Maddie was supposed to carry on his legacy. All her life she'd believed her mother had died when she was a baby. That was the story her father had told her…and since he'd passed away a year ago, there was no way she could ask him why he'd lied.

And according to the gruff-voiced attorney who'd called her two days ago, her father had indeed lied to her. And it had been a whopper. All these years, she'd had a mother she'd never met—a mother who'd been raised in this house and who just happened to be renowned Madison Avenue jewelry designer Eva Ware.

Oh, Maddie was very well-acquainted with the professional persona of Eva Ware. She'd studied the woman's designs ever since she was in junior high and had first dreamed of creating her own line of Southwestern-style jewelry. Her father had known of her admiration for Eva Ware Designs, but he'd never once mentioned that the woman she'd so admired was her mother.

She was still struggling with the idea when the lawyer had told her that five days ago Eva Ware had been struck down by a hit-and-run driver.

No.

The news, shocking and unexpected, had set her head spinning. Sitting down hard on a nearby chair, she'd tried to gather her scattered thoughts as the voice on the other end of the phone droned on. Maddie had caught bits and pieces— her mother's request...fly to New York...reading of the will...claim her inheritance.

Inheritance? She'd still been grappling with that word when the attorney had sprung another one on her. A real kicker. *Sister.* In addition to having a mother she'd never been aware of, she also had an uncle, a cousin and a sister— an identical twin, Jordan Ware.

For a few moments, the attorney's voice had become nothing more than a buzz in her ear. She had a sister? A *twin* sister she'd been separated from since birth?

No. That was straight out of the plot a Disney movie—two of them, in fact. *The Parent Trap* had been one of her favorite films when she'd been a child. A memory flooded her mind of watching the older Hayley Mills/Maureen O'Hara version of the film with her father when she'd been nine or ten. *And he'd never breathed a word.*

No. She couldn't accept that. Her father couldn't have lied to her all these years. Gripping the phone as if it were a lifeline, Maddie had stood up and interrupted the man on the other end of the line. "You're lying. If this is some kind of hoax, or some kind of scam you're running, it won't work."

In a calm voice, as if he'd fully expected that reaction, he'd told her to call information and get the number of the Fitzwalter and Carnegie law firm in New York City and then to call it and ask for Edward Fitzwalter the Third. Pacing back and forth in the living room of the ranch house, she'd debated following his instructions for a full fifteen minutes.

She couldn't, she wouldn't believe that her father had lied to her. The man who'd called her had to be some kind of a con artist. Pausing at the window that filled one wall of the living room, she'd stared out at the land that had been in the Farrell family for five generations.

And then she'd thought of Daniel Pearson, the local real estate agent who'd been pressuring her to put the ranch on the market for the past six months. It was pretty common knowledge that ever since her father had died, she'd been struggling to run the ranch and still grow her jewelry design business. Could Mr. Fitzwalter's call be connected to that? But how? If she had in truth inherited something from her mother, it would only help her hold on to the ranch and carry on her father's legacy.

In the end, Maddie had succumbed to curiosity and a gut feeling that the man who'd called her was indeed Edward Fitzwalter the Third. And he had been. More than that, he'd been patient and kind enough to repeat all the information he'd given her before. He'd even told her that he'd booked an airline ticket for her on the following day. All she had to do was go to the airport and pick it up. A limousine would be waiting for her at JFK airport and it would take her to the Ware family's estate on Long Island for the official reading of the will.

Maddie dragged her thoughts back to the present when the butler man stopped in front of a double set of paneled doors. Nerves jittered in her stomach as he turned the handles and pushed them open.

Still on the threshold, Maddie let her gaze sweep the room. It was cavernous. Three of the four walls were packed with books. The scent of leather-bound volumes mixed with the aromas of lemon wax and lilies from the vases scattered throughout the room. Four narrow stained-glass windows took up the wall directly across from her and let in a gloomy light.

And she was stalling. Screwing up her courage, she stepped into the room and one by one met the gazes of the five people who'd turned to stare at her. She began with the mustached and balding man who was sitting at the desk. She guessed him to be Edward Fitzwalter the Third. Then Maddie looked to the three people seated to the left of the desk.

Fitzwalter had given her a thumbnail sketch of each member of the Ware family. The handsome gray-haired man in the red leather chair must be Carleton Ware, Eva's brother. Carleton wasn't involved in Eva Ware Designs. He ran the Ware Bank, which had been established by his great-great-grandfather and whose branches were scattered all over Long Island. Carleton, his wife and son resided year round at Ware house. Eva, though she'd inherited half of the house, had lived in New York City. Carleton's hazel eyes were cool and assessing as they met hers. The younger man seated to his right had to be her cousin Adam. He had wavy, chestnut-colored hair that he wore long and tucked behind his ears. His brown eyes held hostility.

According to Mr. Fitzwalter, Adam was very involved in Eva Ware Designs. He'd gone to work there right after college and he'd been trained by Eva from the time he was in high school. Fitzwalter had described Adam's mother Dorothy, the woman seated to Carleton's left, as a society matron with a very active social life both on Long Island and in Manhattan. She served on several charitable boards and spearheaded fundraisers for institutions like the Museum of Modern Art. She was a tall slender woman with a model's figure. Her gaze was several degrees cooler than her husband's, and superiority radiated off her in waves. Dorothy Ware's perfectly coiffed brown hair and impeccably tailored black suit had Maddie feeling underdressed.

Growing up on a ranch had never allowed her much time

to spend on fashion, and her khaki slacks, embroidered denim jacket and leather ankle boots were perfectly acceptable business attire in Santa Fe. She shifted her attention to the small Chinese man sitting farthest away from the attorney. He had to be Eva's longtime assistant, Cho Li. He wore his long black hair pulled back into a ponytail, and it had begun to thin on top. According to Fitzwalter, Cho Li had been with Eva even before she'd opened her Madison Avenue store. When he nodded his head and smiled at her, she finally found the courage to turn to the one familiar face in the room—Jordan Ware's.

On the long flight from Santa Fe, she'd imagined this moment so many ways. But she hadn't anticipated the swift punch of recognition in her belly or the instant sense of connection. For a second she couldn't quite catch her breath. It wasn't like looking in a mirror—not exactly. In the dove-gray suit and turquoise blouse, Jordan looked as though she'd stepped right out of a fashion magazine, making Maddie feel even more the country bumpkin.

But the woman who rose from her chair and faced her now had the same blue-violet eyes and the same facial features. And though Jordan Ware wore her hair in a chic style that framed her face in a sleek curve and Maddie wore hers in a long braid down her back, the color was the same honey gold.

Everything that Fitzwalter had told her on the phone was true. For the first time, Maddie felt the reality of that sink in. She really did have a twin. A sister.

Maddie had no idea how long they stood there in that freeze-framed moment taking each other in, nor how many times Fitzwalter cleared his throat before the sound penetrated.

It was Jordan who moved first, rushing forward and taking

Maddie's hands. Looking into her sister's eyes, Maddie saw her own feelings mirrored—curiosity, excitement and fear. Would they have anything in common? Would they even like each other?

"Welcome," Jordan whispered.

For the first time since she'd entered the mansion, some of Maddie's tension eased.

Then Jordan turned to the others in the room. "Uncle Carleton, Aunt Dorothy, Adam, Cho Li, this is my sister, Madison Farrell."

For a moment there was silence in the room.

Cho Li was the first to speak. Stepping forward, he bowed. "It is my pleasure to meet Eva's other daughter."

Maddie found herself bowing back.

Then Carleton rose from his chair. "You'll have to forgive us, Madison. The shock of my sister's death coupled with the news that she had a second daughter tucked away all these years in Santa Fe…well, we're still trying to absorb everything. Until you walked into the room right now, I'm not sure that any of us really believed what Edward had told us. Dorothy, Adam and I want to welcome you to Ware House."

Adam and Dorothy, their eyes cool, remained silent.

Grateful that she didn't have to walk into the room alone, Maddie let her sister lead her to a chair.

As they sat, Jordan sent her a smile and a conspiratorial wink. "Once the will stuff is over, we'll talk."

1

JORDAN WAS still holding Maddie's hand when Fitzwalter opened the file in front of him and lifted the papers. Out of the corner of her eye, Maddie studied her sister. Jordan's lips were pressed tightly together and her eyes were totally focused on the attorney.

She was nervous, Maddie realized. And it went beyond the fact that they'd just met. Since her chair was located at the right of the desk and angled in a way that gave her a view of the other occupants of the room, she took a moment to study the other Wares.

With his arm draped casually over the back of his wife's chair, Carleton appeared to be perfectly at ease. But there was a stiffness in his shoulders and his mouth that belied that. At first glance Dorothy appeared to be bored, but her hands were clasped so tightly in her lap that the knuckles had turned white. Adam sat poker-straight, his hands gripping the arms of the chair.

If there was one thing her father had taught her it was the importance of reading facial expressions and body language. According to Mike Farrell, it was an essential skill in all kinds of activities—from playing poker to bargaining for a price on his cattle. Two things were clear to Maddie. The other Wares' nerves were stretched as tightly as Jordan's were. And the family didn't seem to be very close-knit.

Why not? Had any of them provided support for Jordan as she'd dealt with the terrible news of her mother's death? Something tightened around her heart as Maddie recalled the numbness and the piercing pain she'd felt when her father had passed on a year ago. That had been sudden too. She still felt guilty about the fact that she'd been at a jewelry show in Albuquerque, and Mike had suffered a heart attack while he'd been out checking some fences. Alone. Cash Landry, her neighbor and lifelong friend, had found the body the next morning.

Since she'd never met Eva Ware, Maddie couldn't know exactly what Jordan was going through. Was there someone her sister could turn to as Maddie had been able to turn to Cash? As Edward Fitzwalter donned a pair of reading glasses, she linked her fingers with Jordan's.

Gripping the papers in two hands, Fitzwalter peered over his glasses, first at the Wares and then at Jordan and Maddie. "My plan is to make this brief. If any of you want a complete draft of the document including all the whereases, wherefores and so on, I'll be happy to make a copy. But if no one objects, I'll get right to the bequests."

Silence reigned in the room. When the attorney shifted his gaze back to the paper he was holding, Jordan's fingers tightened on Maddie's. She was worried about the contents of the will. Maddie's heart sank. Of course she would be. So would everyone in the room. The only reason that Eva Ware would have requested her presence today was because she'd left something to the daughter she'd deserted. And that something would be taken out of someone else's inheritance.

"To my personal design assistant Cho Li, I leave the sum of five hundred thousand dollars so that if he chooses, he can retire. But my hope is that he'll remain in his position until the new owners of Eva Ware Designs get up to speed."

Dorothy Ware whispered something to Adam and he

jerked forward in his chair. "New owners? Who are the new owners?"

Fitzwalter glanced up. "I'll get to that part sooner without interruptions."

Adam opened his mouth and then shut it.

"To my brother Carleton, I leave all of my shares in the Ware Bank. I hope that he'll finally make the fortune he's always believed I've prevented him from getting."

Maddie noted that the news didn't seem to make Carleton very happy.

Fitzwalter cleared his throat. "The rest of my estate, including stocks, bonds, cash, Eva Ware Designs, my fifty-percent share of Ware House on Long Island and my New York City apartment, I leave to my two daughters, Jordan and Madison, to be shared equally. It is my sincere hope that they will run Eva Ware Designs together. However, there is one requirement. They must change places and walk around in each other's lives for three consecutive and uninterrupted weeks beginning within seventy-two hours from the time this will is read. If they refuse to fulfill the terms as I've set them out or if they don't stay the course for three weeks, my fifty percent of Ware House will go to my brother Carleton. Everything else, including the business and my apartment, will be sold and the profits divided equally among all my surviving relatives."

Jordan's mouth dropped open, and this time Maddie thought she knew exactly what her sister was feeling.

Dorothy touched Adam's arm and he leapt out of his chair to plant both of his hands on the desk inches from the papers that Fitzwalter had just set down. Anger radiated off of him in waves, causing Maddie to sit forward in her chair.

"That can't be right. I'll be the chief designer now that Aunt Eva is gone. She should have put me in charge. She always led me to believe that one day I would step into her shoes."

"He's right." Dorothy Ware spoke for the first time. Unlike her son's, her voice held no trace of emotion.

Unperturbed, the attorney met first Dorothy's and then Adam's eyes. "I assure you that Ms. Ware's will is in perfect order."

"No," Adam argued. "She had to have changed her mind since she wrote this. She was…busy. She just didn't have the time to see you about it."

Fitzwalter slipped the papers back in the file. "She came to my office two weeks ago and reviewed every detail."

Adam's face had colored to a deep red, and for a moment, Maddie was afraid that he was going to shove the oak desk over on the attorney when Carleton's voice intervened. "Adam."

The younger man drew a deep breath and backed away from the desk. As soon as he was a safe distance away, Maddie turned to Jordan and spoke softly. "I don't get it. Why wouldn't she leave the business to you—and why would she want us to change places after she's kept us apart all these years?"

"I've got a theory about that." Jordan glanced over at the other Wares who'd gone into a small huddle.

Maddie looked too. Dorothy was speaking, but her voice didn't carry, and from the expression on Adam's face, he didn't like what he was hearing.

"Let's blow this scene," Jordan whispered. "I've got a reservation at an inn in Linchworth. I wanted you to myself and I thought staying over would be better than battling rush-hour traffic back into the city."

They'd made it nearly to the front door when Adam caught up with them. He grabbed Jordan by the arm and jerked her around to face him. "You can't get away with this."

The fury in his voice sent Maddie into action. Enough was enough. She gripped the arm holding Jordan. "Let my sister go."

"What?" Adam sent her a startled look.

Maddie placed both hands on his chest and gave him one hard shove into the wall. "Just because you're frustrated by the terms of your aunt's will doesn't mean you can manhandle my sister. Got that?"

Adam stared at her. "You shoved me."

"I did."

"Adam." The cool tones of Dorothy Ware's voice carried the length of the hallway.

"This isn't the end of this," Adam said as he pushed himself away from the wall and strode back to his mother.

Jordan waited until they'd collected their bags from the butler and run down the steps to the waiting limo. Then she whirled to face Maddie. "I've wanted to give Adam a good shove for years." She pulled Maddie into a hard hug. "I guess I've been waiting for my superhero sister to do it for me."

JORDAN LED the way into the suite she'd rented in the Linchworth Inn. She hadn't said a word to Maddie during the five-minute ride in the limousine. In spite of the distracting and somewhat amusing altercation with Adam, Jordan knew her head was still spinning with the contents of her mother's will. Maddie's must have been too. She'd tried to think, to plan her strategy. But in business, the key to any successful strategy always depended on knowing your audience.

And she didn't know her sister very well at all. Oh, she'd done as much research as she could—first cross-examining Mr. Fitzwalter and then checking out Maddie's Web site. In Jordan's opinion, the Web site needed a makeover, but the jewelry didn't. Her sister had talent. Most of Maddie's work was focused on Southwestern belt buckles, tie clips and pins. The designs were dramatic, the workmanship exquisite, using a lot of turquoise and intricately inlaid patterns. There'd also been a few examples of finer pieces—earrings and bracelets. Perhaps she could use her sister's interest in jewelry design as a bargaining chip.

But she needed to know more. And she didn't have a lot of time. The seventy-two-hour clock was ticking.

Leaning down, she opened the door of a small refrigerator and then glanced back at Maddie standing just inside the room, taking it in.

Jordan let her own gaze sweep the area. It was a small suite with two bedrooms. The sitting room had dormer windows with lace curtains and was furnished in antiques. Two chintz-covered love seats faced each other across a small coffee table with a marble top.

"I can offer you some wine. Mom and I always liked white. But I can order up a bottle of red or something else if you'd prefer."

"White's fine," Maddie said.

Silence stretched as Jordan uncorked a bottle of chardonnay and filled two glasses. Stalling. That's what she was doing. What in the world was the matter with her? She was hardly ever at a loss for words.

"This is a lovely room," Maddie said.

Jordan glanced around again and felt her throat tighten a little. "Mom liked it. We used to stay here whenever we had to visit Uncle Carleton and company." She would never stay here again with her mother. But she couldn't let herself think about that right now. Not yet.

"You didn't stay at Ware House?"

Jordan handed her a glass and waved her over to one of the love seats. "The atmosphere there has always been a bit frigid. And things have gotten worse since I got my MBA and started working at Eva Ware Designs. But it goes back further than that. I don't think that Uncle Carleton and Mom ever saw eye to eye even when they were kids. The friction escalated when my grandfather died. Uncle Carleton is one of those old-fashioned men who believes that the oldest son should inherit everything outright. Thank heavens, my grandfather didn't agree. When he died, he divided everything up between Mom and Uncle Carleton—even Ware House. She took her half of the stocks, bonds and cash and invested everything in her design business. She was able to move into the Madison Avenue store."

"Smart decision," Maddie said.

"I agree, but the other Wares didn't."

Maddie grinned suddenly.

"What?"

"What you called them—the other Wares. I'd already started thinking of them that way."

Smart, Jordan thought. Her twin was perceptive. That could work in her favor. Tucking her feet underneath her, she leaned back. "As a sort of peace offering, Mom agreed to let Uncle Carleton, Aunt Dorothy and Adam live in Ware House. She got to use the place for business parties, and she agreed to attend any social gatherings that had to do with Ware Bank."

Maddie sipped her wine. "You said the friction's gotten worse since you went to work for Eva Ware Designs."

"Because before that, Adam thought he had a clear shot at taking over the business one day. He'd been there for three years before I joined the company. He's a brilliant designer. Mom was very aware of that. His parents were disappointed with him because he didn't go into banking, so I think he feels he has to succeed. Aunt Dorothy certainly does. Plus, he has a temper."

"I noticed. He may be a fine designer, but he doesn't have your background in business."

Jordan studied her for a moment. "How do you know that?"

"I looked you up on the Internet. A bachelor's degree from the Wharton School, an MBA from Harvard. Very impressive."

Slowly, Jordan smiled. "Touché. I visited your Web site. It needs some work, by the way. But the jewelry doesn't. What I saw was beautiful."

Setting her glass down, Jordan leaned closer and fingered one of the earrings Maddie was wearing. The silver had been configured into fragile lace surrounding a clear turquoise stone. "This is quite lovely. Mom was always looking for turquoise of this quality."

"She should have come to New Mexico."

Jordan met her sister's eyes and saw a hint of pain that she totally understood. "She was in New Mexico when she gave birth to us. I badgered Fitzwalter until he showed me our birth certificates. We were born in Santa Fe."

"She was at the ranch?"

"I don't know about that, but she was definitely in Santa Fe."

"She should have come back."

"Yes, she should have. And our father should have come here. I'm not sure we'll ever find out why they didn't. Or why they separated us."

"Why does she want us to switch places?" Maddie asked. "You said you had a theory about that?"

"I do. I got it the moment I searched your name. I think she wants you to get an in-depth experience at Eva Ware Designs because she wants you here."

"No. That's impossible."

"I know her. She was a very focused woman. I'm sure she was keeping track of your career, and if and when something happened to her, she wanted you to see what she'd created—to know that you could share in it."

"But why didn't she contact me? Why put it in her will?"

Jordan rose and began to pace. "I've asked myself those questions over and over. She could have been afraid to contact you after all these years. The other thing about her is that designing jewelry was her driving passion." Jordan waved a hand. "She gets—used to get—totally lost in her work. Other things got pushed to the back burner."

"Why three weeks?"

"She probably thought twenty-one straight days would do it." Jordan's smile was wry. "When she first started at her gym, her trainer told her that doing something every day for three weeks was what it took to build a habit."

"But that's…crazy. And it's not fair to you."

"It's not crazy if you knew Mom. Eva Ware Designs meant everything to her." Jordan paced to one of the windows before she turned back. "That's why we have to talk about the will."

Maddie rose also. "Yes, we do. I want you to know that—"

Jordan held up a hand. "Stop right there. Since I'm the oldest, I get to go first."

Maddie's eyes narrowed. "How do you know you're the oldest?"

Not a pushover either, Jordan thought. "I told you I'd seen the birth certificates. I beat you into the world by almost four minutes." Impulsively, she strode over and grabbed Maddie's hands. "I want you to please hear me out before you say a word."

Maddie nodded.

Jordan dropped her sister's hands, whirling away. "I've

been trying to figure out how to say this in a way that will convince you."

"You don't have to."

Jordan glared at her and pointed a finger. "You said you'd hear me out."

"Okay. Okay." Maddie threw both hands up and sat back down on the love seat. Watching her sister made her think of her father. That glare Jordan had just given her had been pure Mike Farrell and her father had always paced when he was trying to talk her into something. But she'd just wanted to make it easy for Jordan. The money, the house, Eva Ware Designs—none of it belonged to her. It should have all gone to Jordan. How could her sister want her to take it?

"I know it's crazy." Jordan sat back down on the love seat. "The thing is, we have to agree to the terms of the will."

Maddie simply stared at her. "How can you possibly want that? It's not fair."

Jordan ran her hands through her hair. "I know it's not. It's horribly unfair. Switching places will be complicated, to say the least. But I don't see what else we can do. I saw on your Web site that you have a jewelry show in Santa Fe in four days."

Maddie did, and in all the turmoil of the last few days it had entirely slipped her mind. "I can't miss it. I've worked for months on those designs, and it's essential that I be there to make contact with new buyers."

"No worries. I should be able to handle the show. I've done several with my mother. Marketing the product is the part of the business I'm good at."

"But there are other things—problems at the ranch," Maddie said.

"What kind of problems?"

Maddie raised her hands and dropped them. "I'm just not the best rancher in the world, and I've been struggling to fill my father's shoes and at the same time grow my jewelry business. My neighbor, Cash Landry, has been helping me, but I can't let that go on forever. And there's this real estate agent, Daniel Pearson, who wants to sell the ranch for me."

Jordan moved back to the couch. "You can't be seriously thinking of selling?"

"No." But Maddie felt a stab of guilt. Wasn't that exactly what she was thinking of doing? After all, she hadn't given Daniel Pearson a flat-out no. And here her sister was, arguing that they keep her mother's business going. How could she even think of doing less for her father?

A gleam of interest leapt into her sister's eyes. "Maybe I can help."

"How?"

"Three weeks will give me a chance to get a feel for what the problems are. Not that I'm a rancher—but I do have those business degrees. Plus I'll bring a fresh perspective. How many people did you tell about flying east for the reading of the will?"

"No one. My foreman Mac and Cash were both away, driving my cattle to market, then meeting with future buyers in Albuquerque. They're not due back for a few days yet. Cash's foreman comes over to tend the horses and check on things when Cash is gone. But I didn't even have a chance to tell him I was leaving."

Jordan took a thoughtful sip of her wine. "I'll bet I could pretend to be you at the jewelry show without anyone knowing the difference."

"Pretend to be me? You're serious about this."

"Very." Rising, Jordan began to pace again. "I know buyers prefer to talk to the designer, and I've learned enough at Eva Ware Designs to masquerade as you. If the ranch is deserted right now, I'd only have to pretend when I go into Santa Fe. You won't be able to pass yourself off as me, of course. The other Wares already know who you are, and so does Cho Li. I'll let everyone else at the Madison Avenue store know. You'll just have to do my job for three weeks."

"But I have no idea what you do for a job."

"My schedule is on my laptop. And Cho Li will fill you in. He's been working with Mom for as long as I can remember. Is there someone who can fill me in at the ranch?"

"Wait. You're going too fast." Maddie felt as if all her objections were being picked off like ducks in a shooting gallery. "I haven't told you all the problems at the ranch. It might not be safe for you there."

"Why not?"

"There've been some incidents of vandalism lately. Minor ones at first—cut fences, graffiti on the bunkhouse. Cash was pretty sure it was the Trainer twins. Joey, the older one, had a sort of a crush on me. But lately, the incidents have gotten more serious. Due to a cut fence, some of my cattle strayed, and we couldn't round them up in time to drive them to market. And a couple of weeks ago someone doctored the feed in my stables and I nearly lost my horse."

"You called the police?"

"They couldn't do much except file a report."

Jordan joined Maddie on the couch. "I'll be careful. Besides, it'll be as safe for me there as it would be for you."

"I can handle myself."

Jordan's eyebrows shot up. "So can I. After all, I've been raised in New York City. But there's something you should know about the store. A month ago Eva Ware Designs was robbed. Someone broke through the security codes and took approximately one hundred thousand dollars' worth of jewelry from the main salon. The police are still looking into it. But in the meantime, the security codes have been changed. And it happened after hours, so you should be fine."

Maddie was more worried about Jordan than she was about herself. But Cash was due back from the cattle drive in another few days, she told herself. She could call him and tell him to look out for Jordan.

Suddenly, nerves tightened in her stomach. Was she really thinking of switching places with her sister?

"Is there anyone at the ranch who can fill me in on what I have to do?"

"Cash and my foreman can when they get back from the cattle drive."

Jordan narrowed her gaze on her sister. "This Cash—are you and he…seeing each other?"

Maddie shook her head. "No. We grew up together. He runs the ranch next to mine. My father and his father had this idea that someday we might fall in love and join the two ranches. But it hasn't happened. Cash and I are just friends."

"Good. Do you think I could fool him into thinking I'm you if he shows up at the ranch?"

Maddie studied Jordan. "You're really getting into the idea of masquerading as me."

"It's a practical approach. I won't have to explain to everyone about the will and switching places. Do you think your cowboy neighbor will buy it?"

Maddie considered, then shook her head. "He's pretty astute."

Jordan grinned at her. "Really? I love a challenge. We'll have to write things up for each other, and we'll keep in touch by phone. That's what the girls did in *The Parent Trap*, and they were only half our age."

"You saw that movie?"

"Only about fifteen times. When I was little I remember watching it with Mom."

"There's one big difference between us and *The Parent*

Trap girls. They switched so that they could get to know the parent they were separated from. We're not going to be able to do that."

"No." Jordan sat down next to Maddie again and took her hands. "We're not. I wish with all my heart that there was a way for you to meet our mother."

The understanding she saw in her sister's eyes helped ease the tightness in Maddie's throat. "Same goes about our father."

"Maybe switching places is the only way we have left to get to know them. We can do this."

Maddie searched her sister's face. "I don't understand. Why do you want to? And why would you want to share your inheritance with me?"

Jordan stared at her. "Because you're my sister, and because our mother wanted it this way. However late it is, she must have had some regrets about separating us, and this is her way of making sure we get to know one another."

"There are other ways for us to get to know one another."

"Maddie, you heard the terms of the will. If we don't change places for three weeks, Eva Ware Designs will be sold. I can't stand by and let that happen. Our mother worked her whole life to create it, and I can't let it be destroyed. I want her legacy to live on. No matter what it takes, we have to fulfill the terms of the will. Please say you'll do it."

Maddie wasn't an impulsive person—at least she didn't think of herself that way. But she could sympathize with what Jordan was trying to do. It was the same thing that made her want to hold on to the ranch and keep it going so that her father's legacy would live on.

And Jordan was right. If she did switch places and step into Jordan's job at Eva Ware Designs, it would provide her with the only opportunity she might ever have to learn more about the woman she so admired. The woman she'd never met. And it was just possible that she could find out why their parents had decided to separate them. Hadn't that been one of the primary questions on her mind since she'd accepted the truth of what Edward Fitzwalter III had told her during that phone call?

"Okay. I'll do it."

"You will?"

Maddie nodded.

"Thanks." Jordan gave her sister a quick hug. "Okay. Now for the practical matters. You can live in my apartment, of course. I have a roommate, Jase Campbell. He was a few years ahead of me in college and we shared an apartment there. He moved into my place when he came to New York and started up his security firm. The arrangement has become sort of permanent."

"Are the two of you involved?"

"No, we're strictly pals. He's like a big brother to me. But you probably won't even run into him. He's off on some mysterious job in South America. I can't even reach him by cell. I haven't been able to even tell him about…"

When Jordan suddenly stopped talking, Maddie took her hands.

"I don't think it's totally sunk in yet that she's gone," Jordan said.

Maddie handed Jordan her wine. "How could it? You had to identify the body." Fitzwalter had told her about that. "Then there were the funeral arrangements and to top it off you find out you have a sister you never knew about."

Jordan met her sister's eyes. "When you lost your father, how long did it take for you to accept it?"

Maddie sighed. "I think I'm still trying to adjust." She raised a hand to her sister's cheek. "But I think that visiting the ranch may help you. There's a kind of serenity there."

"I'm glad I have you, Maddie Farrell."

"Ditto."

"Well." Jordan drew in a deep breath and let it out. "We only have about seventy hours left. We'd better get started."

Maddie blinked as Jordan rose, strode to a desk and pulled out her laptop.

"There's a lot we have to learn before we switch lives."

2

IT WAS nearly midnight when Jase Campbell descended the steps of a small private jet at LaGuardia Airport. After nearly a month in the bowels of the steamy Amazon jungle, he welcomed the stiff breeze that had made their landing a little rough. New York City's humidity level couldn't even begin to compete with what he'd been experiencing.

The Cessna was the third plane he'd been on in the last twenty-four hours and the only one that had provided any amenities. Thanks to Federman Corporation, the company that had hired him as a consultant in their efforts to free three hostages, he'd been able to shower, shave and even change his clothes—luxuries that he'd sorely missed.

The one thing he hadn't been able to do was catch much sleep. The last days of the mission were still too fresh in his mind. It had only been partially successful—one of the men hadn't made it out of the jungle. Each time he closed his eyes, his mind would run through the other options he might have used, other tacks he might have taken with the captors.

He needed sleep, Jase told himself as he strode up the steps of the terminal building. Thank heavens his apartment was only a thirty-minute cab ride. And at this hour of the night, Jordan would be sound asleep. That would save him from being cross-examined on what he'd been doing for the last three and a half weeks.

Jordan and he had been friends since they'd been under-graduates together at Wharton. His lips curved as he recalled exactly how they'd met. He'd been a senior and she a freshman. Off-campus housing had been at a premium, and they'd arrived to view an apartment at the same time. They'd each wanted to sign a lease, so the landlord had suggested they flip a coin. Jordan had flatly refused, claiming that her luck was abominable. Instead, she'd suggested that they share the place and split expenses.

For Jase it had been an ideal solution. Unlike a lot of the trust-fund students, he'd come to Wharton on a scholarship. Jordan had drawn up a set of rules to follow so that they kept out of each other's way. The list with its bullets and high-lighted passages had been Jase's introduction to the highly organized world of Jordan Ware.

And though she was a very attractive woman, their rela-tionship had never progressed down a more intimate path. Instead, she'd become like a sister to him, competing against him for grades, nagging him when he'd gotten so wrapped up in a project that he'd forgotten to keep in touch with his family and even criticizing his selection of dates. In Jordan's opinion, Jase had a tendency to attract what she'd termed "psycho babes."

Jase's lips curved at the memory. The first thing he'd done when he'd left the navy and decided to set up a security business in New York City was to call Jordan. His goal had been to enlist her help in finding an apartment. Instead, she'd suggested he move in with her. If it didn't work out, he'd at least have more time to find a place of his own. That had been a year ago, and so far everything had gone very smoothly. Jordan, who'd worked for her mother's jewelry design studio since she'd gotten her master's degree, had put him in touch with a few clients, and he'd even done some work for Eva

Ware Designs. In fact, there was a job he'd left hanging when he'd taken on the hostage-negotiation project.

Once he entered the terminal, Jase glanced around, spotted a secluded niche and headed toward it. Before he caught a cab, he needed some privacy to check in at his office. He'd been out of contact for far too long, and his patchwork of odd flights home hadn't allowed any calls. Even at this hour, there'd be someone at Campbell and Angelis Security picking up the phone. With any luck, it might even be Dino Angelis, his partner of six months.

Sure enough, someone answered on the second ring.

"Campbell and Angelis Security."

Jase frowned as he tried to place the familiar voice. Not Dino. His partner's voice was much deeper and he didn't speak with a drawl. But it couldn't be who he thought it was. His brother D.C. was currently serving with the military police on a second tour of duty in Baghdad.

"D.C.?" Jase asked.

"At your service. Where are you? Dino and I were getting worried."

"I'm at La Guardia. What are you doing in my office?"

"Since I got here two days ago, I've been holding down the fort and helping Dino out. Got my leg busted up a little, and the army decided that I should take some leave time while I got it back in shape."

Jase frowned. "How bad is the leg?"

"Nothing that can't be fixed."

"Does Mom know?"

"I spent a week in Baltimore and let her pamper me. I gained at least five pounds while I checked out Darcy's latest boyfriend."

Some of Jase's tension eased. If his brother had the time and energy to torment their kid sister, then he must be on the mend.

"Are you going to tell me how bad the leg is?"

"You're as bad as Mom. It's going to be fine. With any luck I'll be back in Iraq by Christmas."

Jase didn't see that as lucky. But he knew he'd gotten as much out of D.C. on the subject of his injury as he was going to. "Let's go back to my first question. What exactly are you doing in my office? And where's Dino?"

"I came to pay you a surprise visit and Dino offered me a temporary job. Right now I believe he's at his fiancée's apartment."

It was thanks to Dino's pretty fiancée Cat McGuire that Jase had been able to persuade Dino, his old navy buddy, to become his partner last December.

"Where are you staying?"

"Dino fixed me up temporarily with an empty apartment in their building. Not that I get to spend much time there."

"Business is good, I take it?" Jase asked.

"So good that you've been missed, bro."

More of Jase's tension eased. If Campbell and Angelis had to take on some extra help, Dino couldn't have found a more perfect person than D.C. His brother had a sharp and inventive mind and the kind of intuition that made for an excellent cop. Unable to stop himself, he yawned hugely. What he needed even more than a good night's sleep was work. One lesson he'd learned when he'd been working special ops was that the best way to dim the images from the previous operation was to immerse yourself totally in a new one.

"By the way, your roommate, Jordan Ware, has been trying to contact you. Mom told me that the two of you are sharing an apartment again."

"When? What did she want?"

"About a week ago. She talked to Dino and asked him to pass on a message to contact her if you called in."

Once again, Jase frowned. Jordan never called him at

work. Then he pushed the small worry aside. No doubt she'd called the office because his cell phone had been worthless where he'd been for the last few weeks. At any rate, he'd see her sometime tomorrow.

"Hold down the fort. If Dino calls in, tell him I'll be in the office tomorrow afternoon." Once Dino brought him up to speed on all their active files, he knew exactly which case he would start on. He'd promised Eva Ware that he'd look further into that break-in and robbery at her Madison Avenue jewelry store. In his opinion, it had to have been an inside job, and that worried him a bit.

"Right now, my aim is to crash for at least twelve hours," Jase said, then added, "Thanks for covering."

"I live to serve."

A BIT DIZZY from sleep deprivation and jet lag, Maddie let herself into Jordan's Soho apartment. During the last few days, she'd managed to lose all sense of time. The only reason she knew that it was shortly after midnight was because she'd asked the cab driver who'd driven her from JFK.

According to her estimate, she'd spent nearly eighteen of the last forty-eight hours on an airplane. Severe thunderstorms in the midwest had delayed her flights both to and back from Santa Fe. She'd barely been at the ranch long enough to pack what she thought she'd need for a three-week stay in New York. Jordan, the lucky girl, had only had to make one flight.

In the very short time they'd spent together before Jordan had insisted she immediately fly back to the ranch and set things in order for the switch, Maddie had learned that her sister was a ruthlessly organized woman who gathered data, made lists, assembled files and was quite used to having her "suggestions" followed. Had Eva Ware been like that? Maddie wondered. Would she ever know? She hoped that Jordan was right and that by switching lives each of them would come to know the other parent better. But she was beginning to feel a sense of loss that she would never have a chance to talk to Eva about her design process.

And Jordan would never hear Mike Farrell's laugh.

Not that her sister wouldn't discover as much as she could about the ranch and their father. The woman was meticulous. She couldn't think of one thing that had escaped Jordan's attention. Jordan had even suggested that since Maddie possessed very few outfits appropriate for the city and Jordan experienced the same lack of wardrobe for ranch life, they could borrow clothes from one another and cut down on what they needed to pack. Maddie figured that was Jordan's subtle way of letting her know not to appear at Eva Ware Designs in her jeans and boots.

Yawning hugely, she muscled her suitcase through the door, then sagged against it for a moment, nearly paralyzed with exhaustion.

"Just a few more minutes," she muttered. "You can do it."

She groped blindly along the wall until she located a switch. The muted light from a Tiffany-style lamp allowed her only a shadowy impression of the living room—stained-glass-fronted bookcases flanking a brick fireplace, an antique desk, a comfy-looking leather couch and a flat-screen TV. The furnishings with their mix of the feminine and the masculine suddenly reminded her about Jordan's roommate—Jase Campbell.

The man's image slipped instantly into her mind. Jordan had provided her with photos of everyone she might possibly meet during her three weeks in New York, and she'd been reviewing them one by one on the long flight from Santa Fe. From the moment she'd glanced at Jase's picture, she hadn't quite been able to get him out of her mind.

Maddie recalled Jordan describing Jase as a big brother. They'd been friends ever since they'd roomed off-campus together in college, and when he'd left the navy to start up his own security firm here in New York, he and Jordan had hooked up as roommates again. Jordan's description of her relationship with Jase Campbell could have fit her own relationship with her neighbor, Cash.

However, as Maddie had studied Jase's photo, her response to him had been anything but sisterly. He had a strong face, lean with sharply defined bones. And though he wore a jacket and a tie, he didn't look quite…tamed. Perhaps it was the longish, windblown hair that hinted at a streak of recklessness. Or maybe it was the eyes. She was baffled by the fact that every single time she'd closed her own eyes and tried to sleep on the plane, she'd thought of those angled cheekbones, the strong jawline and firm lips.

And each time his image had popped into her mind, her palms had tingled with the desire to touch his face. When she'd imagined herself doing just that, a heat had begun to build inside her. She'd even foolishly given into an impulse to run her fingertips over the image in the photo—touching first his mouth, then the rest of those sharp features.

When the heat simmering inside her had rushed to her face, she'd glanced nervously around to see if anyone had witnessed what she'd done. To her great relief, everyone within sight had been sleeping. Something she herself should have been doing. But instead of slipping the photo back into the file, she'd glanced down at it again.

And traced her fingertips over it once more. Her desire to touch the image, to touch *him* was baffling…and unprecedented. She'd experienced a purely chemical reaction to a man before. But no man's photo had ever affected her in such a physical way.

Perhaps it was because she hadn't had any sex in a while. During the past year, between the plans she had to expand her jewelry design business and the extra work she'd had to take on at the ranch, she simply hadn't had the time. Or the desire.

Yawning again, Maddie struggled against a huge wave of exhaustion as she turned and dragged her suitcase down a narrow hallway. The effort of placing one foot in front of the other almost defeated her.

Probably her whole odd reaction to Jase Campbell's photo was due to sleep deprivation and the emotional whirlwind she'd been caught up in during the past few days. When she met him, she'd find him a pleasant man, and her unusual and highly sensual response to his photo would turn out to be much ado about nothing.

Not that meeting Jase was a sure thing. Jordan had mentioned that for the last three and a half weeks he'd been out of the country and out of contact. So she had no idea when he'd be back.

Maddie stopped short at the first door she came to, not sure if she could take another step. If she didn't find a bedroom soon, she was simply going to curl right up on the floor. She bit back a groan when the door to her left opened onto a tiny bathroom. Putting all her effort into the move, she half stumbled into the room directly across the hall. There was just enough moonlight pouring through the window for her to make out a bed. Not bothering to turn on the light, she shoved her suitcase against the wall. Unpacking would have to wait. Using the foot of the bed as her guide, she moved to the side nearest the window and pulled the drapes. Then she stripped down to her tank top and panties. With the last bit of energy she could summon up, she tugged just enough of the covers back to slip beneath them. The moment her head touched the pillow, she fell abruptly into sleep.

IT WAS nearly one when Jase let himself into the apartment. At some point during the taxi ride from La Guardia, the adrenaline that had fueled him for the last few weeks had drained away as surely as if someone had pulled a plug. Setting his duffel down, he shut the door and locked it. Then, without turning on the lights, he made his way to his bedroom, shed his clothes, eased back the covers, and climbed in. Sleep claimed him before his head settled fully into the pillow.

THE DREAM came slowly, slipping into his mind as a lover might slip into his bed. A woman, soft and warm, was nestled against him. With lazy pleasure, he let himself drift in sensations, absorbing each one. The press of a palm against his chest, the silky length of a thigh trapped between his. And the scent—he had to draw her closer to place it—he'd caught that fragrance before on drives through the country—a mix of wildflowers and sunshine.

When she sighed and snuggled closer, Jase ran a hand from her shoulder to her thigh and back again, absorbing the contrasting textures of smooth, soft skin and rougher cotton. Desire tugged at him when she pressed against him and her hands moved to slide over his back.

Drifting with the sensations, Jase touched his mouth to her temple and slipped his hand beneath her shirt. The throaty sound of pleasure she made when he cupped her breast had the tug of desire turning into a sharp pull. Nothing would be simpler than to give in to the temptation to shift her onto her back and make a place for himself between her legs. To thrust into her and lose himself in her.

But equally tempting was the thought of exploring her more thoroughly and discovering how far the dream would take him. Slowly, he ran his hand from her breast down the taut length of her torso, over that firm, narrow waist until he could slip his fingers beneath the band of her panties. The soft moan she made when he found her heat and began to stroke her urged him to take his mouth on a leisurely journey over her face from her temple to jawline and back again. Her breath was hitching now and she began to arch faster and faster against his hand. Desire pulled even more strongly against his control. But first…first, he wanted to take more, to give her more. He traced her mouth with his tongue, then began to tease her lips with his. When he finally allowed himself to fully taste her, the flavor was so sweet, so potent, that he thought he might never get enough. Taking the kiss ever deeper, he slipped two fingers into her and felt her soar.

THE ORGASM shot through Maddie in one glorious wave after another until she was sure she was going to drown. When she finally surfaced, she had only a few moments of respite, barely enough time to register what that clever mouth was doing to hers before those long hard fingers began to move inside her again. She'd never dreamed anything this vividly before. Even as the incredible pressure began to build once more, other sensations bombarded her. She inhaled his scent, something dark and male. The sharp nip of his teeth on her bottom lip. And his body—it was so hot that she felt as if it was branding her at each and every contact point.

The second orgasm was sharper than the first, and before it peaked, he was there, just where she wanted him to be, thrusting into her. And then they began to move together.

Yes, she thought as she wrapped arms and legs around him. This was what she wanted—this wild, fast race. This was what she'd always wanted, and no one had been ever able to give it to her before. Holding on for dear life, she rode the climax, rode him, until they leapt over that final crest together.

3

MADDIE DRIFTED UP slowly through layers of sleep, trying to hold on to each one. The dream she'd been having was so wonderful, so real. With each breath, she drew in her lover's scent—potent, male. His arm held her close, and she felt the length of that hard body pressed against her. The sensations were vivid enough to have her blood heating all over again.

She wanted more than anything to sink back into the dream so that he would touch her, tempt her, tease her again. But there was light beyond her closed eyelids and she could hear muted sounds. Motors rumbling, brakes squealing...

Traffic? Frowning, she struggled to remember.

The insistent beep of a horn, louder than the others, triggered a kaleidoscope of memories. Her sister, the terms of her mother's will, the endless series of plane rides, the detailed files Jordan had insisted she study.

The horn blasted again.

She definitely wasn't in Kansas anymore. Nor was she at the ranch in Santa Fe. She was in her sister's New York City apartment. The last thing she clearly recalled was dragging her suitcase into the closest bedroom and falling into bed.

That's when the dream had begun—and her lover had joined her. And he was still with her. The smooth taut skin on his shoulder was warm beneath her hand, and above the sounds from the street below she heard the steady rate of his breathing.

Was she still trapped in her dream?

A mix of emotions swept through her—fear, excitement. Anticipation? Gingerly, Maddie opened one eye. There was just enough light seeping through the slit in the drapes for her to see that her senses were not deceiving her. Her hand was indeed resting against a man's shoulder. And the rest of her body was totally wrapped around his. Everything about him, the hint of stubble on his chin, the strength of the arm wrapped around her waist—even the erection growing harder against her stomach—seemed to be very real.

Squeezing her eye shut again, Maddie drew in a deep breath and let it out. One thing she'd learned growing up on her father's ranch was that you had to face facts. So the dream lover who'd joined her in bed last night had been real. *Was* real.

And facts had to be dealt with. A cut fence had to be mended ASAP so cattle didn't stray. Still, a real lover in one's bed instead of a dream one presented more complicated problems—one of them being that she didn't seem to want to disentangle herself from him. What she was tempted to do more than anything else was to push him onto his back and taste him again, touch him again.

Not happening, Maddie lectured herself. And why was she even considering the possibility? No man had ever made her feel the way this one had. Ever. And she didn't even know who he was.

Stiffening her resolve, Maddie slowly drew her head back and this time she opened both eyes. Even in the dim light, recognition was instantaneous. After all, she'd memorized those features—the angled cheekbones, that strong chin, the firm lips.

At some point in the night, she'd made love to Jase Campbell. And he'd made love to her.

Heat shot through her. But it wasn't from embarrassment.

Her body was on fire because she wanted to repeat the experience. Right now.

Not going to happen. She had to get a grip. And she had to get out of this bed. If she could just get away before he woke up, maybe she could pretend that the night they'd just shared hadn't happened. If he brought it up, she'd just tell him that he'd been dreaming. That would be one way to mend the fence. Maybe the only way.

Dragging her eyes away from his face, she focused on ungluing herself from him. But her body rebelled, refusing to take orders from her brain. Her hand seemed permanently affixed to his shoulder, her fingers splayed. Maddie faced another fact—she didn't want to stop touching him, and she knew that if her hand moved at all, it would slide down to wrap itself around the length of his erection which was pressing against her stomach more insistently with each passing moment.

When he sighed, his breath feathered along her temple, and his arm tightened more firmly around her waist. Maddie barely managed to stifle a moan. He was waking up. Once he did, the pretend-it-never-happened scenario would no longer be an option. But it wasn't panic she was feeling, it was a wild thrill.

What was happening to her? Why was she reacting this way?

He stirred again. Maybe there was still time to slip away. She focused all her effort on pushing against his shoulder. It was like trying to dislodge a boulder. Then she felt his whole body stiffen. Before she could blink, he slipped a hand beneath her chin and tilted it up so that she had to meet his eyes.

She was aware of several things at once. The body pressed against hers had grown harder, and the heat that seemed to leap from him to her was enough to melt her bones. But it was his eyes she couldn't look away from. The photo hadn't captured the color. The mix of dark green and blue reminded her of some of the rarer turquoise stones she worked with.

Then suddenly his gaze narrowed, darkened, and his fingers tightened their grip on her chin. Their mouths were close, nearly touching. If either one of them moved... Just anticipating the brush of those lips against hers, Maddie felt her brain cells wink off one by one. *Yes.*

No. Jase felt his mind clouding over and fought to clear it. He was holding a woman in his arms, and he had no idea how that had come to happen.

The last thing he remembered was reaching his apartment and falling into bed. Memories began to trickle in. That's when the dream had begun. There'd been a lover waiting for him, hungry for him. What she'd ignited in him had gone beyond anything he'd ever experienced before. Desire had never been so compelling. Passion had never been so consuming.

But what had happened during the night hadn't been a dream.

It was morning now. The sound of traffic floated up from the street below. Her hair was just brushing his chin, her breath was hot on his chest. She was very real. And so was the fresh surge of desire he was feeling. A thin stream of sunlight fell across the delicate line of her cheekbone.

If he gave into temptation and traced a finger along the path of the light, he knew just what her skin would feel like. Soft as the petal of a flower, warm...

Jase clamped down on the heat that shot through him. She wasn't a dream. This was a real woman. And she was wrapped so tightly around him that he wasn't sure he could ever break free.

And he still wanted her. Desperately. Her mouth was so close, barely a breath away. His leg was already nestled between hers, and he could feel that she was ready for him. More than anything, he wanted to sink into her, to lose himself in her again.

No. Gripping her shoulders, Jase disentangled himself, pulling back far enough so that he could see her face clearly for the first time. It was the eyes that drew his attention first. They were dark—a deep blue that bordered on violet. And they were very familiar. The color, the shape—they were Jordan's eyes. And she had Jordan's face. But... Narrowing his gaze, he studied her more closely.

"You're not Jordan."

He would have staked his life on it. Her scent was all wrong. Jordan always smelled like some exotic French perfume. This woman smelled like wild flowers and sunshine. And Jordan's hair wasn't long enough to pull into a braid.

Then there was the chemistry. As long as he and Jordan had known each other, there'd never been any spark between them. And *spark* was far too tame a word for what he'd experienced with this woman.

Those eyes, damn them, were still clouded with desire. The pulse at the base of her throat was hammering. Whoever she was, he could have her again. Right now. Jase wasn't usually one to throw caution to the winds either in his personal or his business life. But for one precarious moment, he was outrageously tempted.

He tightened his grip on her shoulders. "Who are you and what are you doing in my bed?"

THE NOTE of command in Jase's voice snapped Maddie out of the trance she'd fallen into ever since he'd pulled back and she'd looked into those mesmerizing blue-green eyes. A moment ago, she'd been sure he was going to kiss her again. And she'd wanted him to. More than that, she'd willed him to. But he hadn't. And now he seemed to be focused on getting answers. Okay, maybe he had a right. But so did she.

She squirmed backward, intending to get out of bed. But she was naked. Sweeping her hand beneath the covers, she searched for her tank top. Without success.

"I'm still waiting for an answer."

The sudden hint of humor in his tone had her chin lifting and her temper surging. This was not funny. "What I was trying to do here was sleep. When I arrived last night, I was nearly blind with exhaustion and I simply got into the wrong bed. Do you know how many planes I've been on in the past three days?"

"Not as many as I have, I'll wager. Is this what you're looking for?"

She glanced up barely in time to catch the tank top he tossed her. Then her gaze focused on him. Big mistake. He was lying on his side now, his head propped on his hand. The sheet barely covered him to the waist.

An intense wave of hunger shot through her. Why was this happening to her? Baffled, she tore her eyes away from him, slid off the side of the bed, and tried to cover as much as she could with the tank top. If she wanted to think clearly, her best bet was to get out of the room. But the door was on his side of the bed. There was just no way to make any kind of a dignified exit.

"You haven't answered my first question. Who are you?"

She shot him a narrow look. He was definitely enjoying this. "I'm Jordan's twin sister and Eva's other daughter."

It gave her some satisfaction when a bit of the humor faded from his gaze.

"You'll have to do better than that. Jordan doesn't have a twin."

"Yes, she does. Turns out we were separated when we

were babies, and neither one of us knew anything about it until four days ago."

For two full heartbeats silence stretched between them. He was studying her as if he were weighing what she'd told him. And she couldn't take her eyes off him. Worse, she could feel her brain cells start to click off again. She had to get a grip.

"Where is Jordan?" he asked.

Her chin lifted. "She's at our father's ranch in Santa Fe."

"Why?"

Maddie welcomed the surge of temper. "Look. It's a very long story, and if you were any kind of a gentleman, you'd leave right now and give me a chance to get dressed. Then I'll be happy to answer all of your questions."

He smiled slowly, fully.

Maddie felt the heat shoot all the way to her toes.

"Never let it be said that my mother didn't raise me to be a gentleman."

Maddie stared as he threw back the covers and got out of bed. For the first time, she got a good look at what she'd explored with her hands during the night—the broad shoulders, the strongly muscled back, the bronze skin that ended with a clearly defined tan line at his waist.

And his butt. There were muscles there too. She remembered exactly what they'd felt like beneath her palms, tensing and then relaxing as he'd moved inside her. When he turned, Maddie's throat went dry as fresh need thrummed through her.

"My jeans...ah, there they are." He leaned down to scoop them up. "But these are yours, I believe." He laid her panties on the foot of the bed.

She ignored the panties and focused her gaze on his. He knew exactly what effect he was having on her. Damn him.

Still smiling, he took another step toward her, extending

his free hand. "I'm Jase Campbell, by the way. I'm Jordan's roommate. And your name is...?"

"I'm Maddie Farrell." She sent him a thin smile as she shook his hand. The instant he relaxed his grip, she hooked her foot behind his right ankle, then used both hands to shove hard against his chest. His butt hit the floor with a very satisfactory thud. *There,* she thought. *Enjoy that.*

He grinned up at her. "Nice move, Maddie Farrell."

She snatched her panties off the bed. "I believe you said something about your mother raising a gentleman."

He winced a little. "So I did." He stretched out a hand. "You wouldn't want to give me a hand, would you?"

"Do I look as though I have *stupid* branded on my forehead?"

"No. But it was worth a try." He rose in one graceful movement, but she noticed that he took his time walking to the bedroom door. When he reached it, he turned back. "I'll make us some coffee, Maddie Farrell. Then we'll talk."

For a full thirty seconds after he'd disappeared from view, Maddie didn't move. Because she wanted to run after him? What in the world was wrong with her? The man thought this whole situation had a humorous side to it. Maybe—in a hundred years—she could agree with him.

Biting back a groan, she sank onto the bed. Maybe if she burrowed under the covers, she'd wake up and discover that it was all a dream.

But it wasn't. In a few moments she was going to have to join him for coffee and answer his questions. Besides, she wasn't the kind of person who ran from problems. On a ranch you just couldn't do that.

You grew up around men. You know how to handle them.

All she needed was a plan.

4

JASE LEANED his hip against the counter and sipped coffee. He could hear the shower still running in the bathroom, so he had a few more minutes to figure out what in the hell he was going to do. Usually, he wasn't at such a loss. But the night he'd just spent with the woman who called herself Maddie Farrell had been unprecedented. She'd scrambled his brain.

And she was going to be a problem for him.

For the first few minutes after he'd left her in the bedroom, he'd struggled hard against the urge to forget about the questions he had and just walk back in there, toss her onto the bed and make love to her again. Instead, he'd run water in the sink and splashed it on his face. He might not be a gentle lover, but caveman tactics weren't his style.

Then again, no other woman had ever shoved him onto his ass. His lips twitched at the memory, then he sipped more coffee. He'd told her the truth about his mother. His father, a career army man, had died when he was ten. D.C. had been nine and their sister Darcy had been six. Their mother had gotten a teaching job in Baltimore and had proceeded to raise her children the way she managed her classes—with a firm hand.

Problem was, he didn't want to be a gentleman with Maddie. If he did make a move on her, she wouldn't resist.

Just in those few moments that they'd lain together in his bed after they'd awakened, he'd sensed she was as reluctant as he to pull away. And she was just as curious as he was about what it would be like to make love while they were both fully awake. That made the temptation almost irresistible.

If he joined her in that shower now, they could both find out. In a matter of seconds—perhaps ten to get into the bathroom and another five to strip out of his jeans—he could step under the spray and...

With an oath, Jase set his mug down, then gripped the edge of the counter with both hands. Being this enthralled by a woman just wasn't like him. He couldn't deny that he had a reckless streak. He and D.C. had gotten into more than their fair share of trouble in their teenage years. According to his mother, they were responsible for turning her hair prematurely gray. But college with a major in business and four years in the navy, two in special ops, had pretty much drummed recklessness out of his system.

As he glanced down the hall at the closed shower door, guilt moved through him. Hadn't he already taken enough advantage of her? Sure, he'd been exhausted, sleep-deprived, but the bottom line was that he'd allowed himself to be lulled into making love to a woman he'd found in his bed. He should have fought harder against the dream she'd enveloped him in. Making love to her had been a mistake. A big one.

And he shouldn't have to be fighting so damn hard against the desire to repeat the experience. If she was telling the truth, she was his best friend's sister.

Jase refilled his mug and took a long swallow. Time to step back, look at the big picture and come up with a plan. That was what had saved his life several times during his special-ops missions in the navy.

He should be focusing on what she was doing here, not

joining her in that shower. And what in the hell was Jordan doing on a ranch in Santa Fe? He nearly grinned at the thought. Talk about a fish out of water. From the time he'd first met her, Jordan had been a city girl right down to her weekly manicure and pedicure.

While he'd waited for the coffee to brew, he'd tried to contact Jordan on her cell to check out the twin story, but she wasn't picking up. Then he'd typed *Maddie Farrell* into his laptop.

Madison Farrell was a Southwestern jewelry designer in Santa Fe. In addition to her photo, her Web site featured images of finely carved silver pins, belt buckles and rings, all with a clearly Southwestern flair. When he'd searched Santa Fe's newspaper, *The New Mexican,* he'd found an article praising the intricacy and modern artistry of her designs. Like mother, like daughter, he'd thought. He'd also come across an obituary for a local rancher, Mike Farrell, who'd died a year ago and had been survived by his only daughter, Madison.

So, she was evidently who she said she was, and she looked enough like Jordan to be her twin—but he still had questions—a lot of them.

And until he got some answers, he was going to put any plans for taking Maddie Farrell back to his bed on hold.

MADDIE TURNED a complete circle in the shower and let the hot water sluice over her. Her body ached in places it had never ached before, places where Jase Campbell had touched her. And it felt wonderful.

With a sigh she rested her head against the shower wall. She had to think—and not about Jase. What had happened between them in that bed of his during the night had been crazy. Wonderful. Amazing. But it had been a mistake. And mistakes were for learning, not for repeating.

Waking up beside him had distracted her. Big-time. He didn't even know about Eva's death. Jordan hadn't been able to reach him.

Pouring shampoo into her palms, she lathered her hair lavishly, then rinsed it, wishing she could wash the man right out just as easily as soap. It might not be that simple, but she was going to try. She had to be practical, use some common sense. And get herself back on track.

After all, she only had three weeks to walk around in Jordan's shoes, and she had a lot to do. It hadn't been just to please her sister and fulfill the terms of the will that she'd come to New York, she reminded herself. Before she went back to Santa Fe, she intended to find out everything she could about Eva Ware. If Jordan was right and Eva had been truly interested in a daughter who designed jewelry, why had she waited so long to act on that interest? Too long.

Each time she thought about the fact that she'd never really get to meet or talk with Eva, a little band of pain tightened around her heart.

If she could, she was going to find out why she and Jordan had been separated. The key was there. She was sure of it. Though she hadn't mentioned it to her sister, she had a theory that Eva might have confided in someone that she'd had twins. She'd bet that Cash's father had known. But he'd passed on a year before her own father had.

Getting the answers to her questions and getting to know as much as she could about Eva Ware—those had to be her priorities.

Twisting off the faucets, she stepped out of the shower and wrapped her hair in a towel. Then she swiped the steam off the mirror over the sink and faced her image.

"You have too much on your plate right now to fit Jase Campbell in."

And wasn't it possible that Jase felt the same way about her? After all, he'd been out of the country for over three weeks. He must have a lot to catch up on at his office.

Bending over, Maddie began to towel-dry her hair. The more she thought about it, the more convinced she became that she might have hit on the key to extricate them both from an…awkward situation.

Reason and logic—that was the strategy. After all, she'd grown up surrounded by men—her father and Cash, to name two. The business of running the ranch had always been the men's primary focus. Her father had even missed her first jewelry show because he'd had to meet personally with a buyer in Albuquerque.

Though it had hurt at the time, she'd come to understand his decision. How many times during the past year had she prioritized her growing design business over the ranch? Often enough that Cash was growing concerned. He'd taken over more and more of the work she should have been doing, including driving her cattle to market.

It had helped to talk to Jordan about her concerns that she really couldn't run the ranch on her own. How much longer could she rely on Cash's help? She hoped that Jordan would have some ideas on that score, because she didn't want to have to sell.

Maddie hung up the towel and pulled on the clothes she'd unpacked from her suitcase—her old standbys—jeans and a T-shirt. Then she frowned as she glanced at her image in the mirror. Her problems at the ranch had to go to the back burner for now. Jase Campbell was the big issue she had to deal with. Surely he'd understand that what had happened between them was, no, *had* to be, a one-time fling. A mistake that could not and would not be repeated.

Her frown deepened when she felt the sharp twist of regret.

She wondered for a moment just who it was she was trying to convince that the time they'd spent in Jase's bed couldn't be repeated.

WHEN JASE heard the door to the bathroom open, his first instinct was to turn away. But there was no time like the present to discover just what effect Maddie Farrell would have on his senses after their short reprieve. Her walk was a lot like Jordan's—long purposeful strides—but Maddie's was slower. And he'd never found himself staring at Jordan's legs. He slid his gaze up body-hugging denim and over the white T-shirt that revealed everything about that tight compact body he'd only begun to explore during the night. The clothes were nothing that he'd ever seen Jordan in. Even when she went casual, she looked like a fashion plate.

When Maddie finally came to a stop in front of the island that separated the main room of the apartment from the galley-sized kitchen, Jase shifted his eyes to her face. It was there that he noted the biggest difference between the twins.

He'd accepted the fact that the two women were twins. They had to be. Except for the length of their hair, they might be mirror images of each other. And it was just his luck that he found the single braid that fell over one of Maddie's shoulders sexy as hell. Each time his eyes strayed to it, he felt an urge to loosen it and run his fingers through it.

Tucking his hands firmly into the back pockets of his jeans, Jase transferred his attention to Maddie's other features. Jordan's expression was more animated, and her eyes often held a glint of humor. Maddie, with her chin lifted and her eyes solemn, looked as if she were about to face a firing squad. There was a resolve there that he couldn't help but admire.

The little twist of guilt he felt had him putting himself in her shoes for the first time. She'd come to New York, and as part of her introduction to the city she'd found herself in his bed. And he'd taken full advantage of it. No matter that she'd cooperated fully. Quite suddenly, it became his goal to set her at ease and to wipe that facing-the-firing-squad expression off her face.

"We have to talk," she said.

"We do. How do you take your coffee—plain or loaded?"

"Plain—if that means black."

"Good taste. Jordan barely puts a dollop of coffee in her cream and sugar." He filled a mug and handed it to her. "Do you want an apology for what happened in my bed last night?"

Surprise had her nearly spilling her coffee. Gripping the mug in two hands, she said, "No. Of course not."

"Good." He slid onto one of the stools on his side of the narrow island, keeping his eyes steady on hers. "Because I'm not sorry it happened. Are you?"

"I…" She paused as if to consider the question. "I suppose in a way, I am. Because it complicates things."

"But…?"

Twin spots of heat flared in her cheeks. He couldn't recall Jordan ever blushing.

"But in another way, I'm not sorry. Because I've never… It was…"

He smiled slowly. "Yeah, it was for me too."

She could have evaded his pointed questions. Lied. But she hadn't. His admiration for her shot up another notch.

"While we're on the subject, there's something else I need to ask. Are you protected? I didn't use a condom last night."

Two spots of color reappeared on her face. "I'm on the pill."

"You're seeing someone then?" Jase was surprised at how much he disliked that idea.

"No." Her chin shot up. "Not that it's any of your business."

Relief warred with amusement. She certainly had her sister's temper. He was careful to bite back the grin. "I'm not seeing anyone either."

Her eyebrows shot up. "Did I ask?"

How often had he heard Jordan use that same haughty tone?

"Look." Maddie set her mug down on the countertop and sat on the stool across from his. "I think we need to agree that what happened between us last night was a mistake. And when I make one, I don't like to repeat it."

He narrowed his eyes on her. "Why was it a mistake?"

She braced a hand on the counter, fingers spread. "Because it's a complication I don't have time for. I need to explain why I'm here and why Jordan is in Santa Fe."

Yes, you do, Jase thought. And he was baffled at how her mere presence in the room could distract his mind from that pivotal question.

Maddie drew in a deep breath and let it out. "Jordan told me she hadn't had time to contact you, so I'm sorry to have to tell you that Eva Ware is dead."

Jase's eyes narrowed and something in his gut tightened. "She's dead? How? When?"

"An accident. She was killed by a hit-and-run driver in front of her apartment building a week ago."

An accident? Even as he struggled to absorb what she was saying, he reached for her hand. "I'm sorry."

"Thank you." Maddie linked her fingers with his. "I didn't know her, and now I never will. I'm still trying to accept that."

"How's Jordan?" He couldn't stop thinking that he'd been away. Jordan had been alone.

"I don't think she's had time for the loss to fully sink in. She's been busy handling details—the funeral and then the will. The whole thing will probably catch up with her at the ranch. It's a very special place. I'm hoping that being there will help her."

"Why is she there—and why are you here? Why aren't you together?"

"Because of Eva's will."

Her fingers were holding on to his like a lifeline now. "Tell me everything."

Maddie did just that, beginning with the phone call from Fitzwalter, then the meeting with her sister and the other Wares, the reading of the will and their decision to meet its terms.

"And Jordan's alone at the ranch?"

"Yes." A frown furrowed her forehead. "I'm a little concerned about that. We've had some problems lately—vandalism, and my horses had a close call."

"How so?"

"Someone poisoned their feed, but don't worry—Cash is due back tomorrow."

"Who's Cash?"

"My closest neighbor. We grew up together, actually."

When Jase noticed that his knuckles had turned white gripping the handle of the coffee mug, he set it carefully down on the counter and flexed his fingers. "And you're involved with this Cash?"

"When it comes to the running of the ranch, you could say we're involved. Since my Dad died, Cash is always poking his nose in, making suggestions, offering to do things. He's gotten very protective. The last few days he's been helping my foreman get my cattle to market. He doesn't even know about Jordan or about anything that's happened."

Jase found that he didn't like the idea of some cowboy—childhood friend or not—hanging around Maddie. It was the second time that she'd made him come close to feeling jealous. And he'd only known her—what? A handful of hours?

In the silence that stretched between them, Maddie's stomach growled.

"You're hungry." Jase rose from his stool and pulled the refrigerator door open. Nothing except two bottles of energy water. He pulled them out and set them on the island. "When was the last time you ate?"

Maddie shrugged as she opened one of the bottles. "They served some pretzels when we were stranded for three hours on the runway at O'Hare."

Jase began a methodical search of the cupboards. "Jordan doesn't cook, and she's a regular old Mother Hubbard when it comes to stocking provisions. But she usually keeps a stash of cookies." Giving up on the cupboards, he opened the microwave door. "Aha, success." He pulled out a bag. "Chocolate chip. Will these tide you over?"

Maddie selected one from the stack he piled in front of her. "They're my favorite. I always keep some in my studio at the ranch."

Jase smiled. "Another thing you and Jordan have in common besides temper, I guess."

When she'd finished the first cookie, she began to fiddle with her braid. Jase found himself wanting to reach out and touch it too—instead of asking some important questions. Alarm bells had been going off in his head ever since she'd told him that Eva had been the victim of a hit-and-run driver. Three weeks after her store had been robbed.

"Maddie, do you have any idea why Eva made out her will that way?"

"Jordan thinks that in the event of her death, Eva wanted a daughter with a flair for jewelry design to get involved in her business."

Jase didn't much care for the way Eva had set up her will, but all he said was, "Do you know if anyone knew about the terms of the will ahead of time?"

As she reached for another cookie, she considered the question. Then she shook her head. "They all seemed pretty shocked when Fitzwalter read the will. Except for Cho Li. Besides Jordan's, his was the only friendly face in the room."

"Why do *you* think Eva wanted you and Jordan to change places?"

She set down the cookie. "I'm not sure. But I'm not comfortable with Jordan's theory. I don't like the idea of taking something that belongs to her. I'm hoping that Eva's plan had a broader design and that she wanted Jordan to experience what she'd missed all these years by not growing up on a ranch. While she's out there, Jordan's going to try to see what she can do to help me make the ranch more profitable."

Jase studied her. "The ranch is in trouble beyond the vandalism?"

Maddie sighed. "I'm not the rancher my father was. And I can't help feeling guilty about that."

"Guilt can be hard to deal with."

Maddie's eyes flew to his. After a moment she said, "I'm sorry. All I'm doing is talking about myself. Jordan said that you were away all this time because you were trying to free some hostages. Were you successful?"

"Partially. There were three. We lost one of them."

This time, she was the one who reached for his hand. "I'm sorry."

For the first time since he'd left South America, Jase felt something loosen inside of him. Then he said aloud what he'd been telling himself ever since he'd looked down at the body of the man he hadn't been able to rescue. "The two we did free were a man and his son. They were reunited with the rest of their family in Panama City yesterday."

"Sometimes, no matter what you try to do, you lose someone. For months after my father died, I kept thinking if I'd just been with him—or if I'd just done something differently. Maybe if I'd nagged at him more not to ride out by himself. He had a heart attack while he was alone. If he'd just had someone with him…"

His fingers tightened on hers. "You shouldn't blame yourself."

"Neither should you."

As the silence stretched between them, Maddie became intensely aware of the pull between them. She'd felt it the moment she'd stepped out of the bathroom and started toward him. But now she sensed that it was more than a pull. As she looked into those blue-green eyes, something moved through her. Recognition? How could that be? They were strangers.

Dragging her gaze away from his, she glanced down at their joined hands. His was so large that hers was barely visible. And even though her skin was tan, it was shades lighter than his. They were so different, yet somehow her hand felt just right in his. She might be baffled by it, but she couldn't deny it was true.

"Maddie, I don't think what happened between us last night was a mistake."

Even as she jerked her hand away, she met his eyes again. What she saw had her bones melting. She fought against losing brain cells and swallowed hard. She'd had a clear plan when she'd stepped out of the bathroom. She'd just gotten off track. "Whether it was a mistake or not, it just can't happen again."

"Why not? Especially if we both want it to?"

The man was nothing if not direct. And the hint of recklessness she saw in his eyes triggered not panic, but a thrill.

Maddie tried to ignore it. Logic and reason. Those were the keys. "Like I said before, we're both busy. And I only have three weeks."

"But you're not saying you don't want it to happen again." He rose and moved around the island.

She slid off her stool but held her ground. "If you come nearer, you'll end up on your butt again."

"It might not be so easy if you try that a second time."

She felt her temper rise, and she very nearly said, *Wanna bet?* But she swallowed the words.

He took a step closer. "On the other hand, it might be fun to find out."

Maddie absolutely hated the fact that a part of her agreed with him. She detested that she took two steps in retreat. But she couldn't deny that that the way he was advancing on her had excitement streaming through her.

Reason and logic. Reason and logic. She struggled to infuse both into her voice. "That's just it. I don't have time for fun and games. That's not what I came to New York for."

She very nearly sighed in relief when her words stopped Jase. But he was only a couple of feet away. If she reached out, she could touch him again. Disgusted with herself, she fisted her hands at her side.

The recklessness in his eyes faded. "You're right, Maddie Farrell." He reached out to toy with the end of her braid. "I'm not sure why I keep getting distracted by you, but I'll figure it out. In the meantime, there's a phone call I have to make. I want to find out what really happened when your mother was run down."

5

"DAVE, I need a favor." Jase paced back and forth in the small kitchen, his cell phone at his ear. He was very much aware that Maddie's eyes were on him. He knew from the line furrowing her forehead that she was worried. That might be a very good thing.

On the other end of the line, Detective Dave Stanton drawled. "And what can the lowly NYPD do for a top-notch security ace like yourself?"

Stanton was a giant of a man with chocolate-brown skin, and his jovial teddy-bear exterior hid a tough cop. Jase had run into him on a case he'd been working six months ago and they'd since become friends. Stanton had also been assigned to the break-in and robbery at Eva Ware Designs.

"It's about Eva Ware—the hit-and-run. I've been working a case out of the country for the past three weeks or so, and I just heard about her death. Can you check into it and call me back?"

"Won't have to. I've been keeping tabs on the investigation. It's stalled out but the file is still open."

"What do you know?" Jase stopped pacing when Maddie slid off her stool and strode toward him. He switched his cell phone to speaker so that she could hear too.

"She was run down on her way home from the gym when she was crossing the street to her apartment," Stanton explained. "It was part of her regular routine to visit the gym twice a week right after she left the Madison Avenue store. She walked home taking the same route. According to her doorman, she always crossed the street directly in front of her apartment instead of walking to the corner."

"So someone could have been waiting for her?"

"That's the bug I put in the ear of the two detectives assigned to the case. They followed up and someone in her building with a window facing the street remembers seeing a light-colored sedan parked across the street in a delivery zone. Says it was there for some time before it pulled out and clipped Ms. Ware."

"There was a witness to the accident?"

"Several of them, including the doorman of her building. All agree that it was a light-colored car. One insisted it was a Mercedes. But no one got a plate number. That's where things stand."

"So Eva Ware's death probably wasn't an accident."

"That's my gut feeling."

"You know a lot about a case you're not working," Jase said.

"I liked Eva Ware. She was a classy lady. So is her daughter Jordan. How's she holding up?"

That's exactly what Jase wanted to know. He still hadn't been able to reach Jordan on her cell. "I haven't had a chance to connect with her yet. Thanks, Dave."

"No problem. Keep me in the loop if you find out anything."

"Will do."

As Jase closed his cell, Maddie shook her head. "Jordan never said a word about Eva's death being anything other than an accident."

Jase lifted the coffeepot and topped off both of their mugs. "That's probably how the original report read. It sounds to me like Detective Stanton was the one to push looking into it more carefully. By that time Jordan was probably caught up in making funeral arrangements. I wish I'd been here." It ate bitterly at him that Jordan had had to handle everything on her own.

"I wish that I could have been here for her too. I don't know if I could have made it through my father's death if Cash hadn't been there for me."

Tilting her head, Maddie studied Jase for a moment. "You believed that Eva's death wasn't an accident even before you called Detective Stanton. Why? Is there someone who would want to harm her?"

"Perhaps." For a minute, Jase debated how much he wanted to tell Maddie and decided she'd have to know it all. Jordan too. "Have you been able to reach your sister? I tried her cell earlier with no luck."

"Cell signals are seldom available at the ranch. And the land line seems to be out. I called before I showered. There was a nasty storm predicted last night. But she intends to go into Santa Fe today and visit the hotel where they're holding the jewelry show tomorrow. Her cell should work there, and she'll call. It's our plan to keep in daily contact. And you must know how Jordan is about plans."

Jase smiled. "A real stickler."

Maddie set her coffee on the counter. "You haven't answered my question. Why did you instantly suspect that our mother's death might not be an accident?"

"Do you ever have gut feelings that something isn't quite right?"

She met his eyes. "Yes. I get them sometimes when I'm designing a piece of jewelry. Then I know I'm going in the wrong direction."

Jase leaned against the counter and crossed his legs at the

ankles. Maddie Farrell was a good listener, astute too. Maybe it would help him to talk it out. "I got one the minute you told me that Eva had been run down. A few days before I left for South America, your mother's store was broken into and approximately one hundred thousand dollars worth of jewelry was stolen."

Maddie frowned. "Jordan told me about that. She said that they'd gotten past the security. Considering the kind of pieces I've seen on Eva Ware's Web site, I'm surprised they didn't steal more. Some of her individual pieces go for two or three times that."

Smart girl, Jase thought. "The break-in occurred in the main salon. Most of the designs are kept in the safe and only brought out at a specific customer's request. But there were more expensive pieces on display. The police thought that the thief or thieves purposely took small pieces that could easily be fenced. And they only took pieces with gems."

"Which could be taken out and sold."

"That was the thinking. Detective Stanton worked the case, but Eva asked me to look into it also. I would have anyway since I was the one who'd installed the security system. The robbery was a very slick job. Either the thief was a highly sophisticated pro, or he'd had help from the inside. I thought the latter and I told Eva. She hired me to look into it further when I got back from South America. I suggested that she let me turn the investigation over to my partner, Dino Angelis, but she refused."

"Maybe she wanted a little time to gather information herself. Could be she suspected who the insider was and she wanted to be able to confront him or her."

Jase studied her. "Yeah. That's what I thought at the time, but how did you make that leap? You didn't even know Eva."

"I guess because if I were in her place, that's how I'd want to handle it. Jordan tells me that the business meant the world to Eva, that she'd devoted her life to it. On a much smaller scale, I know how I feel about my own fledgling design business. And I can sympathize with Eva wanting to try to handle it herself. Maybe she didn't even want the thief prosecuted."

"Why not?"

"Perhaps she didn't want a scandal. As I understand from Jordan, almost everyone there has been with her a long time."

"Good point."

Maddie climbed on a stool and folded her hands in front of her. "So. How are we going to find out who broke into Eva Ware Designs?"

He frowned at her. "*We're* not."

"We have to."

Jase straightened from the counter. "Maddie, if Eva did figure out who the thief was and threatened exposure, that person might be the one who ran her down. If he or she killed once, they won't hesitate to do it again."

Maddie swallowed hard and tried to ignore the sudden chill that radiated through her. Hearing the words spoken aloud in that blunt tone was a lot worse than thinking it. "You believe the thief killed Eva?"

"It's a strong possibility, and I think that's why my friend Dave Stanton is keeping an eye on the file."

His eyes had gone as flat as his tone. He was purposely trying to scare her. "But you're going to look further into the robbery?"

"Yes."

If he was right and someone had run Eva down, there was no way she wasn't going to do her best to find the person. She just had to find the right strategy to convince him. "I can help."

"No. It's too dangerous. Do what you came here to do— get to know your mother and her jewelry design business. My office will handle looking into who might have been behind the break-in and robbery."

A plan was already forming in her mind. Maddie leaned forward. "But I'm going to be on the inside. And my cover is perfect. Jordan has told everyone about me. I'm Eva Ware's other daughter, the one she left behind. I can play on the sympathy factor. Not from my cousin Adam, but perhaps from the others."

Jase moved to her then and covered her folded hands with his. "I'm sorry. It's got to be rough on you."

"On Jordan too."

"Yes."

"That's exactly what the others are going to think. And I'll be expected to ask a lot of questions anyway. I already intend to talk to people about Eva—what she was like, how she got started in the business, what her creative process was like. It's the only way that I have of getting to know her now. I'm going to insist on a tour of her workroom."

Jase was looking at her, saying nothing. But he was thinking. She could almost hear the wheels turning. Reason and logic. "The break-in could come up as a part of those kinds of conversations. I could find out things that they'll never tell you if you come into the office in your official capacity."

"You're not a trained investigator."

Her chin lifted. "No. But I already have an idea of where to start."

Jase slid onto his stool. "Don't keep me in suspense."

"I'll be right back." Whirling, she raced down the hall to Jordan's bedroom. Once there, she grabbed the file her twin had prepared for her along with her bag.

When she returned, Jase was waiting. She placed the file on top of the island and dug in her purse for her appointment book. It was an old-fashioned leather-bound volume with a ribbon she used as a bookmark. Right now it was stuffed with business cards, paper clippings and sticky notes. Next she drew out the neatly printed papers Jordan had given her. They contained her hour-by-hour schedule for the next three weeks.

Jase regarded them in silence for a moment. "Explain."

"They're appointment calendars. Jordan and I have very different styles. She keeps track of her daily and weekly schedule on some high-tech thing she carries in her purse." She patted the bursting leather book. "I do it in a less high-tech way. My father used to give me one of these every Christmas. I'm betting Eva would have kept some version of an appointment calendar. If not, her personal assistant must keep one." She paused to consult her file. "Her name is Michelle Tan. According to Jordan, she started out as an intern and took over the job of Eva's personal assistant when it opened up. Jordan says she's been with Eva for nearly a year now."

"And you're interested in Eva's appointment calendar because…?"

"If you're right and Eva had some idea of who was behind the break-in, it makes sense that she would have confronted him at some point. And I'm betting that she wouldn't have done it at Eva Ware Designs. But she may have made note of the meeting place in her calendar."

Jase's eyes narrowed as he considered. "You may be right. She came to my office when she decided to hire me to investigate further. And she told me not to mention it to Jordan until we had something more concrete to go on."

"See? She was being discreet."

Too discreet, Jake thought. *It might have gotten her killed.*

Jase pointed to the stack of cookies. "You going to finish those?"

"Help yourself."

He took a cookie and bit into it. He was being manipulated. Living with a mother and a sister, he and D.C. had learned early on what that felt like. The thing was, Maddie made sense. Eva's appointment calendar *was* a good place to start looking. And Maddie did have a good cover. Plus, she was going to poke her nose into this whether he wanted her to or not. If Jordan were here, he'd be facing the same problem. The two of them were as curious as Alice when she'd decided to follow that rabbit down his hole.

Maddie leaned forward. "My father was a firm believer in two heads being better than one. Whenever there was a problem at the ranch, he used to talk it over with our neighbor, Jesse Landry. After Jesse died, he'd talk with Cash and me." She beamed a smile at him. "Admit it. You could use my help."

For a moment, the smile and the way she was looking at him had his thoughts scattering. Jase firmly anchored them in place. He was going to have to learn to deal with her effect on him if he was going to keep her safe.

"I'll go along with this, but I'm going to be your constant companion."

Her brows shot up. "Constant companion?"

"For the next three weeks—or until we get this sorted out—I'm going to be at your side."

"No way. That will spoil everything. You run a security firm. I'll never be able to get any of them to talk freely with you hanging around."

"Jordan has dragged me to Christmas parties and a couple of other events Eva threw at her apartment. So they know me mostly as Jordan's friend and roommate. When I went to check the security system after the break-in, it was after hours. And as I mentioned, Eva came to my office when she decided to hire me to investigate further."

"But that's not going to explain why you're tagging along after me."

He smiled slowly at her. "Here's *my* cover. Even though we just met, it was love at first sight for you and me. And I'm determined to spend as much time as possible with you during the three weeks you're here."

6

"WE'RE SORRY that we cannot complete your call at this time. Please try again later."

Maddie frowned at the handset as she replaced it in its cradle. It was the second time she'd tried the number at the ranch since she and Jase had returned to their separate bedrooms. Both times she'd received the metallic, recorded message. Even if there'd been a storm at the ranch last night, it had to be over. The phone lines should be working.

She needed her sister's help. Her gaze strayed to the small bookcase the phone was perched on and for the first time she noted the framed photo that sat on the first shelf. Jordan was in her cap and gown, and Eva Ware stood close, her arm around Jordan. Both smiled into the camera.

A little band of pain tightened around Maddie's heart. It was immature and not fair to Jordan to be jealous of the fact that Eva hadn't been at her college graduation, nor had she witnessed all of the other milestones in Maddie's life. Her father had been present, she reminded herself. And Mike Farrell had missed all of Jordan's big events.

Maddie swallowed hard as she studied Eva's face and noted the braid that fell over one of her shoulders. She fingered her own. It was hard even now to really get her mind around the fact that Eva Ware was her mother. In her own thoughts and even when talking to Jase about her, she was still referring to her as *Eva Ware*.

Would she ever get used to the idea? She set the photo carefully back on the shelf. Why? Why had her father and Eva decided to separate? Why had they each cut one daughter out of their lives? She was determined to find an answer to that question before she left New York. Maybe she would discover at least a partial answer as she came to know Eva better.

The second shelf of the small bookcase was filled with paperback books. Curious, she ran her fingers along the spines. Her lips curved when she realized that Jordan lined her paperbacks up alphabetically according to the last name of the author.

Didn't that just figure?

But what really surprised her was that she had nearly half the same books in the small bookcase in her bedroom at the ranch— starting with the Brontës and Jane Austen. Then there were more modern writers—Linda Howard, Jayne Ann Krentz, Karen Robards, J.D. Robb, Nora Roberts and Robert B. Parker. Maddie's smile widened as she realized Jordan obviously shared her own weakness for romantic suspense and mysteries.

Then she glanced at the bottom shelf and simply stared. The books there were alphabetized too, but they were all westerns— Zane Grey, Louis L'Amour, Luke Short, Larry McMurtry. She recognized the authors because they were her father's favorites. There were two copies of *Lonesome Dove*—one that was falling apart and another that seemed to be brand new. How many times had she teased her father about rereading that novel? It appeared that her sister might have the same addiction.

Could a taste in reading run in a family? And what else might she and Jordan have in common? Certainly not their taste in clothes. Striding toward the full-length mirror on the open closet door, Maddie studied the outfit she'd selected. She'd searched high and low for a plain pair of slacks and a blazer—but Jordan didn't seem to believe in them. Her twin favored clothes that were either a little too frilly or fashion-forward for Maddie's taste. Her own wardrobe consisted almost entirely of jeans or slacks and jackets and T-shirts.

Simple, flexible—and you seldom had to worry about color coordination.

She'd finally decided on a suit she'd initially been drawn to because of the color—a pale blue that reminded her of a summer sky in Santa Fe. The skirt had a flouncy, fluted ruffle along its hem. Turning in a half circle, she watched it flare out. The jacket had feminine bell-shaped sleeves. It was certainly not something she could wear at the ranch, but it was growing on her.

She dropped her gaze to her bare feet. What she needed now was shoes. She sent a worried glance at the rows upon rows of them that took up a wall in Jordan's closet. So many choices, so little time. The shower in the bathroom had stopped running five minutes ago. Since then, she figured Jase had probably shaved and now was dressing.

And she doubted he was stumped by shoe selection. The problem with Jordan's was they all looked to be ankle-breakers. Still, there was a dark blue pair with a silver buckle that her eye kept returning to. Moving into the closet, she ran her finger over the buckle. But they'd never been worn. She didn't feel right about wearing a pair of shoes that Jordan never had.

Which was one of the reasons she needed to talk to her sister. Striding back to the phone, she once more punched in the number of the ranch. To her surprise, it rang. Then she listened to her own voice telling her to leave a message.

When the beep sounded, she said, "Jordan, this is Maddie. Pick up if you can. Otherwise call me back ASAP."

A glance at her watch told her it was nine-thirty. "I'm

running a little late, but you should be able to reach me at Eva Ware Designs a little after ten. Jase is coming with me."

She'd lost some time trying to talk him out of his plan to become her constant companion, but he'd remained firm. Until they had a clearer idea of what was going on, he was going to stick to her like glue. And he hadn't missed his chance to tell her that two heads were better than one. There was nothing like having your own words come back to bite you.

"You didn't mention in his file that he was mule-headed. Anyway, it's a long story, and there's something else I need to tell you." There was no way she was going to mention what they'd discovered about the investigation into Eva's death on an answering machine.

"So call me." She was about to hang up when she remembered. "One other thing. There's a pair of shoes in your closet that doesn't look as if it's ever been worn. Hope you don't mind if I break them in. Bye."

She stared at the handset for a minute after she'd replaced it. She hadn't exactly asked permission. But those blue shoes were definitely calling her name.

Striding to the closet, she plucked them off the shelf, stepped into them, and winced. Was this what Cinderella's stepsisters had felt like when they'd tried on the glass slipper?

But they were the right size. She'd checked that out. The tight fit had to be due to the fact that she was used to wearing boots. Very comfortable, *worn-in* boots. She took an experimental step out of the closet and had to slam a hand into the door frame to keep her balance. Maddie shifted her gaze to the mirror. "This can't be that hard. You learned to ride a horse, rope a cow and shoot a gun."

She took one step and teetered. This time she didn't reach for the wall. "You can learn to walk in these. Millions of other women have. How hard can it be?"

Turning away from her reflection, Maddie started for the foot of the bed, stumbled, and nearly went down.

"About as hard as learning to walk on stilts," she muttered. Then she focused on her destination. It was less than ten feet away. Concentrating hard, she raised her arms for balance the way a tightrope walker would and put one foot gingerly in front of the other. By the time she reached the bed, she could lower her arms.

And breathe.

So far, so good. She took another breath and started toward the dresser on the other side of Jordan's bed. She raised her arms again, but by the time she was halfway there, she no longer felt the need to use them for balance. Thank heavens the learning curve for navigating around in the shoes was going to be short.

On the surface of Jordan's dresser lay a silver-plated brush and comb, a small box of hairpins and a jewelry box. Raising her eyes, Maddie regarded her image in the mirror and frowned. The hair was definitely wrong for the outfit.

In her mind's eye she pictured Jordan's sophisticated, layered cut. Much better. There had to be something she could do. Quickly, she unraveled the braid and ran her fingers through it. Then using the hairbrush, she pulled it smoothly back from her face into a ponytail. Finally, she twisted the ponytail into a bun and secured it to the back of her head with pins.

Better. But were the earrings okay? With a critical eye, she studied the tiny silver horseshoes that dangled from each of her ears. The sky-blue of the turquoise was fine in terms of color. But her hand was already reaching to open Jordan's jewelry box. What she saw inside took her breath away.

Of course, she'd seen Eva's jewelry in magazines and on the store's Web site, but nothing had captured the delicacy of the designs. In comparison, her horseshoes looked almost gaudy. She was reaching for a froth of lacy gold in a teardrop shape when she suddenly became aware that she wasn't alone in the room.

Turning, she saw Jase standing in the open doorway. How long had he been watching her? The way he was looking at her, the heat in his eyes, had her throat going desert-dry. Quickly she dropped her gaze from his. Not that it helped. He'd changed into a dark blue T-shirt and blazer which only emphasized his broad shoulders. And he wore jeans that fit snugly at the hips and hugged his legs like a second skin.

And, in spite of everything she'd said to him, she wanted him again. For a moment, as the silence stretched between them, she became very aware of the fact that they were separated only by Jordan's bed. If she moved toward it, would he? A wave of longing struck her, so intense that for a second, she nearly lost her balance.

It wasn't the shoes this time.

It was the man.

And she could have him right now. She could tell by the expression in his eyes. An image filled her mind of the two of them on the bed, naked, their limbs entwined, their bodies moving as one.

No! Maddie fisted her hands at her sides. She had to get a grip on the way he was affecting her. Everything she'd said to him was true. She didn't have time to indulge in…this… this…craziness. She had to learn to walk around in Jordan's shoes. Literally as well as figuratively. She had to get to Eva Ware Designs.

Dragging her eyes back to his face, she forced her mind back to the problem that had consumed her before Jase had entered the room—what she was wearing. She raised her hands and dropped them. "What do you think?"

FOR A MOMENT Jase didn't respond. How could he when he simply wasn't thinking at all? His thoughts had scattered the moment he'd caught sight of her on the other side of the bed. He'd stopped in the doorway because he hadn't trusted himself to go farther into the room.

Or perhaps it was because desire had struck him with the force of a Mack truck. When she'd loosened her braid and run her fingers through it, he'd nearly lost it. He'd grabbed the doorjamb with one hand and held on tight as his mind emptied and filled with sensations—of how that long, loose hair would feel between his fingers, on his skin.

He didn't even know how long he'd been standing there staring at her. Long enough for him to weave a nice little fantasy about getting her out of that suit and touching her. Really touching her. He'd pictured them on that bed—this time in the daylight when they were both awake. And he knew exactly how that skin would feel—soft as rainwater, smooth as the petal of an exotic flower one might come across in the steamy jungle he'd just left.

"Well?"

Jase gathered enough of himself to note that her hands had fisted on her hips and one foot was tapping. And still he couldn't get a word out. For the first time, something like fear moved through him.

No woman had ever tied his tongue in knots before.

"If this outfit is that bad, you'd better come right out and say it. I'm used to wearing jeans and slacks, so I don't have much fashion sense when it comes to fancy clothes. I went for the color. But Jordan has lots of other clothes."

Jase pulled himself together. And finally found his voice. "It's fine."

She studied him as she moved toward him, giving the bed a wide berth. He appreciated the strategy and took some satisfaction that he wasn't the only one thinking about tumbling her into it.

"You're not just saying that? You're sure?"

"Yeah," he lied. The only thing he was really *sure* of was that she wasn't going to be wearing the outfit much longer if they didn't get out of Jordan's bedroom. And until he found out exactly who might have run down Eva Ware, he needed to be able to think clearly. Still, he couldn't prevent his gaze from raking her one more time. "Are you going to be able to walk in those shoes?"

She glanced down at them. "Yeah, I've got that under control, I think."

Control. That was the key word, Jase reminded himself. He released his grip on the doorjamb, flexed his fingers to assure himself that they were still there. Last but not least, he dragged his gaze away from the bed and led the way out of the room.

TRUE TO FORM, New York City traffic was crawling along at less than a snail's pace. Out of the corner of his eye, he could see that Maddie was staring wide-eyed out the open window of the taxi, craning her neck to take in the buildings, the people, and breathing in the mix of scents—hot pavement, rotting garbage, exhaust fumes—that he took for granted.

He glanced at his watch and saw that it was nearly ten. Even though it was only a twenty-block walk to Eva Ware Designs, he'd decided in deference to her shoes to hail a cab. But what should have been a five-minute cab ride was stretching into thirty. Even in the ankle-breakers she was wearing, they could have easily arrived at the jewelry store by now.

Brakes squealed as the car in front of them came to an abrupt stop. Someone stepped out of the passenger door and hurried into a small store that specialized in fresh produce. Their cabbie leaned on his horn and shouted something out the window in a language Jase wasn't familiar with. Glancing out the rear window, Jase could see that their taxi was neatly boxed in.

He looked at Maddie and saw that she was staring at a policeman astride a horse. They hadn't said much to each other since they'd left the building. She'd been intent on drinking in the sights, and he'd welcomed the reprieve of just being away from the apartment. They'd have to go back there eventually and good idea or not, he was sure that they were going to end up in bed together again.

He'd never met a woman who pulled at him the way she did. Even now his hand was fisted on the seat because he wanted to reach out and touch her. Just to tuck a strand of hair behind her ear or to run a finger down her throat.

But that wouldn't be enough. He'd need more. And he'd have more. It might be the biggest mistake of his life, but one way or another, he did intend to make love with Maddie Farrell again.

Right now, he had to put that aside and switch gears. She still had her eyes on the mounted policeman, and he reminded himself that she had just switched places with her sister and was feeling her way through a strange, new world. Maybe he could help with that.

"In the file she gave you, did Jordan mention that she keeps a horse on a farm just a little north of the city?"

"No."

For the first time since they'd entered the taxi, she turned to face him. He read both surprise and interest on her face. "It's a stallion. She bought him when she moved to the city to work for your mother. She named him Julius Caesar because he was born on the Ides of March."

Maddie stared at him. "My horse is Brutus. What are the chances?"

"Jordan has always loved horses. She started riding

lessons when she was six, and she was a natural. She began competing two years after that and didn't give it up until she started college."

A small frown creased Maddie's forehead. He'd seen the same expression before when she was carefully considering something.

"A penny for your thoughts," he said.

"It's just...odd. No, ironic is a better word."

"For what?"

The frown on her forehead deepened. "I love riding, and I enjoy living on a ranch, but I've discovered that my real passion is designing jewelry. And Jordan seems to have a passion for horses and riding the way my father did. From what I saw on her bookshelf, they even share a passion for westerns."

"You're thinking they picked the wrong daughters when they made their choices."

She nodded.

Even though he knew it was a mistake, he took her hand in his. "I doubt that either your father or your mother would feel that way."

HE UNDERSTOOD. Something tightened in Maddie's throat. Even though her hand was clasped lightly in his, she was aware of the pressure of each one of his fingers. But it wasn't a sizzle of passion that moved through her blood. This time it was something warmer and much sweeter. He leaned toward her and brushed the merest hint of a kiss over her lips.

Without thinking, she raised her free hand to his face—to push him away? To keep him there?

Before she could decide, he drew back and said, "Do you think you can manage three blocks on foot?"

Maddie frowned at her feet. "No promises, but I'm game

to try. After all, I'm supposed to be walking around in Jordan's shoes."

He grinned at her. "She always wore her sneakers when she walked to work and carried the ankle-breakers in her bag."

Maddie glared at him. "You might have told me that before we left the apartment."

"It's only a couple more blocks." Jase passed the taxi driver two bills. Then he grabbed Maddie's hand again and pulled her with him to the sidewalk. As they blended into the flow of pedestrians headed uptown, a cacophony of noise enveloped them—horns blaring, engines thrumming, one-sided snatches of conversations as passersby chatted into their cell phones.

Jase raised his voice. "How are the shoes?"

"Glorious to look at—but agony to wear." She shot him a determined look. "It's going to be worth every bit of discomfort when I walk into that store not looking like the country bumpkin they're probably expecting."

"You'll be fine. Just remember the roles we're assuming."

"I'll be playing myself—the other daughter."

Taking her hand, he raised it to his lips and kissed her fingers. "And I'll be playing your lover."

Heat shot through her and Maddie was sure that if there had been room in the shoes, her toes would have curled. In spite of the role Jase was playing, she intended to keep her focus.

Suddenly, she stopped short and a startled pedestrian jostled her as he passed.

Gripping her shoulders, Jase pulled her out of the flow of traffic into a doorway. "What is it?"

"I forgot the earrings."

"No, you didn't. You're wearing them."

She shook her head. "I was going to take these off and put

on one of Eva's designs. My style is so…different. Next to hers, my earrings look…" She paused, searching for the right word.

"Beautiful." He reached up and ran his finger down one of the horseshoes.

Her thoughts scattered. He was going to kiss her again. She could see the desire in his eyes, feel her own response rip through her. The noises that had surrounded them since they'd left the cab faded to a dim buzz. Her mind constricted like a spotlight on a stage until there was only Jase.

He slid his hands from her upper arms over her shoulders, then framed her face. It seemed as if it had been forever since he'd touched her. Had it only been a matter of hours?

Using his thumbs, he tilted her chin up. "I want to kiss you. I thought I could wait until later when we got back to the apartment. Back to my bed. But I can't."

He lowered his mouth slowly until it was nearly touching hers. Then he paused.

She should push him away, Maddie thought dimly. She'd always prided herself on having a logical, practical turn of mind. But she'd never experienced this kind of desire before. Each time he touched her or even looked at her, she wanted. It was just that elemental.

"I can't wait either." The words tumbled out of her on a ragged breath as she slipped her arms beneath his jacket and rose on her tiptoes. Finally, *finally,* their mouths were touching, tasting, exploring as hunger deepened into a fierce need.

The kiss was so much more than she remembered. What had happened between them during the night seemed more like a dream. This was reality. Each sensation was so intense—the hard planes and angles of body pressing her into the unyielding glass of the display window, the scrape of his teeth on her bottom lip, the heat of his hand as he slipped it beneath her jacket and ran it possessively from her waist to the side of her breast. Then he changed the angle of the kiss and she sampled again the flavor of his need. Irresistible.

Jase ran his hand down to her waist and then back up again. It seemed that he'd been waiting forever to touch her. She was driving him crazy. That had to be why he was acting this way. It wasn't that he hadn't lived dangerously or taken risks before. He'd made his living so far doing both. But he'd always been in control. Maddie Farrell was draining that away.

The taste of her surrender poured into him. He drew her closer until every curve of her body was molded against his. The thin material of her blouse was tempting, maddening. He wanted her out of it. Desperately.

They were standing in the middle of a busy Manhattan street. In some dim corner of his mind that hadn't yet shut down, Jase reminded himself of that. But it was almost impossible to keep a grip on reality when the concrete sidewalk beneath his feet seemed to shift as easily as sand on a beach. He struggled to keep his balance. Shocked, he tried to strengthen the slim grip he had on his control. He should be damning himself for acting like a hormone-driven teenager. He should be damning her for driving him to this. But all he wanted was more of her.

When it finally struck him that he might not be able to stop himself from taking more, a sharp stab of fear gave him the strength to draw back. Releasing her, he took a step away. Even then he struggled, his mind battling against his emotions, and he very nearly dragged her back and kissed her again. He might have if a woman hadn't chosen that moment to walk by them and enter the store.

Jase backed up another step. The first completely coherent thought that slipped into his mind was that he wasn't capable of controlling this. The realization stunned him.

Maddie spoke first. "This is ridiculous."

Jase studied her closely. There was a vulnerability in her that he hadn't noticed before. And because he wanted badly to reach out to her, he slid his fingers into the pockets of his jeans. "That's not exactly the word I'd choose."

"I don't understand what's happening between us."

"It's a puzzler all right."

"We're on a crowded street and all I could think of was that I wanted to kiss you."

"The feeling was mutual."

She frowned at him then. "That only increases the problem. What we need is a solution. What are we going to do about this?"

Jase dropped his gaze to her mouth, then met her eyes again. "I think we both know the answer to that."

She frowned at him. "I don't like it. It's going to interfere with everything. I have enough on my plate."

"Me too." The fact that the frustration in her tone was such a perfect match to his own eased what he was feeling. He managed a smile. "I guess we'll just have to compartmentalize and work around it. And speaking of work, Eva Ware Designs has been open for a good fifteen minutes. I suggest we resume this discussion later."

Maddie lifted her chin. "Fine. Good. We'll keep our focus on our investigation."

Together, they threaded their way back into the stream of pedestrians.

"I meant to tell you in the car that I have an idea about what we should do when we get to Eva Ware Designs."

Jase glanced at her. "Don't keep me in the dark."

"We seem to have two goals. You're primarily interested in figuring out who on the inside might have robbed the store. Of course, I'm interested in that too. I want to learn as much as I can about Eva, but I also want to find if there's someone there Eva confided in."

"Someone who might have known about you?"

Maddie nodded. "The more I think about it, the more I believe she must have confided in someone. And that someone may be able to shed some light on why Jordan and I were separated."

Jase held his tongue. His impression of Eva Ware was that she was a very self-contained woman. He'd had some time to think in the shower earlier. As he'd turned it over in his mind, he'd become convinced that she'd had some idea of who had broken into her store from the very beginning, yet she confided in no one. Not in Jordan. Not in him. She was a private woman and she knew how to keep a secret. She'd kept a very important one for twenty-six years.

"And I want to see Eva's appointment calendar. It might be better when we get there to separate and gather our information separately."

It wasn't a bad idea, Jake thought. "As long as I don't have to let you out of my sight."

"I have a question," she said.

"Ask away."

"Do you have any thoughts on why my mother asked Jordan and me to change places?"

Jase thought for a moment. "I think Jordan's theory that she wanted the two of you to experience the life she and your father had separated you from is a strong possibility. Did the fact that you're a talented jewelry designer play into it? Perhaps. But I also think she may have been experiencing some regret."

"It that's true, why didn't she just bring us together? Why put it in her will so that our coming together would only occur after her death? Now, I'll never get to know her."

"I don't know the answer to that question, Maddie. But this way she'll never get to know you either. Her loss."

"I'm going to get some answers."

When they stopped at the corner, he ran a finger down one of her earrings. "By the way, I like these. For what it's worth, your mother might have wanted you to experience Jordan's life—but I don't think she wanted you to stop being true to yourself."

7

EVA WARE DESIGNS was housed in a building on the corner of Madison Avenue and 51st Street. Because her nerves had been steadily building during the last few blocks, Maddie slowed and focused her attention on the display windows. As distracting as the man beside her was, she was going to put him out of her mind and concentrate on what she'd come to New York to do—learn as much as she could about Eva and Jordan.

The white marble facade of the building framed four two-foot-square windows, two on each side of the glass-doored entrance. Each window was artfully lit and showcased a single piece of jewelry.

Bait, she thought. The minimalist approach intrigued her, especially when she recalled the more cluttered window displays in the boutiques that carried her jewelry in Santa Fe. Most of the shop owners had no acquaintance with the idea that less might be more.

Maddie moved from one window to the next, not as a delaying tactic anymore, but because she was fascinated. Her eyes widened when they spotted the solitary emerald set in a delicately woven gold band. She guessed the ring to be at least two full carats, and yet the craftsmanship of the design made it look so delicate. Eager to see more, she bypassed the entrance and walked around the corner.

"We haven't even gone inside, and you look like a kid in a candy shop."

She grinned at Jase. "That's exactly how I feel." She waved a hand at a window holding a pair of earrings, each offering a mini explosion of tiny, multicolored gems. "Putting only one piece in each window—it's a brilliant marketing idea. It forces the viewer to focus solely on the artistry of the piece."

"It was Jordan's brainchild. It took her almost six months to win your mother over. Your cousin Adam fought her tooth and nail."

The last window held a pendant, three inches square. The gold was hammered and though it was crafted on a much smaller scale, it still made her think of a breast plate that an ancient warrior might have worn into battle. Wanting to get a closer look, she barely kept herself from pressing her nose against the window. There was a diamond set in the center of the pendant and radiating out from it were four rows of turquoise stones.

Something tightened around her heart. "I didn't know Eva worked with turquoise."

"Sorry," Jase said. "I don't have much information on that. I knew about the display windows because Jordan vented about it for several months."

Maddie pressed her fingers against the glass, wanting very much to touch the pendant. "It's a little like some of the pieces I've designed—except I don't use diamonds or gold. I'd like to know how she developed that hammering technique."

"We should go in. That's the kind of question your cousin Adam should be able to answer."

Yes. She turned to look at him and saw that he was leaning against the white marble wall, regarding her steadily.

She cocked her head to the side and regarded him right back. "You're thinking that I'm stalling. And I have to admit, my window-shopping started out that way. And then I just got caught up in out-and-out gawking. I've been in awe of Eva Ware's jewelry ever since I started to dream of designing some myself."

Straightening her shoulders, she moved past him and around the corner. "And you've made your point. I didn't come here as a besotted fan. I came to get some answers."

She pulled the front door open, then paused and shot him a look over her shoulder. "When I talk to Adam about Eva's techniques, I can ask him other questions too."

Before she could enter the store, Jase took her hand.

Maddie tried to tug it free and failed. "I thought we agreed to postpone our...personal situation until later."

"Our personal situation?" Jase grinned. "Yeah, we'll deal with that later." *Thoroughly,* he thought. "This is work related. Remember my cover?"

When he leaned down to kiss her nose, Maddie froze. She was aware that two people in the store had turned to watch them—a sturdily built, well-dressed woman at one of the display cases and a very distinguished-looking man who must be the manager.

"You're making a scene," she breathed.

"That's the plan. The first time I spotted you, I fell hard. Haven't been able to think straight since. As long as we're in the store, I'm your besotted boy toy. If everyone buys in to that, I won't come off as any kind of a threat."

Boy toy? That much she could see. But even with the wind-blown hair and wearing jeans and a blazer, it was hard for Maddie to imagine Jase Campbell not coming across as a threat.

ONCE THEY were inside the store, Jase released Maddie's hand. Touching her in any way clouded his thoughts, and he needed a clear head. The rather flip description of the role he intended to play as her besotted admirer was a bit too close to the truth to suit his liking.

But he'd worked enough special ops and cases to know that it was sometimes essential to make use of the cards you were dealt. He kept the two occupants of the store in his peripheral vision. The man in the pin-striped gray suit and ruthlessly knotted tie was staring at Maddie now.

Jase searched his memory. Jordan had introduced him as the store manager at a party she'd dragged him to at her mother's apartment. What was his name? Arnold? Albert? His face was tanned, his graying blond hair carefully styled, and he still reminded Jase of Sean Connery.

Arnold Bartlett. That was it. Jase noted that the portly woman who favored the kind of outfits Queen Elizabeth wore, right down to a pink pillbox hat, had turned her attention back to the display case.

Three steps in front of him Maddie twirled in a circle. *A kid in a candy store* didn't quite do justice to the expression on her face. It was such a mix of wonder, excitement, pride—and jealousy?

He could understand all of those. Jewelry was a business to Jordan, but it was clearly Maddie's passion. This was her mother's world. What must it feel like to have been cut out of Eva's life? To have been denied the experience of growing up beside her sister? And now, she would never have the chance to talk to Eva about it.

He thought of his relationship with his own family—his sister Darcy, his mom, his brother D.C. What would his life be like, what would he be like now if he'd been denied a relationship with them?

Maddie moved back to him. "It's so lovely."

Once more she let her gaze sweep the room, drinking in every detail. He'd only been in the store once before, after hours, when he'd come to check out the security system his firm had installed. He'd been impressed. The floor was white marble, the walls a creamy color broken every five feet or so with raised carvings of Greek columns. Potted plants and vases of fresh flowers were scattered throughout the room.

Even here the jewelry was displayed discreetly—just a few pieces in each of the five display cases. That too had been Jordan's idea. Since so much of the store's business consisted of special orders, she'd argued that the display cases as well as the windows should have the purpose of giving their customers ideas.

Scattered throughout the main salon, antique couches and chairs were grouped in conversation areas. On an intricately carved sideboard near the front of the store sat silver urns offering coffee and tea. Another sideboard offered chilled sparkling water.

Over Maddie's shoulder, Jase saw Arnold Bartlett pick up a phone.

"I'm so out of my league," Maddie said.

His eyes cut to Maddie's as anger moved through him. It wasn't directed at Maddie, but at the two people who'd put her in this situation—her parents. He grabbed her shoulders. "You're not. You belong here every bit as much as Jordan does. You remember that." Then he pulled her close for a quick hard kiss.

Maddie tried to keep her focus as her brain clouded and her knees went weak. He was playing a role, she reminded herself. And she had to do her part. Plus, she had to keep her mind on her goals.

A deep masculine voice said, "Ms. Farrell."

When Maddie turned toward him, the dignified-looking man smiled and extended his hand. "Arnold Bartlett—store manager. I want to welcome you to Eva Ware Designs."

Beaming a smile at him, Maddie shook his hand. "Thank you, Mr. Bartlett."

"Call me Arnold. Your sister does." He studied her for a moment. "Even though Jordan told us about you, I... The resemblance is striking. When you first walked in, I was sure you *were* Jordan. She sometimes wears her hair pulled back."

Still smiling, he shot a look of polite inquiry at Jase.

Jase threw a friendly arm around Maddie and pulled her possessively close. "Jase Campbell. I'm an old pal of Jordan's."

"Ah, yes. But I assumed Maddie would be coming here alone."

Jase gave Maddie a little squeeze. "Since she's only going to be here three weeks, I just can't bring myself to let her out of my sight. I'm sure you can understand why."

"Yes, well..."

"Madison?"

Maddie's gaze shifted to Adam Ware who was striding purposefully toward them.

"Adam told me to notify him the moment you arrived," Arnold Bartlett explained. "He wants to give you a personal tour."

Maddie stifled a surge of nerves as her cousin approached. He was even more classically handsome than she recalled. Today he wore a pale gray suit and a silk shirt and tie in varying hues of the same color. His longish chestnut-brown hair was shoved behind his ears revealing a single diamond in his right earlobe. His features were chiseled, his skin tanned and his profile might easily have graced some ancient coin.

Adam reminded Maddie a bit of the real estate agent, Daniel Pearson, who'd been so intent on getting her to let him list and sell her ranch. Both had a sheen of smooth sophistication. Adam was a bit more volatile, but she was reluctant to put her trust in either of them.

The man standing at her side with his arm around her was anything but smooth. Though if he decided to act the role of the city sophisticate, Maddie had no doubt that Jase could pull it off. Her father would have liked Jase, she suddenly realized. If for no other reason than that he seemed to be able to lie like a trouper.

When Adam reached her, he gave her a smile that didn't succeed in reaching his eyes. That was another difference between the two men. Jase's slow and easy smiles always reached his eyes.

"If you'll come this way, I'll show you to Jordan's office." Then he turned to Jase. "You'll have to stay here. We don't allow anyone but employees or family beyond the main salon."

A little flare of anger began to build inside Maddie. Jase tightened his arm around her, and Maddie knew he was going to say something. To warn him off, she shifted her balance and pressed one of her narrow heels into his foot.

He stiffened, but he kept silent.

Maddie brightened her smile. She wasn't going to allow herself to be intimidated. She might not have been a part of Eva's life for the past twenty-six years, but she was here now.

"I came here for more than a tour, Adam. I'm stepping into Jordan's shoes for the next three weeks, so you're going to see a lot of me and Jase. And Jase will be accompanying me beyond the salon as my special guest."

Drawing Jase with her, she strode toward the elevator she'd seen Adam step out of.

"Nicely done." Jase spoke in a voice only she could hear.

She jabbed a finger into the call button. Once they were all in the elevator, Maddie said to Adam, "Before you take me to Jordan's office, I want to see where Eva worked."

Her cousin stared at her. "No one is allowed in there

except members of the design team. That's a strict rule that Aunt Eva made."

Maddie raised her eyebrows at him. "I'm sure that Jordan has been allowed into the workroom?"

Now Adam frowned. "Occasionally, but she doesn't work there. She's not a designer."

"Well, I am. And since I'm Eva Ware's other daughter and a fellow jewelry designer, I'm certain she wanted me to visit."

"Oh, very well." Adam's tone was less than gracious as he punched the button for the second floor. "Our workroom is adjacent to our office." Once again he shot a look at Jase. "But I can't allow your friend access to the design studio. It's one of Aunt Eva's hard and fast rules that outsiders are never allowed in her workroom. No one is permitted to see works in progress. She's even kept my parents out."

"The thing is, Eva Ware isn't in charge here anymore," Maddie said.

Adam's face turned red. He opened his mouth, shut it and finally said, "Very well."

The elevator door slid open on a small, high-ceilinged room with three offices opening off it. Desks and cabinets were partially visible through the open doorways. Oriental rugs in muted pastel shades dotted the marble floors. Sunlight poured through narrow windows. An antique cherry desk sat in the center of the room, and a young Asian girl glanced up, then rose and moved toward them. "Welcome to Eva Ware Designs. I'm Michelle Tan."

Maddie summoned up the name from the notes Jordan had given her as she shook the hand the young woman extended. Then as the Michelle's gaze shifted to Jase, Maddie said, "This is my friend, Jase Campbell."

"Ah. Jordan's roommate," Michelle said. "She's spoken of you."

"I hope in a positive way," Jase said.

Michelle smiled, but Adam interrupted before she could speak. "They've asked to see Aunt Eva's workroom. We'll be back shortly." Then he turned and led the way down a short hall.

"You're doing a nice job of handling your cousin, darlin'," Jase murmured for Maddie's ears only. "The pushier you are with him, the more easily I can fade into the background."

"His mother isn't here to prompt him. He seems more assertive when she is." Then she shot him a look. "Darlin'?"

"Payback for my foot."

The short exchange eased the nerves in Maddie's stomach.

"When we get in the studio," Jase continued, "I'll distract your cousin so you can take your time."

Adam opened the door and strode into the room. Over his shoulder, Maddie could see Cho Li, her mother's long-time assistant, bent over something at a desk. He wore jeans and a loose-fitting chambray shirt.

"Cho, what are you doing working in Aunt Eva's space?"

Adam's voice had the small man swiveling in his chair.

Cho Li wore rimless glasses.

"I was finishing a design that Eva was working on," Cho replied in a calm voice. "She would want it completed."

For a moment the gazes of the two men clashed. In the end, it was Adam who dropped his. "You remember Madison Farrell."

Cho rose from his chair and moved toward Maddie. When he reached her, he bowed.

Jase released Maddie's hand as she also bowed. He knew from Jordan that Cho Li was in his midseventies, but he looked younger and his eyes were smiling. Jase quickly scanned the room. It was large, nearly twice the space of the office area where they'd left Michelle. Tall narrow windows along two walls let in plenty of light, and there were three clearly defined workspaces.

"Welcome, Ms. Farrell," Cho Li said. "What can I do for you?"

Maddie smiled at him. "Please call me Maddie."

He nodded his head. "Maddie then."

"I'd love to see the design that you were completing for Eva."

A smile spread over Cho's face. "Come."

When Adam started to follow them, Jase put a hand on his arm. "I wonder if I could have a word with you."

"What about?"

Jase glanced at Maddie, then lowered his voice. "In private?" Then he drew Adam over to the far end of the room. He settled his hip against a worktable so that Adam would have to face him. "The thing is, I need some help."

Adam's eyes narrowed. "With what?"

Over Adam's shoulder, Jase could see Maddie and Cho standing in front of the worktable. Cho was holding up a ring of yellow gold with a smaller ring of white gold inside it.

Jase met Adam's eyes. "Maddie and I have only just met. Jordan and I have been pals for years, and they look so much alike. But when I met Maddie, something just clicked. You know what I mean?"

"Your relationship with Madison is of no interest to me. Now if you'll excuse—"

Jase put a hand on Adam's arm. "The thing is, I'd like to buy her something while we're here. Can you help me with that?"

Adam frowned at him. "Do I look like a salesperson? If you came to purchase something, Arnold could have taken care of you in the main salon."

Jase shrugged. "You're one of the designers, aren't you?"

Adam's chin lifted. "Yes, I am. Now that Eva is gone, I'm the head designer at Eva Ware Designs."

"And you're Maddie's cousin. Family's important to her. I was thinking that one of your creations might be just the ticket. Something exclusive that hasn't made its way downstairs yet? Do you have some pieces that I could look at?"

Adam was torn. Jase could see the struggle in his face, but in the end ego won out. He opened a drawer in his worktable, took out a thick ring of keys and led the way to a cabinet in the corner. "I can show you three of my latest creations."

MADDIE TOUCHED the pendant of concentric gold rings that Cho had been working on when they'd entered the room. "Would you mind if I picked it up?"

"Go ahead," Cho said.

Maddie examined it more closely. The larger ring was yellow gold and the smaller circle dangling inside it was white gold. Cho had nearly completed hammering the finish onto the larger ring.

"There's the sketch your mother was working from."

Maddie shifted her gaze to the corkboard that formed the walls above each workspace. There were at least a dozen sketches pinned to the wall, and it took her a moment to locate the right one. She saw that the inner circular ring was supposed to be hammered too.

She looked back at the pendant now nestled in the palm of her hand. "It's beautiful. Just beautiful. I've been experimenting with a technique like this one."

"Why don't you try your hand on the silver?"

"Silver?" Maddie's eyes narrowed on the inner ring. "I thought it had to be white gold." But it wasn't. She could see that now. "I didn't know that Eva worked with silver."

"She had just started." Cho held out the small hammer. "Go ahead."

Her fingers itched to take it. Instead, she met Cho's eyes. "You knew her for a long time."

He nodded. "I worked with her for a year before she opened this store."

Maddie drew in a deep breath. "Did she ever tell you about me?"

"No. I'm sorry."

Maddie read both sadness and understanding in Cho's eyes. Swallowing her disappointment, she glanced back at the tool he held in his hand. "I think you'd better finish this. I'm not sure she'd want me to work on her pieces."

"But she brought you here," Cho said.

Maddie stared at him. He was right. Eva *had* brought her here with the terms of the will. She must have wanted her to be here. When Cho swiveled the chair and she felt it at the back of her knees, she sank into it.

He sat down beside her. "One thing I can tell you. I worked with her for a year before she signed the lease on this building. There were three other places she looked at, but she told me that she wanted a store on Madison Avenue. She believed it would bring her luck. It did."

Maddie took the tool that Cho offered and turned back to the circular rings. Then, drawing in a deep breath, she hit the first stroke.

8

WHILE ADAM had waxed on and on extolling the design values of first a ring and then a bracelet, Jase had taken the time to study the room. The worktable that Cho and Maddie sat at ran nearly the length of one wall. It had two workspaces. Adam's desk and worktable sat on the opposite wall.

Occasionally, Adam would glance over to see what Maddie was doing. Jase had used those opportunities to take a quick inventory of the sketches that nearly covered the walls. He knew from Jordan that Cho didn't create any original jewelry, that he worked on executing and occasionally modifying Eva's designs.

Adam's jewelry was bolder than Eva's, and his use of gems was more dramatic. Jase glanced down at the piece Adam had described as a tennis necklace of multicolored gems nestled between stations of etched gold. It was a stunner, and it was the only piece Adam had shown him that might suit Maddie.

"How much?" Jase asked.

"One hundred and fifty thousand." Adam glanced over his shoulder to check on Maddie and Cho again.

Jase took advantage of his distraction to pull open a second drawer in the small chest. It held hundreds of gems separated by colors into different compartments.

"Stop that."

It was only his lightning-fast reflexes that kept Jase's fingers from being caught when Adam slammed the drawer shut.

"That's a lot of bling," Jase commented.

"Yes." Adam held out his hand for the tennis necklace. "If that tennis necklace isn't to your taste, Arnold has more on the main floor."

Instead of handing it over, Jase poured the necklace from one hand into the other. "I heard there was a robbery here about a month ago. I guess they didn't get in here."

"No," Adam said shortly, wiggling his fingers impatiently for the necklace. "The thieves hit the main salon."

"I heard that what they took roughly amounted to fifty thousand less than the price of this necklace. But I suppose something like this would be harder to fence than the smaller pieces that were taken."

Adam stiffened. "Every piece that was taken was one of a kind. It was a terrible loss."

"Were some of your pieces stolen?"

Something flashed into Adam's eyes. Anger, or maybe fear. "As a matter of fact, none of my pieces were stolen. If your theory is correct, the thieves might have found my designs a little too pricey. Now, if you'll give me that necklace?"

"Actually, I like it. But it's a little large for Maddie. Could you make one a little bit daintier with smaller stones?"

Though Jase hadn't supposed it possible, Adam grew even stiffer and his voice rose slightly. "Absolutely not. I never alter one of my designs."

Jase allowed a puzzled expression to fill his face. "But Jordan told me that was why so few pieces were on display in the main salon—so that customers could consult with the designer and place special orders."

Adam snatched the necklace, placed it back in the cabinet

and locked the drawer. "That's Jordan's strategy. Aunt Eva went along with it. I didn't."

"But wouldn't you have made more money in the long run by following Jordan's strategy?"

Adam's chin lifted. "I'm an artist. I won't modify my designs."

Jase would grant Adam was creative. But if he had to choose two other words to describe Maddie and Jordan's cousin, they would be *arrogant* and *rebellious*. The rebelliousness was something he and his aunt Eva had shared. According to Jordan, both had shunned going into the family banking business. Perhaps Eva Ware had seen a bit of herself in her nephew. But in the end, she hadn't seen enough to leave him her business.

At the far end of the room, the first hit of a hammer sounded. Adam whirled toward Maddie and Cho. "Wait a minute. You can't—"

Jase gripped his arm and kept him firmly anchored in place. He pitched his voice low. "Actually, she can. You have no authority to stop her."

Adam's face went red with fury. But whatever he would have said was interrupted by the ringing of his cell phone. He glanced impatiently at the caller ID and then took the call. "Mother, I'm… No… Yes. I can explain."

Adam glanced once more at Maddie and Cho; then with frustration radiating off him in waves, he whirled and left the room.

What exactly did Adam Ware have to explain to his mother, Jase wondered. Whatever it was, he didn't seem happy about it. On the bright side, it had gotten Adam out of the room.

Jase shifted his attention to Maddie and Cho. Their heads were bent low over the pendant Maddie was working on, and

Cho was speaking in a low murmur. They were so absorbed in their work that he doubted they were aware that Adam had just stormed out.

Satisfied, Jase moved to a far window that looked down on 51st Street. Pedestrians moved quickly along the sidewalks in steady streams interrupted only by the changing traffic lights.

Adam Ware was going to be a problem. Jase knew from Jordan that Adam was twenty-nine and he'd joined Eva Ware Designs right out of college. He'd already been working there for three years and designing his own line of jewelry when Jordan had come on board. He'd resented her presence from the beginning and complained regularly about any changes she wanted to make.

And Jordan hadn't been a jewelry designer. How much more resentment was Adam feeling about Maddie? And just how dangerous was that temper that flared so close to the surface? Frowning, he glanced back at Maddie, saw her hold the pendant she was working on up to the light. Cho murmured something to her before she set it back on the worktable and once more picked up the small hammer.

The more Jase thought about it, the more he was convinced that Eva had stirred up a real hornet's nest of trouble with the terms of her will. In college, Jordan had described her mother as having an acute case of tunnel vision. And while it might have interfered with her personal life and relationships, Eva's ability to focus almost solely on her designs and business had served her career well. Jase had no doubt that the woman hadn't considered even for a minute the problems her daughters might encounter as a result of her desire to reunite them. Toss Eva's probable murder into the mix, and the terms of the will made a real recipe for disaster.

Jase didn't like any of it. But part of the Adam Ware problem could be solved—temporarily at least. The best way to get Adam off Maddie's back for a while was to distract him. And Jase had an idea of just how to do that.

Assured that Maddie and Cho were too engaged in their work to pay attention to anything he said, he turned back to the window and pressed a number into his phone.

"Campbell and Angelis Security."

Jase recognized his brother D.C.'s voice immediately. "Holding down the fort, are you?"

"So you've finally risen from the dead? From the way you were talking last night, I didn't expect to hear from you until at least midafternoon."

"Is Dino there?"

"He's due back momentarily. But I'm available," D.C. said. "And bored. Answering the phone is not really my true calling."

"I've got a list of names I want you to write down." Keeping his voice low, Jase rattled off the names of everyone they'd met so far at the store. "They all work at Eva Ware Designs."

"Sounds like you're working on a case."

"Yeah. It was one I agreed to before I left for South America. There was a break-in at Eva Ware's Madison Avenue jewelry store. That's Jordan's mother. She was struck down by a hit-and-run driver last week. I'm playing catch up and keeping an eye on Maddie, Jordan's sister."

"Wait a minute. Jordan has a sister?"

It occurred to Jase then that D.C. didn't yet know about Maddie. Hell, he'd only known about the will and Maddie's existence himself for what? Less than twelve hours? Quickly, he gave D.C. a condensed version of what Maddie had told him and then filled him in on what he'd learned from Dave Stanton.

D.C.'s reaction was summed up in a low whistle.

"What do you need?"

Jase nearly smiled. He knew D.C. had a million questions, but for now, he'd focus on the job. "Have Dino or one of the other men get financial information on all of those names—look for the disappearance or appearance of significant sums of money from their accounts. The jewelry that was stolen from the store had a value of approximately one hundred thousand dollars. And see what else pops."

There was a silence on the other end of the line, and Jase could picture D.C. writing everything down in the small notebook that he always carried with him. Cops, even of the military variety, always seemed to carry notebooks. There had never been much opportunity for jotting down notes on a special ops assignment, so Jase had learned to keep track of everything in his head.

He let his gaze sweep the street below. It was shortly after eleven, and pedestrian as well as vehicular traffic had picked up. He was about to turn around and check on Maddie again when he shifted his eyes back to the corner diagonally across from the store on Madison. Something had caught his attention. What?

Then he spotted her—the same matronly woman who'd been examining jewelry when he and Maddie had first entered the salon. She was wearing the same pillbox hat, the same pink suit. She stood in the recessed entranceway to a designer leather-goods store, but she wasn't window-shopping. Instead, she seemed to be watching Eva Ware Designs.

"Earth to Jase. Are you still there?"

The woman in the pink suit chose that moment to turn and walk into the Louis Vuitton store. Jase refocused his attention. "I'm here."

"Anything else you need?"

"Yeah." Jase flicked a glance toward Maddie. She was chewing on her bottom lip and beginning to wield that hammer like a pro. A few strands of hair had fallen loose from the knot she'd twisted it into.

"This is a job for you and it takes priority over the research for now. I want you to call Eva Ware Designs and ask to speak with Adam Ware. Identify yourself as a freelance writer. You're working on an article for *Vanity Fair* on up-and-coming jewelry designers. Ask him for an appointment ASAP." Jase glanced at his watch. Eleven-ten. "As soon as you hang up, if possible."

D.C. laughed. "Sounds like fun. I suppose you're not going to tell me why."

"Later. Just put the plan in action."

"Dino just came in so it shouldn't take us long. Anything I should know about this Adam Ware?"

"He has an ego the size of Australia."

"That should work. What do they say—the bigger they are, the harder they fall? Am I stuck with your scenario or can I make up one of my own?"

Jase bit back a grin. "Going to improvise, are you?"

"When we were kids and got into scrapes, I always came up with a better story than you did."

Jase wouldn't admit it out loud, but it was true. Not only was D.C. inventive, but he had a real flare for playing his audience. "Just keep it believable. And while you're creating your scenario, see if you can keep Ware busy for the next few days or weeks if possible."

"Got it. You know the military police never get assignments like this. Maybe I ought to get out and come to work for you."

"Anytime," Jase said before he closed his cell. If D.C. was serious, he and his brother would have to have a talk.

Later.

Cho and Maddie were now holding up the pendant to compare it to the sketch of the design. Neither of them glanced up when he moved to Adam's chair, sat down and propped his feet on the desk. It was his favorite position for thinking—and there were several things he needed to mull over.

At the top of the list was Maddie Farrell. Even now when he should be thinking of solving the puzzle of who'd robbed Eva's store and then run her down, he couldn't keep his eyes from returning to Maddie.

What he was feeling for her was growing beyond that initial chemical connection that had ignited between them. Little by little he was coming to know her as a person. She was smart, brave, certainly not afraid to try new things. Her spunk reminded him of his mother and sister. His lips curved as he thought of the game way she'd taken on the challenge of walking in Jordan's killer shoes, then handling her cousin. And now, she was also throwing herself into the task of working on one of her mother's designs.

As he watched, she picked up the pendant again and held it against the sketch. Though her back was to him, he knew that a little line was furrowing her brow. She'd inherited at least some of her mother's focus. And she shared Jordan's energy. And he'd experienced both of those qualities when they'd made love.

Just thinking about the night they'd spent together had his body hardening and desire moving through him with rusty claws. It wasn't just that he wanted to make love to her again. He had to. He needed to taste her again, touch her, to thrust into her when she knew it was him and not some dream lover.

The only question was, how long could he wait?

IT WAS two hours later when Jase and Maddie walked out of the work studio. Adam had checked on them once early on. Other than giving Maddie and Cho a frustrated look, he'd done nothing to interrupt them before leaving. "That was quite a design you finished."

"Thanks," Maddie said. "How did you manage to keep Adam distracted for so long?"

"Charm."

Maddie snorted. "I didn't think your brand would work on him."

"Piece of cake. All I had to do was ooh and ahh over his designs. And then he got a phone call from his mother and left."

"My impression is that she rides him pretty hard."

"He certainly didn't look like a happy camper when he got the call. What did you learn from Cho?"

She drew in a deep breath and let it out. "That my mother wanted me here."

Jase stopped dead in his tracks and turned to her. "That's the first time you've referred to Eva as your mother."

"I know."

"Did Eva tell Cho she wanted you here? Did he know about you?"

"No. Cho says Eva never mentioned me. He never knew that Jordan had a sister until I was invited for the reading of the will. But Cho said the will proves that my mother wanted me here. I hadn't thought about it quite that way before."

"He's right."

"I still have questions, hundreds of them, but it helps to look at the will that way—as proof that she really wanted me here. That she wanted to unite Jordan and me. Cho also told me that she specifically wanted a store on Madison Avenue because she believed it would bring her luck. Am I foolish to think that means she was thinking of me?"

Jase raised their joined hands to his lips and kissed her fingers. "No, it's not foolish at all. You've had a good day, Maddie Farrell."

"Yes. The next thing I'm going to do is to ask Michelle about my mother's appointment calendar."

But when they stepped into the office area, Michelle was on the phone and Dino Angelis was filming her with the video camera he had resting on his shoulder. Jase realized that when D.C. had promised fast action, he'd obviously meant it. Through the open doorway to one of the offices, Jase spotted Adam sitting behind his desk. Facing Jordan's cousin, with a cane hooked over the arm of his chair, was D.C. Adam seemed to be hanging on his every word. Jase wondered if the cane was a prop or if D.C. needed it for that leg injury he'd mentioned. The latter, he bet. He made a mental note to stop by the office later in the afternoon.

Putting down her phone, Michelle waved them over, and Dino moved toward the door to Adam's office.

"What's going on?" Maddie asked.

Michelle leaned closer and though her voice was pitched low, there was a thread of excitement running through it. "Those two men came to talk to Mr. Ware. The one with the cane is Mr. Duncan Dunleavy. He's producing a new reality TV show about artists in the city. They want to feature Mr. Ware on it. They've already taken some footage of him downstairs in the main salon."

"Wow," Jase said.

Maddie shot him a look, then turned back to Michelle. "And they just showed up out of the blue?"

"Oh, no. They phoned first, but they were in the area, and Mr. Ware told them to come right over. And he told me to send them right in when they arrived even though he was still talking with his mother."

"Dorothy Ware was here?" Maddie asked.

"She still is." Michelle put her fingers to her temples. "I was supposed to fetch you from the workroom, but I forgot.

Then we all got distracted by the filming. Mrs. Ware too. She had a lot of questions for Mr. Dunleavy. She's waiting in Jordan's office to talk to you."

Maddie's nerves began to jitter the moment that she entered Jordan's office and saw Dorothy Ware sitting ramrod-straight in one of the chairs. The older woman was wearing a linen suit in raspberry red, a pair of black patent-leather pumps and her hands were resting over a designer clutch bag on her lap. It was ridiculous to be intimidated just because she looked as if she'd just come from a cover shoot for *Vogue* magazine.

Reminding herself of the things that Cho had told her and of how she'd felt when she'd been working on the pendant her mother had designed, Maddie circled around Jordan's desk, sat down in the chair, and folded her hands in front of her. "What can I do for you, Mrs. Ware?"

"I'm here because I want to know what your plans are for my son. He doesn't seem to have the capability or the ambition to ask that question himself. If he's not marked for success here, his father can always find a place for him at Ware Bank."

The cool detached way Dorothy Ware was speaking about her son and his future sent a little chill through Maddie. "From what I've seen, Adam is a talented designer and he's been very successful here."

"Not successful enough for my sister-in-law to leave him the business. And when I called him a few hours ago, he felt threatened. I had to cancel a very important meeting to come over here. Carleton and I are chairing a fashion show to benefit a new children's cancer wing at Mount Sinai Hospital." She glanced at her watch. "I'm due back there right now. So I'd like to clarify this matter once and for all."

What matter? Maddie wondered. "Adam didn't look

threatened when I last saw him. In fact, he appeared to be excited and very engaged with the man in his office."

"Yes. Adam introduced me. Mr. Dunleavy wants to feature Adam in a TV show." Dorothy raised a well-manicured nail and pointed it at Maddie. "That ought to give you some idea of how valuable Adam is to Eva Ware Designs. Eva depended on his genius."

"I know how valuable Adam is."

Dorothy met Maddie's eyes steadily. "He believes that you intend to take over as head designer and push him out."

Maddie drew in a deep breath. "I don't know where Adam got that idea. For the next three weeks all I intend to do is fulfill the terms of my mother's will."

"I understood that you were to merely step into your sister's shoes and do her job. Jordan doesn't work in the design part of the business."

Maddie raised her chin. "Well, I do. And I intend to work with Cho Li to bring the sketches my mother left to fruition. However, I have no intention of getting rid of Adam or pushing him out. From what I've seen he's a brilliant designer. I assure you his job is secure."

There was a beat of silence, then Dorothy Ware rose from her chair. "Thank you. If Adam was able to speak for himself, I wouldn't have had to waste my time with a trip over here."

Maddie managed to suppress a shiver until Dorothy Ware had swept out of the room and Jase had closed the door. "Is it my imagination or did the temperature in the room just warm up a few degrees?"

"She's a cold one," Jase murmured. "I wonder if Adam ever pleases her."

"We're not seeing any of them under the best conditions. The terms of the will must have thrown everyone in the family a curve ball." She turned to him then and gave him a speculative look. "Speaking of curve balls, Adam seems to be completely caught up in this reality-TV thing. Did you have something to do with it?"

Jase smiled slowly. "You're a sharp one, Maddie Farrell. What tipped you off that I had something to do with it?"

"The timing. It was very convenient. Do they work for you?"

"Duncan Dunleavy is my younger brother, D.C. And the man toting the video camera is my partner, Dino Angelis. I phoned and asked D.C. to come up with a distraction while you were working with Cho."

"It's not going to be pretty when Adam finds out it's all a hoax."

"No worries," Jase assured her. "When the time comes, D.C. will have a plausible exit strategy. It won't come back to bite you. And it may give Adam the time he needs to stop feeling so paranoid."

Maddie rose, walked to him. Then, rising on her toes, she kissed him lightly. "Thanks."

Jase found it took some effort not to grab her and deepen the kiss. *Later,* he promised himself. Then he wondered how much longer he could wait.

MADDIE SANK onto one of the luxuriously upholstered couches in the ladies' room. With D.C. and Jase's partner filming, the only way Maddie could get Michelle alone was to bring her here. The restroom was a true lounge. In addition to three stalls as well as a double sink, there was a comfortably furnished outer sitting area. A mirrored wall allowed ample room for retouching makeup, and Michelle was making good use of it. Maddie made a mental note to use some tomorrow. In Santa Fe, she rarely bothered with anything more than a moisturizing sunscreen and a touch of lipstick.

When Michelle finally turned, Maddie said, "Before we go back out there, would you mind if I asked you a question?"

"Anything. I can't imagine how difficult this must be for you, and Adam is being so rude."

"Does that surprise you?"

Michelle shook her head. "No. He's very absorbed in his work. In himself. But he doesn't treat Jordan the way he's treating you. Maybe it's because you design jewelry and he sees that as a threat to his position here at Eva Ware Designs." Michelle glanced at her watch. "I'd better get back. I'm not supposed to be away from my desk for long."

"Just one question," Maddie said. "I'm assuming that Eva kept some sort of appointment calendar?"

"She had a Palm Pilot."

"I'd like to see it. I don't want anything important to slip through the cracks while I'm here."

Michelle grimaced. "The Palm Pilot should be in her desk drawer—top right. That's where I put it each time I updated it from her desktop. But she never really got the hang of it. She always used one of those old-fashioned leather-bound books with a ribbon to mark the current page."

Something tightened around Maddie's heart. She reached into her tote and pulled out her own day planner. "Was it like this?"

Michelle's eyes widened. "Just like it."

"Do you know where I could find Eva's?"

"That's yours?"

Maddie nodded.

Michelle thought for a moment. "Eva always took it home with her at night. I imagine it would have been with her…effects. Jordan might have a better idea."

As she followed Michelle out of the room, Maddie reminded herself that she needed to talk to her sister.

LEANING AGAINST a doorjamb, Jase watched the two women walk out of the restroom. A ringing phone had Michelle rushing for her desk.

It was only as Maddie drew close that he noticed how tired she looked. Little wonder with the emotional roller-coaster ride she'd been on all morning. There were dark smudges under her eyes. He reached out and rubbed a thumb over one of them. "Tough day."

"But I'm making progress. I just learned that my mother kept an appointment calendar in a book very similar to mine."

Jase tucked a loose strand of her hair behind her ear. "Like mother, like daughter."

She swallowed. "Maybe. I'm still getting used to thinking about her as my mother. And every time I do, I can't help but wish I could have met her, talked to her. Had a chance to work at her side."

Jase traced a finger along her cheek. "I know." He experienced a sudden urge to take her away and give her a break. Give them both a break.

Behind them, the phone rang again, and Michelle said, "Eva Ware Designs."

Maddie glanced around. "Where's Adam?"

"They're in the work studio. D.C. wanted to get some footage of the designer at work. The reality-TV gig should keep Adam out of your hair for a while."

"Jordan?" The excitement in Michelle's voice had them both looking at her.

"Yes. Yes, she's right here." Turning to Maddie, Michelle continued, "It's your sister. Why don't you take it in her office?"

Maddie hurried into the room and picked up the phone.

Closing the door, Jase said, "Put it on speaker."

Jordan's voice filled the room. "Maddie, something terrible has happened. Are you alone?"

"No," Maddie said. "Jase is here. I've put the phone on speaker so he can hear."

"Jase is back?"

"I'm right here, Jordan. We're in your office. What's happened?"

"It's Maddie's design…" Jordan's voice broke, and suddenly there was a man speaking on the other end of the line.

"Maddie, this is Cash."

The cowboy, Jase thought as he stepped closer to the desk. "Jordan never cries," he muttered to Maddie. He raised his voice. "Is Jordan all right?"

"She's fine. Who are you?"

"Jase Campbell."

"Jordan said you were in South America."

"Maddie said you were out on a cattle drive."

"I'm back."

Maddie stared at Jase. Not only had he tensed up, but he'd used a more polite tone with Adam.

"Is Maddie all right?" Cash asked.

Maddie shifted her gaze to the phone. There was an edge to Cash's voice too. "I'm fine. Put Jordan back on—or better still, push the speakerphone button."

"Maddie?" Jordan's voice was stronger now. "I don't want you to worry. I can get it all fixed while I'm here. As far as we can tell, nothing was stolen. I wasn't even going to tell you about it, but Cash said I had to."

"Tell me about what?"

"Your design studio. Someone broke into it and…destroyed everything."

Maddie felt Jase's hand close around hers, and she gripped it hard. "But you're all right?"

"She's fine," Cash said. "She told me about this will her mother left. I was thinking that perhaps someone vandalized the place to upset you enough to have you flying back here. Or perhaps to scare Jordan so she would leave. So stay right where you are, Maddie. I'm going to stick close to Jordan for the next three weeks. We'll hire Mitch Cramer to repair the damage. And I'll get one of my men to stand guard."

"Cash, you insisted Jordan tell us because you're afraid that something similar might occur on this end too?" asked Jase.

"Something like that."

"Good thinking."

Maddie studied Jase. The tension she'd sensed in him earlier had faded.

"You should stick close to Maddie," Cash said.

Jase squeezed Maddie's hand. "I intend to. We've got some bad news on this end too."

"What? Has something happened at the store?" Jordan asked.

"Everything's fine at the store except that Adam isn't happy that Maddie's here."

"Surprise, surprise," Jordan said in a dry tone.

Maddie exchanged a look with Jase and saw the quick flash of humor in his eyes. She might not have known her sister for very long, but she sounded more like Jordan now than she had when she'd first called.

"It's not good news," Jase warned. "You might want to sit down."

"I'm fine standing."

Maddie kept her fingers laced with Jase's as he told Cash and Jordan about the investigation into her mother's death.

"It wasn't an accident." Jordan's voice was steady, and since it wasn't a question, Maddie and Jase remained silent. "The police are investigating a homicide."

"A possible homicide," Jase corrected. "I have a hunch the hit-and-run is connected to the break-in and robbery at the store. Your mother and I both suspected that it was an inside job."

"She never mentioned that to me."

"I don't think Eva wanted anyone to know."

"Who in the store would do something like that?" Jordan asked.

"That's the million-dollar question. Any ideas?"

"No," she replied.

"She hired me to look into it, and I told her I could put someone on it while I was in South America. She refused the offer. She insisted I handle it personally. Hindsight is twenty-twenty. I think she had some idea of who the thief was."

"Then she definitely would have followed up on that," Jordan said. "Eva Ware Designs was her baby. If she was right and someone on the inside had robbed the store, she would have wanted to avoid scandal at all costs. I wouldn't have agreed. That's probably why she never mentioned it to me. Maybe I should fly back."

"No." Cash, Jase and Maddie spoke in unison.

For a moment there was silence. Then Maddie said, "Remember why we agreed to change places, Jordan. I've only just seen the store and Eva's workplace, but you don't want her work and her legacy to die. I don't want that either. And you haven't had a chance yet to explore the ranch."

"Okay. Okay, you're right," Jordan agreed.

"And I'm working with Jase," Maddie continued. "We're going to find out who did this."

"What can I do to help?" Jordan asked.

Maddie was relieved to hear that her sister's voice was calmer. "Eva's appointment calendar—the leather-bound volume—we're trying to locate it."

"That old thing. Even with Michelle's help, I couldn't drag her into the twenty-first century."

"Where is it?" Maddie asked. "Michelle said she took it home every night. Do you know where we could find it?"

"She always put it in her tote bag." There was a pause at the other end of the line. "When I picked up her stuff at the morgue, I couldn't bear to bring any of it back to my apartment. So I dropped the box off at hers. You'll find everything in the front hall closet. Why do you want it?"

"If she confronted whoever it was she suspected, she may have noted it in her calendar. It's the kind of thing that I would do."

"If you're right that someone at Eva Ware Designs murdered Eva, and he or she discovers that you're looking into it, you could both be in mortal danger," Cash commented.

"Yeah," Jase said.

There was a knock on the door.

"Just a minute," Jase called out. Then he said, "We've got to go."

"You take care of Maddie," Cash said.

"You got it," Jase said. "Same goes for Jordan."

"Got it covered."

As the connection went dead, Jase said, "I like your Cash Landry."

Maddie raised an eyebrow at him. "Good to know that he has your stamp of approval. I like him too. He's been like a brother to me. And he'll take good care of Jordan. It's thanks to his careful instruction that I was able to knock you on your ass this morning."

Jase grinned at her and slung a friendly arm around her shoulder. "I don't think he has the same 'brotherly' feelings toward your sister. And she's such a city girl."

Maddie was still trying to absorb Jase's implication when the knock sounded at the door again.

"Yes?" Jase said.

Michelle popped her head in. "I'm about to order in for lunch. Would you like me to get something for you?"

Before Maddie could answer, Jase said, "Nah. I'm going to take Maddie out for lunch. I think she needs a break."

9

JASE'S IDEA of a "break" was an impromptu picnic in Central Park. Maddie was delighted. The morning had been intense and so much had happened, her mind was still whirling with it. They'd used the 60th Street entrance, and the first thing that had caught her eye was the long line of tourists waiting for a horse-and-buggy tour.

"Don't even think about taking a carriage ride," Jase said.

"I wasn't."

"Liar. I can tell by the way you're looking at those horses. If you want, we can come back tonight when the traffic is lighter. In the meantime, you need something besides chocolate chip cookies to sustain you." He waved a hand at the array of vendors hawking their wares. "What are you adventurous enough to try?"

She met his eyes. "Surprise me."

"Do you have objections to onions?"

"Not as long as you eat them too."

With a laugh, he leaned down and kissed her. It was brief, friendly, and it shouldn't have made her knees melt. Still, she couldn't trust her legs to carry her, so Maddie stood where she was and watched Jase join a long line at a hot-dog stand. Even at a distance, she could feel the strong, steady pull he had on her senses.

And on her.

What had happened in his bed had connected them in a way that she'd never before experienced with a man. And over and above the strength of the chemistry that existed between them, she was beginning to know him as a person.

He'd made his way to the head of the line, and as she watched, he leaned against the cart and said something to the man behind it that had the vendor suddenly grinning. Beneath that easygoing, laid-back persona he projected lurked so many other qualities. She'd glimpsed the hint of recklessness in his eyes and there'd been a no-nonsense toughness in the way he'd initially handled Cash on the phone. There wasn't a doubt in her mind that Jase could be ruthless when he wanted to. But she'd also been on the receiving end of his kindness. She thought of the way he'd searched the kitchen for Jordan's stash of cookies, the way he'd hailed a taxi to save her from having to walk over twenty blocks in Jordan's killer shoes, and of the creative way he'd gotten Adam Ware off her back for the time being.

Her stomach did a little flip. And it wasn't merely from hunger. Being involved with Jase Campbell had the potential to be the biggest mistake she'd ever made in her life. But she'd gone way past the point of being able to draw on reason and logic. There'd be a price to pay when she had to go back to Santa Fe, but that was not going to stop her from making the most of the time she had with Jase.

But for now, she was going to stop staring at him like a gawking teenager. Turning, she found a space to sit on a nearby bench and eased her feet out of Jordan's super-stylish shoes.

Glancing down, Maddie saw that her toes had turned red where the shoes had put pressure on them. She was beginning to think that the only way that the *Sex and the City* women had managed to survive their fabulous footwear was to walk in the shoes only while on camera.

Then pushing the thought of her aching feet away, she simply tried to drink in everything around her. Though she'd seen plenty of pictures of Central Park on TV and in the movies, none of it had accurately captured the experience of being here.

A wide range of sensations bombarded her—from the familiar aroma of horses and leather to the more foreign smells of exhaust fumes and sunbaked pavement. Layered through those were the scents of food—onions, pizza—and humanity.

The sun beat down and moist heat bounced up from the cement sidewalks. Flowers bloomed everywhere, spilling out of pots and neatly bordering the walkway. Others grew among the rocks and boulders.

But it was the people who fascinated her. Throngs of them passed by pushing strollers, riding bikes, clicking cameras. There was such a variety of voices, accents and foreign languages. She recognized Spanish easily but was hard-pressed to identify most of the others.

And there were so many different types, ages and sizes— from teenagers racing around in skimpy halter tops to elderly couples walking at a more leisurely pace. A dignified-looking older man using a motorized wheelchair caught her attention. A portly woman in a pink suit hurried by him carrying two large shopping bags. Maddie had to look twice, but she was sure it was the same woman she'd seen in Eva Ware Designs when they'd first entered the main salon. It seemed to her that perhaps half the population of New York had chosen to take a lunch break in the park.

"C'mon, we have to find a picnic spot." Jase reached for her hand.

She glanced down at the shoes. "Can't we eat here?"

Leaning down, he scooped the high heels up and handed

them to her. Then he urged her off the path onto the grass. It felt cool and soothing beneath her feet.

"*Barefoot in the Park.* There's an old Neil Simon movie by that title," he remarked as he led her further away from the footpath.

"Starring Jane Fonda and Robert Redford when they were in their twenties. You know that film?"

"Jordan has a copy of it. She's a real movie buff. One of her favorite ways to relax is watching old films."

"I used to watch movies all the time with my dad. He has an amazing collection. Some of them are really old—*The Thin Man* and some Charlie Chan movies."

"You'll have to look through Jordan's collection. How about here?" Jase asked.

"Great." He'd chosen a circular stretch of grass at the foot of a hillside banked with large boulders. A line of trees branched off on either side providing plenty of shade, and a soft breeze offered respite from the heat. Maddie glanced over her shoulder. The footpath was still visible, but it was a couple hundred yards away and the sounds were muted.

Jase settled himself cross-legged on the grass, and after hitching up her skirt, she joined him.

"Sorry there's no picnic blanket." He dug into the bag and handed her a hot dog and a bottled water.

"I'll complain later when I see the grass stains. Right now I'm too hungry to care." She turned her attention to the hot dog. The spicy aroma of onions and chili had her stomach growling.

"I ordered it loaded," Jase explained.

She licked mustard off her thumb, then bit into the hot dog. The explosion of flavors on her tongue had her closing her eyes and sighing. "It's great. I can even taste some of the flavors of Santa Fe."

"It's the chili," Jase said around a mouthful. "Although I like mine hotter."

"So that it cauterizes your throat."

"Exactly."

"Me too."

The second time she paused to lick condiments off her fingers, Jase dug in the bag and produced napkins.

For a few moments they ate in silence, except for the muted sounds from the footpath. And farther away, she could hear the sounds of New York City traffic—the horns, the revved motors. But here in this spot, the buzzing of bees was louder.

She'd eaten nearly the whole hot dog when she set it carefully on a bed of napkins and opened her water bottle. As she swallowed the cold liquid her thoughts slipped back to the four-way conversation they'd had with Cash and Jordan.

"Penny for your thoughts," Jase said.

She met his eyes. "Ever since I got that phone call from Mr. Fitzwalter, my mind has been filled with questions."

Jase used one of the napkins to wipe his mouth. "Maybe I can help. Ask away."

Maddie hesitated. She didn't want to return yet to the questions that had been plaguing her about her parents' separation, about Eva, about Eva's death. Not when the sun was shining so brightly and they'd found a little oasis of seclusion in the teeming city. So she asked, "Tell me about your family."

His eyebrows rose. "I'll bet that's not the question at the top of your list."

"Maybe not." She smiled as she stretched out her legs and leaned back on her hands. "But I asked it. I already know you have a brother."

Jase gathered up their trash and put it in the empty bag.

"D.C., aka Duncan Dunleavy, is a captain in the army's military police. He's served two tours of duty in Iraq, and he's currently on leave because of a leg injury. Last night when I landed at LaGuardia, I called my office and he picked up the phone. He visited my mother and sister in Baltimore for a while and then a couple of days ago he decided to drop in on me."

"But you were out of the country."

Jase nodded. "He decided until I got back that he'd work at my office. My partner being the smart man that he is took D.C. up on the offer. My brother likes to keep busy. You might have a chance to meet him in person later today—depending on how long his charade runs with Adam."

"And the rest of your family?"

"My father was a career military man in the marines. Nineteen years ago, when he was just a year short of early retirement, he was killed by friendly fire."

"I'm so sorry, Jase."

"It was a long time ago. D.C. and I were nine and ten, and we were very close to him, which is probably why we both ended up joining a branch of the military. Then there's my mother, who's a high-school principal in Baltimore." He smiled. "You'd like her. She's a petite woman—but tough. She takes no prisoners. And there's my sister Darcy who's still in college. She's not sure yet what she wants to be when she grows up. Currently she's torn between law school and joining the staff of our congresswoman. D.C. and I don't want her going into the army or the navy, so we're bad-mouthing lawyers and politicians."

Maddie's eyes widened. "Why?"

"We learned when she was two that anytime we offer advice, she does the exact opposite."

She laughed, and he joined her. The way he described his family, she could almost picture them.

"I've got a cousin too. Sloan Campbell. He trains horses out in the San Diego area. His father and mine were step-brothers. I haven't seen him in years."

She tilted her head to one side. "How did you end up in the security business?"

Jase's eyes grew more serious. "I guess one answer is that my father's dream was to open his own private-investigation firm once he got out of the army. I always thought that one day D.C. and I might join him—a sort of family business. That's why I went to Wharton and majored in business. But I also got into security and investigation because I like solving puzzles."

"Puzzles?"

"It was the same thing that drew me to special ops in the navy. Oh, I liked the action and adventure, the adrenaline highs, but it was coming up with a plan that I liked best. There'd always be this goal, and I'd enjoy coming up with more than one way to get to it. Because a good op always needs back-up plans."

Maddie studied him for a moment. The man had a natural bent for making light of things—even serious issues. But there was something more serious in his eyes when he talked about his work. "It sounds a bit like designing jewelry. I get a vision of the finished product in my head, and then I have to figure out a way to get there."

"It's a lot like that." Jase reached out and took her hand. "Now, why don't you ask me the question that put that frown on your face when you were eating?"

Maddie sighed. It helped that Jase had taken her hand. It was a question that had been nagging at her ever since she'd started to get to know her sister. "What can you tell me about Jordan's relationship with Eva?"

"Jordan never talked much about it, but I sensed it wasn't as close as she may have wanted it to be."

"Why not?"

"Eva was a very self-contained woman, very focused on her art. Jordan never put it into words, but I think your sister believed that if she had inherited her mother's talent for designing jewelry, she and Eva would have been closer."

Something tightened around Maddie's heart. "Do you think that's true?"

Jase shook his head. "I think Eva distanced herself from everyone because the most important thing to her was her art and Eva Ware Designs. Your sister called it tunnel vision. That's why Jordan's description of how your mother might have wanted to handle the robbery rings so true to me. I should have anticipated that Eva would have wanted to keep it quiet and minimize the scandal."

Releasing Maddie's hand, he rolled to his feet and paced to the boulder. "That's why she came to me instead of going to the police. I should have pressed harder to convince her to let my partner Dino work on it. But I was scheduled to leave the next morning and I was thinking about the three hostages they were holding." He whirled to face her. "I'm betting Jordan's right and Eva did some investigating on her own."

Maddie got up off the ground and moved to him. "You believe she figured out who broke into the store."

"Yes. And I'm betting it was someone we met today."

The faces ran through Maddie's mind on a little video loop—Arnold Bartlett, Cho, Michelle Tan, Adam. She didn't want it to be any of them.

"If I hadn't taken that case in South America, if I'd just been here…"

Maddie lifted her hands to his face. "The father and the son you helped rescue might be dead. It won't do any good to blame yourself for Eva's death. We've got to concentrate on solving the puzzle. Who ran Eva down and why?"

AT HER TOUCH, Jase felt his temper and frustration with himself ease. "You're right. And we should get on it."

"So what's the plan? I was thinking before we go back to the office, we should go to Eva's apartment and find the appointment calendar. I'm sure it will tell us something."

He took her wrist in his hand intending to guide her out, but then he felt her pulse speed instantly at his touch and it drew an immediate response from him. They had places to go, people to see. But what he felt when he looked into her eyes had him backing into the boulder and drawing her closer.

"Jase?"

It wasn't objection he heard in her tone. It was invitation. That alone had fire moving through his veins and whatever good intentions he had went up in the smoke. He'd promised himself that he could wait until they went back to the apartment.

But wasn't this why he'd brought her here to this out-of-the-way spot?

He drew her closer until her body was pressed fully against his. Then, wondering if he'd had any choice at all, he murmured, "Maddie," and touched his lips to hers.

If she had protested in any way, made a sound, put those hands on his chest to push him away, he might have been able to keep it short, quick and simple as he had earlier when he'd kissed her in the office. But her mouth went from cool to hot in an instant, burning with an urgency that mirrored his. Her arms went around his neck, she threaded her fingers through his hair and pressed herself close to him, pushing him harder into the granite boulder.

He simply had to devour her. He ran one hand down her back to her hip and splayed his fingers, drawing her closer. Her body was so strong, so soft, so supple. Just as he remembered. And those sounds she made in her throat. It seemed he'd waited forever to hear them again. He ran a greedy hand over her. More heat surged through him, incredibly, impossibly.

Suddenly frantic, he grabbed her hair, drawing her head back so that he could plunder the sweet, moist recesses of her mouth. Then, murmuring her name, he spun her around and rammed her against the granite boulder. In some part of his mind that was still functioning, he knew that he should draw her around to the other side of the rock where they would have more privacy. Then he could have her. He was skilled enough, she aroused enough. It would be crazy, wild. Wonderful.

He could raise her skirt and sink into her, lose himself in her the way he had during the night. He spun her again, moving her closer to the other side of the boulder. The second time he turned her, he felt a chip of rock sting his face.

There was only one thing Jase knew of that could dislodge a piece of granite like that. A bullet.

While his mind rocketed to full alert, his body operated on instinct, pushing Maddie behind the outcrop of rock and shoving her down.

He heard her suck in air. "What?"

"Shh." He clamped his hand over her mouth and listened hard.

Nothing.

He glanced down at Maddie. Her face had gone white, and her eyes held both questions and fear.

He lifted his hand from her mouth and shifted his weight a bit so she could breathe.

She touched his cheek. "You're hurt. What happened?"

"Someone shot at us."

"I didn't hear—"

"They used a silencer."

"And they hit you?"

"No." Relieved that she wasn't going into shock, he continued, "The bullet dislodged a piece of granite."

"Who?"

"It's a pro," he said, thinking aloud. "He may think we ducked behind here to make love." Jase figured that thanks to him their actions had pointed in that direction.

"In that case, he'll wait us out," Jase mused. "But if the shooter doesn't buy into that idea, it's not going to be long before he circles through the trees to come at us from the other side to finish the job. That's what I'd do."

Maddie's lip trembled, but her eyes stayed clear and focused on his. "What are we going to do?"

Jase wriggled out of his blazer, took his gun out of its holster and stuffed it in the back waistband of his jeans. "*I'm* going to see if we can sell him on the fact that we're back here having at each other. And *you're* going to stay put."

Rolling off her, he crumpled up his jacket and lobbed it so that half of it fell just beyond the edge of the boulder. Hopefully, it would lie well within the sight line of the shooter.

"Now, give me yours."

Maddie levered herself up and tugged off her jacket.

Jase took it and tossed it a little to the left of his blazer.

"Now what?" Maddie asked.

Jase's eyes shot to her face. Her lips weren't trembling anymore. The trace of fear was still in her eyes, but so was a gleam of determination. She was game for anything. He took her chin in his hand and kissed her quickly. Then he took his cell phone out of his pocket and handed it to her. "You're going to dial 911, fill the operator in and describe our location. We're about half a mile into the park off the 60th Street entrance. Then cross your fingers and pray that the shooter thinks we're back here having a good time."

She moistened her lips. "What are you going to do?"

"I'm going to use the rocks for cover, crawl into the trees and circle behind him."

"No." She grabbed a fistful of his T-shirt. "You stay here too until the police arrive."

"He's a pro, Maddie. He might not have waited to see me toss our clothes. He could already be heading this way to fulfill his contract."

"Then it's too dangerous."

He gripped her shoulders and let his eyes go hard. "You have to trust me. I've done this kind of thing before. Besides, it could be more dangerous if I stay here. We could both end up dead."

He waited until he saw acceptance in her eyes, and then he crawled away.

WITH TREMBLING HANDS, Maddie set the cell phone on the ground beside her. The police were on their way. Talking to the 911 operator and focusing on describing their location had distracted her. But she'd lost track of the time. Plus the adrenaline that had flooded her system when Jase had told her they'd been shot at had faded.

Only the fear was left. She was still looking at the spot where Jase had crawled into the trees. How long ago had that been?

Too long.

As fear raged through her, images and snatches of what he'd said to her before he left drifted back into her mind. She pictured the way he'd handled his gun before he'd stuffed it into the waistband of his jeans. He was a pro too, she reminded herself.

You have to trust me, he'd said. *I've done this kind of thing before.*

And he had, she lectured herself. He'd worked special ops.

He'd be all right. He had to be. But why wasn't he back? Why hadn't the police arrived yet?

Fisting her hands at her sides, Maddie listened hard. But all she heard was the distant traffic and the muted sounds of park visitors as they passed by on the footpath below. No sirens. No gunshots.

A sudden thought occurred to her. The man who'd shot at them had used a silencer. He could have already killed Jase without making a noise.

Then she heard the shots. One. Two. Three.

Without another thought, she shifted onto her hands and knees and began to crawl toward the trees just as she'd seen Jase do.

10

JASE HAD KEPT crawling for a good hundred feet before he'd gotten up. As long as he'd been on hands and knees, he'd been able to keep the sounds of his progress to a minimum. Once he had started to run in a zig-zag pattern through the trees, there was a good chance the shooter could hear him.

The upside of that was that it would take the hit man's attention away from Maddie. The downside was that it increased Jase's chances of getting shot. He hadn't let himself think about that. When he thought he'd covered enough distance, Jase took cover behind a thick tree trunk and listened hard.

Nothing. Even the birds and squirrels had been silenced by all the noise he'd made. While he listened and caught his breath, he focused on the grid he'd imagined of an equilateral triangle. The boulder where he'd left Maddie and the shooter's position lay at opposite ends of its base and the point of the triangle was about a hundred yards into the trees just where he was now.

Initially, the woods had been cool, but there was no breeze. Sweat trickled down his back. When a bird returned to a tree overhead and began to sing, Jase began to make his way slowly and carefully toward the point of the triangle where he'd figured the shooter had positioned himself.

Of course, nothing was certain. The man could be long

gone by now. But Jase didn't think so. He'd always figured that being a hired assassin required almost unlimited patience. And he was betting that the shooter had decided to wait Maddie and him out. After all, how long did it take for a little lunchtime quickie in Central Park?

When Jase figured he was nearly where he wanted to be, the hair on the back of his neck stood up and a coolness settled over his mind. He slipped behind the nearest tree. Though his instincts weren't as sharp as his partner Dino Angelis's were, he trusted them.

He waited. The shooter wasn't the only one who could be patient. One minute stretched into two and then five. As each one passed, Jase became more certain that his opponent was nearby.

The intermittent soft breezes he felt told him that he was close to the treeline. The shooter had to be somewhere in that direction. Very carefully, he edged his head out enough to scan the trees.

He saw nothing. And if he'd given his position away, some bark would be flying off the tree. Jase glanced at his watch. If Maddie had followed his instructions, the police should be here very soon. There'd be sirens. Once warned, the shooter would take off.

Should he wait? Jase pondered that for a couple of seconds. Nah, he decided. Squatting very carefully, he picked up a small rock, then straightened and tossed it to his left.

The moment Jase heard the thud, he poked his head out again and scanned the area. Out of the corner of his eye, he saw bark fly. He figured he had about five seconds to spot the shooter while his attention was focused on the place where the rock had fallen.

But there was no one. It was only after he'd pulled his head back out of sight that he realized he'd seen something in his peripheral vision—a black canvas bag at the base of a tree about ten feet away. He was betting his shooter was in that tree.

Drawing his gun, he clasped it in both hands, drew it up, and risked another quick look. He spotted the man on a branch about fifty feet off the ground. He wore all black. A bullet thudded into the tree inches away from his face. Operating on instinct, Jase threw himself to the ground, rolled twice, then took aim at the tree limb and fired three times.

The branch swayed, then cracked, and the shooter fell. Jase kept his position and counted to ten. The man had dropped his rifle and it was lying on the ground about two yards out of reach. So far he'd made no move to retrieve it.

Slowly, Jase got to his feet and walked forward. Nothing moved. There was absolute silence. The shots that had been fired had sent birds flying out of the trees. When he reached the prone body, he realized two things. The hit man was a woman, and she'd been playing possum.

Too bad he didn't realize the latter until she'd hurled a rock at his forehead. He fought off the grayness that threatened to envelop him while she leapt to her feet, grabbed his gun hand and flipped him to the ground.

MADDIE WAITED only until she reached the cover of the trees before she hauled herself to her feet and ran directly to her left. That was where the shots had come from. Shots from Jase's gun, she told herself. He was all right.

But she never would have heard the shots from the other gun because it had a silencer, nagged a little voice at the back of her mind.

A fresh jolt of fear had her hitching up her skirt and forcing more speed into her legs. Being barefoot slowed her down. The carpet of dried leaves helped, but stones and branches still cut into the soles of her feet, causing her to skid and stumble. Once she saved herself by grabbing the trunk of a tree. The next time she went down on all fours. She stayed there for a moment dragging breath into her burning lungs.

And she listened.

She heard it then—grunts and thuds, the crunch of leaves. Sounds of a struggle. Hope blossomed within her, and she pushed herself up again. She raced for the line of trees and tore across the grass toward the noise. She'd just dashed into the trees again when she heard the sirens. The police were coming.

Maddie skidded to a halt the moment she saw them. A woman and Jase were rolling over the ground locked in a vicious struggle. First one was on top, then the other. Blood pouring from a gash on Jake's forehead was putting him at a disadvantage.

The sirens grew louder, but they weren't going to arrive in time. Maddie glanced around quickly and spotted Jase's gun. She raced toward it, picked it up and whirled. The woman was on top again. Raising the weapon in both hands, Maddie took aim. They rolled over once, then again.

Her hand was steady. She knew how to handle a gun. Her father had seen to that. But she didn't want to hit Jase. She glanced around the area again. Then she spotted something. Trading the gun for a fat tree branch, she cocked it over her shoulder and dashed toward them.

The woman rolled on top and wrapped her hands around Jase's throat. He grabbed for hers. The sound of ragged breathing filled the air.

Maddie evened her stance and swung the branch. The woman fell forward onto Jase. Dropping her makeshift bat, Maddie dragged her off him.

"Maddie?" Swiping blood out of his eyes, Jase got to his knees. "You were supposed to stay put."

"I heard shots. I didn't think the police were going to get here in time." She dropped to her knees too and forced herself to take a closer look at the wound on his forehead. "Did she shoot you?"

"Nah. She suckered me by playing possum, then threw a rock. I'm going to have a hell of a headache. What did you take her out with?"

"A tree branch."

"Good job."

With great effort, Maddie shifted her gaze to the woman who lay facedown in the dirt. "Is she...dead?"

As if in answer, the woman moaned.

"Evidently not. But I'm not taking any chances this time." Jase drew a pair of plastic restraints out of his pocket and fastened her hands behind her back, then secured her feet.

The sirens that had been growing steadily louder abruptly stopped.

Jase shoved himself to his feet and moved to a nearby tree where he knelt down beside a black duffel Maddie hadn't noticed before. "Before we go out to talk to them, I want to take a quick look in our shooter's bag."

He unzipped it and the first thing he drew out was a pink pillbox hat. Then he lifted a pink jacket and a padded vest. He shifted his gaze to Maddie.

"It's the woman who was in the main salon of the store when we arrived."

"I saw her later across the street watching the front entrance," Jase said as he stuffed everything back into the duffel.

"And I saw her enter the park with two shopping bags."

"To carry the duffel and the rifle." Jase rose, slung the bag over his shoulder. When he reached her, he pulled her close. She wrapped her arms around him and for a moment they stood still and merely held on. It wasn't passion that moved through her. It was something else, warmer, sweeter. Maddie knew that she could have stood there for a very long time.

But there were footsteps approaching, so she lifted her head. Jase met her eyes, and his were cool and hard. "One thing we know now. Only someone who knew you were visiting the store this morning could have set this up. And that someone wants you dead."

Then to Maddie's surprise, he gripped her shoulders hard and gave her a hard shake. "So the next time I tell you to stay put, follow orders."

IT WAS with some relief that Jase opened the door and let Maddie precede him into his office. Thanks to Dave Stanton and the fact that he'd done some favors for a few detectives at the precinct, they'd been delayed less than two hours giving their statements. While one of the policewomen had helped Maddie wash up in the restroom and had lent her a pair of sneakers, Jase had called Michelle Tan to explain why they wouldn't be returning to the store. Then he'd called Dino and D.C. to fill them in and ask them to join him ASAP at the office.

Maddie hadn't talked to him during the taxi ride to his office. She was annoyed. But he was the one who had a right to be annoyed. She should have stayed behind the boulder. Every time he thought of what might have happened, what almost *had* happened…

Mostly, he was angry with himself. He should have taken better care of her.

Dino rose from his chair as they entered and walked toward Maddie, his hand extended. "You must be Maddie. I only met your sister Jordan once, but the resemblance is striking."

"Thank you."

To Jase's annoyance, Maddie beamed a very warm smile at Dino. Dino not only returned it but he held on to her hand a moment before releasing it. If Jase hadn't been sure that Dino and Cat McGuire were totally in love, he might have been jealous. But he wasn't.

"I hear you saved my partner's life," Dino said.

Maddie sent Jase a look. "He's mad at me about that."

"I'm not mad," Jase said.

She turned back to Dino. "Instead of saying thank you, he told me to follow orders next time. Can you picture that?"

Much to Jase's annoyance, Dino grinned. "He's a stickler for following orders." Then he shifted his gaze to Jase. "Any news on your hit woman?"

"She's not talking. But they've got her fingerprints and the gun, and they're running a background check. Soon as they give me a name, we'll run our own."

Dino nodded and held Jase's gaze then. "Right before Christmas, we were involved on a case, and you gave me some good advice. At the risk of taking a left to the chin, I'm going to return the favor."

Jase knew exactly what was coming. Dino was about to tell him that playing the blame game was only going to interfere with solving the case. Jase already knew that. He also knew that if Dino was ready to duck a punch, Jase was allowing his temper to bubble too close to the surface. He rarely allowed that to happen. It was a delayed reaction, he told himself. "It was close. I nearly lost her."

"I nearly lost you too," Maddie said, striding toward him. "But I didn't." She poked a finger into his chest. "And if I had just sat there by that boulder waiting for the police, you might not be here."

Summoning up more control, Jase drew in a breath. "You're right. Thank you." Then he drew her into his arms and for the first time since that chip of granite had sliced his face, he felt some of his tension begin to ease.

"Should I come back later?"

At the sound of his brother's voice, Jase released Maddie and turned to find D.C. leaning on his cane.

"No. Join the party," Jase said with a smile. "And meet Maddie."

Jase noted that in crossing the room to take Maddie's hand, D.C. moved with only a slight limp. A little knot of tension inside him eased.

"Sorry I'm late. It took me a little time to turn Adam Ware over to Tony and Carter. They'll be on-site from now on filming. That ought to help with security issues for Maddie."

"Thanks, bro."

"No problem." Easing himself into a chair, D.C. looked first at Dino and then Jase. "What did I miss?"

Jase leaned a hip against his desk. "We're just getting started. On the surface there seem to be three cases. The first is the robbery at Eva Ware Designs. Before she died, Eva Ware hired me to investigate that. Detective Dave Stanton worked the case. He and I believed it was an inside job. Someone not only had the security codes, but they knew how to disable the alarm. A top-notch pro could have done it, but the thief was very selective about what he or she stole. Eva estimated the value of the jewelry at somewhere around a hundred thousand dollars. Another half a million dollars worth in the display cases was left there—untouched."

"Interesting," Dino said. "You're thinking someone had a certain sum in mind, knew the value of what he or she was stealing?"

"That's my hunch. I have a contact who may be able to give us a line on who might have fenced the jewels locally. I'll put him on it. The next thing we have is the strong possibility that Eva's hit-and-run wasn't an accident but a homicide. Perhaps connected to the robbery. Maddie, Jordan and I all think that she either guessed or discovered who the thief was and perhaps confronted them. Finally, we have the attempted hit on Maddie."

D.C. stretched out his good leg. "The question is, do we really have three separate cases?"

Maddie studied the three men continuing to discuss details as if she weren't in the room. All three were good-looking, with Dino being the most classically handsome. On the surface, D.C. and Jase didn't look at all alike. D.C. was a little shorter and his coloring was darker. She also sensed that the hint of recklessness she'd seen in Jase might be more pronounced in his younger brother. Her gaze returned to Jase. In the park she'd gotten her glimpse of his ruthlessness. And now she was seeing a focused intensity as he and his partner and brother picked away at the puzzle.

"Good question," Dino was saying. Leaning back in his chair, he laced his fingers behind his head. "A mother killed and a daughter almost killed within a week? Hard to believe there's not a connection."

"I'm not a great believer in coincidence," Jase put in. "But there's plenty of motivation to get rid of Maddie without it being connected to her mother's death and the robbery."

Maddie felt a chill move through her. "Why would someone want to kill me?" Her mind had been trying to avoid that question ever since Jase had given her that hard shake and told her that someone wanted her dead. Of course, that hadn't been much of a problem because her mind kept returning to those endless minutes when Jase and the hit woman had been rolling around on the ground.

"The will."

When the three men spoke in unison, Maddie steadied herself by leaning against a desk.

"If you're dead, the terms of the will can't be fulfilled, and there are others who benefit," Jase said. "Money's a powerful motivator."

Maddie swallowed hard. This morning her biggest worries had to do with getting to know her mother, finding out why her parents had separated her from her sister and figuring out what to do about Jase Campbell. And now someone wanted to murder her. Mentally, she gave herself a shake. One thing she'd learned from her father was that it never worked to play ostrich and try to ignore a problem.

"Okay. Someone wants to kill me because of the will. So far, we've been thinking about the robbery being connected to my mother's death. Could it be connected to the will also?" she asked.

"She may be onto something," D.C. said. "What if someone expected to get a lot more when Eva died and they wanted to hurry her along?"

"That's a possibility," Dino agreed.

"It still goes back to money," Jase said. "We have to find the money trail."

"I'll get right on it." D.C. pulled his notebook out and turned to a computer.

Dino moved to look over his shoulder. "Why don't I take Cho Li, Michelle Tan and Arnold Bartlett. Then you can concentrate on the Wares and the Ware Bank."

Maddie turned to Jase. "You suspect Cho Li?"

"Until we learn otherwise, everyone's a suspect. It pays to be thorough."

"We have to warn Jordan," Maddie said.

All three men turned to stare at her.

"If someone is trying to kill me over the will and they haven't succeeded, they could try her instead."

"Or perhaps the plan is to get rid of both of you." Jase picked up the office phone and handed it to her. "Call the ranch. Leave a message if you have to. Tell Jordan it's urgent. Tell her to use my cell number to get back to us."

Maddie nodded and her stomach knotted when she got the answering machine. "She was planning on going into Santa Fe today to visit the venue for the jewelry show. If they're there, Jordan's cell might work."

She punched in the number, and to her relief, Jordan answered. "Jase?"

"No, it's Maddie. We're at his office."

Jase punched the button to turn on the speakerphone.

"It's Jase too, Jordan. Something more has happened at this end. Is Cash with you?"

"Yes, he's listening."

"Someone—we think someone at Eva Ware Designs—hired a hit woman to shoot Maddie this—"

"Maddie, are you all right?" Cash interrupted.

"I'm fine."

"I'm worried about Jordan," Jase explained. "So's Maddie. It could be that the attempt on her life is connected to Eva's hit-and-run—and we're thinking all of it may be connected to the will."

"The will," Cash said. "Because if one or both of them is eliminated, someone else inherits?"

"Correct."

"That's what I've been afraid of. Can you keep Maddie safe?" Cash asked.

"I've put extra men on it. I want to send my brother out to Santa Fe to play back-up on your end."

There was a beat of silence on the other end of the line. "That might be a good idea."

"I'll take care of it," Jase said and disconnected.

"I'll handle the background checks." Dino got to his feet.

"I'll book my flight," D.C. said.

Maddie wanted to feel relief but Jase merely frowned at the phone. "What's wrong?" she asked.

"The cowboy," Jase said. "He agreed pretty easily to the back-up. My impression before was that he thinks he can handle pretty much everything."

"That would describe Cash in a nutshell. He's a lot like my father was."

Jase met her eyes. "I'm thinking that something has happened that Cash and Jordan haven't shared with us yet."

11

WHEN THEY LEFT the office, Jase bypassed the elevator and opted for the stairs. Her borrowed sneakers helped Maddie keep pace with him. At ground level, he steered her to an exit door that opened onto an alleyway.

The scents of beer, human sweat and ripe garbage assaulted her senses. "I see we're taking the scenic route back to the apartment."

"We're not going back to the apartment."

"I really need to change my clothes."

"We'll buy something." At the end of the alley, he drew her with him toward the nearest corner. "For the time being, I'm not letting you go anywhere near that place. Whoever is behind this has to know you're staying there. And they also know who I am and where I work. This time we're not going to give anyone the opportunity to tail us—or to know where we're staying."

The light changed and they crossed the street.

"So your cover of acting as my brand-new lover probably didn't fool the killer."

"It didn't have to. The hit had to have been set up before we got to the store. It might have been arranged as soon as Jordan told them when your first day at Eva Ware Designs would be. This way." He drew her with him into a coffee shop on the corner.

At three-thirty in the afternoon, the lunch crowd had thinned. A black woman in a deep purple waitress's uniform was leaning over the counter, flipping through a newspaper.

"Edie," Jase said when he reached it.

The woman straightened and her face lit up. "Long time no see, sweet cakes. I missed you."

"I've been working an out-of-town case for a couple of weeks. Just got back." Jase circled behind the counter, gripped her shoulders and kissed her cheek. "I missed you too."

"Go on now. You missed my apple pie."

Maddie could have sworn that the woman was blushing. And Jase…well, it was the first time since they'd left the park that she'd seen the easygoing Jase Campbell. She wasn't sure which side of the man fascinated her most.

Jase grinned. "That too."

"Sit down. I'll fix you a piece."

"No time. I just stopped in to say hi." He slipped a folded bill into the pocket of her uniform. "I need to use your back entrance."

Edie glanced at Maddie, then back to Jase. She waved her hands in a shooing motion. "You're working another case. Go ahead."

At the swinging doors to the kitchen, Jase paused and looked over his shoulder. "If anyone comes in and asks, the lady and I are—"

"Using the facilities," Edie finished. "I know—the usual cloak-and-dagger stuff. I'll save you that piece of pie."

A few of the people working in the kitchen smiled or waved at Jase as they headed toward the back door.

"Get followed a lot, do you?" Maddie asked as they exited.

"Now and then."

She noted that the moment they left the coffee shop, Jase

was back in security mode. After cutting through another alley, he crossed to the edge of the sidewalk and hailed a cab. Once inside, he leaned forward and said, "The Donatello."

Five minutes later, Maddie found herself walking into one of the most luxurious hotels she'd ever seen—except in the movies. Couches and chairs offered spacious seating to guests in the lobby, and the soft sounds of a Mozart string quartet could be heard beneath the muted conversations.

They passed an array of shop windows displaying high-end clothes and jewelry. Everywhere she looked, mahogany shone and brass gleamed. Three crystal chandeliers hung from a carved ceiling, and a vase of fresh flowers as tall as a Christmas tree graced a marble-topped table.

When they arrived at the registration desk, a young woman wearing a black suit with a nametag that read *Jessie* beamed them a smile.

"I'd like to speak to Mr. Benson," Jase said.

"Certainly, sir." She disappeared through a door and a few minutes later a man of medium height with dark hair and a perfectly trimmed mustache stepped out of the same door. He wore the black suit that seemed to be the uniform of the hotel staff and the same nametag. His read *Louie*. The moment he saw Jase, Maddie noted that the serious expression on his face lightened just a bit.

He bowed slightly when he reached the counter. "Mr. Campbell, welcome to the Donatello."

Jase leaned forward. "Louie, I need a favor."

"Certainly, sir."

"I need a room for a few days. The lady here is in a bit of a jam, and I need a place to keep her on the q.t."

His expression still perfectly serious, Louie Benson raised one eyebrow. "You're using the Donatello as a safe house?"

Maddie detected a slight note of horror in his tone.

"So to speak," Jake said. "And I can't use a credit card. It's too easy to trace them. You'll have to bill my office."

"Very well." Louie typed rapidly into a computer and within seconds tucked a plastic key into a folder and passed it to Jase. "Your suite is on the top floor. You access it by taking the private elevator down the corridor to your left. Press the button for the penthouse."

Jase nodded toward the row of shops. "Can you make some credit arrangement with the shops? I'll have to get her some clothes."

"No problem," Louie said. "I'll tell them to put any purchases on your bill."

Jase smiled at him. "Thanks, Louie."

"No." Louie's smile was thin, but it reached his eyes. "Thank you, sir."

"How did you do that?" Maddie whispered as they moved down the short hallway to the private elevator.

"What?"

"Get us a room in this hotel with no reservation. We don't even have any luggage."

"I know," he said on a sigh. "There goes my reputation."

Maddie couldn't prevent a laugh. "I'm serious."

Jase punched the elevator button. "I did a favor for Louie about six months ago. Someone was stealing from the guests by breaking into the in-room safes. The police had been called in twice and everyone was being discreet. But if the thefts had continued, it was bound to get into the papers, and the reputation of the Donatello would have been irreparably damaged. Louie called my office and asked me to solve the problem. I did. The thief turned out to be one of the hotel detectives."

The elevator doors slid open, and they stepped through them. The three walls were lined with mirrors. As the car began its ascent, it was suddenly very quiet, and the air seemed closer. No Mozart, no chatter of guests. For the first time since they'd left Jase's office, Maddie let herself think about the fact that she and Jase would be alone once they reached the suite.

She could see Jase reflected endlessly in the mirrors. Perhaps that was why he seemed to fill the space. He was leaning against the brass rail on the wall across from her. He'd been easy and relaxed when he'd been talking to Louie, but he wasn't now. There was tension in his jaw, in his shoulders, and the knuckles of one hand showed white where he gripped the railing. The fact that his face looked a bit battered from their encounter with the hit woman made him look tougher and sexy as hell.

In the back wall of the elevator, she could see the profile of that lean face and the length of that rangy, male body. A body that she had touched. A body that she could touch again. All she had to do was take a few steps to close the distance between them and she could slip her arms around him, run her hands over those taut muscles and feel his heart pound against hers.

Her bones were already in meltdown when she met his eyes. What she saw stopped her breathing. She was trembling, aroused by the fantasy she'd spun—and by the man.

It was shocking how much she wanted to make love with him. Terrifying. In her mind she'd always been practical, cautious. She should be worried that her life was in danger— that her sister's life might be in danger too. But right now all she could think of was making love with Jase again. It was as if she was a totally different woman with Jase Campbell.

Worse yet, she had no desire to return to what she'd been before she met him. What she wanted was for him to touch her again, really touch her. To feel his hands skimming over her naked flesh, making it burn, taking her to a place where there were only the two of them. Only the now.

"Maddie?"

His voice was hoarse, raw.

Her throat went dry. "Yes?"

"I promised myself that when we got to the room, I would let you sleep. I'm not going to do that. The moment we get to the room, I'm going to make love to you."

Maddie wondered if her heart had actually stopped. Somehow she found her voice. "Why do we have to wait until we get to the room?"

He moved then, very quickly, first to punch the button that stopped the elevator between floors. As the car jerked to a halt, Maddie felt her heart skip a beat. Then he trapped her against the wall. And at last, his body was pressed against hers.

A scorching wave moved through her. Everything about him was so hard—his hands, his chest, the angle of his hip, even the long length of his thigh as it moved between hers. She arched helplessly against him.

His mouth hovered a breath away from hers. "I was going to bring you here for lunch. You looked so tired. Instead, I took you to the park. I told myself it was so I could keep my hands off you."

She wrapped her arms around his neck and threaded her fingers into his hair. "That didn't work out."

"No. I can't stop wanting you."

"Same here."

"I have to figure this out."

"Me too."

"*Later.*" They spoke the word in unison.

He brushed his mouth over hers, drawing back just enough to nip her bottom lip before sliding his tongue between her lips.

She arched helplessly against him. Even his mouth had grown harder, more demanding, as if he believed that there was some flavor that he had yet to discover.

And all the while his hands, his clever, ruthless hands were moving over her, pressing, molding, claiming. When those lean fingers slipped beneath the hem of her skirt and pushed it up, flames seared her nerve endings.

Still gripping her waist, he sank to his knees, slipped her panties down her legs and tossed them aside. In her peripheral vision, Maddie saw the white lace arc before settling on the floor of the elevator. The sight had a hot thrill shooting through her.

To steady herself, Maddie wrapped both of her hands around the brass rail as he eased her thighs farther apart. With his thumbs, he separated her folds, then he began to use his mouth on her.

She was sinking, drowning in a storm of sensations, each one more erotic that the last—the soft texture of his tongue, the scrape of his teeth. First she burned, then she shivered.

And still she wanted more. Widening her stance, she arched her hips to give him more access. His fingers dug into her buttocks at the same instant that his tongue pierced deeply into her.

He knew exactly when her orgasm began, and when she peaked he heard her cry his name. The sound urged him to send her flying again. And again.

When she went limp and lost her grip on the handrail, he caught her and guided her to the floor. Need battered him as quick and hot as lightning flashes. His fingers fumbled as he tore his belt free and lowered his jeans. Then he moved over her and drove into her.

The sharp stab of pleasure nearly stopped his heart. For a moment he held himself still, wanting the moment to last. But when she wrapped arms and legs around him, when she opened her eyes and met his, she filled his vision, his mind, his world. Together they began to move, quickly, desperately.

"More."

Had he said the word? Had she?

All he knew was that there was more. Impossibly more. The single word became a drumbeat in his head as he drove her, drove them both higher and higher until they reached the peak together and shattered.

LAYER BY LAYER, Jase's mind found its way back to reality. The scents were the first to penetrate—body heat—a mix of his and hers and sex. His mouth was at her throat, the memory of her taste still haunting him. Beneath him, her heart beat fast. One of his hands was tangled in her hair though he had no clear recollection of how it had gotten there.

It had all happened so fast.

Opening his eyes, Jase confirmed what he already knew to be true. He'd just made love to Maddie Farrell in an elevator at the Donatello. And he was still sprawled on top of her. In spite of that, he didn't seem to have the will to move.

With great effort, he managed to lift his head. Her eyes were open, her face flushed and her mouth still moist and swollen. In his peripheral vision, he could see their reflections in the mirrored wall. Their clothes were in disarray, their hair wildly mussed. They each looked as if they'd just survived some kind of natural disaster. Barely.

He plucked a twig out of her hair. He hadn't been gentle with her—not here and certainly not when he'd shoved her against that boulder in the park. He frowned. "I was rough with you. Are you all right?"

"Better than all right." She studied him for a moment. "I'm a lot tougher than I look."

"Yeah." He thought of how she'd clocked the hit woman with that tree branch—and how she'd knocked him on his ass earlier that day.

Earlier that day? It seemed impossible that he'd known her for less than twenty-four hours. So much had happened.

"How about you?" she asked. "Are you all right?"

Something in her tone finally eased the knot of guilt that had tightened inside him. "Much better than all right." He grinned down at her. "I haven't done anything like this since I was sixteen." And he'd been a randy teenager then.

"I've never done anything quite like this—ever."

"Good." He didn't want to imagine her making love in semi-public places with anyone but him.

Her eyes widened. "You're..."

"Yeah." Incredibly, he could feel himself growing hard inside her again. Experimentally, he rocked into her and watched her eyes cloud.

"Jase."

The word was half question, half demand.

With a groan, Jase eased himself up to his knees. First he did his best to rearrange her rumpled clothes. Then he managed to pull up his jeans. Finally, he got to his feet and helped her up. "I think we'd better take act two to our suite. Louie might decide that the elevator has malfunctioned and if anyone sees us like this, he might not ever do me a favor again."

He shoved a button, and the elevator began to climb.

MADDIE WOKE to the sound of rain, the hard, pounding kind that often produced flash floods at the ranch. She was going to use it as an excuse to spend an extra hour in bed before she went to her studio. Burrowing more deeply into her pillow, she tried to slip back into her dream.

But the scent was all wrong. It wasn't the lavender from the fabric softener she used on her sheets, it was stronger, male.

Jase.

Opening her eyes, she sat straight up and found herself in the middle of a bed. Alone. The covers were tucked neatly around her. The last she recalled the bedding had been rumpled, some of it on the floor.

Come to think of it, she and Jase had been on the floor too. Using both fists, she rubbed sleep out of her eyes and tried to clear the fuzziness out of her brain. Then she looked down at the bed again. He must have tucked her in. Something inside her softened at the sweetness of the gesture.

How long had she been out? She was reassured when she spotted a sliver of sunlight sneaking through the drawn drapes. That's when she realized that what she'd mistaken for rain was the sound of the shower in the next room. The last thing she remembered, Jase had been on his cell phone, first with Dino and after that, she was pretty sure he'd talked to someone about who might have fenced the jewels. That was when she must have shut down.

A double-toned chime sounded.

Not Jase's cell, she decided, glancing at the small table near the bed where he'd left it.

The chime sounded again.

Maddie crawled from beneath the covers and reached for the hotel robe Jase had thoughtfully left on the foot of the bed.

When she reached the door to the suite, she used the peep hole. On the other side was a tall woman in her late thirties wearing a black suit. Her long dark hair was curly, and she reminded Maddie of Julia Louis-Dreyfus from *Seinfeld*.

"Yes?" Maddie said.

"I'm Sabrina Michaels and I'm delivering some packages Mr. Campbell ordered from the shops at the Donatello."

Maddie opened the door and took the bags.

Sabrina smiled at her. "If there's any problem with the selections, just let me know. Mr. Campbell was pretty specific
with his requests, but I can certainly bring up more for you
to look at. You can reach me through the hotel operator."

As soon as she shut the door, Maddie couldn't resist. Jase
was still in the shower, and she didn't want to wait. She
carried the bags further into the main room of the suite, and
set them on one of the long glass-topped coffee tables. Jase
had been pretty specific with his requests, Sabrina had said.
That must have been after she'd fallen asleep.

In the first bag she found a pair of jeans and a short-
sleeved blue chambray shirt that Jase had evidently ordered
for himself. Beneath those, she found a black scarf and a pair
of sunglasses. For disguise purposes? Setting the first bag
aside, she lifted a pair of cream-colored strappy sandals out
of the second one. Unable to resist, she ran one finger over
the buttery soft leather and sighed. The heels were only half
as high as those on Jordan's blue shoes, but they were still
very stylish. And she was dead certain they'd be easier to walk
around Manhattan in. At least for her.

In the second bag, she found a summer-weight blazer in
the same creamy white. And instead of a matching skirt, she
found a pair of slacks.

Slacks.

Hugging them to her, she sank down on one of the sofas.
Jase had remembered her saying that she felt more comfortable in them. Maddie felt her heart take a little tumble. She'd
grown up around men, and her impression of them was that
while they were well-meaning, they weren't the most attentive of creatures.

But Jase was different. With a little sigh, she rose and laid
the slacks carefully over the back of the couch.

When she peeked in the third bag, she found lace panties, a bra and a silky black nightgown. Definitely more seduction-wear than sleepwear. There wasn't a doubt in her mind that if Jase had ordered the slacks to please her, he'd ordered the frothy black nightgown to please himself. She made a mental note to wear it that night.

That night.

After the hours they'd just spent together, she was actually thinking of making love to Jase Campbell again. Something must have happened to her brain. Perhaps the pollution in the Manhattan air had affected her synapses. She'd never before developed an intimate relationship with a man she barely knew.

Correction. She hadn't known Jase at all when they'd first made love. That had been a mistake made by two strangers because she'd accidentally crawled into the wrong bed.

Maddie sighed again. But making love to Jase Campbell never felt like a mistake. It always felt so right.

Jase was different for her. In so many ways. And because of him, she was becoming different too. She'd never known she could be this way—happy, sexy, desperate, crazy. Every time he touched her she felt something new.

It wasn't just the sex. Not when she looked at him or thought of him and something inside her tilted. That was emotion.

Maddie thought of the strategy she'd developed to handle Jase when she'd been in the shower this morning. Logic and reason. Hah! Being logical and reasonable just wasn't part of the equation where Jase was concerned. She wanted him and he wanted her. It was just that simple. Just that elemental.

She also recalled telling him that she only had three weeks to accomplish her agenda in New York, and that making love again with him would only complicate things.

Maddie turned and walked toward the bedroom. Like it or not, making love again with Jase Campbell had become an important part of her new agenda in New York.

And she was certain that she was going to like it. A lot.

12

JASE STARED at himself in the mirror. He couldn't remember the last time he'd spent this much time in the bathroom. He'd showered and shaved. He'd even considered using the hotel hair dryer to do something with his hair.

Pitiful.

But Maddie needed some sleep. And he hadn't trusted himself to stay in the same room with her and not make love with her again.

Even when she'd finally fallen asleep, he hadn't been able to stop himself from watching her. Finally, he'd moved to the bed and stroked her hair. He couldn't seem to prevent himself from touching her.

That's when it had happened. It was while he'd stroked her hair that he'd felt something move through him, something that had nothing to do with the fact that he wanted very much to make love with her again.

Trying to figure it out, he'd studied her sprawled across the bed. She slept with the same intensity that she did everything else. And she *was* a lot tougher than she looked. He'd experienced the strength and passion that she brought to their lovemaking. But right then as he'd looked down at her, what he'd wanted more than anything was to protect her. To cherish her.

The fact was that he was coming to have feelings for her

other than those of a casual lover. Feelings that went far beyond making sure that she wasn't killed.

He thought of what she'd said to him that morning in the kitchen—that if they made love again, it would complicate things. Well, she sure as hell had been right about that. But he hadn't brought her here to the Donatello just to make love to her. And though it had been a long day, they still had a call to make. After what Dino had told him on the phone, he very much wanted to see what Eva Ware had written in her appointment book.

He ran his hands through his hair and started toward the door to the bedroom just as it opened and Maddie entered the bathroom. Both of them stopped in mid stride.

MADDIE'S THROAT went dry, and the air in the room was suddenly thick. Jase's shoulders still glistened with droplets of water from his shower. The towel was tucked low over his hips.

The silence stretched between them.

Maddie finally broke it. "I want you again."

"Ditto. But we need to get to your mother's apartment."

"I know. The clothes you ordered came. I need to shower." But hadn't she known what she really wanted when she'd stepped into the bathroom?

"Right." On his way to her, he dropped the towel and then he shoved the bathrobe down her arms. Finally, he scooped her up into his arms.

"What are you doing?"

"We might as well try the age-old solution." He twisted the faucets. "A cold shower."

Maddie screamed as the icy water sluiced over them. "Turn it off! I'm freezing!"

"That's the idea." He set her down but used his body to block her in.

Through the wet hair plastered to her face, she glared at him. "I don't like this idea."

"It does have its drawbacks." There was laughter in his voice. "But I thought you were tougher than you look."

She raised both hands and gave him a hard shove. She might have had more luck with the boulder in Central Park. Sputtering, she made a blind grab for the faucets.

He grabbed her wrists. "No cheating."

"I'm sure I'm turning blue."

"That *is* one of the drawbacks."

He backed her farther into the shower, and a fresh spray of icy needles pelted her.

"I'm going to get even for this."

"I'm looking forward to it. But for now, since you don't like a cold shower, I thought we'd shift to plan B."

"No, you—"

He cut off her protest by covering her mouth with his. With one arm holding her close, he slathered soapy lather all over her body.

Incredibly, her skin began to heat. When his fingers slipped between her thighs, found her, pierced her, she began to burn. Wrapping her arms around him, she drew him even closer. The fire he'd ignited built rapidly then. With his hand alone he took her on a desperate ride, driving her up and up until the climax shot through her with a violence that left her trembling.

That was enough to drive him to the edge. When she whispered his name, he lifted her and wrapped her legs around him.

"Maddie, open your eyes."

She did as he asked, and he looked into those blue-violet depths. When he drove himself into her, he knew she thought only of him.

When she murmured his name, he thought only of her.

He pulled out, thrust in again, over and over. She shuddered again and again. When he could no longer help himself, he drove them both into the madness.

MADDIE WAS just slipping into her new shoes in front of a full-length mirror when Jase's cell phone rang.

He tucked it under his chin and listened silently while he shrugged into the new blue shirt, then buttoned it. He left it hanging loose and tucked his gun into the back waistband of his jeans.

The man was definitely efficient. As a security agent, as a lover, as a friend. And he seemed to be able to shift between his various roles effortlessly. Since they'd left the bathroom, he'd been all business again and she was learning to follow his lead.

But something had happened while they'd been in the shower. It was as if some question between them had been asked and answered. Maddie just had to figure out what it was.

Jase shut his cell phone, then tucked a strand of hair behind her ear. "D.C.'s plane is boarding. He'll be in Santa Fe tonight. Between him and Cash, Jordan will be all right."

She'd already told herself that, but it helped to hear Jase say it.

"Ready to hit the road?" he asked.

"Yes." They'd decided while they were dressing that they were going to go to her mother's apartment and get the appointment calendar. But it wasn't finding the calendar that had nerves knotting in her stomach. It was the idea of seeing the place where her mother had lived.

"There's a strong possibility that whoever it is we're dealing with will have Eva's apartment staked out. In their place, that's what I'd do. They have to know by now that the hit failed, and they may have a back-up plan."

"What are you saying?" Maddie asked.

"We have to take precautions. I already asked Dino to post one of our men near the entrance. His job is to see if anyone else is watching. But we're going to have to be fast. We can ditch the taxi a few blocks away, and I'll pay the driver to wait for us across the street from the apartment so we can make a quick getaway. You're going to wear the scarf and the sunglasses I had sent up." Plucking them out of the bag, he tossed them to her. "It's standard celeb wear."

His eyes when they met hers were sober. "I don't suppose there's any way I could talk you into waiting here and letting me get the appointment book?"

Maddie shook her head firmly. "No way at all."

"Figured." He took her arm and they were halfway to the door when his cell rang again.

He checked the caller ID, then said, "Yeah?"

For a few minutes, Jase said nothing. He merely listened. When he finally repocketed the phone, he opened the door of the suite.

"That was Dino checking in again. While you were sleeping, he called to tell me what he'd found out about Michelle Tan."

"Michelle?"

"About a month ago, three days after the robbery, in fact, a bank check for one hundred thousand dollars was deposited into Michelle's bank account. The money was withdrawn in cash two days later."

She shot him a look. "Can Dino hack into a bank's computers?"

Jase grinned at her. "Sure. He's getting better at the technical stuff. But it was a bank check, so he doesn't know yet who it came from."

"I see."

"Even more intriguing, it turns out that Michelle's the granddaughter of Cho Li."

"GOOD JOB," Jase murmured as they rode up the seven flights to Eva Ware's apartment.

"Thanks. It seemed the easiest way."

And it had been. She'd gotten them past the doorman by lowering her scarf and pretending to be Jordan. It had also saved them some time. And Jase wasn't sure how much time they had. Whoever was behind this was smart and prepared. In his experience, people who were prepared always had a back-up plan.

He glanced sideways at Maddie. She'd been very quiet during the short cab ride to Eva's place. Because she was trying to absorb the news about Michelle and Cho? He could understand that. He was trying to figure it out too. The two least likely suspects for robbing Eva's store had risen like cream to the top of the group.

He was positive Jordan hadn't known about the relationship between the two. She'd certainly never mentioned it to him, nor had she put it in the notes she'd given Maddie. Had Eva known? Or perhaps suspected? The appointment calendar just might tell them something.

But Jase had a hunch that what was bothering Maddie now went a little deeper.

"Have you ever been in Eva's apartment?" she asked as they left the elevator.

"No."

"After we find the appointment calendar, I'd like to take a little time to look around."

When he didn't immediately reply, she continued, "I know you'd prefer to get in and out, but I won't take long. I'd just like to get...an idea of how she lived."

Jase thought of the doorman, a fit enough looking man. But he was in his fifties and a pro could take him out in seconds. He reminded himself that Dino had stationed a man across the street who was a pro also. "Sure."

She unlocked the door with the key Jordan had given her and hesitated a moment before stepping into the foyer. Then she simply looked around. Jase had noted before that she was good at standing still and absorbing her surroundings. Perhaps every artist had to have that quality.

The foyer opened into a short hallway with high ceilings. The apartment itself was located in one of Manhattan's oldest buildings, but the wainscoting and the chair railings had been artfully restored. Beneath the rich hues of an oriental carpet lay gleaming dark hardwood floors.

Jase tried to put himself in Maddie's shoes. She'd been to her mother's workplace and seen the professional side of Eva Ware. But this was personal. Intimate.

First things first. He opened the double doors of the closet and found the cardboard box on the floor just as Jordan had described.

"So far, so good." He quickly pushed aside the clothes that Eva had been wearing the night of her accident and found a tote. Inside was a leather-bound appointment calendar. Like Maddie's, it was stuffed with folded notes and newspaper clippings. Handing it to her, he thought, *like mother, like daughter.*

She ran her fingers over the cover and then tucked it into her own tote. Linking his fingers with hers, they started down the hallway together. At the end of it, Jase could see the kitchen. The reddish hues of the setting sun poured through louver-covered windows, glinting off stainless-steel appliances and black granite counter tops. An archway to their right opened into a formal dining room, but Maddie drew him through the archway to their left.

Here the light was dimmer, but Jase could make out on the wall facing them a brick fireplace flanked by two bookcases with leaded-glass doors. And there was a desk to their immediate right, its surface stacked high with sketch books. One was open, a pencil lying on its surface.

Maddie was already moving toward the desk as he felt along the wall for a switch. When he flicked it on, his attention was drawn immediately to the oil portrait over the mantel.

His eyes went first to Eva, seated in a delicately carved armchair wearing pale gray slacks, a matching jacket and a pink sweater. Her long blond hair had been twisted into a braid that fell over one shoulder. Next to her a much younger Jordan stood in a pink dress trimmed in ruffles at the neck, sleeves and hem. Her hair had been fastened back from her face with bows and fell in curls to her shoulders.

It was a family portrait, Jase supposed. Mother and daughter. He shifted his gaze to Maddie and saw that she was studying it also. Was she imagining what the portrait might have looked like if she'd been in it too, standing on the other side of Eva?

The surge of anger took him by surprise and had him striding toward her and taking her hand. Why in hell had two sane people who'd obviously loved both their daughters each cut one out of their lives?

"You should be in that portrait. They were stupid to split the two of you up," he said.

"I'd like to think that they loved us so much that they couldn't bear to part with both of us."

Jase turned to study her. "Is that why you think your father kept you?"

"It's what I'd like to believe." She moved closer to the portrait, drawing him with her. "It's odd."

"What?"

"My father never had a formal portrait done. But on my eleventh birthday, he had a photographer come to the ranch. Dad insisted that the man take the picture outside near the stables. I'd been riding Brutus, the horse he'd just gotten me for my birthday. We didn't dress up or anything. Dad posed the picture with me on the horse and him standing beside it. Later, he framed the photo and kept it on the dresser in his bedroom. Jordan will see it the moment she walks into the room."

"Your sister looks to be about eleven in the painting."

"That's what I was thinking. It's an odd coincidence that they'd both decide to have a formal picture taken when we were about the same age."

Jase turned to her. "Do you think your parents kept in touch over the years?"

With a sigh, she shrugged. "Maybe that's just what I'd like to believe. There has to be some explanation for what they did. Why they did it."

Jase traced a finger along her jawline—so strong, so stubborn. "If there is, you'll find it." Whatever else he might have said was interrupted by a sound—metal scraping against metal.

"What's that?" Maddie whispered.

"We're going to have company," he whispered back. Motioning her to one side of the archway, he flipped off the light, then flattened himself to the wall on the opposite side of the arch. From his position, he had a partial view of the door to the apartment as it swung open. In the dim light, he saw a shadowy figure move into the hall. He or she turned immediately to the closet door, opened it and pulled out the same box that he had searched earlier. By that time, his eyes had adjusted to the dimmer light and he recognized who it was.

Flipping the light on, he stepped into the hall and said, "Can we help you, Michelle?"

MADDIE FOLLOWED Jase into the hallway in time to see Michelle Tan drop Eva's tote bag. The contents—wallet, a matchbook and a small sketchpad—clattered out onto the floor.

"I—" Michelle placed a hand to her heart and took a deep breath.

Maddie wasn't sure who was more surprised—Michelle or herself, but she managed to ask, "What are you doing here?"

Without answering, Michelle dropped to her knees and began to stuff things back into the tote.

"Yes, what are you doing here?" Jase repeated.

"I came to see if I could find Ms. Ware's appointment calendar," Michelle mumbled.

Maddie noted that the young woman's hands were trembling. She put a hand on Jase's arm as she moved past him, caught his eye and mouthed, "Good cop." Then she dropped to her knees in front of Michelle and stilled her hands. "Why did you think the calendar would be here? And how did you get a key?"

Michelle's head popped up at that, and her voice was suddenly stronger. "Ms. Ware gave me a key. Sometimes she would get to work and remember that she'd left a sketch of a design at home. She'd ask me to come here and pick it up."

Okay, Maddie thought. That jelled with Jordan's description of Eva as a bit disorganized. Plus, she'd seen the sketches littering Eva's desk. "She trusted you then?"

"Yes. Yes, she did."

"Why did you think the journal was here?"

Avoiding Maddie's eyes, Michelle sat back on her heels and folded her hands together. "I knew you were interested in finding it. I was on my way home from work when I remembered Jordan saying that she'd brought everything that the police had returned to her to this apartment because she couldn't bear to go through it yet. It's right on my way home, so I decided to stop in and see if it was here."

Liar, Maddie thought.

"I don't think so." Jase's voice had turned so clipped and cold that it nearly sent a shiver down Maddie's spine. "I think you eavesdropped on Maddie and me when we were talking on the speakerphone with Jordan."

Michelle shook her head. "No."

"Yes. Then when I told you that we were going to be tied up for some time at the police station, you saw an opportunity to get hold of it before we did."

Michelle shook her head again.

"Jase," Maddie said. "Can't you see she's upset?"

"She should be upset. What's so important about that appointment calendar that you had to sneak in here to steal it, Michelle?"

Michelle looked at him then. "Nothing. I wasn't going to steal it. I was just trying to help."

"Help yourself, maybe," Jase said. "You were worried about something that it might contain."

"No. Why should I be? I have nothing to hide."

"Jase." Maddie injected a note of warning into her tone. Then she took Michelle's hands in hers. "We know that you deposited one hundred thousand dollars into your checking account three days after Eva Ware Designs was robbed of over a hundred thousand dollars worth of jewels."

Michelle's eyes went wide with shock, then flooded with tears. "You think—no. You can't. I didn't."

The young woman's emotional reaction could be fake, Maddie told herself. "Then where did you get the money?"

Michelle opened her mouth, shut it, then shook her head. "I can't tell you."

When Jase didn't say anything, Maddie pushed forward.

"You're going to have to. We already know that Cho Li is your grandfather."

Michelle dropped her head into her hands and began to cry.

A HALF HOUR later, Jase stood next to Maddie beneath the awning of Eva Ware's apartment building watching as two uniformed policemen helped Michelle into the backseat of a patrol car.

She hadn't said one more word while he'd called Dave Stanton and they'd waited for the police. Neither had Maddie.

Stanton had sent someone to pick up Cho Li and he was going to question Michelle personally as soon as she reached the precinct. He and Maddie had been invited to come down and watch.

"I don't like it," Maddie murmured as the patrol car pulled away.

There were quite a few things that Jase wasn't liking, the top one being that they'd stayed a lot longer than he'd intended at Eva's apartment, plenty of time for someone watching the place to put a plan into operation. And he had a bad feeling about that.

He'd insisted that she put on the scarf and sunglasses again, but the disguise was a thin one. He scanned the street, spotted a taxi blocking the entrance to an alley across the way, and recognized the driver as the one he'd tipped heavily to wait for them.

"C'mon. Our ride's over there." He took Maddie's elbow and urged her toward the curb. The street in front of Eva's apartment was narrow. Vehicles took up every parking space and two were double-parked. Since it wasn't a Manhattan thoroughfare, traffic was minimal at this time of night. Still, Jase paused to look both ways. His bad feeling hadn't eased.

A car was moving slowly toward them from the left. Jase

eased Maddie to his other side, using his body to block hers. Once the vehicle had passed by, he said, "Let's go."

"I can't believe that she robbed Eva Ware Designs, can you?"

"A good investigator keeps an open—" The roar of an engine cut him off, and he caught the sudden blur of movement to his right. He had just enough time to register that the cream-colored sedan matched the description of the car that had run Eva down.

Maddie turned her head and he felt her freeze. The head-lights flashed on, blinding them both.

There was no time to think. No time even to panic. He just let his reflexes take over. Whipping his arm around Maddie's waist, he lifted her.

The roar of the motor grew louder, the lights closer. Jase leapt into the air and twisted his body to take the brunt of the impact as they landed on the taxi's hood. Holding Maddie tightly, he rolled and brought her with him to the sidewalk on the other side of the cab. This time it was his shoulder that took the hit and his breath whooshed out. For a second, he just held on tightly. Then he said, "You all right?"

"Yes. You?"

Easing her next to the side of the taxi, he got to his feet. But all he could see were the taillights of the car just before it careened around the corner.

MADDIE LAY flat on the sidewalk, her mind still spinning while she tried desperately to process what had just happened. Her body was cold and numb. And all she could hear was a sort of soft buzzing sound like white noise.

Someone had tried to run her and Jase down.

When she'd heard the racing motor and turned her head,

those blinding lights had been so close. She'd even been able to see the hood ornament.

Voices began to penetrate. She recognized Jase's. Someone else was speaking with an accent.

"I saw part of the plate number. You blocked my view when you landed on the hood of my car."

"What kind of car?"

Jase's voice again.

"A light-colored sedan, a Mercedes," replied the voice with the accent.

"Did you see the driver?"

"He was wearing a jacket with a hood."

It had really happened then. Someone had almost succeeded in running them down. If it hadn't been for Jase's quick reflexes, they would both be lying out in the street. Bleeding. Dead.

And the driver of the car would have gotten away with it. Again.

The bastard.

Fury gave her the energy to scramble to her feet.

Jase turned to her and joined her on the curb. He ran his hands up and down her arms as he studied her. "You're all right."

"You too." She wrapped both arms around him and simply held on. Something else moved through her then, something that had the fear and anger fading. And another kind of fear building. She realized that she didn't want to let Jase go. Not now.

Maybe not ever.

13

MADDIE STOOD with Jase and Detective Stanton in a small anteroom. In the adjacent room, beyond the one-way glass, Michelle sat with her hands folded on a table, her face drawn, her knuckles white. Although the detective had questioned her for over an hour, Michelle hadn't varied from the story she'd told Jase and Maddie.

"I'll keep after her for a while," Stanton said, "but she's pretty stubborn. She denies ever having the security code to the Madison Avenue building or having anything to do with the robbery."

"Cho could have had the security code," Jase pointed out.

"True. She refuses to talk about the hundred thousand in her account."

"It didn't stay in her bank account very long," Jase said. "According to my partner, the money appeared via a bank check, but was withdrawn in cash two days later."

"It's the amount and the timing that are so incriminating," Maddie said.

"I agree. It looks as though she needed some cash fast and she knew just how to get it," Stanton replied.

"My partner is tracking down where it came from," Jase said. "And I'm expecting to hear back from an informant who knows a lot of fences in the area."

The detective turned to Maddie. "You look better than you did when you came in."

She managed a smile. "Thanks. I want to know who was driving that car."

"Working on it. I've sent a couple of uniforms to go door to door. The bastard had to be waiting for you. Same way he waited for your mother. We're running the partial plate number. Your description of the hood ornament matches well with the taxi driver's certainty that it was a light-colored late-model Mercedes, so that should narrow the search."

Jase slipped his hand into hers. "Maddie, the car that ran down your mother was also described as a light-colored sedan."

She turned to him. "You think it might be the same driver?"

"Could be," Stanton said. "Killers are unbelievably cocky. The bastard got away clean the first time. Probably figures he can do it again."

"The one thing we know for sure is that Michelle wasn't behind the wheel," Maddie pointed out.

"Right. But she could have an accomplice," Stanton said. "We haven't been able to locate Cho yet."

Maddie shook her head vehemently. She'd already had this discussion with Jase on the ride to the station. "I can't see Cho running anyone down. I'll bet he doesn't even drive."

Stanton glanced at Jase and then back at Maddie. "I'm checking all possibilities. I'll be at Eva Ware Designs with a search warrant when it opens tomorrow morning, and I'll be questioning everyone again about the robbery. Nothing like a couple of suspects to jog everyone's memory."

Turning, Maddie studied Michelle through the one-way glass. "My guess would be that she's gone silent because of her loyalty to her grandfather. I never should have mentioned Cho's name."

Stanton's eyebrows shot up. "You don't like him for the hit-and-run, but you suspect him for the robbery?"

"I don't want to," Maddie said. "They make a pair of unlikely jewel thieves."

He snorted. "They didn't have to be pros if they had the security codes. And Eva Ware trusted Michelle enough to give her the key to her apartment."

"She may open up when you get Cho in here," Jase said. "Or he may open up once he sees that she's under suspicion."

Stanton glanced at his watch. "I've had men stationed outside his apartment ever since you called. There's no sign of him. The apartment is dark, he's not answering his phone or his door."

"Maybe he skipped," Jase said.

Maddie turned from the window to face Stanton and Jase. "Even if Cho or the two of them robbed Eva Ware Designs, I still can't see either of them running Eva down."

"Money does strange things to people," Stanton said.

"Maybe Eva was onto them and confronted them. With her gone, their jobs are secure, Cho's reputation is golden." Jase frowned. "The thing is, neither of them has a motive to hire a hit woman to kill Maddie."

"The two things don't have to be connected," Stanton said.

"No," Jase mused. "But something tells me they are."

Once again Stanton sighed. "Me too."

There was a knock at the door, and a young uniformed officer poked his head in. "I've got something on the plate that you might be interested in, sir."

"Report," Stanton ordered.

"A cream-colored Mercedes sedan with a license plate containing the three numbers we have on the partial is registered to a Ms. Eva Ware."

For a moment there was dead silence in the room.

Stanton finally turned and said what they all were thinking. "That means that Eva may have been run down by her own car."

Maddie dug into her tote for the ring of keys Jordan had given her. "I have the key. Jordan told me that Eva kept it in a garage on the block directly behind her apartment building."

Stanton pulled the key off the ring when she handed it to him. Then he glanced through the one-way glass at Michelle Tan. "The question is whether Eva was as generous with her car keys as she was with the key to her apartment."

SITTING cross-legged on the sunken floor of the suite's living room, her back against one of the sofas, Maddie once more pored over the last weeks of Eva Ware's life as they were minimally recorded in her calendar. After assigning two uniforms to check out the garage and see if the Mercedes was there, Dave Stanton had sent them home.

But the excitement she'd been feeling when they'd arrived at the Donatello and first opened the leather volume had steadily drained away.

Dino had dropped off some things at the desk for them while they'd been out. In addition to clothes for both of them, he'd left Jase's laptop and a file of the financial information he'd been able to dig up so far on everyone either related to or employed by Eva Ware. Nothing had popped on any of them except for the hundred thousand dollars that had briefly resided in Michelle Tan's bank account.

Eva had used a personal shorthand, mostly consisting of initials, but they were pretty easy to decipher. And there were very few appointments. On Monday mornings at nine there was an *S.M.*, a staff meeting. Wednesday noon, lunch with J. Jordan. Maddie ran her finger over the initial. Had Eva been so focused on her business that she'd had to pencil Jordan in to spend time with her? She thought of the easy relationship she'd always had with her father, the constant companionship he'd offered. And she felt sorry that Jordan had missed out on that.

"Find something?"

Maddie met Jase's eyes. He was seated on the floor across the coffee table from her, his long legs stretched out. "Just that Eva has Jordan penciled in for lunch every Wednesday."

"That was your sister's doing. They'd go out to lunch, and Jordan would either produce tickets for a matinee or she'd make your mother go shopping with her. She thought Eva spent too much time focused on her work and insisted that she take at least Wednesday afternoons off. Jordan had some theory that the time they spent visiting a museum or seeing a play would actually foster Eva's creativity."

"Jordan sounds just like my dad. He was always nagging me that I worked too much."

"Was he right?"

"I didn't think so at the time. I wonder if Eva's focus on work was one of the reasons they broke up."

"You may never find out the answer to that," Jase said.

"But if I find enough pieces, maybe I can put the puzzle together by myself."

He smiled at her then, slowly. "You're absolutely right."

She nodded and shifted her gaze determinedly to the appointment calendar. "For tonight, I have a big enough challenge with this particular puzzle."

"Patience is a requirement if you want to find all the pieces."

Maddie would have settled for just two pieces that would lock together. Every puzzle needed that first match.

The week after the robbery Eva had jotted *J.C.* in the five-o'clock Wednesday slot. Jase had confirmed that was the day she'd come to his office. The next day he'd left for South America.

Twice a week, on Mondays and Thursdays, *P.T.* had been noted in the same time slot. Since Eva's routine had been to visit the gym on her way home from work, Maddie guessed that *P.T.* stood for *personal trainer.* Except for lunch with J., none of the initials jotted in various time slots seemed to connect to anyone who worked at Eva Ware Designs or members of the Ware family who stood to profit from the will.

Scattered randomly on each page were doodles that Maddie suspected were the beginnings of design ideas. Some were elaborated upon in more detail on a later page. Others were abandoned or scratched out.

In Maddie's mind, Eva had used the semi-empty pages of her appointment calendar to test out new ideas—or perhaps to help her think through problems. On a hunch, she flipped through the earlier months and noted that the doodling had increased after the date of the robbery.

And that meant exactly what? Hadn't they already surmised that Eva suspected someone on the inside of pulling off the robbery? Maddie had been so hoping that the appointment calendar would provide them with a new clue.

Discouraged, she glanced again at Jase who was sorting through the clippings and sticky notes that Eva had stuffed inside the appointment calendar. On the dining table on the upper level, they'd dumped the contents of Eva's tote bag and discovered nothing more than what had tumbled out when Michelle had dropped it—a wallet, a pack of matches and a sketch pad half-filled with embryonic designs.

Every so often Jase would pause and scribble something on a piece of hotel stationary. Maddie was doing the same on a message pad she'd located by one of the phones. His list was longer than hers. But then he was a trained investigator.

Jase glanced up at her, then at the pizza they'd smuggled into the Donatello. "Do you want another piece?"

"Go ahead."

He reached for the last slice, folded it neatly in half with one hand, and took a bite. With his other hand, he continued to lift and examine the various pieces of paper Eva had stuffed into her calendar.

She glanced back down at the two pages that captured the last week of Eva's life. It was the fourth time she'd gone over them. There had to be something she'd missed....

The only unusual thing was that on the day before Eva had been run down, she'd scratched out *P.T.* and replaced it with another doodle. This one looked vaguely familiar. Perhaps it was a revision of an earlier sketch.

Frustrated, Maddie tapped her pencil on the notepad. "I'm getting nowhere. If Eva confronted either Michelle or Cho at work with her suspicions, she wouldn't have had to write it down. All she records are standing appointments. Other than that, she used her calendar to sketch design ideas."

Jase swallowed a last mouthful of pizza. "It's the same with the papers she slipped into the book." He held up an advertisement torn from a glossy magazine. In the margin was what Maddie guessed to be an earring in the shape of a spiderweb.

Eyes narrowing, she reached for it.

"What?"

"The design." The moment Jase handed it to her Maddie placed it carefully next to the page she'd been studying. "It's the same one she drew in the five o'clock time slot the night before she was run down."

Rising, Jase stepped over the coffee table and knelt down next to her so that he could study the drawing too.

"I don't think it's a design," he said. "It's the logo for the club that's being advertised—the Golden Spider."

Quickly, Maddie scanned the ad. There were quotes from newspapers and magazines extolling the virtues of the Golden Spider club as one of Manhattan's premier night spots—"the latest place to be seen in the Big Apple." The in place to be. Then she saw it. The text was layered over a faint drawing that matched what Eva had doodled in her appointment calendar and again in the corner of the ad.

Frowning, she flipped back through the pages to the night of the robbery. Then using one finger she began to skim down each page until she found what she was looking for. A week after the robbery, on the day she'd visited Jase at his office, Eva'd sketched the same spiderweb. "Here it is again. I assumed it was an idea for a piece of jewelry, but maybe not."

Jase strode to the dining table on the level above them. "Something's tugging at the back of my mind. I've seen it before someplace."

Maddie studied him. The energy that he always seemed to keep tightly leashed was much closer to the surface. "You think it means something?"

"Maybe." First he leafed through the sketch book. "Nothing here." Then he picked up something from the table. "Well, hello." He tossed it to her.

Maddie caught the matchbook, and her heart skipped a beat when she got a close look. "The Golden Spider." She glanced up at Jase.

"I'd say we have a clue." He descended the two steps and began to pace. "I'm still thinking that I saw that design before. Some place besides the matchbook. I saw a lot of jewelry sketches pinned to the wall while we were in the workroom at Eva Ware Designs. Would your mother have seen a logo like that one and purposely sketched it with the idea of turning it into a piece of jewelry?"

"I…don't know. We'll have to ask Jordan."

"No." Moving forward, Jase dropped to his knees beside her and grabbed her shoulders. "I'm asking *you*. You're more like your mother than you realize."

A skip of panic moved through her. "I don't think so."

"You're both designers. Your brains are hard-wired in a certain way."

"That doesn't mean I know her."

"Fine." But he disagreed with her. Maddie was coming to know her mother more and more. The problem was she wasn't quite comfortable with that knowledge. Releasing her, he picked up the message pad she'd been taking notes on and held it for her to see.

Maddie studied the doodles she'd made in the margins. She hadn't even been fully aware of drawing them. A few were designs she'd been experimenting with for quite a while.

She drew in a deep breath and let it out. "I sometimes do that when I'm worried or thinking through a problem."

"Yeah. From the looks of it, your mother had the same habit. So now I want you to take your best guess. Would your mother have seen something like the spider design and 'borrowed' it as the basis for a piece of jewelry?"

"No," Maddie said firmly.

Jase nodded. "Then she had to have some other reason for her doodles. My theory is that your mother came across it in the ad or on the matchbox, or some other place. Either way she started thinking about it or worrying about it. I can't imagine that she was doodling this because she was a regular visitor at the Golden Spider. You with me so far?"

Maddie thought of the desk in Eva's apartment, piled high with sketch books, littered with drawings. It had been a potent testimonial to what Eva had done when she got home from the gym or the store every night, and it argued forcefully against her mother having had any nightlife. Come to think of it, Maddie herself didn't have a nightlife either. How many evenings did she return to her studio to work? There was a sudden tightness around her heart that had her rubbing her fist against it.

"In the morning, I'll have Dino see what he can dig up on this club. And I want to get to Eva Ware Designs before anyone else does, including the police. I'm still thinking that I saw the spider logo somewhere when we were there today. I'll also fill Stanton in. He's going to be questioning everyone at the store tomorrow. He might as well ask if any of them have been to the Golden Spider." Jase smiled slowly. "That may just stir something up."

Maddie narrowed her eyes. "You *want* to stir something up, don't you?"

Jase's smile faded. "You bet I do."

He pressed down hard on the anger that had been simmering inside him ever since he'd seen that car in his peripheral vision. "I want to get my hands on the bastard who nearly ran us down and who killed your mother."

Just saying the words had an image he'd been battling against for hours running through his head—Maddie lying in that street, bleeding. Lifeless.

Ruthlessly he blanked it out, but beneath his rage something else—determination—iced.

"Me too. Got any ideas?"

"Not yet." That was the hell of it. "I'm drawing a blank. Not even the spiderweb makes sense—yet. But it will. Investigative work is a matter of gathering pieces that don't seem to fit and then finally seeing the whole picture."

His cell phone rang and he fished it out of his pocket. The caller ID told him it was Stanton; he tilted the phone so that Maddie could hear too. "Yeah?"

"Mixed news. I've gotten nowhere with Michelle Tan, and Cho Li has yet to appear at his apartment."

"Could something have happened to him?" Maddie asked.

"I doubt it. One of the uniforms watching the building chatted up the doorman. The guy claims Cho stays out all night two or three times a week."

"Maybe he has a lady friend," Jase said.

"That's my first guess. I'll have my men bring him in as soon as he shows up. We're having better luck with Eva Ware's car. It was parked in her garage. The dent on the hood and the fabric we found on the undercarriage suggest that it was used to run her down. I hope to have lab results confirming that tomorrow. There's no garage attendant on duty. The gate can only be opened with an electronic key card. You find anything like that in her effects?"

"No. No spare car keys either," Jase said.

"So someone close to her could have seized an opportunity to lift both," Stanton mused. "There's a surveillance camera that takes pictures of anyone leaving or entering the garage. I'm hoping to have the tapes early tomorrow, and we may get lucky. Anything new on your end?"

"Have you ever heard of a night club called the Golden Spider?"

"Can't say that I have."

"Eva referred to it a few times in her appointment calendar, and I'm going to have Dino check it out in the morning."

"I've got a friend over in Vice. I'll see what I can find out."

Jase repocketed his cell, then turned to Maddie. "My gut instinct tells me that things are going to start to move quickly tomorrow. That's one of the reasons I want to arrive at Eva Ware Designs before anyone else does. I always found when going into an op, it paid to get there early."

"How can I help?"

"Depending on how the morning goes, we may have to improvise on the spot." He thought of what she'd done with Michelle, playing the sympathetic cop. "Think you can follow my lead?"

She met his eyes, lifted her chin. "You haven't lost me yet, have you?"

"No." He leaned down and kissed her mouth softly. He meant to keep it short, sweet, but he couldn't resist lingering, luring. *I nearly lost her.* When he felt himself sinking, he reluctantly drew away.

"Let's try a different tack." He pushed aside the notes he'd jotted down and handed her a blank piece of hotel stationary. "How good are you at sketching faces?"

She stared at him. "Sketching faces?"

"Yeah. I want you to draw likenesses of the people who may have had access to the security codes at Eva Ware Designs."

Maddie began with a quick drawing of her cousin Adam. Jase passed her a second sheet and she attacked Cho.

As he watched her pen fly across the page, he marveled at how good she was. She was biting down on her lower lip, concentrating hard. He'd seen Jordan do the same thing sitting at her computer.

"I have photos of everyone in the files that Jordan prepared for me."

"That would spoil the experiment. You're like your mother. You think while you draw."

"Oh."

Her hand paused for a moment, then continued to fly across page after page. The sketches were clever and insightful caricatures. She managed to accurately capture Adam's ego, Arnold Bartlett's pomposity, Cho's serenity and Michelle's eagerness and seeming innocence.

"Where did you learn to do this?" he asked.

She glanced at him. "In high school, I worked on the school newspaper."

"Try Carleton and Dorothy."

At her raised eyebrow, he elaborated, "If Adam had access to the security codes, theoretically so did they."

When she'd finished, he lined the sketches up in two lines. "If Michelle, Cho, or Arnold robbed the store and Eva suspected one of them, their jobs would be at stake and there would have been a scandal that would have made the front pages of the newspapers."

"But if family was behind it—" Maddie lined up Adam, Dorothy and Carleton next to the others "—then the scandal would go even deeper. Eva might have been afraid that the store or the business would have been hurt."

For a few moments, silence stretched between them as they studied the two columns they'd fashioned out of the drawings.

"It all comes back to the same old suspects—someone in the family or someone employed by Eva Ware Designs."

"The question is, who has the most at stake?" Jase said.

"And if Eva's murder is related to the robbery, who stood to gain from both?"

Jase gave her shoulders a squeeze, then gathered up her sketches and stacked them into a pile. "Enough for tonight. Sometimes I find the best way to shine new light on a problem is to sleep on it." He rose, drawing her to her feet with him. "Let's go to bed."

14

TAKING her hand, Jase drew Maddie with him into the bedroom. When they reached the bed, he said, "I haven't let you sleep much."

Maddie smiled at him. "I think that I made my contribution to the no-sleep agenda."

When she reached for him, he took her hands and raised them to his lips. "Something's happening between us, Maddie. Something I don't quite understand." But he thought he did understand. He was very much afraid that he was falling in love with Maddie Farrell. And it had him feeling jittery.

It gave him some satisfaction when he saw the change in her eyes. Perhaps he wasn't the only one feeling a bit out of his depth.

"You feel it too," he said.

"Yes. A little. I've given it some thought, and I think it would be wrong to make too much of it. We've been on a roller-coaster ride, emotionally, physically."

Impatience flared but he tamped it down.

"We're smart. We're adults."

Her fingers had tensed in his.

"What we're feeling right now—"

"Is real," he insisted.

"Perhaps. But it could fade when the crisis is over."

Knowing the value of keeping an opponent off balance, Jase raised their joined hands and kissed her fingers. "You may be right. We'll just have to wait and see."

But he was pretty sure his feelings weren't going to fade. He'd just have to convince her that hers weren't going to either. "We have an early morning. I think we should go to bed."

"I thought you'd never ask." Her hands were already busy, gripping the hem of his T-shirt and pulling it up and over his head. But he intended to keep the pace slow. Even when they tumbled onto the bed and began to strip off the rest of their clothes, he kept nibbling her mouth, tasting, teasing. He wanted, no, he needed to savor her—something he hadn't allowed himself to do before.

Her taste was familiar now, sweet, potent, drugging. And yet each time their mouths clung, separated, then fused again, there was something new.

Her hands moved faster than his and he felt the energy in her, heard her moan his name and sensed the imminence of the all-consuming fire. Still, he fought to keep it at bay.

"You don't have to seduce me," she whispered.

But he did. He wasn't sure if it was for her or him. But he did.

She framed his face with her hands and whispered against his mouth, "I want you."

The three words took his breath away as surely as a sucker punch to the gut. He felt his head spin, his heartbeat quicken. He levered himself up far enough that he could see her. In the moonlight pouring through the window, her skin was pale, delicate. Her hair the color of spun gold. He took out the pins and threaded his fingers through it.

"Jase…"

"I just want to look and touch." With one finger, he traced her forehead, her cheekbones, then moved along her jawline to her throat where her pulse beat hard and fast. He continued to touch her—breasts, stomach, thighs—and then he took his mouth on the same journey. Desire stabbed through him when the hands on his shoulders went lax and she began to tremble. Little by little he lost himself in the sound of her breath catching, then releasing on the whisper of his name.

STEEPED in sensation, Maddie felt herself begin to float. This wasn't what she'd expected, wasn't what she'd thought she wanted. Even when his mouth finally returned to hers, there were so many new things to absorb. The flavor of his lips was different, and it went to her head like wine. Totally seduced, she began to run her hands over him, learning his secrets just as he was learning hers. Wherever she touched, he trembled. Wherever she tasted, he shuddered.

"Maddie," he murmured as he made a place for himself between her legs and entered her. His face, his eyes filled her vision, her world.

Even then, they moved slowly, watching each other as they climbed higher and higher. When they drew close to the edge, he lowered his mouth to hers and with one final shudder, they tumbled over together.

AFTERWARD, Jase held Maddie tightly, her head resting on his chest, her legs still tangled with his. One of his hands was pressed against the small of her back, holding her in place; the other was in her hair. The steadiness of her breathing told him that she was sleeping. But his own mind wouldn't shut down.

Instead of trying to fight his wakefulness, he let his mind run through some of the things they'd learned. His gut instinct told him that Maddie had been right all along, and Eva's appointment calendar had given them a vital clue.

His instincts also told him that time was running out. Eva's hit-and-run had been carefully and methodically planned. Hiring a professional hit had also taken planning. But the person who'd tried to run Maddie down had taken a huge risk by using the same car.

A killer driven to desperate measures was more dangerous than a careful and methodical one.

Maddie sighed, then settled.

And they hadn't narrowed their list of suspects down one bit.

The digital clock on the night stand read 2:53 a.m. If he wasn't going to sleep, there was work he could be doing. Instead of waiting until morning to give Dino the job, he could be finding out what he could about the Golden Spider club and why Eva had been so worried about it during the last few weeks of her life.

But he simply didn't want to move.

As long as they were here in bed together, he could keep her safe.

And she was his. She'd been his from the moment she'd climbed mistakenly into his bed. Only it hadn't been a mistake. It had been right. She'd been right for him from the beginning. The certainty of that moved through him like a slow-running river. There were things he wanted to tell her. Needed to tell her. But it wasn't the time. Not just because a killer still had her in his sights, but because her life had turned into chaos.

Instinctively, he held her even closer. Patience was a virtue he'd cultivated over the years. He'd needed it when he'd been working special ops. He also needed it in his business.

But he wondered just how long he could wait before he settled things with Maddie.

MADDIE STIFLED a yawn as Jase hurried her along 50th Street. He'd woken her at six-thirty and told her to get ready. The attentive lover from the night before had morphed into security-agent man again. He'd already showered and shaved, and while she gulped room-service coffee and struggled to catch up, he'd been on his phone—to Dino and Stanton she supposed.

It wasn't until the cab had dropped them off on Fifth Avenue around the block from Eva Ware Designs that the caffeine finally began to clear the fog out of Maddie's brain. She'd asked why the taxi hadn't dropped them off directly in front of the store, and Jase explained that the store was probably being watched.

The blunt reminder that she was still a target had her nerves knotting and her mind going on full alert. Somehow working to decipher her mother's appointment calendar and then making love with Jase had pushed fear about the imminent danger to her life onto the back burner. Quite suddenly, as if everything had shifted into sharp focus, Maddie was very much aware of her surroundings. Brownstones lined up like so many soldiers on either side of the street. In spite of the early hour, a few people were out and about. They passed a man in work clothes fiddling with an awning. A young woman in shorts and flip-flops was walking her dog. A taxi pulled up about three buildings down, and a woman in a business suit hurried down the steps. Jase's hand tightened on her arm, and she was very much aware that his other hand had slipped beneath his jacket to his gun.

Even as her throat went dry, the cab pulled away. Jase picked up the pace and drew her into a narrow alleyway. "We're going in the back way to the store."

"Why are we here so early?"

"I want to make sure no one is lying in wait for you. This is the one place that they can depend on you showing up to today."

Maddie glanced sideways at him. His mouth was set in a grim line, and she could see that his attention was focused on their surroundings. She forced herself to look where he was looking, but she couldn't see anything out of the ordinary. The alley appeared to be deserted.

"I also want to tour the place without being interrupted. I can't rid myself of the idea that I saw something similar to that Golden Spider logo yesterday."

When they reached the back entrance to the store, Jase positioned her between himself and the wall of the building while he dealt with the security code and opened the door.

"Can you get in any place this easily?" Maddie asked.

"It helps that I installed the system and the codes." His voice was pitched low. "I'll go in first. No noise. No conversation. You stay behind me until I make sure that each area is clear."

"You really think someone is in there waiting for us?" she whispered.

The eyes that met hers were cool. "I'm playing it safe. I didn't play it safe enough yesterday when I took you to the park. I changed the security codes for Eva the day after the robbery, but Arnold Bartlett has the new code, and I imagine Jordan has it. There's no way to be sure that Eva didn't give it out to someone else."

Maddie swallowed hard and they slipped into a room that appeared to function both as storage and a break room. Jase led the way into the main salon. The faint scents of coffee and lilies lingered in the air. Lit only by the early-morning sun, the room lacked the glitter and fantasy that she'd experienced the day before, but for Maddie, it still had a quiet elegance.

She followed Jase past the elevator to the stairwell and together they climbed to the second floor and exited into the office area. It was empty. Maddie kept half a step behind Jase as he moved silently from office to office, scanning each one. Satisfied that they were deserted, he moved down the short hall to the door of the workroom. Then he stopped and listened. Maddie counted ten beats before she heard it—a faint tapping. Even muffled, she recognized it as the sound of a hammer striking against metal and it was coming from inside the workroom.

Jase motioned her to stay where she was, then took out his gun and stepped forward to open the door.

"Cho?" he said.

Startled, the man whirled in his chair. The small hammer clattered to the floor when his eyes fastened on Jase's gun.

IT WAS shock and fear that Jase recognized on Cho's face. Gut instinct told him that Maddie had been right about him. Whatever was going on, Cho wasn't behind it. The moment he lowered his gun, Maddie rushed past him.

"Cho, what are you doing here?" she asked.

Cho rose from his chair. "I often come in early to catch up on work. I got behind yesterday because of the cameraman."

Maddie motioned him into his chair and then sat in her mother's. Perfectly willing to let her play good cop again, Jase left the door behind him open and moved to a far corner between two windows. From his position, he could keep his eye on both Madison Avenue and 51st Street and still be ready for anyone who tried to enter the workroom.

He'd learned a long time ago to trust his instincts and they were still telling him that something was going to go down today.

"You haven't spoken to the police then?" Maddie asked.

"Police?" Cho's gaze shifted to Jase, then back to Maddie. "Why would I speak with the police?"

Maddie quickly filled him in on what had happened at her mother's apartment and later at the police station. While she did, Jase scanned the room, searching for what had been tugging at the corners of his mind ever since he'd come across that ad for the Golden Spider and seen Eva's doodle in the margin of her calendar. Maddie had been right, it wasn't among her mother's sketches.

After glancing down on both streets, he moved to Adam's desk. He'd done the same thing yesterday, then turned and leaned his hip against the corner so that he could talk to Adam and still keep his eyes on Maddie and Cho. He repeated the movement and was midpoint in turning when he caught it out of the corner of his eye. On the shelf above Adam's desk was a framed photo of the Golden Spider logo.

A tingle of excitement moved through him as he moved back to the corner between the windows and refocused his attention on Maddie and Cho. Instead of growing agitated about his granddaughter's troubles, Cho appeared to have become more relaxed as Maddie finished.

"The police know she's your granddaughter, and it's the timing that looks so bad," she explained. "The money went into her account three days after the robbery, and she won't tell the police where it came from or what she needed it for."

"I gave her the money," said Cho. "Michelle is very proud. She was embarrassed to have to ask me for help."

"Where did you get the money?" Jase asked.

Cho's chin lifted slightly as he shifted his gaze to Jase. "Eva lent it to me."

"Eva lent you the money?" Maddie asked.

Cho nodded. "Michelle needed it right away, and it would have taken time for me to get that amount out of my retirement fund. I would have had to sell some stocks at a loss. When Eva died, I told Jordan everything. You'll get the money back."

They hadn't had a chance to tell Jordan about the money in Michelle's account, Jase thought. But the fact that Cho had told her would give his story more credibility.

"Why did Michelle need the money so quickly?" Maddie asked.

Cho shook his head. "As I mentioned before, she's a very proud girl. That was the reason she didn't want anyone to know that we were related. She was determined to get this job on her own. She was still living in a dorm when she interned here. But as soon as she was hired full time, she decided she needed to find her own place to live. And since she was working here and was being paid well, she decided to buy a place. She needed thirty thousand dollars for a down payment. Instead of coming to me for help or advice, she borrowed the money."

"Not from a bank," Jase said.

"She tried and was turned down. Then a friend told her about a place where they were more understanding about young people starting out on good career paths." Cho raised an eyebrow. "I believe they call them loan sharks in this country. She says she read the paperwork and that she was given an amount to pay monthly. Which she did. Then a month ago, she was told that she wasn't even covering the interest on the loan and that her current balance was a hundred thousand dollars. Michelle's a proud girl, but she's not stupid. She knew that she was in trouble. That's when she came to me for help."

Maddie studied him for a moment. "Did Michelle know that you borrowed the money from Eva?"

"No. Eva withdrew the money from her account on the day we talked and she gave me a bank check. There's no way that Michelle could have known. It would have shamed her even more to know that Eva was involved."

Maddie glanced over her shoulder at Jase and then back at Cho. "I think that the reason she won't talk to the police is because she wants to protect you."

"From what?" Cho asked.

"It's the timing again. I'll bet she thinks you robbed the store and that's how you got the money."

Cho thought for a minute. "Perhaps."

"You'll have to go down to the police station and explain everything," Jase said. A flash of movement on Madison Avenue caught his attention—two men getting out of a taxi. He recognized his operatives, Tony and Carter. If they were arriving, Adam Ware wouldn't be far behind.

When he turned back, Cho was clearing his desk. On a hunch, he took the photograph from Adam's desk and showed it to Cho. "Do you know anything about this photo?"

"Yes. That's a design Adam created for a nightclub. It's also the place where Michelle went to pay back her loan. I insisted on going with her to deliver the hundred thousand."

THE WINDOW in the hallway outside the workroom led to a fire escape and offered a view of the alleyway. Through it Jase watched Cho exit through the back door and head towards 51st Street. He'd already phoned Stanton to let him know that the man was on his way, and he'd given him a brief summary of Cho's story.

In return, Stanton had explained what he'd learned about the Golden Spider club and its owner from his friend in Vice. Then Jase had checked with Tony and Carter, who were still hanging out at the front of the store, and confirmed that Adam was due to arrive any minute.

He relayed that information to Maddie and added, "Tony and Carter are here on the pretext of getting some shots of Adam in the workroom before the store officially opens. It's as good a time as any for us to discover if your cousin has the new security code. Or if he's going to have to cool his heels until Arnold Bartlett arrives and opens for business."

The moment Cho disappeared from view, Maddie turned to study Jase. "There's something in your eyes—a sort of excitement. Have you fitted the puzzle together yet?"

"No. But I'm closer than before."

"Because Adam designed that logo for the Golden Spider?"

"Yes. It proves he had a connection with the club's owner, John Kessler, and/or that club. Stanton says that Kessler has been under investigation for some time. The problem is that they can't get any hard evidence on him. Socially and politically, he's very well-connected here in the city. The Golden Spider is the place to be seen in New York right now. All the big movers and shakers hang out there. But the man is suspected of using the club as a front for a very sophisticated loan-sharking business. Kessler finds his client base there. So far he's kept his distance from the shadier side of the business. The two victims who have gone to the police have gone missing. But those two clients seem to have been selected very carefully. They were young, they worked in the city at upwardly mobile jobs and they had access to money."

"Michelle didn't."

"She worked here. We know that it wouldn't have been hard for her to get her hands on one hundred thousand dollars' worth of jewels. That's eventually what she might have been pressured to do. They may even have thought that's what she'd done when she was able to produce the money. And if encouraging their young clients to steal money from their workplaces is their modus operandi, that may be why the police haven't been able to get any hard evidence. The victims aren't going to admit to being thieves."

"Michelle can give them hard evidence. She didn't steal anything."

"True." Jase watched a cab pull up at the mouth of the alleyway on 50th Street. "Stanton will encourage her to do just that if Cho's story checks out. In the meantime, Stanton is going to put both Michelle and Cho in protective custody for now."

"And what about Adam? He has a connection to the Golden Spider club too. The thing is why would he need to steal jewels or borrow money from a loan shark? Jordan told me he has a trust fund, and his father runs a bank."

"Good question. But he fits the profile of the victims Kessler targets," Jase pointed out. "Everything we just said about Michelle is true about Adam in spades. He might even be the "friend" who told her about Kessler's operation. Plus, for the last two years he's seen Jordan as a threat to his future here at Eva Ware Designs. With Eva gone, he probably assumed he'd step into her shoes. Then he learns that you're a designer also. Last but not least, with you or Jordan out of the way, Adam stands to inherit a lot more money because of the terms of your mother's will. He's under pressure from his mother, he has a temper and a rebellious streak. You can bet that Stanton will question him very closely about his connection to Kessler."

A man emerged from the taxi and started down the alleyway. Gripping Maddie's shoulders, Jase turned her so that she could see.

"Adam," she murmured.

Together they watched as he let himself easily into the back door of the store.

"That answers one question. He has the new code. So he could stage another robbery at any time."

"Or he could just pilfer a few pieces here and there, hoping that no one would notice."

He turned to her, smiled and tucked a strand of hair behind

her ear. "Good theory. Have I told you that I like the way your mind works?"

Then Jase opened the window and climbed out onto the fire escape. There was an ominous creaking sound.

"What are you doing?" Maddie asked.

"Getting out of here."

"We're going down the fire escape?"

Jase held out a hand. "C'mon. While two of my best operatives are keeping Adam occupied, we're going to go on a little field trip to your cousin's apartment."

"Why?"

"We may find another puzzle piece there. And I want you out of the store. I took a chance even bringing you here. This is where that hit woman picked you up yesterday."

As she placed her hand in Jase's and threw her leg over the sill, Maddie made the mistake of glancing down. Her head spun once, and the moment she shifted her full weight onto the grated flooring, it creaked again.

"Don't look down."

"Already did."

"Think you can make it?"

She met his eyes. "You haven't lost me yet."

"No. And I don't intend to." Leaning down, he kissed the tip of her nose. "I'll go first." He shut the window. "We have to move fast. Do you think you can run in those shoes?"

"Sure."

Jase turned and led the way down a flight of steps.

Keeping her eyes fastened on Jase's back, Maddie took a firm grip on the hand railing and followed one tense step at a time. Rattles and groans joined the creaks. She was surprised that no one had run into the alleyway to find out what all the noise was about. When Jase reached the first landing, the whole fire escape swayed.

Maddie's head spun again. "I don't think this has been used in a while."

"Hang in there. It's almost over." Dropping to his knees, Jase lowered the ladder. It made a little shrieking sound and particles of rust rose in a fine spray. "I'll be right beneath you." He turned and began to climb down.

Maddie braced a hand against the brick wall of the building as the fire escape groaned and swayed. Then she heard the sound of the impact as his feet hit cement followed by a soft grunt.

"C'mon. I'll catch you."

For a minute, Maddie closed her eyes. *Don't think about it.* Then, drawing in a deep breath, Maddie gripped the railing, ignored the slight sway. *Think of something else. Jase.* In her mind, she pictured him standing beneath her, ready to catch her if she slipped. With that thought in mind, she turned around, dropped to her knees and found the rung of the ladder with her feet. Slowly, she began her descent.

"Atta girl," Jase said.

She kept his image in her mind as she located the next rung and the next. She pictured what his face looked like when he was above her, thrusting into her, the crinkles that formed at the corners of his eyes when he was grinning. She recalled the concern she'd glimpsed briefly in his expression when he'd watched D.C. walk with that cane. The cold steel she heard in his voice when he went into security mode.

She'd known him less than forty-eight hours and yet she knew so many sides of him. Her right foot dangled in the air and she gripped the ladder tightly.

"Just drop. I'll catch you."

For only a moment, she hesitated. But even then, she didn't picture the distance to the ground. The image in her mind was

Jase below her, his arms outstretched, that long, lean body braced to catch hers.

When she let go and fell, she felt her heart take the same fast tumble.

Arms as strong as steel clamped around her. "Gotcha."

For an instant, she felt him sway. Then he set her solidly on her feet.

"Ready?"

She turned to him then. And the fear that snaked up her spine had less to do with the fact that her life was in danger and much more to do with the man. She wasn't sure she *was* ready for what she was coming to feel for Jase Campbell. But she was going to get ready. Taking his hand in hers, she said, "Yes."

Side by side, they raced for the end of the alleyway.

15

TWENTY MINUTES later, Jase and Maddie climbed the stairs in Adam's apartment building.

"You've given me a whole new perspective on the lack of security in New York City dwellings."

Jase slanted a look at her. She hadn't commented as he'd gotten them into the basement of the building through an emergency-exit door. The alarm had sounded, but before anyone had appeared in the hallway, he'd urged her into the stairwell. "This one has excellent security at least at the front end. A doorman and another man on duty at the desk." That was why he'd chosen a different entrance.

"Can you get into any building this easily?"

"Depends. I was in a hurry, and I was lucky." He knew enough not to depend on luck for everything. He'd been able to hail a cab on Fifth Avenue and he'd switched taxis twice before arriving at Adam's building. He was as sure as he could be that they hadn't been followed, but he couldn't shake the feeling that he'd overlooked something.

On the fourth-floor landing, he pushed through the exit door. "Another time I might have pulled a D.C. and spun a story for the doorman that would have gotten us into Adam's apartment in a more legitimate way."

When they reached apartment 457, Jase motioned her to

one side of the door. Then he knocked loudly. He counted ten beats, then knocked again.

Nothing.

Only then did he take the small case out of his back pocket and begin to work on the lock. Less than two minutes later, he had the door open. Still on the threshold, he scanned the living room. Something had his gut clenching, but there was no sound, no movement and nothing to be seen but dust motes dancing in a slant of morning sunlight.

Hurry, he told himself as he stepped into the small foyer. All he caught was a blur of movement, but it was enough to have him turning slightly. As a result, the blow hit him in the side of his head instead of the back.

"Maddie, run." He managed to choke out the words as the pain, immediate and fierce, grayed his vision. Then his world went black.

MADDIE STOOD frozen as she watched Jase crumple to the floor. Then a hand grabbed her arm and jerked her forward into the room. Even then, she wasn't able to shift her eyes away from him. Blood was oozing from a cut on his head.

A shove from behind had her stumbling past Jase's lifeless body. A spurt of anger freed her from paralysis. She whirled on her attacker. She would have lunged forward had it not been for the gun in the woman's right hand.

"Dorothy?" Maddie stared at the impeccably dressed woman standing in front of her, taking in the details as her sluggish mind raced to keep up. Adam's mother was wearing a royal-blue suit today. The color contrasted nicely with the blood dripping from the fireplace poker Dorothy held in one hand. Jase's blood.

Maddie swallowed the hysteria threatening to bubble up. She had to think, she had to find a way to help Jase. She'd been trained in self-defense tactics by Cash. The first rule was to distract your opponent. For now, she just had to stall. Keep Dorothy talking.

"What are you doing here?" Maddie asked.

"Adam called me."

Dorothy took two steps forward, and Maddie backed up in retreat. They were out of the foyer now, farther away from Jase. That was good. But in the stronger light, what Maddie saw glinting in the older woman's eyes had fear nearly freezing her again.

"He saw you leaving by way of the fire escape," Dorothy continued. "I was still on my cell talking to him when the police arrived to take him in for questioning. That was your doing. Don't bother to deny it."

Dorothy's voice was calm, composed, making the lethal weapon in her hand seem surreal. Keeping the gun steadily aimed at Maddie, she moved sideways to the fireplace and hung the poker on its hook. *Good,* Maddie thought. There was only one weapon to worry about now. "I don't know what you're talking about."

"Don't play innocent." Dorothy moved closer, and this time Maddie held her ground. She had to if she was going to get that gun away.

"I know what you're doing. Your friend runs a security firm. Jase Campbell. Adam recognized the name the moment you introduced him."

"He's also Jordan's apartment mate," Maddie said. "And a good friend."

"But that's not why you brought him with you to Eva Ware Designs. Before she died, Eva told Adam that she'd hired Jase Campbell to investigate the robbery. And I knew when I saw him with you yesterday that you intended to stir everything up again. It's all part of your goal to push Adam out of Eva Ware Designs. And for that you have to die, just as Eva had to die."

DIE. That one word penetrated the fog clouding Jase's brain. Then he remembered. The woman standing just inside the foyer. Maddie was in danger. How long had he been out? Experimentally, he opened his eyes just a little and rode out the wave of pain. He could just make out the two women standing in a slash of sunlight about ten feet away.

Dorothy Ware had a gun aimed at Maddie. Anger and fear flooded through him. Jase shoved both aside and resisted the urge to get up. When he moved, he'd have to be fast. And he had to be sure that he wouldn't get dizzy. Wouldn't stumble. Slowly, carefully, he raised his head off the floor. Pain spiked at his right temple, but there was no dizziness.

MADDIE SAW two movements at once. Jase lifting his head and Dorothy raising the gun slightly. *Don't panic. Stall.*

"Is that why you hired the hit woman?" Maddie asked.

Surprise flickered for a moment in Dorothy's eyes. "I don't know what you're talking about. I prefer to handle things on my own."

Maddie didn't let herself look at the gun. "You still haven't told me why you're here."

With her free hand, Dorothy gestured toward the purse that sat on the arm of one of the sofas. "Adam asked me to come and take away the jewels."

"The jewels?"

"Adam is not entirely stupid. He knew he wouldn't get away with another robbery. So instead, he's been bringing pieces here one at a time. Eventually he'll sell them in the same way he sold the others. He couldn't afford to leave them here now that the police are involved."

A chill snaked its way up Maddie's spine. Dorothy spoke

about her son's actions in the same matter-of-fact tone she might use to discuss the weather. *Don't panic. Just keep her talking.*

"Adam robbed Eva Ware Designs? Why? He's rich."

Dorothy sighed. "Not anymore. He has a gambling problem, and he hasn't conquered it yet. He's gone through his trust fund, and Carleton wouldn't help him out. He claims he can't because money has become very tight at the bank. Plus he's still annoyed with Adam for not taking a job at Ware Bank. He could be a VP by now. So Adam had to borrow money elsewhere."

"At a high interest rate?" So Jase had been right.

"Yes. Luckily, I sit on the MOMA board with a man who helps people in Adam's situation."

"John Kessler?"

Dorothy frowned. "How did you know?"

"The man's a loan shark," Maddie said.

"Nonsense. He helped Adam when his father and I couldn't. Of course, I did what I could to help him with the payments, but I couldn't go on doing that forever. I told him he had to be a man and take care of the problem. And for once in his life, Adam stepped up to the plate."

The pride in Dorothy's voice had Maddie's blood turning even colder.

"He robbed Eva Ware Designs of a few baubles to take care of the debt once and for all. Everything would have been fine if Eva hadn't figured it out. When she confronted him about the robbery and discovered that Adam was still gambling, she actually threatened him. Adam, in spite of his faults, is a Ware."

"Did she threaten to have him arrested?"

"Of course not. Adam's family. She told him that she would settle his additional debt, but that he would have to leave Eva Ware Designs. Can you imagine that?"

For the first time, Maddie heard a thread of emotion in Dorothy's voice.

"She was going to fire Adam! Adam, whose dream was to run Eva Ware Designs one day. I couldn't allow that to happen. That's why I had to kill her. That's why I have to kill you."

Beyond Dorothy's shoulder, Maddie saw Jase spring to his feet and lunge forward. Later, she remembered everything in freeze-framed moments. Dorothy started to turn. Jase was still too far away to reach her in time. Without any thought on her part, Maddie flew forward and brought the edge of her hand down hard on Dorothy's gun arm. The gun fired into the floor.

The shot was still ringing in Maddie's ear when she grabbed the arm she'd just hit and kicked Dorothy's feet out from under her.

Jase flipped the woman over and sat on her while he put plastic restraints on her wrists and ankles. Then he pulled out his cell, punched in a number, and handed it to Maddie. "You talk to Stanton. He's going to yell at me and my head hurts."

As she took the phone, he smiled at her, then winced and said, "Is that one of the moves your friend Cash taught you?"

"Yes."

"I owe him one."

It took a lot of charm, arguments and dogged determination, but in just three hours Jase was letting Maddie lead him down the hall to his bedroom. The stop at the emergency room had been at Maddie's insistence. Stanton had joined them there and questioned them both in the waiting room.

While he'd been X-rayed, poked, prodded, stitched up and given a prescription for twenty-four hours of bed rest, she had stayed by his side.

That's when Maddie had asked the question that was foremost in his own mind. "You don't think that it's over, do you?"

"Hard to say," he'd replied. "That's why I haven't called D.C. yet. I don't want anyone in Santa Fe letting down their guard until we know more."

According to Stanton, Carleton Ware had been shocked when he'd heard the news about his wife and son. Stanton's take was that the reaction rang true. Neither the wife nor the son had implicated him. Carleton was out of town attending a conference, but he'd sent a team of lawyers to the station. However, the hard evidence had started to dribble in. The security cameras at Eva's garage had caught a good shot of Dorothy behind the wheel of Eva's car on the same night that Eva was run down. And Dino had tapped into Eva's bank account and found a withdrawal of two hundred and fifty thousand dollars two days before her death. Apparently that had gone to Adam to pay off the additional debt he'd incurred since he'd robbed the store. Jase's informant had also phoned in. One of the fences he'd contacted had given a description of Adam.

"I don't believe Dorothy hired the hit woman who shot at us in the park," Maddie said. "I don't think she could have faked the surprise I saw in her eyes when I asked her about it."

"I'm not so sure she hired the hit either. Perhaps Adam did," Jase said.

"The terrible thing is his mother would be proud of him if he did."

They'd reached his bedroom, and Maddie steered him through the door and onto the bed. He let her fuss over him, rearranging pillows. But when she turned to go, he took her wrist and pulled her down on top of him.

"Jase," she said. "The doctor said bed rest. You have a possible concussion."

"That doctor was only twelve years old. Besides, it's equally possible that I don't have a concussion."

"Either way, you need rest."

With one hand he held her in place. With the other he drew her head down and brushed his lips over hers. "Stay with me."

When she melted against him, a little of his tension eased.

Lifting her head, she said, "We're just going to rest."

He smiled slowly. "For now." He eased her to his side and turned to face her. It occurred to him that they were in the same position as when he'd opened his eyes and first seen her. He tucked a strand of hair behind her ear. "I've waited a long time to get you back here in my bed, Maddie."

When he saw the nerves flash into her eyes, he felt his own knot more tightly in his stomach.

"We don't need to talk now," she said.

Patience. He'd thought he could draw on it. Promised himself that he would. But he couldn't.

"I know that you have a lot on your plate. Your aunt has been arrested for murder, your cousin for robbery. You've just begun to get settled in at Eva Ware Designs and get your questions about your mother answered. We haven't even had time to search Eva's apartment or office to see whether there's any evidence that she and your father kept in touch over the years."

"I have an idea about that. A hunch. We can check it out later. Right now you need to rest."

Hadn't he promised himself during the eons of time they'd spent in that emergency room that he'd wait for later, too? There were so many reasons why he shouldn't push her now. And one reason why he had to.

"I can wait to make love with you, Maddie. But I need to settle something. I thought I could give you time, but I have to say this. We both thought that making love that night was an accident, a mistake. But it wasn't. There's something about you that's felt so right—from the beginning."

When he paused and she merely stared at him, impatience bubbled over. "Dammit, Maddie. I love you."

For a moment the words hung in the air between them while Maddie's head took a bigger spin than it had on the fire escape. *Jase loves me?*

He gripped her shoulders. "I want you here in my bed. Not just for tonight or the next three weeks. I want you here permanently."

Permanently? Wasn't that the word that she'd been afraid to let herself think about? Hope for?

Jase began to look panicked when she still remained silent. "I know that we come from different worlds. But we'll find a way to build a bridge between them. I figure even after the terms of the will are met, you'll want to keep your hand in at Eva Ware Designs. And who knows how Jordan will feel about ranching? Maybe Dino and I could open a branch of our business in Santa Fe. We can work something out." He was babbling, Maddie realized. Jase never babbled.

"Wait." She placed her hand over his mouth. "I think it's my turn to say something."

She smiled at him and framed his face with her hands. "I love you too. Let's build that bridge." She drew his mouth to hers.

The kiss was filled with promise and joy. Not just right, but perfect.

Epilogue

"THIS COULD have waited until tomorrow," Maddie said as they stepped into Eva Ware's apartment.

"I rested for nearly four hours."

She shot him a look. "Some of what we did in your bed didn't qualify as resting."

He grinned at her. "You're an irresistible temptation to me, Maddie Farrell. Besides, I think making love to you was just what the doctor should have ordered. I feel much better now."

The truth was he'd felt wonderful ever since she'd said she loved him. Foolish as it might be, he wanted to shout it from the treetops. Before they'd left the apartment, he'd settled for calling his brother, but D.C.'s phone had gone straight to voice mail. So had Jordan's. It wasn't enough to worry him. If there were serious problems at the ranch, D.C. would have found a way to contact him.

"You said you had a hunch," he continued. "I know what it's like to have one of those and not be able to act on it right away. You're not going to rest easy until you check it out."

She led the way out of the foyer and paused in the doorway to Eva's library. Outside, the early-evening light was dimming, so Jase flipped on a switch. They were facing the portrait of Eva and Jordan.

"I could be wrong," Maddie said. "I still don't really know her all that well."

Jase took her hand. "You know her better than you think you do."

"You said that before, and it started me thinking. I want to believe that my parents kept in touch all these years—that they had some interest in the daughter they didn't raise. But that may be wishful thinking."

"Or it could be the reality. You're not going to know until you follow your hunch. Tell me what it is."

"It may come to nothing. But my mother and I did use the same old-fashioned appointment calendar, and I have this box at the ranch—something my father gave me when I was little—to keep photos, souvenirs and mementos in. I was wondering if Eva might have something similar."

"Good idea. Where do you want to start looking?"

"We could start here…but that would be stalling. I've always kept mine on a shelf in my closet."

"Let's go."

Eva's bedroom opened off the library. Maddie gripped Jase's hand tightly as they crossed to the closet. "It might not be here. She could have rented storage space. It could be at Eva Ware Designs."

"Let's see." The moment Jase opened the door, he heard Maddie's breath catch. There were two boxes on the shelf above the neatly hung clothes. One was labeled *Taxes;* the second box was red and unmarked.

"The red box—it's exactly the same as the one my father gave me. What are the odds? He must have sent it to her."

Without a word, Jase lifted down the box and carried it back to the library. Then they sat down on one of the leather couches and Maddie opened it.

It was filled with photos and letters from Mike Farrell. Maddie lifted them out one by one. Most of them marked milestones in Maddie's life—her birthdays, graduations.

"This was my very first jewelry show," Maddie said, giving him the picture.

"The photos have been handled, Maddie. Look at the worn edges. Eva looked at them."

She met his eyes. "But she never called, never came to visit. And I can't just blame my mother. My father went along with whatever it was they decided. I don't understand it."

Jase lifted an envelope out of the box and examined it more closely. "This one is addressed to your father, and it's never been mailed."

"Open it."

When he did, they read it together.

May 15th
Dear Mike,
It seems strange to be writing to you after all these years. You, of all people, know what a coward I am. I'm afraid to pick up the phone. And if you don't answer this letter, I'll understand.

I'm regretting the agreement we made all those years ago. You told me I would, and you were right. I just couldn't see it at the time. Of course, keeping me informed about Maddie's life through photos helped. I've been to her Web site, and her designs are beautiful.

I haven't been nearly as good about sending pictures of Jordan. But at least you have the ones when she was competing in horse shows. And when you've sent presents, I've seen that she's gotten them—even if I didn't tell her who they were from. She's a talented young woman with a very good head for business. I'm fortunate to have her with me. You were right about that—and so many other things. I owe you a great deal.

Enough stalling. I'm writing because I wonder if it's time that we brought the girls together. I've been struggling with the idea for over a year now. They're both out of college, independent young women. What do you think? I'm so afraid that they'll hate me for what happened.

And perhaps after all these years, you're happy with the way things are. Let me know and I'll abide by your decision.

I hope this letter finds you well.

All my best,

Eva

Jase waited while Maddie skimmed the letter a second time. "She wrote it but she didn't send it. He wouldn't have gotten it anyway because he died on the twelfth of May that same year. But I would have received it, and I would have probably opened it and read it."

"Perhaps she changed her mind and called your father after all."

Maddie sighed. "There were so many calls after he died."

"And if she'd asked for Mike, you would have told her that he'd passed."

"Yes." She glanced again at the letter. "This raises even more questions than it answers. *I'm so afraid they'll both hate me.* Why would we hate her? Because it was her idea to separate us?"

"Perhaps." Jase took the letter and placed it on the table. Then he took her hands in his.

"So a year ago, she was thinking about bringing us together, and when my dad died, she changed first her mind and then her will? Why wait until she was dead to bring us together?"

"You may never get all the answers, Maddie. And you may not get the ones you want. But I can theorize about the timing. You've discovered how focused Eva was on her work. But at the time she wrote the letter Jordan had been working at the Madison Avenue store for about a year. She'd come back after six years in college and graduate school, and she was insisting that she and Eva spend time together—having lunch, going to the theater, shopping. Eva was getting to know Jordan as an adult, and perhaps she wanted to know you too. Then when your father died, she may have lost her courage. Perhaps she was afraid of losing both of you if she revealed what she and Mike had done."

"So she arranged to have us meet after she was dead? What a waste."

"I agree." Jase leaned down and brushed his mouth over hers. "You know, we don't have all the answers yet. You were both born in Santa Fe and there may still be people who remember your mother being there, however briefly. I'm betting Jordan is investigating that possibility."

"We have to call her, fill her in. And find out why she's had her cell phone off for the past few hours. But now that Adam and Dorothy are in police custody, she should be safe, right?"

"She should be, but I'm going to ask D.C. to stay out there for a few more days."

Maddie drew out her cell phone. But before she punched in the numbers, she turned to him. "Whatever questions or criticism I have about my mother, she did one thing right with her will."

"What's that?"

"She brought you into my life. I'll be forever grateful to her for that."

"Ditto," he said, and he pulled her closer for a kiss. He would be forever in Eva's debt for bringing him Maddie.

* * * * *

TWIN SEDUCTION

BY
CARA SUMMERS

To my lovely niece, Sarah Fulgenzi, a new
June bride. Congratulations! I wish you a true
"happy ever after" and I know you'll work
hard to achieve it. I love you!

Prologue

WARE HOUSE.

Jordan gave the Long Island mansion a cursory inspection as she slammed the taxi door behind her. The overcast sky shrouded the place in even more gloom than usual. With its turrets and weathered gray stones, the three-story structure her great-great-grandfather had built looked as mysterious as ever. She'd always thought it could have served as the setting for the Gothic novels she'd enjoyed reading as a young girl. The kind of house that held lots of secrets.

At least that much hadn't changed. Because in the last week, everything else in her life had.

When pain squeezed her heart, Jordan rubbed her fist against her chest. *You've gotten this far. You can get through the rest.*

Seven days ago, two policemen had come to her apartment door with bad news. Her mother, renowned jewelry designer Eva Ware, had been killed by a hit-and-run driver as she'd crossed the street to her apartment building.

Her mother was dead.

A week had gone by and she was still struggling to accept that. Eva should be with her right now. They'd always come to Ware House together. But her mother wasn't here. She would never be here again.

Closing her eyes, Jordan ordered herself to take a deep

breath. She couldn't fall apart. She had too much to do. It would be her responsibility to make sure that her mother's legacy lived on.

A quick glance at her watch confirmed she was a good half hour early for the reading of her mother's will. She could take a moment to gather her thoughts, her strength. Turning, she began to pace on the flagstones in front of the huge entrance door.

You can get through this.

And she could. Hadn't she made it through identifying the body at the morgue and making arrangements for the funeral? Her Uncle Carleton and Aunt Dorothy had insisted on helping her with that.

Jordan had been both grateful and surprised when they'd contacted her because her mother and her uncle hadn't been on the best of terms for as long as Jordan could remember.

From what her mother had said, the little feud stemmed back to her grandfather's will. Carleton and Eva had each inherited half of Ware Bank, half of Ware House and half of his stocks, bonds and cash. Carleton had wanted his sister to invest her share in Ware Bank, the family business, but Eva had insisted on putting her cash into her fledgling jewelry design business.

To Jordan's way of thinking, it had turned out to be a wise decision since Eva Ware Designs was one of the most exclusive jewelry stores in New York City. Eva had tried to placate her brother's feelings by moving out of Ware House and letting him have the place to himself. Her Uncle Carleton, Aunt Dorothy and cousin Adam had lived there ever since, but the strain on family relations had never quite faded. Every time she and her mother visited, the chill in the air was so noticeable that her mother had rented a room at a small inn in nearby Linchworth when ever they intended to stay overnight.

In spite of all that, her aunt and uncle had been helpful in planning the funeral. Dorothy Ware had a great deal of expertise when it came to organizing social events, and Eva Ware's funeral had turned out to be just that. Thousands had come to pay their respects to the award-winning jewelry designer.

But the one person Jordan had wanted there hadn't been able to come—Jase Campbell, her apartment mate and closest friend.

She and Jase had first met during her freshman year at the Wharton School of the University of Pennsylvania. Jase had been a senior and they'd met by accident when they'd both shown up to rent an off-campus apartment. Instead of flipping a coin to see who'd get it, they'd moved in together and become fast friends. A year ago when Jase had left the navy to start up his own security business in Manhattan, they'd become apartment mates again. But for the last three and a half weeks, he'd been in some remote area of South America negotiating a hostage situation. She hadn't even been able to talk with him via cell phone.

He didn't even know that Eva was dead.

And he certainly didn't know about the other big change in her life. She'd acquired a sister.

Edward Fitzwalter III, her mother's longtime attorney, had called with *that* shocking news on the day after her mother's funeral. Even now, Jordan was tempted to pinch herself to see if the last week had been a nightmare that she could just wake up from.

She had a sister she'd never met. Madison Farrell. And she was coming here today for the reading of their mother's will.

Each time Jordan thought about it, her heart took a little leap and nerves knotted in her stomach. She'd only had two days to try to absorb it, and although she prided herself on her efficiency and adaptability, she wasn't sure she had.

How *did* one process the fact that one had a sister—an identical twin—who'd been raised all these years on a ranch in New Mexico by a father Jordan had never known? A father she would *never* know because he'd died a year ago.

The whole situation was straight out of a Disney movie. At first, she hadn't believed Fitzwalter. She'd nagged him until he'd shown her the birth certificates. She and Madison had been born in Santa Fe. She was older than her twin by almost four minutes.

Fitzwalter had also shown her a wedding license. Eva Ware had married Michael Farrell approximately eleven months before she and Madison had been born.

Immediately after seeing the paperwork, she'd looked Madison Farrell up on Google and begun a file on the sister she'd never met. Within an hour, she'd amassed quite a bit of information. Her sister went by the name of Maddie. In addition to being a rancher, her twin was an up-and-coming jewelry designer in Santa Fe. And except for a difference in hair styles, she and Maddie could have been mirror images of each other.

What would her sister be like? Would they have anything in common? From the looks of her Web site, Maddie had inherited their mother's genius for designing jewelry. Had Jordan inherited her father's talent for business?

Jordan sighed. Instead of answering her questions, her research had only brought more. Why had their parents separated them? Why had they been kept apart all these years? Why had her mother told her that her father died shortly after she was born? Would her sister have any answers?

Pushing back a fresh wave of frustration, Jordan whirled to glance back at the house. It still seemed impossible that her mother wasn't here right now. Today Jordan had faithfully followed their old routine, taking the train from Manhattan, then hailing a taxi. She'd even stopped in Linch-worth and checked in to the suite she and Eva always stayed in.

Why? Oh, she'd told herself it was so she had some-place to take Maddie after the reading of the will so that they could talk privately. In spite of her aunt and uncle's help with the funeral, she didn't think that the family dynamics had changed. But she wondered if she'd fol-lowed her mother's routine because she was having trouble letting go and accepting her death.

And what would Maddie Farrell make of the family dynamics? To say the Ware family wasn't close-knit was an understatement. Jordan rarely saw her uncle or aunt, and the only reason she saw her cousin Adam was because he worked as a designer at Eva Ware Designs.

The sound of a sports car roaring up the driveway drew her attention. Speak of the devil, she thought as her cousin Adam braked in front of the house.

Sending him a little wave, she marched up the steps. There was still time to get inside—depending on how quick Lane was to answer the door.

It had opened just a crack when a car door slammed behind her. "Jordan, wait up. I want a word with you."

Adam Ware sounded annoyed. Jordan couldn't remem-ber a time in the two years since she'd gone to work for Eva Ware Designs that he hadn't.

By the time Lane had fully opened the door, Adam was at her side. "What in the hell are you trying to pull?"

Jordan tamped down on her annoyance and sent her cousin another smile. "I'm here for the reading of my mother's will." Then she shifted her smile to the butler. "Good afternoon, Lane."

The butler, who'd always reminded Jordan a bit of Michael Caine, bowed slightly and stepped aside. "Ms.

Jordan, Mr. Adam, the family has gathered with Mr. Fitz-walter in the library."

"Has my sister arrived?" Jordan asked.

"Not yet."

"Your *sister,*" Adam snorted. "That's the very person I want to have a word with you about." He urged her through an open doorway to the left.

With an inward sigh, Jordan gathered what patience she could. Ever since she'd joined Eva Ware Designs, Adam had opposed every single marketing strategy she'd proposed. During the three years he'd worked alone with her mother while she'd pursued her graduate degree, her cousin had come to expect that he would one day take over and run Eva Ware Designs. And for some reason, her presence in the company had made him paranoid.

She'd tried to approach him on a rational level and pointed out that their talents lay in different areas—that while he brought his design expertise to the company, she brought a business background. But nothing she said or did seemed to assuage his fear.

Eva had mostly viewed the friction between them as a sort of sibling rivalry and gone back to work. But each time her mother had approved one of Jordan's marketing ideas, Adam had seemed to feel more and more threatened.

The spacious room Adam had ushered her into was furnished with antiques from the Victorian era. Velvet drapes in a rich shade of burgundy had been pulled back to allow in the dim light. When they'd reached the far end of the room, Adam turned to face her. Even in the dim light, he was incredibly handsome. He had his father's tall, athletic build, and his mother's rich chestnut-colored hair, worn long enough to push behind his ears.

"I want an explanation," Adam said in a tight voice.

"An explanation of what?"

"I want to know what you're up to with this sister you've manufactured. My father said that he'd received a call from Fitzwalter and that you're suddenly producing someone you claim is your long lost sister."

"I received the same call from Fitzwalter." Jordan worked to keep her voice calm. "I believe my parents are the ones who must be given the credit for producing her. Fitzwalter can show you the birth certificate. At my mother's specific request, he contacted Madison and arranged for her to travel here today because my mother wanted her here for the reading of the will."

"Why? Why reveal this second daughter now?"

Excellent questions, Jordan thought. "Your guess is as good as mine."

"I want to know what it means."

Jordan studied him for a moment. There was a hint of near panic in his eyes. "It means you have a cousin you never knew about."

He made a dismissive gesture with his hand. "That's not what I mean. I want to know how this person is going to affect my position at Eva Ware Designs."

"Very little, I would think." Adam wasn't the only one asking these questions, Jordan decided. He was probably only parroting his parents' concerns. She suspected there was a lot of parental pressure on Adam, particularly from his mother, to one day take over Eva Ware Designs.

"From what I've been able to gather, Maddie has her hands full running her ranch and her own jewelry-design business out in Santa Fe."

"She designs jewelry?" Adam's tone was incredulous.

"You can check out her Web site." She made a point of glancing at her watch, then turned to stride toward the door. "My sister is due to arrive any minute. So I think we ought to join the others in the library."

Before she could step into the hallway, Adam grabbed her hand and jerked her around. "You don't know any more than that?"

She met his eyes steadily. "No." Then she pulled herself free and led the way out of the room.

Lane was waiting down the hallway, and as they approached, he reached for the handles of the paneled double doors and pushed them open. As she entered the library with Adam a step behind her, the scents of lemon wax and lilies assaulted her senses.

Jordan paused for a second to let her gaze sweep the room. It was huge. Three walls were lined with bookshelves, and four stained-glass windows nearly filled the fourth. Fitzwalter sat behind a carved oak desk with his back to the windows. Red leather chairs had been arranged in two semicircles around the desk.

Cho Li, her mother's longtime assistant at Eva Ware Designs, had chosen a seat in the second row of chairs, and she returned the warm smile he sent her.

Uncle Carleton and Aunt Dorothy had already taken their seats to the attorney's right. Adam strode directly to them and said something to his mother. A report on their conversation, Jordan thought.

As always, she was struck by how handsome her uncle was. And how quiet. For as long as she'd known him, he'd been a man of few words. Her mother had always claimed that he was totally focused on Ware Bank, which had been established by his great-great-grandfather and whose branches were scattered all over Long Island. Considering her mother's focus on Eva Ware Designs, Jordan privately thought that brother and sister had a sort of tunnel vision in common. She wondered if Maddie would turn out to be the same way.

Carleton's hazel eyes were cool and shuttered as they

met hers. Jordan wondered what her uncle thought of the news of Madison Farrell's existence. Dorothy, too, for that matter. Her aunt was even harder to read than her uncle.

Jordan took her seat to Fitzwalter's left.

"It's two o'clock. Surely we can get started now." Dorothy Ware spoke in the same cool, unruffled tone she always used. As usual, her aunt looked as if she'd just walked away from a cover shoot for *Vogue,* but Jordan noted her hands were folded tightly on her designer bag.

Fitzwalter removed his glasses as his cell phone rang. Picking it up, he said, "Yes?"

After a moment, he disconnected the call, took his glasses off and said, "Ms. Madison Farrell will join us shortly. Her car has just pulled up."

A mix of nerves and anticipation jittered in Jordan's stomach. There was a part of her that wanted to dash out of the library and greet her sister at the front door. But there was another, more cautious part of her that was still struggling to accept what Fitzwalter had told her and what she'd seen when she'd examined the birth certificates.

Her sister. In a matter of seconds, she was going to meet her *sister.* How many times had she let herself imagine the moment? But this was real.

The grandfather clock ticked off the seconds. On the other side of Fitzwalter's desk, the Wares sat in silence, their eyes on the library door. Did they all suspect what Adam did—that she'd somehow conjured up a sister after all these years? Or knowingly kept her existence hidden?

A sudden spurt of anger had Jordan springing to her feet and turning to face the door. She'd had grown used to Adam's paranoia, but this was ridiculous. And her sister was about to walk into this frigid, hostile atmosphere. In her mind, she pictured Maddie entering the house, then following Lane down the long hallway to the library doors. Her own nerves paled in comparison with what she imagined her sister must be feeling. She started toward the doors.

When they opened, Jordan froze, and suddenly she and Maddie might have been alone in the room. As many times as she'd let herself imagine this moment, nothing had prepared her for the instant sense of connection and recognition that hit her like a punch in the gut. She felt winded—as if she'd just sprinted up a steep hill. It was one thing to see a photo on a Web site and quite another to come face-to-face with your mirror image.

Well, almost your mirror image.

Maddie Farrell had the same blue-violet eyes, the same facial features and hair color, but she wore a different hairstyle. Jordan kept hers cut just below chin length, while Maddie wore hers in a long braid just as Eva had done. How many times had she tried to convince her mother to switch to a more modern style?

Just as she had countless times in the past few days, Jordan pushed aside the little twinge of pain near her heart. She and Maddie had different taste in clothes, too. But Jordan liked the casual Southwestern style of Maddie's khaki slacks and embroidered denim jacket.

Jordan had no idea how long she and Maddie stood there taking each other in. Taking the reality in.

Everything that Fitzwalter had told her was true. She did indeed have an identical twin sister. And she was here.

And she was standing on the threshold like a deer caught in the headlights.

Jordan rushed forward and took her sister's hands. What she saw in Maddie's eyes—curiosity, excitement, anticipation—mirrored her own feelings so well. Once again, the sense of recognition struck her and some of her nerves settled. It was going to be all right. Whatever else happened, they were going to be all right.

Suddenly filled with joy, she whispered, "Welcome."

Then she turned to the others. "Uncle Carleton, Aunt Dorothy, Adam and Cho, this is my sister, Madison Farrell."

Cho rose and bowed. "It is my pleasure to meet Eva's other daughter."

There was one long beat of silence before Carleton Ware rose from his chair. "You'll have to forgive us, Madison. The shock of my sister's death coupled with the news that she had a second daughter tucked away all these years in Santa Fe...well, we're still trying to absorb everything. Until you walked in right now, I'm not sure that any of us really believed what Edward had told us. Dorothy, Adam and I want to welcome you to Ware House."

Jordan shot her uncle a grateful smile. For a man of few words, he could sometimes be counted on. Then she squeezed Maddie's hand and led her to a chair and whispered, "Once the will stuff is over, we'll talk."

1

THE SKY was still pitch-black when the limo pulled up to the JFK terminal at 6:00 a.m. When Jordan got out with Maddie, her sister turned to her in surprise. As she met her twin's eyes, she experienced that same odd sense of connection that she'd felt the moment she'd first seen her.

Maddie smiled. "Jordan, I can get onto the plane back to Santa Fe by myself."

"I know." Jordan led the way through the revolving doors of the terminal. "You must think that I'm some kind of control freak, not to mention a nonstop talker. But I still have some things to say. I'll walk you to the security check."

In the little inn in Linchworth where she had taken her sister after they'd left Ware House, they'd stayed up most of the night talking and talking and talking. But when Maddie had finally drifted off to sleep, Jordan's mind had replayed over and over the voice of Edward Fitzwalter III reading Eva Ware's extraordinary will.

Eva had left a sum of money to her longtime personal assistant, Cho Li. And to her brother Carleton, she'd left all of her shares in Ware Bank. Both of those bequests had seemed reasonable to Jordan.

Then Fitzwalter had gotten to the part that was going to turn her and Maddie's life upside down.

The rest of my estate, including stocks, bonds, cash, Eva Ware Designs, my fifty-percent share of Ware House on Long Island and my New York City apartment, I leave to my two daughters, Jordan and Madison, to be shared equally. It is my sincere hope that they will **run Eva Ware Designs together**. However, there **is one requirement**. They must change places and **walk around** in "each other's lives" for three **consecutive weeks** beginning within three days (seventy-two hours) from the time this will is read. If they **refuse to fulfill the terms** as I've set them out— or if they don't stay the course for three weeks—my fifty-percent share of Ware House will go to my brother, Carleton. Everything else, including the business and my apartment, will be sold and the profits divided equally among all my surviving relatives.

Her first reaction to the terms of her mother's will had been shock. Even her Uncle Carleton had been ruffled. Dorothy had said something to Adam in a low tone, after which he'd jumped from his chair and planted both his hands on Fitzwalter's desk. He'd insisted that there must be a mistake, that Eva had intended that he step into her shoes as head designer.

But there was no mistake. Her mother had wanted Maddie and her to switch places for three weeks, and she'd talked her sister into actually doing it. They were going to switch lives just as those girls had done in that Disney movie *The Parent Trap*.

Maddie had been reluctant at first, and Jordan couldn't fault her for that. Switching lives was going to be complicated, to say the least. But she'd explained that if they didn't fulfill the terms of the will, Eva Ware Designs, the company that her mother had devoted her entire life to building, would be sold. Jordan couldn't let that happen.

When they reached the escalator to the security check, Jordan drew Maddie aside. "I know I shoehorned you into this."

"You're not making me do anything I don't want to do. I've idolized Eva Ware ever since I was in junior high school." Maddie's brows knit together. "My father knew that and he never breathed a word."

"Mom never said a word, either. I've gone over and over it in my mind."

Maddie met her eyes steadily. "I know I was a little reluctant at first, but I understand that we can't let her business be sold. I feel the same way about the ranch."

Maddie had confided she was in a little trouble on that point. Ever since Mike Farrell's death a year ago, she'd been struggling to keep the ranch financially in the black. And lately there'd been some incidents of vandalism—cut fences, wandering cattle—and, more recently, an attempt to poison her horses' feed. A real estate agent, sniffing trouble, had been after her for the past six months to sell.

Maddie took her hands. "We only have to switch lives for three weeks."

To Jordan's way of thinking, that was the strangest part of Eva's stipulations. Why three weeks? She'd told Maddie it was something their mother had picked up from her personal trainer. Some behavior theorists believed that it took twenty-one consecutive days to build a habit.

Jordan squeezed her sister's hands. "You'll be careful and not stay late at work?"

"I'll be careful. I'll leave at closing time," Maddie promised.

There'd been a break-in and robbery at the Madison Avenue store about a month ago. The police were still looking into it. And Maddie wasn't used to the risks of living in Manhattan.

"I'll feel better when Jase gets back from South America," Jordan said.

"I'm more worried about you being alone on the ranch. I'll breathe easier when I know that my neighbor Cash Landry and my foreman are back from driving our combined herds to market."

One of the things they'd learned about each other during the brief time they'd spent together was that each had a guy pal as a best friend.

Cash Landry had been a part of Maddie's life ever since she could remember. He was like a brother to her—and a little overprotective at times. Jordan had described her relationship with Jase using nearly the same words.

"Cash may be back by the time you fly out the day after tomorrow," Maddie said.

"That reminds me. You've got your ticket for the return flight?"

Maddie smiled. "I do."

Jordan took a deep breath and let it out. "We can do this." And looking into her sister's eyes, she believed that they could.

"Don't worry," Maddie said. "I have the easiest part of this. All I have to do is live in your apartment and work in a jewelry-design studio. You have to survive three weeks on a ranch."

"I'll manage. I'm a quick learner."

"I have to go," Maddie said, releasing her hands.

For a second, Jordan felt the loss of contact. "You've got the notes I made."

"Right here." Maddie patted the duffel she was carrying over her shoulder.

"And I've got yours. And we'll talk," Jordan said. "Any questions, you just call."

"Right."

They moved toward each other at the same time, hugged, held on.

"Love you," Maddie said.

"Same goes." And Jordan realized that she meant it.

Then Maddie turned and stepped onto the escalator.

Jordan watched her sister until she was out of sight.

JORDAN TOOK one last look in her closet, then closed the door and checked her watch. 3:00 p.m. Glancing around her bedroom, she ticked things off her mental list. Her suitcase was packed. On the foot of her bed sat a stack of items still to be tucked into her open briefcase. And she had nearly an hour to wait before the limo service was due to take her to the airport.

Plenty of time for the nerves jittering in her stomach to have a field day. Jordan paced to the window and back. Had she been wrong to pressure her sister into agreeing to the switch? Frustrated, she strode to the window and stared down at the sluggishly moving traffic on the street below. She hated second-guessing herself. Usually, she never wavered once she'd made a decision.

But she and Maddie weren't the carefree preteens of *The Parent Trap*. They were adults with serious responsibilities. She really had no experience running a ranch, and Maddie had said that it was in a bit of financial trouble. But while she was there, Jordan intended to at least look into the business end of things and see if she could come up with a plan to help her sister out.

The easiest thing on her agenda would be to stand in for her sister at a big jewelry show where store owners would be placing orders for the next year. And she'd had an idea about that. She was going to impersonate Maddie at the show. She'd even purchased a hairpiece that she could fasten to the back of her head so it would look as if she'd tied her hair back into a bun. She was sure that potential buyers would be much more comfortable dealing with the designer, "Maddie Farrell," than they would be with Jordan Ware.

There wasn't a doubt in Jordan's mind that she could handle that side of the job. And Cho Li would be a great help to Maddie at Eva Ware Designs. But, well, her sister was going to be a fish out of water in New York City.

It wasn't that she was overly worried about Maddie's safety. Before they'd left Ware House, Adam had accosted them in the hall, and Maddie had actually shoved him into a wall. The shocked look on Adam's face was something Jordan would treasure for a long time. But living in New York City was a far cry from the life Maddie was used to.

If only their mother had given them more than three days before they had to make the switch. Then she could have eased her sister into the fast-paced life of the Big Apple. But thanks to their deadline, Maddie was going to have to face everything alone.

Jordan felt guilty about that. From the very first moment she'd seen Maddie framed in the doorway to the library, she'd felt this odd compulsion to protect her. Could it be simply because she was the older sister? For the life of her, she couldn't find a rational explanation for the instant sense of connection she'd felt with Maddie.

Jordan began to pace again. What choice had she had? If they didn't change places, Eva Ware Designs would be sold and the money divided among the other Wares, Maddie and her.

She simply couldn't allow that to happen. The business her mother had created and devoted her life to would have been destroyed. She and Maddie were doing the only thing they could do.

Moving to the bed, Jordan sat down again. She needed someone to talk to. And Jase wasn't here.

Jordan picked up a framed photo off the bed table. Jase had taken the picture at her college graduation. In it, she was fully decked out in her cap and gown and her mother was standing next to her.

"What were you thinking?"

It wasn't the first time she'd asked her mother that question in the past two days.

"And why in the world did you gamble the business you devoted your life to on an assumption that Maddie and I would go along with this ridiculous idea?"

At least Jordan had a theory about that. In addition to being a brilliant designer, her mother had been astute about people. And she would have known that Jordan would have been very tempted by the idea of living on a ranch for three weeks. Not to mention curious about the life her sister had been living all these years. And visiting the ranch would be the only way that she would get to know the father she'd been separated from.

But how could Eva Ware have been equally sure about Maddie, the daughter she'd cut herself off from all of these years? Had she kept track of the little girl she'd left in Santa Fe? Had her father kept track of her? Mixed in with the unending loop of questions was a keen sense of loss. In a way she'd lost two parents in the space of a week.

"Why did you and Mike Farrell get married and then break up? And why did you split Maddie and me up?"

Anger moved through her as she thought of the most important question—a question she wanted desperately to find the answer to.

"Why did you keep us apart all these years?"

It was unfathomable to her that her mother, a woman she'd thought the world of, could have kept her sister Maddie a secret all these years. And now there was no one to demand the answer from. Both Mike Farrell and her mother were gone.

Absently, Jordan rubbed at the little twinge of pain near her heart. Then rising, she moved to the foot of the bed and placed the items she'd previously stacked there into her briefcase: a guide to Santa Fe and the surrounding areas and a manila folder containing Maddie's notes on the people she might run into on the ranch and in Santa Fe.

Jordan had provided the same information to Maddie, but she'd organized it into separate files with photos. Her sister, like their mother, took notes on whatever came to hand—napkins, some pages from her sketchbook, the stationary from the bed-and-breakfast they'd stayed at after the reading of the will...

Last but not least, she bent down and grabbed a few well-worn paperbacks from her bookshelves. The books were all westerns by her favorite authors—Zane Grey, Louis L'Amour, Luke Short and Larry McMurtry. Guilt rippled through her. She was going to Santa Fe to make sure Eva Ware Designs went on to thrive. But she hadn't shared with her sister her lifelong obsession with ranches and cowboys.

She wasn't sure how it had begun, but there'd been a surprise Christmas gift from Santa when she'd been six. A miniature ranch, complete with buildings, fences, horses and, of course, cattle. She'd ignored the dollhouse her mother had given her and set up her ranch in a corner of her bedroom. How many hours had she spent reconfiguring those buildings and weaving stories in her mind about what life would be like on the range? And it wasn't long after that her mother had given into her pleas to take riding lessons.

Only Eva had known that she'd always fantasized about living on a ranch one day. It was a dream she'd never expected to come true.

But now it was.

When her cell rang, she reached for it and flipped it open. "Yes?"

"Hi. It's Maddie."

Panic bubbled up. Her sister should be en route to New York. "You've changed your mind? Look, I know I bullied you into this."

"You didn't bully me," Maddie said. "Maybe you plied me with some wine…"

At the humor in her sister's voice, some of Jordan's tension eased.

"I was late getting out of Santa Fe, and thanks to bad weather, my connecting flight to JFK is delayed here in Chicago."

"It's good to hear your voice." And it was, Jordan realized. Hadn't she wanted someone to talk to?

"Same goes. What about you? Having any second thoughts?"

"Not a chance. I'm packed and the limo is due in half an hour."

"We're really going through with this."

It wasn't a question. Jordan smiled and felt more of her worries and guilt fade. "Yes, we are."

"You remember where the key to the ranch house is?"

"Underneath the terra-cotta planter on the porch."

"And my latest designs for the jewelry show are—"

"In the safe."

"Sorry. Are you as nervous about me forgetting something?"

"No. All you have to do is consult the notes I gave you. And if you have questions, you can call me."

"Right. I've been thinking. Maybe Eva knew what she was doing. This is a good chance for me to get to know Eva and for you to get to know our father."

"It's our only chance." Something tightened around her heart. But Jordan knew that in business as in life, sometimes you had to play the cards you were dealt. And she was looking forward to learning what she could about her father.

"Would you believe it if I told you I'm looking forward to walking around in your shoes?" Maddie asked.

Jordan smiled. "Absolutely. Same goes for me."

It was the truth. And for the first time, Jordan believed that everything was going to work out.

2

EXCITEMENT WARRED with curiosity as Jordan drove the SUV into the small lean-to on the side of the ranch house. Thanks to the GPS system on her rented vehicle, she'd arrived safely at the Farrell Ranch in just under the hour predicted by the rental agent at the airport. So this was Maddie's home for the last twenty-six years.

It could have been her home.

The words had formed a chant in her mind ever since she'd stepped off the plane in Santa Fe. She could have been raised here instead of in Manhattan. Living in the wide-open spaces that she'd been driving through for the past hour wouldn't have been just a fantasy, it would have been her life. And she would have grown up knowing her father.

Although Eva had tolerated Jordan's love of horses, she'd never shared it. And now she'd lost out on knowing someone who would have. Why?

Jordan pushed down the surge of grief. This wasn't the time to indulge in it. While she was here, she would find answers.

So far, what she'd discovered was that everything—the landscape, the sky, even the air—was so different. On her drive from the airport, the rocks and sand had stretched away for miles on either side of the road. Unfiltered by even a trace of a cloud, the unrelenting light had bounced off her windshield and shimmered upward in a glimmering haze. Sunglasses had offered little protection against the blinding brilliance.

The hills in the distance had seemed so far away. But eventually, she'd reached them and begun the climb. The road had wound upward for several miles in a corkscrew. To her right had been the brownish rock of the hillside. To her left, the land fell away sharply at times into deep gulleys.

The vastness of the landscape awed her. She'd never seen anything like it except in her favorite movies.

Once past the hills, the road had flattened again, and as she drew closer, she caught glimpses of the ranch. The only building she'd been able to identify clearly was the house—a one-story sprawling expanse of stone, glass and wood. Now, thanks to the little bit of shade provided by the lean-to, she could finally get a closer look at the outbuildings.

To her far right was a long building, painted red with white trim. The stables, she guessed. Maddie must have a horse. It was one of many subjects that had never come up in the short time they'd spent together. She'd neglected to tell her sister that she kept a horse in a stable just north of the city. Jordan made a mental note to tell her the next time they talked. Julius Caesar would love it if Maddie paid him a visit.

Next to the stable sat a two-story structure that she supposed served as a bunkhouse. To her left and closer to the house was a smaller building—one story high and fashioned out of the same building materials as the main house. It had to be Maddie's design studio.

Then she let her gaze move to the land beyond the buildings. It stretched far into the distance, flat for a while, then gradually lifting into more hills. Something moved through her then. Was it envy that her sister could call this place home and she couldn't?

Ridiculous. She loved her life in New York. It had to be curiosity. And while she was here, she was going to satisfy it thoroughly by exploring every aspect of Maddie's life, starting tonight with the house.

A glance at her watch told her that she was right on time—8:00 p.m.

And she was stalling.

What in the world was she waiting for? Drawing in a deep breath, Jordan opened the door of the SUV and slid to the ground. The heat hit her like a punch, and she lost her balance as her heels sank into the sand. Slapping a hand on the side of the car, she steadied herself, slipped out of her shoes and tossed them into the car. Thank heavens she and Maddie had decided to share each other's wardrobes because her city clothes weren't going to serve her well in this new environment.

After grabbing her briefcase, she turned and stopped short. In the distance, the hills she'd just driven over were a stunning shade of orange as the sun dipped closer to their peaks.

She made her way, barefoot, to the trunk, muscled out her suitcase and circled to the front of the house. The ground felt hot and gritty beneath her feet, but at least she could walk. A wide porch with a railing stretched the length of the building. Before climbing the short flight of steps, she paused to study the house more closely. The intricately carved entrance door was framed by huge floor-to-ceiling windows that extended the length of the porch on either side. Whoever had designed the place had loved the land, Jordan decided.

And who wouldn't, she thought as she glanced over her shoulder to take another look at those brilliantly orange hills. There was a peacefulness here that appealed to her. Was it because she'd always had that secret fantasy about living on a ranch? But a fantasy was just that. She'd been born and bred in a city—with all its bustle and noise and constant excitement.

Still…there was definitely something about the place that was reaching out to her, tantalizing her.

Had her mother known that this would happen when she'd created that will?

Think about that later.

Knowing that she was stalling again, Jordan frowned and climbed the steps. It wasn't like her to be so hesitant. The key was just where Maddie had left it—under one of the terra-cotta planters. Jordan sighed and shook her head. No self-respecting Manhattanite would leave a key in such an obvious place. She'd had the foresight to give Maddie a whole ring of keys before her sister had flown back to Santa Fe the morning after the will had been read.

Very carefully, Jordan inserted the key into the lock and turned it. As she pushed the door open, she suddenly realized why an uncharacteristic caution had been dogging her ever since she'd convinced her sister to agree to the switch.

Whatever she was going to discover beyond this door, whatever happened to her on this ranch was going to change her life.

Drastically.

So be it, she thought as she strode into the room. But the feeling that moved through her was so surprising that she very nearly backed up onto the porch. The instant that she'd walked into the cavernous room with its steepled ceiling, she'd inexplicably felt at home.

TWO HOURS LATER, Jordan stood in front of one of the huge windows in the spacious living room of the ranch and watched lightning flash in the distance. The floor-to-ceiling windows offered a wide-screen perspective, and the display rivaled the Fourth of July fireworks in Manhattan's harbor.

It was nearly ten o'clock, and that meant it was 1:00 a.m. New York time. Still, she felt wired. After she'd finally gotten over her initial surprise, she'd been like a kid in a candy store, wandering from room to room, trying to take everything in. There were three bedrooms—a master suite she guessed had belonged to Mike Farrell, another one that probably served as a guest room and a third that definitely belonged to Maddie. The closet was full of her clothes.

Jordan had discarded her sweaty city clothes, taken a quick shower and then changed into a set of her own fresh underwear. Maddie's taste ran to plain white cotton. Hers never had. But she had borrowed her sister's robe. Then she'd spent the most time in a cozy room that served as a study or library. But everything she found raised new questions.

She glanced down at the photo of Mike Farrell she'd taken from a table next to his bed. In the picture, Maddie was on a horse. She looked to be about eleven or twelve. The horse was a beauty—black with white spots. Mike Farrell was standing next to her. Something tightened around Jordan's heart as she studied the images. Mike was handsome in a rugged, solid John Wayne kind of way, and he appeared to be a man who was comfortable in his own skin. His hand rested on top of Maddie's on the pommel of the saddle. There was something about the gesture that spoke of an easy camaraderie. And love. What had been the occasion for the photo?

Her mother had stood next to her in a similar fashion the first time that she'd shown her horse, Julius Caesar. They'd obviously loved their daughters. Or at least the one each had chosen.

Why had they separated Maddie and her? Why had Eva

and Mike split? The more the questions spun in her mind, the more determined Jordan became to find answers. Where had her parents met? Where had they lived when she and Maddie were born? Here on the ranch? If that was so, there might be someone in the area who remembered Eva Ware.

Frustrated and annoyed by the never-ending loop of questions, she strode into the kitchen. It was state-of-the-art, and the freezer and large pantry were well-stocked. Who was the cook, she wondered. Maddie? That was another question she'd have to ask.

But what she discovered when she opened the door to the refrigerator was that her twin was thoughtful. In spite of all the things that Maddie must have had to take care of to make the "switch," she'd taken the time to leave cheese, plump grapes and wine. A chardonnay from the same vineyard that they'd shared at the bed and breakfast in Linchworth.

Jordan tired to ignore the guilt she felt as she uncorked the bottle and poured herself a generous glass. Then she fixed a plate with brie and crackers.

She hadn't even thought about leaving food for her twin. Jase Campbell was the one who usually stocked the cupboard and refrigerator, and in the three and a half weeks he'd been in South America, she hadn't replenished anything. On her own, she either ate out or brought home take out.

That was probably not such a convenient option here on the ranch. After taking a sip of her wine, she picked up the bottle and the plate of food, then moved back to the window to watch the show. The lightning seemed to be closer now, and for the first time, she heard a faint rumble of thunder.

Good thing she wasn't afraid of storms.

But watching the show nature was providing wasn't going to relax her enough to sleep. Taking another sip of her wine, she moved to Plan B. A movie. She wasn't sure if it was Maddie or Mike, but she'd discovered earlier in her exploration of the library that someone shared her love of westerns. In spades. Not only was there an extensive collection of old paperback westerns, but she'd also unearthed a large cache of old cowboy movies. She'd run her fingers over the Clint Eastwood classics *Pale Rider* and *The Unforgiven*, before settling on one of her all-time favorites, *The Big Country,* with Gregory Peck. The movie centered on ranchers feuding over access to a river that meant the survival of their cattle, but there was also a strong love story.

A perfect way to end her day. Setting her food and wine on the big coffee table, Jordan lit a fat white candle and used the remote to turn on the big flat-panel TV. Finally, she settled herself comfortably on the leather couch and started the film. She couldn't prevent a smile as the movie's familiar theme music filled the room.

When the rumbling thunder drew closer, she merely upped the volume, took another sip of her wine and spread brie on a cracker. Within minutes, she was swept away to the ranch in the midst of the vast land that served as the setting for the movie.

THE STORM was finally tapering off when Cash Landry turned onto the highway. The sky was pitch-black, and the rain was still pouring down in sheets. Visibility was poor, but about an hour ago, the electrical fireworks had moved on to the east.

The problem was that parts of the road could be flooded, and there wasn't much chance of seeing that in advance. Bottom line, it was not the best time to be driving, but he had to check on Maddie. Mac McAuliffe, her foreman, lived several miles away with his family, so for the last year since Mike had died, Maddie had lived alone on the ranch.

Cash didn't like it. He liked it even less when he was out of touch with her as he'd been for the last ten days. His parents and then his father had been close friends with Mike Farrell, and he and Maddie had grown up together. Three years her senior, he'd early on taken on the role of looking after her. In his absence, he'd had his foreman, Sweeney, check on her daily when he came to feed the horses and check on the stock. When Sweeney had told him that he hadn't seen Maddie today, Cash had only delayed long enough to shower before climbing into his pickup and heading for the Farrell Ranch.

Truth be told, he was worried about her. Her ranch had been plagued by vandalism for the past few months, and the incidents had been increasing in frequency and severity. At first, he'd blamed the occasional cut fence on the Trainer twins. One of them—Joey—had an obvious crush on Maddie, and Cash figured he was making a bid for attention. He'd had a heart-to-heart with the boy. He'd explained that time was money on a ranch and that Maddie couldn't afford to lose manpower rounding up straying cattle and repairing fences.

But Joey Trainer had vehemently denied having anything to do with it. Cash had believed him. And there'd been other kinds of occurrences. Most recently, her horse, Brutus, had gotten ill. The vet had discovered that some of the hay had been poisoned. Since then, Cash had told Sweeney to bring over hay from the Landry ranch.

The most recent cut fence had allowed about a hundred head of her cattle to stray, and he hadn't had time to round them all up before he had to take their combined herds to market.

Pressing his foot on the brake, Cash turned onto the drive that led to the Farrell Ranch. When he hit the first rut and heard the water splash up into the undercarriage of his pickup, he slowed. The driving would be tricky from now on.

What had bothered Cash most was that whoever had poisoned the hay had come close to the house. Too close. So he'd taken to sleeping in the guest room a couple of times a week. It wasn't the perfect solution, but he was hoping that it would give whoever was behind the incidents pause.

Cash had his suspicions about who might be causing Maddie problems. Top of the list was Daniel Pearson, a real estate agent who'd been after her to let him put her ranch on the market for the past six months. Cash knew that Maddie didn't want to sell the ranch, but Pearson had been persistent, and he might believe that she would cave under pressure.

He'd checked and no other ranchers in the area were experiencing any problems. Only Maddie. Hitting another rut, Cash slowed his vehicle to a crawl. Ten days away had given him some time to think, and he'd come up with what might just be a solution to the problem, or at least a way to get Pearson to back off.

He and Maddie could get engaged.

He had to admit that when the idea had first come to him, it had given him pause. More than that, it had given him a good-sized jolt. An engagement hadn't been on his immediate agenda. It wasn't even in his five-year plan. He liked his life just the way it was. Being single suited him to a T. And he was pretty sure Maddie was happy with hers.

But it wouldn't be for real. Just a ruse so the incidents stopped until he could get some hard evidence about who was behind them.

Oh, his father and Maddie's had shared a lifelong dream of having the two of them marry and unite the two ranches. But it wasn't a plan that he and Maddie had bought into. Their relationship, even during their teens when his system had been hormone-driven, had never taken that turn into intimacy. Perhaps because he'd always thought of her as his kid sister and best friend.

But a fake engagement between the two of them wouldn't surprise their neighbors in the least. Most of them would think that Mike Farrell and Jesse Landry had been right after all. It shouldn't be hard to talk Maddie into it. He'd just lay out the logic of it and then give her a little push. Over the years, he'd learned that sometimes Maddie had to be pushed. Especially since she'd become so focused on her jewelry-design business.

Cash frowned as the dark outline of the ranch house came into view. The flood lights that normally lit up the stables and the house were off. And he couldn't see any other light coming from the house. The place must have lost power during the storm.

Chances were she was asleep. The last thing he wanted was to wake her up. But the more he thought about it, the more he wanted to talk to Maddie about the engagement thing tonight and get it settled.

Cash parked in front of the house. That was when he caught a glimmer of light. Some of his tension eased. She'd probably lit a candle. From the time she was a child, electrical storms had frightened her to death.

Not wanting to wake her if she was asleep, Cash didn't bother knocking. Instead, he looked for the key under the terra-cotta pot. When he didn't find it there, he frowned and some of his tension returned. He should have told her to find a better hiding place.

His frown deepened when he tried the door and found it unlocked. He'd have to have a word with Maddie about that, too. He saw her the moment he stepped into the living room and felt a surge of relief. She was stretched out on the sofa, one arm flung over her head. The fat white candle burning on the coffee table allowed him to see the half-empty plate of cheese and grapes and the opened bottle of wine.

His lips curved. She'd probably decided to weather the storm with a little help from a good chardonnay. It was only as he drew closer that he sensed there was something different about her. What was it?

Puzzled, he studied her more closely in the flickering candle light. Perhaps it was the clothes—or the lack of them. Her robe had fallen open. Beneath it, she wore a silk-and-lace tank top that skimmed the tops of her breasts. The matching panties left long, slender legs and narrow ankles bare. Then he saw it. Her toenails were painted a sexy shade of red.

Awareness and heat rippled through him. Cash frowned and glanced at the hand that she'd flung over her head. Her fingernails were painted, too—in the same sexy color. This time the heat was sharper, and an image planted itself in his mind of that hand moving over his bare skin.

He shook his head to clear it. This was Maddie. What was the matter with him? Narrowing his eyes, he let them drift over her again. This time he noted her hair. That was different, too. She'd cut it. The long braid she'd worn ever since he could remember was gone. Spread out as they were on the leather cushion, the honey-colored strands of her hair looked as if some man had just run his hand through them.

When he realized that he wanted to run *his* hands through them, he fisted them at his sides. What in the world had happened while he was away? Had she had some kind of a makeover? That was the only explanation that occurred to him.

Much harder to explain was the way his body was reacting to her. Why would painted nails and a change of hairdo affect him this way? When he finally dragged his gaze from her hair, it froze on her breasts. She wasn't wearing a bra, and so he could see the nipples beneath the thin swatch of silk that covered them.

Heat didn't ripple this time. It punched through him as if he'd stepped from an icily air-conditioned room into the blazing New Mexico sun. His knees nearly buckled.

What in hell had happened to him on that cattle drive? He was still the same man he'd been when he'd left. Wasn't he? But something had changed. What was it? He couldn't remember responding to any woman with this kind of intensity. And he hadn't even touched her.

He wasn't going to, either. He'd come over here to see that she was safe. And she was. So he was going to pick her up and carry her into her bed. Then he was going to bed down himself in the guest room.

Still, Cash hesitated for a moment, wishing he had more of a handle on what was going on. Finally he moved toward her and lifted her up off the couch.

JORDAN WILLED HERSELF to sink deeper into the dream. In it, she was with Gregory Peck, the tall, quiet tenderfoot who'd just fought a duel to save her life. They'd ridden back to her place, both knowing that all the obstacles between them had been removed. After they'd climbed the porch steps, he'd lifted her to carry her through the front door and across the room.

She heard the sound of his footsteps, felt the strength in his arms. It was the first time he'd touched her, and her head spun a bit as sensations arrowed through her with such clarity. She was intensely aware of the hardness of his chest and the heat from the press of his fingers on her stomach. Flames licked outward from that spot until her whole body burned.

Every detail was so real. The collar of his shirt was

rough beneath her palm, the skin on his neck damp. And he smelled simply wonderful—a mix of leather and horses and soap. She nuzzled closer. She had to get closer. When he stopped, she lifted a hand to his face, absorbed the sensation of that firm chin, the sharply angled cheekbone. Then unable to resist, she ran kisses along the line of his jaw. She wanted to taste him. She had to taste him.

As if he'd read her mind, he turned his head until his lips were just brushing hers. For a moment, she hesitated, and she sensed that he was hesitating, too. She was tempted to open her eyes, to try to see what he was thinking. But she knew, didn't she? And if she opened her eyes, he might disappear.

She couldn't let that happen. She had to keep him here. Tightening her fingers on his face, she drew him closer and whispered, "It's all right. I want you to kiss me."

When he did, she pushed everything else out of her mind and let herself plunge into the pleasure. His mouth was so soft. Different than she'd imagined. His flavors were different, too. Dark and hot and dangerous, they exploded on her tongue, shooting through her with such force that she was suddenly filled with him. Everything inside her sped up.

Never had a dream seemed so real. But reality had never brought this kind of pleasure before.

When he drew away, she knew a moment of pure panic. Of aching loss.

"Maddie, I—"

She felt the name whisper across her skin. It registered for a fleeting moment, but her desperation to taste him again shoved any thought ruthlessly aside. "I want more." She needed more. "Make love with me."

As he lowered her to the bed and joined her, he kissed her again. She nipped his bottom lip and threw herself fully into the dream. This time, beneath the flavors she'd sampled before, she tasted hunger. Was it his or hers?

They had to break off the kiss again and again as they rid themselves of clothes. Each time their lips rejoined, they demanded more. Received more. Their hands, desperate now, touched, tormented and took. Pleasure escalated, and the fire between them blazed more fiercely.

In some dim, recessed corner of his mind, Cash knew that he shouldn't be doing this. He shouldn't be in Maddie's bed making love to her. She'd had some wine. He'd seen the half-empty bottle. And she'd been frightened by a storm.

He'd never been an impulsive man. It wasn't in his nature to throw caution to the wind. But this was different. She was different. And his grip on anything rational had begun to slip the moment he'd stood at the foot of her couch and felt that first incredible punch of heat.

No woman had ever aroused him that quickly or that fully. When he'd kissed her, his system had been totally shocked. Never in his life had he imagined that her flavor would be this exotic, this addictive. Each time he sampled, he seemed to find something new. And now he couldn't stop himself from wanting more. Or from taking more.

His hands had taken on a will of their own, racing over her, touching, tempting, claiming. Hers were no less busy, and each place her fingers pressed or her nails scraped, he felt twin ribbons of fire and ice race along his skin.

Speed seemed to be a necessity for both of them as if, like greedy children, they had to grab all the pleasure they could before someone snatched it away. Desire hammered at him with sharp, piercing blows until the pain of not having her became so intense that he rolled her beneath him and drove himself into her.

She wrapped herself around him, matching his rhythm

so perfectly that they moved as one, driving each other higher and higher. Even when they reached the peak, they paused as if to keep themselves there. As if they *had* to keep themselves there so that they wouldn't lose each other. Finally, sharp explosions of pleasure shot through them and pushed them over the edge.

3

AS CASH drifted up through layers of sleep, he was sure he heard a phone ringing. From far away. Gradually, bits and pieces of reality settled into his mind. But the biggest one was the fact that there was a woman in his bed. She was pressed against him like a spoon, her back to his front. Her hair tickled his chin, and each time he took a breath, he inhaled that wild exotic scent.

Maddie?

Everything that had happened the night before flooded his mind. This was not his bed. It was Maddie's, and he'd never expected to be in it.

Opening his eyes, Cash became aware of several things. He could tell by her even breathing that she was still asleep. He was used to rising at dawn, but the strength of the sun pouring through the window told him that the day had a couple of hours' head start on him.

Gradually, as his senses became more alert, he realized that his arm was still around Maddie, holding her close almost as if he'd been afraid that she'd leave at some point during the night.

Cash frowned. Could that have been the reason for the very odd dream he'd had? In it, he'd been standing at an altar watching Maddie as she walked toward him in a white dress.

No. The dream had to have been triggered by the fact

that he'd spent the last few days deciding that he and Maddie should announce their pretend engagement.

And now that they'd become lovers, well, the fake engagement plan held even more appeal. It had become more logical, he told himself. But there was a little voice in the back of his head that told him he wanted an engagement ring on Maddie's finger because he didn't want her to walk away. Ever.

Which was ridiculous. He and Maddie had been friends since childhood. Cash could hardly recall a time that she hadn't been a part of his life. She would always be there for him, just as he'd always be there for her. Not that he was going to delude himself into thinking that their relationship hadn't changed. Drastically.

She stirred.

Cash lay perfectly still as she sighed and snuggled even more closely to him. He caught her scent again—exotic, different. Odd that he couldn't remember Maddie ever smelling quite this way. One of his hands still covered her breast, and he became aware of her nipple pressing into his palm. His body hardened and he realized he wanted her again with the same sharp hunger that had consumed him last night.

What he'd experienced had been unprecedented, and it had been with *Maddie*. Shouldn't there have been some sign that their relationship was going to change this way? For the life of him, Cash hadn't seen one indication.

For a moment he was tempted to lift her hair and wake her by nibbling on her neck. But he knew that anything he started he would finish. He'd already experienced firsthand her ability to destroy his control. And before they made love again, they had to talk. He needed to know that she wanted that to happen as much as he did.

For now, he'd content himself with just holding her.

JORDAN ALWAYS woke quickly, as if someone had thrown a switch. So she was immediately aware that she was not alone in the bed.

Very much not alone. A man's hand covered her breast and his erection was pressed firmly against her backside. Her naked backside. Ignoring the panic that was bubbling in her stomach, she kicked her mind into overdrive. The last thing she remembered was lying on the couch and watching one of her all-time favorite movie couples— Gregory Peck and Jean Simmons and the wonderful romance that had blossomed between them in *The Big Country.*

But the hand on her breast was very real, and it was currently causing her whole system to go into a meltdown. She'd never experienced anything like what she'd felt during the night with another man. Was that why she'd let herself believe that it was a dream?

Jordan prided herself on not being prone to self-deception. And the hardening erection at her backside was knocking the dream theory out of the ballpark.

For a moment, she closed her eyes. Okay, somehow on her first night in Maddie's house, she'd slept with a stranger. Mentally, she ticked off the reasons why that might have happened—she was under stress, she'd always had secret fantasies about cowboys and ranches and she'd had some wine.

Maybe years from now when she was one hundred, she would be able to look back on this and laugh. Right now, she had to get through this the best way she could and that meant finding out just who the man behind her was.

Removing his hand from her breast, she wiggled forward enough to put some distance between them before she turned and found herself looking into a pair of gray eyes gazing at her intently. Panic bubbled up again. He definitely wasn't Gregory Peck. But he was dark-haired and not just a little handsome. His face was just the way her hands remembered—lean, with sharp cheekbones and a firm chin. And if the rest of what she'd touched ran true to memory, he was definitely a hunk.

And there was that scent—dark, irresistible, with just a hint of danger.

"Maddie, are you all right?"

Maddie? For a moment, Jordan was too shocked to think or speak. She had to jump-start her mind.

Maddie? Of course, he thought she was Maddie. She'd been on Maddie's couch, wearing Maddie's robe. Drinking perhaps a bit too much of Maddie's wine. But who—

"Do you want an apology?"

"No," she managed. Maybe Maddie would, she thought giddily.

"Are you protected? I didn't use any—"

"I'm on the pill." Thank heavens.

He narrowed his eyes. "And you're sure you're all right?"

All right? Oh, she was fine. She was lying in bed with a man she didn't know, a man she'd had hot, sweaty sex with, and she wanted to do it again in spite of the fact that he obviously thought he'd just made love to her sister. Jordan managed a nod.

"Good. Because I've got something to say."

"Wait." She pressed her fingers against his lips, intending to set him straight about who she was. The sharp heat that arrowed through her froze her.

He took her hand away from his mouth. "I've spent a lot of time since I last saw you thinking about this. And I believe that the best way to deal with the vandalism problem you're having is for the two of us to get engaged."

"No." Jordan snatched her hand away, scrambled out of

the bed and raced for the closet to grab a pair of jeans. "We can't get engaged."

"Why not?"

"Because I'm not Maddie." Hopping on one foot and then the other, she struggled into the denim.

Seconds ticked by, and Jordan felt his eyes searing into her skin for every single one of them. She'd never been this intensely aware of a man before. Why did it have to be this man? She snatched a T-shirt out of a drawer and pulled it on. If he was waiting for more info, so be it. This was not a conversation she wanted to have while she was stark naked.

"Then who are you?" His tone was patient, even.

Turning from the dresser, she met his eyes and said, "I'm Jordan Ware, Maddie's identical twin."

He was looking at her in an intent way that made her think he could see right through her. Nerves jittered in her stomach.

"Maddie's twin."

"That's right."

His eyes narrowed. "Maddie doesn't have an identical twin."

Jordan planted her hands on her hips. "Yes, she does. We just found out about each other a few days ago. And as far as being *identical* goes, I certainly fooled you."

There was another stretch of silence, and Jordan could have sworn she saw something flash in his eyes. Acceptance? Amusement? Both? Whatever it was, he was taking this a lot more calmly than she was.

"I knew there was something different about you." Narrowing her eyes, she watched him adjust a pillow against the headboard and settle himself against it.

"Turnabout's fair play. Who are you?" But even as she phrased the question, Jordan suddenly knew. He had to be—

"Cash Landry."

"The neighbor." Her heart plummeted. Her knees would have buckled if a sudden spurt of anger hadn't stiffened her spine. "Maddie told me you were just friends."

"We were. We are."

Jordan waved a hand at the bed. "What we did last night goes beyond the parameters of simple friendship."

"I agree."

Unable to contain herself, she began to pace between the bed and the dresser. "She said that she thinks of you as her big brother. I thought your relationship was just like the one I have with Jase."

"Who's Jase?"

Though he hadn't moved a muscle, Jordan sensed danger. "Jase Campbell is my apartment mate. We've been friends since we first shared an apartment in college. But there's nothing…". She waved a hand again at the bed. "We've never slept together."

"Neither have Maddie and I."

"Until last night," she shot at him.

"But it turns out that I wasn't making love to Maddie. I was making love to you. And I want to do it again."

There was a note of determination in his tone that had Jordan throwing her hands out in front of her. "No way." She might have been more successful in keeping the panic at bay if she wasn't right on the same page that he was. And the way he was looking at her, she bet he was reading her like a book.

"You thought you were making love to Maddie, and then you asked her to marry you."

"No, I asked her to get engaged to me."

"Whatever!" Jordan waved a hand. "The proposal makes this whole situation even worse. I just met my sister a few days ago and since then I've slept with the man who wants to get engaged to her. Way to go, Jordan."

"Where is Maddie?"

"She's in New York City. We've changed places. It's a long story."

"I've always liked stories."

When Cash moved as if to get out of bed, Jordan's panic grew, and she started toward the bedroom door. "You stay right there. I'm going into the kitchen and I'm going to make some coffee. Then you'll have your story."

Cash rose from the bed and reached down to scoop up his jeans. "Sounds good."

Keep your eyes straight ahead. But before she made it out of the room, Jordan caught a good glimpse of him out of the corner of her eye. It was enough to trigger a barrage of sensations. Heat. Lust. Longing.

She could feel him grinning at her as she hot-footed it through the door.

CASH TWISTED the faucets to the off position and reached for a towel. After a ten-minute cold shower, his mind had cleared a bit. While he'd been in the same room with her, fantasies had pushed and then lingered at the edge of his mind. More than once, he'd been sorely tempted to scoop her up and tumble her back into bed.

After hanging up the towel, he pulled on his clothes and shoved his feet into his boots. He'd used the bathroom off what had been Mike Farrell's room so that he wouldn't run into her. And so he could think.

He had a lot of questions about the things Jordan Ware hadn't yet told him. Like who exactly she was, why she and Maddie had changed places and why they hadn't known about each other for twenty-six years.

It surprised him a little that he was leaning toward accepting that she was indeed Maddie's identical twin. It would certainly explain his response to her, but not once in all the years he'd known Mike and Maddie Farrell had he heard a hint of a sister. The story he'd been told was that her mother had died when she was an infant.

He had to wonder if his parents had known about a twin. His mother had passed on when he was twelve, but he figured she must have been aware of the situation. So must his father. But there'd never been a word spoken.

If Jordan Ware was telling the truth, why all the secrecy? Who had finally revealed the secret and why?

Exiting the bathroom, he heard the faint sound of running water from the direction of Maddie's bathroom. So he had a short reprieve before he saw her again. Good.

Cash strolled into the large, open space that housed both the living room of the ranch and the kitchen and headed straight for the coffeemaker. The carafe was still half-full, and Jordan had been thoughtful enough to set out a mug for him. Grateful, he filled it to the brim and took a long swallow.

He should have known that she wasn't Maddie. Why hadn't the change in hairstyle tipped him off? As long as he'd known her, Maddie had worn her hair long and in a braid. Either that or she'd twist it up into some kind of knot at the back of her head. She didn't like to fuss much about her appearance, perhaps a result of being raised surrounded by males. No manicures and pedicures for her.

Jordan looked as if she took quite a bit of time with her appearance. Probably had regular appointments for those nails. Had he simply not questioned the differences because of the way that Jordan had blindsided his senses last night?

Maybe. It was hard to be sure because he'd never experienced anything like Jordan Ware before. Her effect on him was baffling. But he was going to figure it out.

At the sound of a door closing, he took another quick

swallow of coffee, then turned and leaned his hip against the counter. To brace himself? If he'd had any question about how she'd affect his senses this morning, it was more than answered when she stepped into view and strode toward him. He felt an immediate snap and sizzle in his blood, and a hard tug of desire. Basic. Elemental.

"I tried to phone Maddie, but the phone's dead."

For a moment, Cash didn't answer. He was too caught up in absorbing her. In the sunlight pouring through the windows, he could see more differences between the women. Maddie's presence was quiet, perhaps more controlled. Jordan radiated a certain energy. And she was wearing makeup. He'd never noticed any on Maddie. Jordan's was subtle, but she'd done something to make her eyes seem larger, and her mouth was painted a soft shade of rose. Hunger stirred sharply inside of him. When he found his gaze lingering on her lips just a bit too long, he took another swallow of coffee.

"Did you hear what I said?" she asked.

Cash dug for what she'd said. "The phone's dead. I thought I heard it ringing earlier. It's what woke me up, in fact." He shrugged. "Lots of time service is intermittent after a storm. It's not unusual for it to go on and off for up to twenty-four hours."

"My cell doesn't work, either." She moved to the coffeepot, and her arm nearly brushed against his as she refilled the mug she was carrying.

Her scent was just what he remembered—flowery, exotic—and it rekindled memories of the hot, sweaty sex they'd shared. He was surprised at how much he wanted to reach out and touch just a strand of her hair. He wasn't sure whether to be relieved or disappointed when she moved to the other side of the granite-topped island.

Cash drew in a deep breath. Growing up on a ranch,

he'd had to learn to adapt and go with the flow. The weather changed, the price of beef varied. So he was just going to have to learn to handle Jordan Ware's effect on him. Problem was, he just wanted to handle her, period.

JORDAN SIPPED COFFEE and made herself meet Cash Landry's eyes across the expanse of granite. It had been a mistake to get that close to him. Especially when he looked so good. With that long lean body, that ruggedly handsome face and those intent gray eyes, the man gave the words *boy toy* new meaning.

And the fact that she was even thinking of him that way shocked her. She'd never been a boy-toy kind of woman, but the idea was becoming very seductive. She thought that she'd pulled herself together while she was showering, but as she refilled her mug, she caught his scent again— pure cowboy, soap and leather and horses—and she'd wanted to jump him.

Wasn't that what had gotten her into this mess?

Very firmly, Jordan reminded herself of the conclusion she'd arrived at while she was showering. She was going to treat this as a business problem—solve it and put it behind her. Boy toys were off the agenda. She and Cash Landry were not going to repeat the little scenario they'd enacted during the night.

"Does your cell work? I need to talk to Maddie."

Cash regarded her steadily over the rim of his cup. "I've never been able to get a signal on the Farrell Ranch. It's in one of those blackout zones. Why do you need to talk to Maddie?"

"Why?" Setting her mug down, Jordan began to pace. "I need to talk to her about you and me." She waved a hand. "Us. And what we did last night."

"Why?"

Jordan paused to glare at him. "Because I just slept with a man who wants to get engaged to her."

"I can explain that."

She raised a hand, palm outward. "I don't want an explanation. I just want my sister to know that I didn't sleep with you on purpose. I thought you were a dream. I have a weakness for westerns, and I was watching *The Big Country*—"

"Gregory Peck, Jean Simmons and the feud over the Big Muddy."

She stared at him. "You know the movie?"

"It was one of Mike's—your father's—favorites. Maddie didn't like westerns, so he roped me into watching it with him a few times."

"So it was my father who read all those westerns in the library?"

"Whenever he could find the time."

Something inside of her warmed. Then she refocused. "I want to explain to Maddie that it was because I was watching that movie that I had this dream."

"About me making love to you."

She fisted her hands on her hips. "No. I wasn't dreaming of you. I was dreaming about making love to Gregory Peck."

"I wasn't dreaming, Jordan."

She pointed a finger at him. "No, you believed you were making love to Maddie. And then you proposed to her. I just have to figure out a way to explain it to her."

"It seems to me that we were both victims of circumstance."

Jordan's temper flared. "I don't know about you, pal, but I don't like to think of myself as a victim."

To her surprise, Cash Landry threw back his head and laughed. The bright, infectious sound of it filled the room and had her anger fading. In fact, she barely kept herself from smiling. "What's so funny?"

"Us. This situation. And the fact that you're absolutely right. It's hard to picture you as a victim of anything."

"I don't think Maddie will see the humor in this."

Cash's expression sobered. "I told you, there's nothing but friendship between Maddie and me. I've never touched her, never even thought about touching her the way I touched you last night."

The words and the way he looked at her when he said them had little thrills rippling over her skin. And her concentration was fading. No man had ever affected her this way. He only had to be in the same room with her to make her want.

"And I don't think you have to explain anything to your sister. What happened between us can remain just that— between us. No one has to know."

Jordan ruthlessly refocused. She couldn't deny that the idea of not having to confess to Maddie appealed to her. "But what about the fact that you want to get engaged to her?"

"I'll explain that. But first things first." His eyes never left hers as he set his cup down on the counter and straightened.

For a moment, Jordan was sure that he was going close the distance between them. If he did… Her hand trembled and coffee sloshed over the rim of her mug.

Then he asked, "Do you cook?"

"No."

He sent her a slow smile. "It's a good thing that I do. While I rustle us up some breakfast, you can tell me all about how you and Maddie discovered that you're twins and why you're here and Maddie's in New York City. Deal?"

Jordan let out a breath she hadn't been aware of holding as he moved to the refrigerator and began unloading bacon and eggs. "Deal."

CASH WATCHED HER scoop the last forkful of food into her mouth. She'd only wanted toast at first, but he'd ignored her request and filled a plate with bacon and eggs, as well. She'd made a second pot of coffee, poured orange juice and set places for them on the granite island.

The pull between them hadn't lessened as far as Cash could tell, but they'd been able to work in harmony as they'd prepared the meal.

Jordan had told the story of the last few weeks of her life in a straightforward manner with no trace of emotion in her voice. He'd promised himself that he wasn't going to touch her, but when she'd spoken about the visit she'd received from the two policemen telling her that her mother was dead, he'd reached over to cover her hand with his, and she'd immediately linked their fingers.

She still hadn't pulled her hand away. Cash glanced down at their joined hands. Hers was delicate-looking, her skin paler than his. Maddie had calluses on her fingers. Jordan didn't. Holding her hand felt...right.

Shifting his gaze to her face, he studied her as she took another sip of coffee.

From what he could gather, she'd been going nonstop ever since she'd received the news of the tragic hit-and-run. He knew something about the success of Eva Ware Designs because Maddie had talked about the famed Madison Avenue designer. So on top of absorbing the shock of losing her mother, she'd arranged a funeral for a celebrity, taken over the reins of a business and then had to make sure her newly discovered sister was prepared to step into her shoes.

His admiration for her had grown with each new detail that she added to the story. But Cash was also worried. To his mind, the terms of her mother's will and the decision she and Maddie had made to fulfill them could be a recipe for disaster. What had possessed their mother to put them in this position? If something happened to either of them—or if either of them backed out of the switch before the three weeks had elapsed—three of Jordan's relatives stood to profit. A lot.

He knew that Maddie wouldn't have thought of that. He wondered if the possible danger had occurred to Jordan.

"So Maddie is alone in your New York City apartment?"

"As far as I know. I haven't been able to reach my apartment mate, Jase, because of the hostage rescue job he's on in South America. He doesn't even know that my mother died, let alone the terms of her will. If he comes home, he's going to have a big surprise in store for him."

Cash could sympathize fully with that. Jordan had been quite a surprise for him. "What's this Jase like?"

Jordan smiled. "He's great. He's a good listener, and he lets me use him not only to vent, but as a sounding board for new ideas that I want to try out at Eva Ware Designs. I couldn't ask for a better roommate."

Hearing her sing the praises of Jase Campbell was leaving a bad taste in Cash's mouth. Was he jealous? That was ridiculous. In spite of that, he wished that the man was there in the apartment with Maddie.

"So Maddie's on her own?"

Jordan frowned. "She won't be once she gets to Eva Ware Designs. My mother's assistant, Cho Li, and Michelle Tan, our receptionist, will take good care of her. And I printed up all these files to fill her in. I even included photos."

"How about the rest of the family? How do they feel about Eva's other daughter suddenly showing up?"

A little frown appeared on Jordan's forehead. "Not so good, I suppose. Uncle Carleton was civil, as always. My cousin, Adam, may give Maddie some problems at work. He was obnoxious at the reading of the will. He's a brilliant jewelry designer, and my mother admired his work. I think that's why he always thought he had a clear shot at stepping into her shoes one day and running the business."

"And he's lost that because in her will, your mother suddenly produced a daughter who's also a brilliant jewelry designer and left her half of the business."

Jordan frowned. "Yes. If we both live up to the terms of the will."

"Depending on how ambitious he is, he could pose a real threat to Maddie."

Her frown deepened. "Adam? I don't think so. Basically, my cousin is a wimp. After the will was read, he followed Maddie and me to the door and grabbed my arm. Maddie unfastened his hand and gave him a shove that nearly had him bouncing off the wall. I have no doubt that she'll figure out a way to handle him."

She tilted her head to one side. "She's smart, and she's not the pushover she seems at first. I had to really do some fast talking to persuade her to switch places. She thinks I should have all the money and Eva's design business."

"You don't agree."

"No. We're sisters. The fact that Eva Ware and Mike Farrell split us up and kept us apart all these years doesn't change that."

If he hadn't already decided that he liked Jordan, her statement sealed the deal. "Maddie's lucky to have you for a sister."

"The luck is mutual." She set down her mug. Then, as if realizing for the first time that her other hand was still linked with his, she withdrew it and crossed her arms on the counter. "Now I think it's your turn to answer my question. Why did you propose to Maddie this morning?"

Cash ran a hand through his hair. "I knew we'd get

back to that. There've been some incidents of vandalism on the ranch lately."

"Maddie told me about them. Cut fences and someone doctored the feed in her stable."

"Maybe she didn't give you a clear enough picture. The poisoned feed in her stable nearly killed her horse, Brutus."

"Brutus? That's her horse's name?"

Cash nodded. "Your father gave him to her for her twelfth birthday."

When Jordan simply stared at him, Cash asked, "What is it?"

"I keep a horse just outside of the city. His name is Julius Caesar. What are the chances?"

"You're twins. You may have been separated since you were babies, but that doesn't mean you don't have a lot in common."

"I suppose." Then she frowned. "What else should I know about the vandalism?"

"The last cut fence was timed so a hundred head of her cattle strayed just before her foreman and I were going to drive them to market. We didn't have time to round them all up and that's going to cost her money. Money that she can't afford to lose."

She studied him for a moment. "You don't think the incidents are random, do you?"

"Maddie's problems have all occurred in the past six months, and during that time, there's a local real estate agent, Daniel Pearson, who's been urging her to sell the ranch. I don't like his timing."

Jordan wasn't sure that she did, either. "Maddie told me that she was having trouble filling her father's shoes. I can understand that. I can't step into my mother's, either. But she doesn't want to sell the ranch. I promised her I'd try to help with that."

Cash's eyes narrowed. "How?"

Jordan's smile was wry. "Good question. How does a Yankee tenderfoot think she can solve her sister's ranching problem? But I am a business major. And I want to help. I'll need to see the ranch first. Take a look at the books."

"I'll take you on a tour day after tomorrow. The best way to see it is on horseback. Think you can handle Brutus?"

"Yes." He was taking her seriously. Something inside of Jordan softened. "Why would you think that I might come up with something?"

He shrugged. "Gregory Peck was a tenderfoot in *The Big Country,* and he solved the feud over the Big Muddy."

"True." She grinned at him. "Now finish explaining why you proposed to my sister."

"It's pretty well-known around here that our fathers always had this dream that one day Maddie and I would marry and join the two ranches." He raised a hand. "Maddie and I agreed long ago that wasn't a possibility. Our relationship never took the turn that yours and mine has. But if we put it out there that we were engaged, I figured people would believe it and since Maddie would no longer have a need to sell, that might put an end to the incidents."

Jordan tilted her head to one side. "I've heard of a marriage of convenience. So this was sort of an engagement of convenience?"

"A fake engagement of convenience."

"Would Maddie have agreed?"

Cash sighed. "Maybe. After some serious and figurative arm-twisting on my part."

Jordan smiled at him. "That's how I got her to agree to switch places with me. You're a sweet man, Cash Landry."

Color rose in Cash's face, but before he could reply,

they were interrupted by a sharp knock on the door. Jordan moved quickly and opened it before Cash could.

Although he couldn't have explained it rationally, he was relieved to see it was his foreman Sweeney standing on the porch. But once Cash noticed the sober expression on Sweeney's usually jovial face, his tension returned.

The tall man took off his hat and nodded to Jordan. "Mornin', Ms. Maddie." Then he shifted his gaze to Cash. "Glad you're here, boss."

"Problem?" Cash asked.

Sweeney's eyes never left Cash's as he nodded. "I finished with the stock, and I was on my way over here to check on Ms. Maddie the way you asked me to. When I passed by her studio, I noticed that the door was ajar. So I went in."

"What is it?" Jordan asked.

"I'd better show you," Sweeney said.

4

JORDAN ALMOST had to run to keep up with the men's long-legged strides. The look in the older man's eyes had triggered a cold dread deep inside of her. The sun beating down from a clear, steel-blue sky wasn't enough to chase away the goose bumps that had broken out on her skin.

Maddie's studio had been broken into? Why? And by whom? Had something been stolen?

She thought she'd steeled herself. In the past few weeks, she'd developed a skill for doing that, but when Sweeney pushed the door open and she saw the devastation, her knees nearly buckled and she couldn't keep from crying out.

The open shelving that must have lined the walls had all been shoved over. Boxes had been overturned, their contents scattered. Gems and silver wires littered the floor. And scattered over everything like freshly fallen snow were shreds of paper. Maddie's design sketches? Something in Jordan's stomach twisted. Eva had always pasted her latest designs on the wall over her workspace. Would Maddie be able to replace them?

Leaning down, she picked up a chunk of turquoise the size of a baby's fist. A quick glance around confirmed that other stones—garnet, lapis, tiger's eye, some even larger than the turquoise—had been thrown helter-skelter throughout the debris. They had to be quite valuable.

"Why didn't they take the stones?" she asked.

"Good question."

She hadn't even been aware that Cash was touching her until he gave her shoulders a squeeze.

"Take a deep breath."

She did and felt her lungs burn. Control. She reached deep for it. When the backs of her eyes began to sting, she blinked rapidly and carefully picked her way further into the room. Cash moved with her.

Her heart thudded painfully in her chest as she thought of her mother's studio, pictured Eva's reaction if something like this had happened to her. A flame of anger began to burn inside of her. While thieves had broken into the main salon of the Madison Avenue store a few weeks back, they hadn't destroyed the place.

Taking another breath, she said in a low tone, "We can't let her see this."

"She won't have to," Cash said equally quietly. "I'll call my housekeeper. Mary's known Maddie since she was a child. She'll gather some friends and they'll put the place in order. Her husband will have the shelves back up in no time. This can all be fixed."

"Good. Okay. We won't have to tell her it happened."

"Yes, we will. She has a right to know about this, Jordan. And we need to know if anything like this is going on in New York."

A ripple of fear moved through her. "You think she's in danger, don't you?"

"I don't know what to think. But I don't like the terms of your mother's will."

She looked at him then. He had a take-charge attitude that she was grateful for. In most of her relationships, including the one she'd had with her mother and in her job, she'd been the person who usually called the shots. She was relieved in this case that she didn't have to figure out everything.

As she turned back to face the piles of debris, a thought suddenly occurred to her. "The jewelry show—the one that's coming up tomorrow in Santa Fe. Maybe those pieces were what they were after." Panic jolted her system. "I told her I'd substitute for her at that show. She said the new designs were in the safe, but—"

Cash ran his hands from her shoulders down her arms and back up again. "They are in the safe. She keeps all her finished work there."

The relief Jordan felt nearly had her knees buckling again. She knew that. Maddie had told her that. She wasn't going to fall apart. She couldn't. Very deliberately, she let her gaze sweep the room again. Someone had done this to scare her sister.

Behind her, Cash moved to speak to the older man who'd remained outside. "Go back to the ranch. Let Steven and Mary know. Tell them I'll call them as soon as the phones come back on line. If you could pack me some clothes and bring them, I'd be grateful. I'll be staying here until we figure out what's going on."

"Yes, boss."

Jordan heard the older man's footsteps fade, but she was still focused on the destruction. She pictured her sister sitting at the worktable. Then she scanned the studio again. The carelessness of the destruction, the meanness of it jump-started her anger.

When the first wave moved through her, Cash said, "C'mon. We're getting out of here."

She turned to face him, temper blazing in her eyes. "We're not just going to repair this place. We're going to find the bastard who did it and make him pay."

"Deal," Cash said.

As Jordan pushed off the speakerphone button ending her call with Maddie, Cash slipped his arm around her and pulled her close. She looked shell-shocked. And no wonder. The news in Manhattan was even worse than it was in Santa Fe.

The message light on the phone had been blinking when they'd reentered the farm house, signaling that the phone was working—at least temporarily. The message had been from Maddie, and the machine must have picked it up when they were still in bed. That had been the phone call that had awakened him. According to Maddie, Jase Campbell had returned. When Jordan had reached Maddie at Eva Ware Designs, Cash was relieved to learn that Campbell had been with her.

He'd thought for a moment that Jordan was going to lose it when she'd told Maddie about the vandalism in her studio. But she'd rallied. She was an extraordinarily strong woman.

Then Jase Campbell delivered the bad news from their end. Eva Ware's death was being investigated as a homicide. A witness had seen a car parked across the street and claimed that when Eva Ware had crossed to her apartment building, the car had been aimed straight at her.

On top of that, Jase believed that Eva's death might be related to the robbery at Eva Ware designs. In Cash's opinion, that news, added to the terms of Eva Ware's will, put both Jordan and Maddie in grave jeopardy. It didn't comfort him that Jase Campbell was on the same page on that score.

"She was murdered," Jordan said as she turned into him and laid her head on his shoulder.

He wrapped his arms around her. When she tipped her head up to meet his gaze and he saw a tear roll quietly down her cheek, he had a moment of raw panic.

He had no experience handling a woman's tears. After

his mother's death, he'd been totally surrounded by men. But he had to do something. Jordan had just been dealt a bull's-eye blow. When Maddie and Jase had given her the news, her face had gone ghost-white. Even now, her breathing was shallow.

Was she going to faint on him? Panic nearly swamped him again.

Easing away, he kept an arm around her shoulder as he led her to the couch. Once he had her settled, he strode back into the kitchen and pulled a bottle of Mike Farrell's single-malt Scotch out of a cabinet. Carefully, he poured three fingers' worth into a glass and drank one of them himself.

He recalled that when his mother had died, Mike had brought a bottle to his father, and they'd shared a drink.

It wasn't the same. He didn't kid himself about that. His mother had died after a long illness. Even though her passing had been anticipated, the loss had nearly leveled him. Jordan hadn't had time to prepare herself—not for the hit-and-run and certainly not for the probability that her mother had been murdered. Glass in hand, he strode toward her and sat down on the coffee table facing her. She still hadn't moved. Praying it would help, he pressed the glass into her hands and said, "Drink it."

It didn't make him feel better when she followed his orders like a robot and shuddered.

"I'm going to be all right," she said. Reaching for his hand, she linked her fingers with his. Who was comforting whom, he wondered.

"I'll be fine. I just need a moment."

"I know."

A second tear rolled down her cheek.

"Take another sip."

She did. "I thought my mother's death was an accident.

Inexplicable. Tragic." Jordan sipped again. "Maddie's so strong. I almost caved. She didn't. For a moment after they told me, all I could think of was flying back to Manhattan to help them find whoever murdered my mother."

Poor kid. She had to feel like Chicken Little with huge chunks of the sky falling on her head. She'd lost her mother, then discovered she'd been kept from her father and had a sister she'd never met. And now this.

"Do you think they could be wrong?" Jordan asked.

"How smart is this Jase Campbell?"

"Smart as they come."

"Then I'm betting he's right. Can he take care of Maddie?"

"Nobody better," Jordan said. "I'm so glad that Maddie is with him. She can lean on him, and he'll make sure she's safe."

That had been his own take on the situation. But it occurred to him that during her long ordeal, Jordan hadn't had anyone to lean on. That much at least, he could change.

Another tear rolled down her cheek. This time she rubbed it away, then glanced down at her hand. "I never cry."

Good, Cash thought. If he could just keep her talking, perhaps she could ride out the storm that was swirling around inside of her.

"If we go with the theory that your mother was run down on purpose, do you have any idea of who?" His own mind was racing. Her mother had been murdered before the will had been read. What if someone had not benefited as much as they'd hoped or expected? "Who in your family might have wanted her dead?"

Jordan shook her head. "No one. I mean, I told you that my cousin, Adam, always wanted to step into her shoes one day. But I can't see him doing something like that. His own mother is always complaining that he lacks spine." She shook her head again. "I don't know. I just don't know."

Tears were rolling down her cheeks now. Cash doubted she was even aware of them. Taking the glass from her hand, he lifted her, then sat on the couch and settled her on his lap.

The floodgates opened. Not sure of what else to do, he kissed the top of her head and simply held her close. When he felt her relax against him and her tears began to soak his shirt, Cash realized that this was better for her than the Scotch.

JORDAN WASN'T SURE how long her little crying jag lasted. It was as if someone had turned on an inner faucet and then just as suddenly turned it off. When Cash pressed a clean hankie into her hand, she blew her nose, then settled back into the crook of his arm.

Letting a shaky sigh escape, she listened to Cash's heartbeat sure and steady beneath her ear. He didn't say anything, and she was grateful for that.

As the seconds ticked by in silence, she knew she should move. All her life she'd stood on her own two feet. Because her mother had always been so focused on her art and her design business, Jordan had had learned to take care of herself at an early age. Oftentimes, she'd watched out for her mother, too. During the last few years when she'd worked for Eva Ware Designs, she'd done more than improve the store's profits. She'd also insisted that she and Eva have a steady lunch date every Wednesday afternoon. After lunch, they would take in a matinee, visit a museum or simply shop. Artists needed breaks from their work to recharge and her mother seldom took one.

Toying with one of the buttons on Cash's shirt, she thought about her relationship with Jase. She didn't recall ever using him to lean on, either. Oh, when he'd been around, she'd used him as a sounding board, but she couldn't recall him ever holding her like this. In fact, she couldn't recall anyone holding her quite like this. Had she ever let her guard down quite this far? Had she ever felt quite this comforted? Or comfortable?

A trickle of unease moved through her. She had things to do. She'd made a promise to Maddie that she'd handle the jewelry show tomorrow. To do that, she needed to look at the pieces Maddie had stored in the safe, and then she wanted to go into Santa Fe and check out the venue of the jewelry show. She simply couldn't stay here any longer.

One more minute, she promised herself. His arms were so strong. From her present position, she could see the sharp line of his jaw and his chin. Stubborn, she thought. In that sense, he was like Jase. She'd never won an argument with her apartment mate. There'd been a few draws, she recalled. She had a hunch that if she crossed swords with Cash, he would prove to be just as much of a challenge. This time, it wasn't unease, but anticipation that moved through her.

Enough. She drew in a deep breath, intending to sit up, but his scent distracted her. Why was it that she couldn't seem to get enough of it?

Time to move, Jordan. But first...

"I'm sorry," she murmured.

"For what?"

"For falling apart on you. I never do that."

"No problem."

Beneath her ear, his voice was a comfortable rumble. It reminded her of her dream.

Which hadn't been a dream at all, she reminded herself. She really, really had to get back to reality and what she still had to do today.

"You're a kind man. I want to thank—" When she raised her head and her mouth accidentally brushed his jaw, her heart gave one good thump and then skipped a beat.

His eyes were so close she could see blue flecks in the gray, and they reminded her of a deep shade of lapis. It occurred to her for the first time how small the world became when you were looking into someone's eyes.

There was something very important she still had to say. And to do. But for the life of her she couldn't seem to get a handle on it. Not when his mouth was so close that she could feel his breath on her skin. Not when his earthy scent of leather and sun and soap surrounded her.

"Cash?"

His hand slipped under her chin, tipping her head up, and it seemed the most natural thing in the world when his mouth closed over hers. His lips were so soft. They didn't demand. They merely caressed. More than anything, she wanted to sink into the comfort they offered and into that odd feeling of coming home.

Then, he suddenly changed the angle of the kiss, and Jordan felt herself swept into that same uncharted territory Cash had taken her to during the night. For a moment, she was incredibly tempted to forget everything else and to lose herself in him and what they could do to each other.

But what had happened during the night had been a fantasy, she reminded herself. And she wasn't the woman she'd been in her dream.

She pulled back. "We can't."

"Why not?"

"Because." His mouth was barely an inch away, his hand still firm on the back of her neck. *Focus, Jordan. Treat this like a business decision.* "I don't have time. There are things I have to do today. Maddie's jewelry show is tomorrow, so I have to look at her designs and then I want to go into Santa Fe and check out the hotel where the show is being held."

"The day is still young."

He wasn't arguing, she noted, not in any vehement way.

He was merely studying her in that intent way he had. And she was outrageously tempted to just shut up. But she had to get a grip. "My life is complicated right now. I have to focus on walking around in my sister's life. I shouldn't be sitting here. I should be taking her designs out of the safe and making sure that they're ready for that show tomorrow."

She had to get up off his lap and move. She always thought more clearly when she was pacing. But she couldn't seem to push away. The man didn't have to do a thing. He just had to *be* to seduce her.

"Look, you need to know something. What happened last night, the way I was?"

"Yes?"

"That was because of the fantasy I was weaving. I don't leap into relationships, especially sexual ones. Normally, I'm very cautious. You assumed I was Maddie. I was imagining Gregory Peck. We should just chalk it up to some strange anomaly caused by the storm and forget it happened."

"Now, that's a problem." He leaned close enough to brush his lips over hers. "I can't seem to get what happened out of my mind. Speaking for myself, I want it to happen again."

Jordan desperately tried to gather her thoughts. But all she could think about was that she was poised on a cliff and the plunge had never seemed so tempting. Nor so dangerous. Finally, she just went with a lie. "That's just it. You're only speaking for yourself."

"If last night was a fantasy, aren't you the least bit curious to find out what the reality would be like?"

She'd been right about the challenge of arguing with him. The real problem was that she wasn't even sure she believed in her side of the argument. She *was* curious. And his mouth was so close. She was pretty sure she felt her brain cells shutting down. "I…can't think."

"Good. Maddie and Gregory aren't here. Let's not either of us think for a while."

This time when his mouth took hers, it wasn't a caress. It was a demand. Passion flared as immediate and urgent as it had been during the night. If she'd thought that she'd exaggerated the experience in her mind, she was wrong. If anything, what she was feeling now was sharper and much more intense. Her pulse had never hammered this hard. And her body had never ached this desperately. His flavors, rich and dark, exploded on her tongue, and she wrapped her arms around him, demanding more.

Knowing that the wide windows allowed them no privacy, Cash lifted Jordan in his arms and strode toward the nearest bedroom. Everything she'd said had made sense. The woman had a real way with words, and he was developing a keen admiration for the way her mind worked. Under ordinary circumstances, he was a cautious man himself. He didn't start up casual relationships. Perhaps last night they'd both been caught up in a fantasy of sorts.

And thanks to the damn will, things *were* complicated. But what he was feeling wasn't rational. He wasn't sure that it was even controllable.

He wanted her, and she wanted him. In fact, the urgency that he tasted as her mouth moved on his had him nearly stumbling as he stepped inside the bedroom. Kicking the door shut behind him, he turned and steadied them both against it.

He wasn't going to take her to the bed. Not yet. He didn't want any lingering memories of the night before clouding what they were going to do now. As he set her on her feet, their lips parted and she slid down his body. He hadn't thought he could get any harder. But he did.

Fingers fumbling, they worked together to get her out of T-shirt, bra, boots and jeans. The panties came last. He took one step back as she hooked her fingers into the lace waistband, pushed them down over her hips. The instant she kicked the panties away, he stepped forward, trapping her against the door. His eyes stayed on hers as he took his hands on a slow journey from her hips upward to the sides of her breasts, her throat. Finally, he framed her face with his hands. "Say my name."

"Cash. Say mine."

"Jordan."

5

AS IF THEIR EXCHANGE of names were a signal, Cash closed his hands around her hips and lifted her. She felt the brand of each long finger burn her skin. She wrapped her legs around him, arching into his hard length.

Desperation had built so quickly on the short walk to the bedroom. Hadn't she just told him that she wasn't like this? She'd never before plunged into a risky sexual relationship with a man. But *no* wasn't a word she could seem to summon up—not when there was such raw heat in his lips and certainly not when there was such a wildfire of need in her own body.

She struggled to hold him close when he pressed her roughly back against the wall.

"Now." She arched against him again.

"In a…minute." Using his weight to keep her in position against the door, he gripped her thighs and eased her back a bit.

She heard the rasp of a zipper. Oh.

His knuckles brushed between her legs as he unfastened his jeans and let them drop. Her breath stopped when that last physical barrier between them had been removed. But it seemed to take him forever to toe off his boots and step out of his jeans. Finally, the head of his penis was pressing against her, so hard, so hot. So close.

The sensations careening through her intensified. No one had ever made her feel this way.

Now. Right now. She wasn't sure if she said the words or thought them.

He gripped her waist, adjusting his position. Then he eased his support and let her sink onto him. As she took him in, inch by searing inch, the enormous pressure sent whirls of pleasure arrowing through her. Desperate for even more of him, she arched. He shoved her back against the door and thrust into her fully.

He began to move then, his rhythm fast, right on the edge of violent. She welcomed the speed and met him thrust for thrust until the climax ripped through her. Once again, he let her body drop. She hadn't thought she could take any more of him, but incredibly she did as he pushed into her a final time and found his own release. A second orgasm, even stronger and longer than the first shot through her.

Afterward, she clung to him. The room was silent except for the sound of ragged breaths being dragged in and released. She couldn't distinguish which was his, which was hers. He kept her braced against the door, and as her head cleared, Jordan figured that it was as much for his own balance as hers. The darkness in the room was broken only by the thin shafts of sunlight slipping through the edges of the drapes. As the moments spun away, she decided that she could be content to stay this way for a very long time.

What was it about this man that he could make her feel wildly desperate one minute and sweetly comforted the next? She was going to have to figure it out.

It was Cash who moved first. He tightened his grip on her. Then with one arm around her back and the other under her bottom, he carried her to the bed. He was still inside of her when he lowered her and settled himself on top of her.

And he was still hard.

Using all the energy she had at her command, she opened her eyes, and what she saw in his had the fever building in her once more.

"Again," he murmured in her ear. "You'd think that would have done it, but I want you again."

She could feel the proof of that as he hardened inside of her. Heat built once again to wildfire proportions. "Me, too."

He began to move, pushing in and pulling out. His rhythm was slower this time, but no less compelling. As the need began to build between them, she wrapped her legs around his and dug her fingers into his butt to pull him closer, deeper. Gradually, the speed built as they rode each other, moving as one until they both shattered.

Afterward, he rolled off of her, then slid an arm beneath her to pull her close. For a while neither of them spoke. Her hand rested on his chest and she could feel the gradual slowing of his heartbeat. Cash Landry was a man who was comfortable with long silences. She never was.

"It seems I was wrong," she finally said.

"About what?"

"I thought that I wasn't the woman you were with last night. It seems I was. I am."

"I can't be anything but grateful for that."

"Me, either. I guess."

He tilted her chin up then so she had to meet his eyes. "You guess?"

She frowned a little. "Well, we're going to have to figure out what to do about this—about what's happened between us."

He tucked a strand of hair behind her ear. "I vote for just enjoying it."

"I suppose we could do that. For the three weeks I'm here. As long as the ground rules are clear."

"Ground rules?"

Something in his tone had a ripple of unease moving through her. But surely, he had to understand. "Cash, we come from different worlds. At the end of three weeks, I'm going back to New York and Maddie's coming here. Whatever it is that we have will end then."

His eyes had that intent look again. "Why talk about the end when whatever we have is just beginning?"

"Because I like to know where I'm going. I need to know. I'm where I am today because I developed a plan and followed through on it to the letter. Can you understand that?"

"Life isn't as predictable on a ranch. Things happen that you can't foresee. The price of cattle goes up and down. A hard winter can make it difficult for the herds to find enough to eat. A dry spring can cut back on the water supply. I'm used to rolling with the punches and coming up with solutions on the spur of the moment."

"Well, we could think of our…relationship…as rolling with the punches, I suppose. As long as we agree that at the end of three weeks, we can roll with ending things between us. That way, we don't have expectations that might hurt us."

"What if the punch rolls us in a different direction?"

"It won't. My mother's business is very important to me, and I'm needed in New York, especially now that she's…not there. I have to see that her legacy lives on."

When Cash said nothing, Jordan's frown deepened. "I'm not going to get you to agree to anything, am I?"

He lifted the hand that was pressed against his chest and brushed his mouth over it. "I certainly agree that we should enjoy each other as long as you're here."

"And the rest?"

"Why don't we agree to disagree on the ending part?"

She studied him for a moment. There was just a hint of recklessness in his eyes—something that she hadn't seen before. And damn it, she was attracted by it. She was suddenly struck by the realization that no matter what they agreed to, this man was trouble for her. Hadn't he already made her discover things about herself that she'd never known before? "I'm glad you're not a client of mine."

"I can agree with that." He shot her a smile that was so charming she forgot she was annoyed with him.

"C'mon." He took her hand and pulled her from the bed. "You need to see Maddie's designs, and then we should head into Santa Fe so you can check out the venue for the show."

Her brows shot up. "You're awfully agreeable all of a sudden."

He turned to her. "The day isn't getting any younger, and if I stay anywhere near the bed and you, we may not make it into Santa Fe."

She said nothing because her throat had suddenly gone dry as dust. She was very tempted to grab his hand and pull him back into the bed. Or onto the floor. Had the man turned her into some kind of sex maniac?

He shot her that bone melting smile again. "However, I'm flexible. If you want to change your plans…"

When he took a step closer to her, she threw up both hands palms outward. "No. I need to go into Santa Fe."

But she held her breath until Cash grabbed his jeans and boots off the floor and left the room.

Then she nearly ran toward Maddie's bathroom. A cold shower. It would help her think and get her back on track. Hopefully.

JORDAN WAS FAIRLY CERTAIN that she had herself back on track when she climbed into Cash's pickup truck. First of all, she'd taken the time to open the safe and examine the pieces that Maddie intended to showcase at the jewelry show. There had been a wide range—from intricately designed silver belt buckles to delicate necklaces and earrings featuring the turquoise that New Mexico was famous for.

Maddie had clearly inherited their mother's talent for design. But like Eva, she might need help in the marketing department. Jordan intended to give it to her. She was already thinking of the best ways to display the pieces at the show.

"Buckle up," Cash said.

"Sorry," she said. "I was miles away."

"You have been ever since you opened that safe."

"I didn't know until I did how much talent Maddie has."

The moment she fastened her seat belt, he started the motor and turned down the long lane that led to the highway. The searing noontime sun pounded down and the air conditioner blasted out more heat.

"You don't design?"

"No. My job at Eva Ware Designs is marketing. I've made a lot of changes since I joined the business. I intend to come up with some ideas for Maddie while I'm here. For starters, she needs a total makeover of her Web site."

Cash said nothing. One thing she was coming to know about him was that he only spoke when he had something to say. So he probably agreed with her on the Web site. If he'd ever taken a look at it.

The first thing she'd decided during her cold shower was that she wasn't going to argue with him over anything that was nonessential. He'd suggested they take his pickup. Since who drove whom in which car into Santa Fe was very low on her list of priorities, she'd agreed. In fact, taking Cash's truck would give her a chance to study her sister's notes again. In Santa Fe she was going to have to pretend to be Maddie full-time.

It wasn't until she'd gauged Cash's reaction that she'd thought she just might pull the masquerade off. The way he'd stared at her when she'd joined him in the living room of the ranch had finalized her decision.

"You look just like her," he'd said.

She should. She'd tried on three of Maddie's more formal outfits before she'd made her choice. Then she'd selected the newest and most feminine pair of boots. In her opinion, her sister needed a serious wardrobe makeover. She'd had to constantly coax her mother into keeping her clothes updated, and it seemed that Maddie favored Eva in that respect.

Still staring at her, Cash had moved closer. "What did you do to your hair?"

"Hair piece." She'd pulled her hair back from her face and concealed the short ends beneath a braid that was twisted in a circle. As Cash had circled her, she'd caught his scent, fresh from the shower, and firmly put it out of her mind. "Once I talked Maddie into switching places and going along with the will thing, I picked it up in a wig store and had my hairdresser dye it to match."

"I've seen her wear her hair exactly like that." When he'd completed his circle and stood in front of her again, he'd said, "You're going to pretend to be Maddie in Santa Fe, aren't you?"

She met his eyes directly. There was nothing slow about the way his mind worked. She hadn't wanted him to try to talk her out of it, so she'd gathered her thoughts and made her case. "It will be simpler. And better for Maddie. I know a lot about marketing jewelry, but buyers at the show will have more confidence if they believe they're talking to the designer. Maddie gave me some notes so I have names and backgrounds on buyers she's dealt with before. And even without the wig, I fooled the man who told us about Maddie's studio."

"Sweeney. I forgot to introduce you."

"I'd just as soon you didn't. I'm only going to be here for three weeks. I think it will be easier all around if everyone just assumes I'm Maddie. I think I can handle the boutique owners. Maddie gave me some notes on their names and their stores. I'm really interested in seeing what I can do to help my sister improve her marketing. And I'd rather not have to waste time explaining that I'm her twin and the terms of the will and so forth."

"That might make it easier."

"And if we run into that real estate agent, Daniel Pearson?"

Cash had frowned at her then. "That might be trickier. He's been out to the ranch, even took Maddie out to dinner a couple of times."

Jordan's brows had shot up. "He's putting that much pressure on her?"

"He is. In fact, if we run into him, he might be so focused on getting you to list with him that you might be able to fool him after all."

As Cash slowed at the highway, Jordan twisted in her seat to get a look at the ranch. Even through the spew of brown dust the pickup was leaving behind it, she saw that the neat cluster of buildings in the middle of a vast open space with a blue sky overhead made a perfect picture for a postcard. Something she couldn't quite put a finger on stirred at the edges of her mind. And she experienced the same feeling she'd had when she'd walked through the front door.

Home.

Why? She'd only been a baby when her mother had taken her away. Had some memory of the place lingered deep inside of her all this time?

She shifted her perspective to take in the blue-gray hills in the distance, the miles and miles of grazing land. It was so vast, so beautiful. Her throat tightened with an emotion she couldn't quite put her finger on. Longing? What she was certain of was that she had to figure out a way to make sure that Maddie didn't have to sell the place.

"Would my father have ever considered selling off part of his land?"

"Never."

"I don't suppose he would have considered leaving here."

"Ranching to Mike Farrell was like a religion. I think he thought of it as his calling. It's a perception that a lot of ranchers have, my father included."

And you have it too, Jordan thought. Something tightened around her heart. "So if my mother thought that she had to leave here and go back to New York, my father wouldn't have followed."

Cash glanced at her. "My best guess would be no."

Jordan sighed. "I can't blame him for that. In a way, my mother's jewelry design business was like a religion, too. She had such tunnel vision about it. They came from such different worlds, I can understand why they split but I don't understand why they separated Maddie and me—and why they kept it a secret."

Cash's only answer was to reach over and run a hand down her arm. They were beginning the climb into the hills and to distract herself, Jordan tried to concentrate on the view. But her rebellious mind kept returning to Cash.

She glanced sideways at him. Sweeney must have brought him the clothes he'd requested because he was wearing a white shirt and black jeans. The belt sported a silver buckle that she bet was one of Maddie's designs. He'd rolled his sleeves up in deference to the heat and the white cotton contrasted sharply with the sun-bronzed color of his skin. She had a sudden desire to reach over and run her hand down the length of that muscled forearm. God, she wanted to touch him. To get him out of that shirt and run her hands very slowly over every inch of him. They hadn't taken much time to explore each other during their frenzied lovemaking against the door or in the bed. Clearly, she hadn't had nearly enough of him yet.

And what exactly was wrong with that? Just as long as she kept their relationship in the proper perspective.

Bottom line—anything that developed between them had a three-week expiration date. But that wasn't all bad. She'd never taken the time to have a fling in her entire life. She'd been too busy going to school and then planning the changes she'd wanted to make at Eva Ware Designs. Those goals had been her focus. But there was absolutely no reason why she and Cash couldn't enjoy one another while she was in Santa Fe. As long as it didn't interfere with her other plans.

Cash glanced at her. "Is there anything else you want to ask me?"

Jordan felt her face heat. Could he have read her mind? *Get a grip.* Turning her attention to the road, she saw that they had started their descent down an incline. To the right, the land began to drop away.

"I'm assuming because of the dates on the marriage license and the birth certificates that my mother spent at least eleven months on my father's ranch starting around twenty-seven years ago."

She frowned. "Of course, I could be wrong about that. But they married a good eleven months before Maddie and I were born—so the marriage wasn't because she got pregnant. You said you didn't know anything about me. Do you think your father might have? Could he have known that there were two of us at one time?"

"He never said anything, but that doesn't mean he didn't know about you. My mother might have known, too. Your father could have sworn them both to secrecy. I've been giving it some thought. Ranch life is pretty isolated. It's hard work, too. There isn't a lot of time for socializing. So very few people might have known about you."

"Can you think of anyone I could talk to who might have known about my mother and about Maddie and me?"

Cash thought for a moment. "Maddie's foreman, Mac McAuliffe, has only been working here for ten years. Sweeney was around twenty-six years ago, but he never had any call to come over here. I was only three at the time and pretty much confined to the house. But there's old Pete Blackthorn."

Jordan dug her sister's notes out of her bag. "I don't think Maddie mentioned him."

"She probably figured you wouldn't run into him. He doesn't stop by the ranch as often since your father died. They used to play the occasional game of chess together. I think Pete misses him."

"Where does Pete live?"

"He keeps a trailer in a park south of Santa Fe. But he's rarely there. Pete's spent his whole life as a sort of free-lance prospector. His great-great-grandfather worked some of the Navaho turquoise mines in the area. A lot of people believe that he has some old maps that were passed down in his family that show the location of some of the old mines. He certainly seems to find more than his share of turquoise."

"Is he the source of those beautiful stones in Maddie's studio?"

"He's her only source." Cash grinned. "Even when she was a kid, he used to bring her stones to play with."

"I'd love to meet him. Not just to see if he knows anything about Maddie and me, but I'd like to buy some of that turquoise for Eva Ware Designs."

"When I take you on a tour of the ranch the day after tomorrow, we might run into Pete. I've seen him frequently in the hills to the southeast."

Jordan sent him a smile. "Thanks."

"Are you up to riding Brutus?"

"I'd love to ride him."

Cash glanced in the rearview mirror and frowned.

"What is it?"

"We've got company. There's a van behind us that's coming up fast."

Jordan twisted in her seat. In spite of the brown dust Cash's pickup was leaving in its wake, she could see the van clearly. It was black with dark windows. Sun glared off them as it closed the distance.

Cash eased his foot off the gas and pressed the brake. "There's a couple of curves coming up that are tricky. No one familiar with this road would be driving that fast." He pressed the brake again. "Maybe he'll take the warning and slow down."

The van closed the distance to ten yards, then five, then three. "He's not slowing. If he wants to pass—" But he wasn't trying to pass them, Jordan realized.

"Turn around and hang on."

Jordan didn't argue. She had a second to absorb the way the land fell away to their right. Then the van rammed into their rear bumper.

The impact slammed Jordan forward into the seat belt and had the rear wheels of the pickup fishtailing wildly. With her heart in her throat, she listened to them spin. She couldn't scream, couldn't think. All she could do was grip the seat with one hand, the armrest with the other and hold on for dear life.

6

TIRES SCREAMED and the truck then skidded onto the narrow shoulder. Dust and gravel erupted in a huge fan. Cash gripped the steering wheel hard as it threatened to rip out of his hands. Easy, he told himself. If he pulled too hard to the left, he'd send the car careening into the rock face.

"That wasn't an accident," Jordan exclaimed.

"No. He's trying to run us off the road." Cash didn't even consider lying. The problem was, the bastard behind them had a good chance of accomplishing his goal. At this point in their descent, the road was a narrow corkscrew, all sharp with angles and little or no shoulder. There was rock on one side and drop-offs to the right, some more sheer than others.

Once the truck was steady again, Cash risked a glance into his rearview mirror. The road had flattened a bit, and the van had backed away.

Jordan twisted in her seat. "He's not so close. What are we going to do?"

Cash shot her a quick glance. "Hopefully spoil his fun. Want to know the good news?"

"Bring it on."

She was frightened, but she was holding together. Another woman—perhaps even Maddie—would have panicked by now. "In my reckless youth, I did a little drag racing on this very hill." More than a little, truth be told.

"So you know the road."

"Like the back of my hand." Even as he spoke, Cash pictured a map in his mind, just as he had as a teenager.

"So what's the bad news?"

"I know the road."

Two beats of silence went by.

"You've got a plan?"

"You bet." It was a risky one. He hoped to hell it would work.

"What can I do?"

"Keep your eyes on the van. I need to keep mine on the road."

"Done." She twisted in her seat. "He's about fifteen yards behind us."

A sign flashed by with a warning of the upcoming double S curve. Cash was happy Jordan didn't see it.

"I want to know when he's out of sight." He eased his foot down on the gas pedal.

"You're going faster?"

"Yeah. He's going to hit us again, but he'll wait until we're farther down the incline where the drop-off is steeper."

"Good to know."

He couldn't prevent his lips from curving. She was a trouper. "There are two possibilities."

"So he has two chances?"

"Not if I can help it."

"He's speeding up, keeping pace."

"Good." On the map he had in his mind, Cash pictured the two places on the road where the land fell away sharply. In the first, the ground plunged into a series of gulleys, each one lower and deeper. There was a chance of surviving. The second option offered a sheer drop-off. Nothing but air for about one hundred feet. Barring a miracle, death would be certain.

If the guy in the van was a pro, and Cash was beginning to suspect he was, he'd have scoped the route out and chosen his spot. The second one. Cash would have put good money on it.

But if his plan worked, neither of them would get that far.

He let his gaze drop briefly to the speedometer and saw the needle inch past sixty. He reminded himself that the truck wouldn't corner as well as the car he'd driven in his teens. Swallowing fear, he took the first curve at close to sixty-five. His fingers dug into the steering wheel as he fought for control. The truck teetered briefly on two tires. After three heart-stopping beats, the other two slammed back onto the pavement. Heart pumping, Cash tightened his grip on the wheel and steered the pickup into the next curve. As his adrenaline spiked, his mind cleared, and he fine-tuned the image of the downward spiral of turns in his mind.

"Where's the van?" he asked.

"Still with us."

"Good." He wanted his pursuer to keep pace. For now. In the most acute angle of the spiral, the back tires skidded, screeching on the asphalt. They slid onto a narrow line of gravel edging the drop-off and spun for an endless moment before gripping the pavement again. Then the pickup shot forward.

"Can you still see it?" Cash asked.

"No. Too much dust."

Perfect. Cash was banking on the driver having to slow for a bit. But he didn't glance back himself. Nor did he look to the right. He knew there would be nothing to see but air.

Eyes narrowed, body tense, he focused all his attention on the winding road, matching it to the map in his head as he zigged and zagged into the next two turns. He'd done this before, he reminded himself.

"There's a bump ahead," he warned Jordan. When the pickup smacked into it and shot into the air for a few seconds, the bottom dropped out of his stomach—just as if he were on a roller coaster. He recalled the thrill it had given him when he was younger. This time, he swallowed fear again. The truck slammed back onto the pavement with a bone-jarring jolt.

In seconds, they'd reach the steepest part of the incline. This was it. Gritting his teeth, he anticipated the next stretch. *Hairpin* didn't even begin to describe the curves. "Hang on tight."

"I still can't see the van. Oh, there he is."

Cash pressed his foot harder on the gas pedal. A sign flashed by. He knew it cautioned a speed of thirty. With luck, he'd make it through the first turns. If he tried to take the last curve at this speed, they'd skid off the road.

But he didn't plan to take that last curve at all. Just ahead, right where he'd been picturing it, was a wide circular area of the shoulder that had been cut into the rock face. It was the only section of the road where a vehicle could pull off. Timing would be everything. Sweat beaded on his forehead and he prayed that his maneuver would work.

He began to tap the brake just before the wide arc of shoulder came into view. When they reached it, he eased the pickup closer to the opposite side of the road before whipping his vehicle to the left and into a spin. Tires spit gravel. Holding on to the steering wheel for dear life, Cash let the momentum take them.

JORDAN WOULD HAVE SCREAMED if her heart hadn't been trapped in her throat. They were going to die. Her mind was numbed by the thought. Her life didn't flash before her eyes. What did was a stream of scenes blurred by the dust the truck was spewing up, each one freeze-framed for an instant in the windshield of the truck. One second a solid wall of granite was dead ahead, the next a dizzying spin of road. Then nothing but air. Her stomach plummeted, and before the images could flash by again, she shut her eyes.

When metal screamed against rock, she knew the end was near. Now she'd never get to know Maddie or her father. Or Cash. She felt the sudden lurch of the truck, knew that he was doing his best to save them. He was the last thought in her mind before the truck suddenly shuddered to a stop.

Cash's hand gripped hers. "Are you all right?"

"Yes." And it was true. She opened her eyes. The scent of burning rubber filled her lungs. It was real. They weren't dead. As her vision cleared, she saw out of the corner of her eye that the rock face was to their right and they were facing up the hill.

Then through the haze of dust, she saw the van lurch around the curve ahead of them—the same one they'd just taken. The back end fishtailed, sending the vehicle into a fast skid. It was a little like watching a movie, Jordan realized. For an instant as the tires spun, the car careened down the road sideways—the front facing the rock face, the rear end spewing up gravel on the nearly nonexistent shoulder.

"He took the curve too fast," Cash said.

Jordan caught the grim satisfaction in his tone. She might have said something then, but she couldn't take her eyes off the van. It was still about fifteen yards away them when the tires found traction. For one horrifying moment, the vehicle shot forward, and she was sure it would crash into the granite wall. But at the last moment, the driver avoided the collision, by jerking the van back onto the road.

"He's overcompensating," Cash murmured.

As if to prove the point, the van tipped crazily to one side, the roof kissing the rock face and sending off sparks.

Then the vehicle careened forward, weaving drunkenly down the road.

"He's not going to make it," Cash predicted.

He was right. The driver had clearly lost control, and he was going way too fast. As the van whipped toward them, it shimmied and shuddered. When it tore past them, she and Cash both twisted in their seats. Together they watched it shoot sideways into the air at the side of the road. There was a sudden and complete silence, and for a moment, as it hovered in space, Jordan half expected the vehicle to fly.

Then, as if a magician had waved a wand, the front end pointed downward and it plummeted out of sight. The sound of the impact shattered the silence.

Releasing her hand, Cash unfastened his seat belt and opened the door. "Stay here."

"No way."

He waited for her to join him on the other side of the truck. Then he gripped her hand in his and led the way across the two lanes.

The van was about fifty yards below them, lying on the passenger side with two of its tires spinning.

Cash pulled out his cell. "I hope I can get a signal." He breathed a sigh of relief as he punched in 9-1-1.

A moment later, Jordan listened to him give the information and their location to someone on the other end. Everything had happened so fast. She was still trying to get her mind around it. By the time he slipped his cell back into his pocket, the van's tires had stopped spinning, most of the dust had settled, and she'd figured out what had happened.

Turning to him, she said, "You intended for him to go off the road, didn't you? That was your plan."

He met her eyes. "I won't deny that I was hoping it

would work out this way. That bastard was trying to kill you."

He half expected her to cringe or pull away, but she didn't. Instead, she wrapped her arms around him and pulled him close.

Cash couldn't have described the emotions that tumbled through him at the simple gesture. His knees nearly buckled. No woman had ever been able to push so many of his buttons so fast. She was taking him into uncharted territory. There was none of the fire or desperation he'd felt when they'd made love during the night or this morning. Now as he held her close to him, it was warmth that spread through him. And he felt suddenly and completely at home.

When she drew back, he didn't want to let her go.

"Thank you," she said simply.

Cash gathered his thoughts. "You helped, you know."

Her eyes narrowed. "How? You're the one who ought to start a new career as a race car driver."

He managed a smile. "You did everything I asked. You didn't ask useless questions, and you didn't fall apart."

She tilted her head to one side. "I don't usually fall apart. But I'm not sure you should depend on me not asking questions or being so obedient all the time."

He threw back his head and laughed. The sound was still lingering in the air when he pulled her close for a quick, hard kiss. At least his intention was to make it quick. But the softness of her lips, the flavors in her mouth tempted him to linger. Just for a moment. And that was all it took to have the heat igniting and spreading like a flash fire in a drought. Before he could think, he'd pulled her close and his hands were running over her, pressing, teasing, tormenting. It was as if his will had been snatched completely away.

It was the sudden feeling of helplessness that gave him the strength to pull back.

She was as breathless as he was, her eyes as surprised. "This is happening so fast."

"Can't argue with that." Another moment and he might have taken her right there where they stood. And he was damn sorry that he'd had to put on the brakes. Another time, another place he promised himself as he dropped his hands.

"You remember what you said about my not counting on you being so obedient all the time?"

She nodded.

"Why don't we give that a little test? What would you say if I asked you to stay here while I climbed down and checked on the driver?"

She shook her head firmly. "No way."

"See? One simple statement and you've totally adjusted my expectations."

Keeping her hand gripped in his, Cash led the way down to the wreck.

AN HOUR LATER, Jordan stood on the narrow shoulder of the drop-off giving her statement to Detective Shay Alvarez. He hadn't introduced himself, which made her suspect that Maddie knew him. How well was the big question. She'd made it her business to get his full name by the tried and true method of eavesdropping.

As Alvarez reviewed the notes he'd been taking, Jordan watched the scene below where a helicopter was lifting a stretcher carrying the injured body of the van's driver. For a moment, Alvarez also turned to watch until the man was safely pulled inside.

Earlier, when they'd reached the van, Cash had climbed up to the window and found the man still had a faint pulse.

They hadn't dared to move him. Not that they'd have been able to. The police had used some sort of a pulley to get the van upright before the medics could deal with getting him out.

The sun beat down ruthlessly, and the dusty breeze stirred up by the helicopter as it lifted brought even hotter air. Jordan felt sweat trickle down her back.

Detective Alvarez glanced down at his notebook. "You're sure you have no idea why this man tried to run you and Cash off the road?"

"No." That much was true, but she was beginning to feel little pangs of guilt because neither she nor Cash had admitted to him that she wasn't Maddie. That constituted lying to the police, didn't it?

"There have been some incidents of vandalism at the ranch," she said. "Someone tried to poison my horse, and this morning, my studio was vandalized."

Shay Alvarez took a moment to study her. "Cash told me."

Jordan figured that conversation must have taken place right after he'd arrived and taken Cash aside for a few moments. She'd gotten the distinct impression from their body language that they knew each other. But she could hardly ask. Maddie would know something like that.

After talking briefly to Cash and turning him over to one of the uniforms who'd accompanied him, Detective Shay Alvarez walked up to the curve that had ultimately sent the van out of control and examined the skid marks.

The man didn't look Hispanic. He was tall and lanky with broad shoulders and blue eyes. The moment he'd climbed out of his car he'd had her thinking of Matt Dillon from *Gunsmoke*.

Now as she met his penetrating gaze, she thought again of the sheriff in the old TV series. Matt Dillon had been one smart man, and she had a hunch that Shay Alvarez was, too. As the silence stretched between them, Jordan finally felt compelled to say something. Anything. "Do you know who the driver of the van is?"

"Not yet. He wasn't carrying any ID. Most professionals don't. But we may be able to trace him through his fingerprints."

"Do you think this incident might be related to the destruction of my studio?" Jordan asked.

In her peripheral vision, she could see Cash striding toward them. Relief surged through her. But it was short-lived.

"Perhaps. I might have a better idea about that if you'd tell me who you really are and why you're pretending to be Maddie Farrell?"

Cash reached them in time to hear the end of Shay Alvarez's question. With a grin he slapped the detective on the shoulder. "I was wondering if you'd figure it out."

"Were you going to tell me if I didn't?"

Cash shrugged. "Maybe."

Shay shook his head. "Knowing her identity is pretty crucial if you expect me to find out why the man in the van tried to kill her."

Cash's expression sobered. "I think he was trying to kill Maddie."

"Perhaps."

"When did you figure out she wasn't Maddie?"

Only then did Alvarez send him an answering smile. "It took me a bit. But she didn't seem to remember that I came out to the ranch when Brutus's hay was doctored."

Annoyance surged through Jordan. "Hey. I'm here and I don't appreciate being talked about as if I'm not."

"Yes, ma'am." The detective turned his charming smile on her and extended his hand. "I'm Shay Alvarez."

Jordan took the hand. "I'm Jordan Ware, Maddie's twin sister."

Shay's expression sobered. "Twins. That would explain the fact that you're a dead ringer for her. But why the impersonation?" He glanced at Cash again. "Or was that just a little joke on me?"

Cash shook his head. "Always so suspicious."

"The two of you have known each other for some time, I take it?" Jordan asked.

"Since high school," Shay said. "I didn't know Maddie had a twin."

"Neither did Maddie until a few days ago. Neither did I." Jordan explained her situation as concisely as she could.

"And I decided to pretend to be Maddie while I'm here because I want her jewelry show to be a success. I'm not sure her potential buyers would be as impressed if they discovered she'd skipped out on the show and they were left to do business with her twin."

"In that case, I won't rat you out," Shay promised. "But who else knows about the switch?"

"Only my mother's attorney, family members and the employees at Eva Ware Designs. Why?"

"Last night or this morning, Maddie's studio was broken into and destroyed. This morning you're nearly driven off the road. Clearly, the vandalism plaguing Maddie and her ranch has increased since you arrived in Santa Fe," Shay said. "And if someone is determined to break the will, getting rid of either you or your sister would work."

Jordan swallowed hard. "You think someone wants to kill Maddie or me because of my mother's will?"

He jerked his head in the direction of the wrecked van. "It's not the only explanation, but it does leap to mind. Money's always a powerful motivator."

"Jordan just found out this morning that her mother's hit-and-run death is being investigated as a possible homicide," Cash said.

Shay let out a low whistle. "You think there's a connection between that and this."

It wasn't a question, Jordan noted.

"I'm not a fan of coincidence, but as you say, it's not the only possibility," Cash said. "What do you know about Daniel Pearson?"

Shay's eyebrows shot up. "The real estate broker and wannabe mogul?"

Cash nodded.

"Mostly what I read in the society pages. He's well-connected socially, serves on a couple of museum and gallery boards, and he's using those connections to establish a thriving real estate business. Why?"

"Because for the last six months he's been pressuring Maddie to sell the ranch."

Shay thought for a minute. "I've met him a few times. He appears at all the events my mother bugs me to attend."

While Shay went on to describe Pearson as a social climber who thought he had a great deal of charm with the ladies, Jordan studied the two men standing in front of her.

Physically, they were similar. Both were tall and dark haired. Shay was a smoother dresser. His khaki slacks were neatly pressed. Cash's jeans were well-worn and fit like a second skin. Both radiated competence. In addition, the cowboy and the cop talked with the ease of old friends, their minds in tune, their respect for each other's ideas clear.

"You think Pearson is involved in this?" Shay asked.

"I think it's possible." Cash glanced up the road to the skid marks. "He could have hired the guy in the van. The same guy could have destroyed Maddie's studio last night and then waited around for us to go into Santa Fe. It was a good bet that she'd drive in today because of the big jewelry show tomorrow. And once Maddie's out of the picture, it's a pretty sure thing that the ranch will go on the market."

"Could be," Shay said. "But if he's been pressuring Maddie for six months, why all the urgency?"

"Perhaps he's under pressure, too," Jordan said. If Pearson is so anxious to list the ranch, he must have a buyer on the line."

Shay and Cash both turned to her.

"You've got a point," Shay agreed. "It's not enough for me to question Pearson. However, I could make some inquiries about who his buyer might be. My mother is on a couple of boards with Pearson's broker."

Cash smiled at him. "You do that."

"I assume you'll be sticking close to Ms. Ware."

Before Cash could reply, Jordan said, "I'm Maddie, remember?"

"Point taken." He took a step closer to her. "Cash won't tell you, but you were lucky to have him behind the wheel today. He knows every inch of this road."

"I know."

When a uniformed officer approached, Shay said, "Duty calls," and strode over to talk to the young man.

"You'll get back to us?" Cash called after him.

"Soon as I have something."

Turning, Cash took Jordan's hand. "Do you want to call it a day and go back to the ranch?"

She shook her head. "I want to go to Santa Fe. I came here to walk around in my sister's shoes, and I gave my word to Maddie that the jewelry show would go off without a hitch. I'm not letting anyone prevent me from doing either of those things."

He gripped her chin and brushed his mouth over hers. "I like your style, Jordan Ware."

7

CASH HANDED JORDAN a frozen cinnamon latte and set his coffee down on the table before he took the seat across from her.

She glanced up. "Thanks." Then she shifted her attention back to the notes Maddie had given her. It had been her idea to stop at the small restaurant across the street from the hotel where the jewelry show was scheduled to open on the following morning. She'd wanted a chance to prep herself in case she ran into anyone she should recognize.

He reached over to lay a hand on one of hers. "You'll do fine."

"I hope so." She linked her fingers with his. "There are a lot of people I'm going to have to keep straight. Some of them Maddie only sees at shows, but there are others she runs into more frequently."

"I might be able to help with some of them."

"Do you know Joe Manuelo?"

He thought for a moment. "We've never met, but I believe he's the man who cuts a lot of Maddie's stones."

"Yes. Maddie says he often visits the shows to see the end products of his work."

As she shifted her attention back to the notes, he studied their clasped hands. Hers was slender, delicate almost, a stark contrast to the woman he was coming to know. And he'd nearly lost his chance to know her better.

As Cash sipped his coffee, he glanced around the small outside patio. He'd taken less than three minutes to fetch their drinks, yet as he'd watched her sitting in the shade of a potted tree with the sunlight dappling over her, nerves had knotted tightly in his stomach. They'd had a close call.

And it didn't help that she was masquerading as Maddie. While he'd been waiting on their drinks, he'd considered pressing her to let him go forward with his idea of announcing their engagement. But there were problems with that plan. He was no longer sure it would be enough to protect her, and, more importantly, he no longer wanted to become engaged to Maddie. That was something he'd have to think about later.

The rational side of his mind told him that she was safe for now. After all, they were in the center of Santa Fe, and there would be some delay time before whoever had hired the thug in the van would learn that the mission had not been accomplished.

Unless the thug had an accomplice right here in Santa Fe. That might shorten their reprieve considerably.

They'll try again, nagged the tiny little voice at the back of his head. His gut instinct was to get Jordan as far away as he could. It was a sort of caveman response, and he couldn't recall ever having one with regard to a woman before.

But then he'd never responded to a woman the way he had to Jordan. He'd had some time while Shay had taken her statement to think about his reaction when he'd kissed her on the side of that road right after the accident. The strength and speed of his desire, the draining away of his willpower—both had been unprecedented. He was still baffled by it.

Even now as he watched her pouring over Maddie's notes, he wanted to reach out and touch her—just to run a finger down her cheek or tuck a strand of hair behind her ear. How long would it take him to erase that totally focused look from her face, he wondered. And how long could he wait to do it?

The current time and the place were all wrong, but that didn't stop his mind from conjuring up a fantasy. In it, they were alone. Not in Maddie's bedroom this time, but in his. It was only as he pictured it in his mind that he realized how much he wanted to see her in his home. She was standing in front of the fireplace dressed in nothing but those seductive scraps of lace and silk she'd been wearing the first night he'd seen her. The punch of heat was just as strong as it had been then—in spite of the fact that he knew what he'd find when he touched her and lowered her to the floor. Or he thought he knew. But every time he tasted her, wasn't there something new, some flavor that he hadn't discovered before…?

"Do you want more coffee?"

Her question snapped his mind back to reality and he silently cursed himself. "No." Quickly, he glanced around the patio. No one seemed to take notice of Jordan. No one seemed out of place.

But a pro would know how to blend in.

For a second, Cash toyed with the possibility of giving into his caveman urges and just carrying her off. And not merely because he wanted to be alone with her. Where could he take her so that she would be safe? To Albuquerque to a luxury hotel? His experience with the kinds of places Jordan must be used to were limited. Because of the ranch, his leisure time was always borrowed, and his idea of a great evening with a woman would be to spend it somewhere under the stars. He figured Jordan's fantasy would be a far cry from that.

She glanced up suddenly and there was curiosity in her eyes. "You're staring at me. It's distracting."

"Sorry. I like the view."

She took a sip of her latte. "Penny for your thoughts."

Cash decided to go with at least a partial truth. "I was wondering what your idea of a perfect romantic evening would be."

She blinked. "A perfect romantic evening? You're kidding, right?"

He felt heat rise in his neck. "No. I was thinking that I'd like to get you away from here where you'd be safe. Some place you'd enjoy. Some place where there'd be just the two of us. And I don't have a lot of experience with women like you."

Jordan set her drink down on the glass-topped table and folded her arms on its surface. "First of all, you're not going to get me away from here. Not for at least three weeks."

"Figured." He stopped himself before he could say more. He'd already dug a hole that might get deeper even without his help.

"Don't you get all overprotective on me."

He said nothing, and her eyes narrowed.

"Look, we're both smart, and we've been forewarned."

"Yeah. But I'm not a professional bodyguard. And you need one."

She waved that away with a little snort. "You've already saved my life once. Plus, anyone who can drive like you has good instincts. So do I. I thought we made a good team during the hair-raising ride down that hill."

"We did." And this wasn't the time for fantasy, he reminded himself.

"Then we'll handle this." She took another sip of her latte.

"I'm not leaving you alone—not even for a moment until we know who hired that thug."

She opened her mouth, shut it and then said, "Okay.

Okay. Now tell me what you meant by not having much experience with a woman like me?"

Cash held back an inner sigh. He'd known they'd get back to that, just as they'd gotten back to his fake engagement proposal. Once again, he went with the truth. "You're different for me, Jordan. It goes beyond the fact that I can't look at you without wanting you. There's something about you that's felt right for me from the beginning."

She swallowed. "We haven't really had a chance to talk about what's going on between us. Maybe we should. I've given it some thought. Not much." She traced one finger through the frost on her glass. "I have trouble thinking when you're around. But I did manage to decide something when I was in the shower. You're different for me, too. Having impromptu flings or affairs…" She paused to wave a hand. "I don't do that."

"Now there's something we have in common."

She drew in a deep breath. "But I want to make love with you again. I can't seem to keep myself from wanting that."

"Same goes for me."

"But that's about the end of the list of what we have in common."

"Oh, I don't know about that. We both love to ride. We both like ranches."

The corners of her mouth lifted, and the little line of worry faded from her forehead. "I like ranches in movies and books. But I'm sure fiction doesn't even crack the surface of what it's like to run a ranch, to live on one."

"You're thinking of your parents, of what you're beginning to suspect happened to them."

"They came from different worlds. And it didn't end happily for them. I'm not sure what we've begun here, but it can't last. We should both be honest about that. It would make things less complicated when I go back to New York."

He picked up her hand and raised it to his lips. "I'm not sure what we've begun yet, either. But why try to predict the ending? I'd rather see where it leads. Unless you're afraid."

Her chin lifted at that. "You don't scare me, cowboy."

"Good." He wished he could say that she didn't scare him, either. But she did. He was almost getting used to the jittery feeling in his stomach. Just as he was almost getting used to the fact that he couldn't be near her without experiencing that steady thrum of excitement in his blood. She felt it, too. He could see it in her eyes. They were darkening into the same deep shade of purple that coated the mountaintops as the sun dropped behind them. He took her hand. Maybe he couldn't carry her off to Albuquerque, but surely he could take her somewhere...

Then beyond her shoulder he caught a glimpse of Daniel Pearson approaching with a woman on his arm. Cash searched for the name and found it. Margo Lawson. Though he'd never formally met her, he'd seen her photo on Maddie's Web site, and Maddie had talked a lot about her. Margo owned one of the premiere boutiques in Santa Fe that showcased Maddie's jewelry.

"Don't look now but we're going to have company," he said to Jordan. "Daniel Pearson and one of the shop owners who carries Maddie's jewelry—Margo Lawson."

JORDAN IGNORED the nerves that danced briefly in her stomach. Her masquerade hadn't fooled Shay Alvarez. Would she be able to fool the two people who were approaching?

As if reading her thoughts, Cash squeezed her hand and whispered, "You'll be fine. You're a dead ringer for your sister. Just remember not to say too much. Maddie is quieter than you."

"Maddie?"

The male voice was still some distance away. Cash squeezed her hand and whispered, "Show time. Knock 'em dead."

"This is a pleasant surprise."

With a smile, Jordan rose from her chair and turned to study Daniel Pearson. He was medium height and handsome in an Ivy League, preppy kind of way. In the light suit, he looked every an inch a city boy, right down to the diamond winking on his pinky finger. "Daniel, it's good to see you."

Then she very nearly stiffened when the man hugged her and kissed her cheek. Maddie's notes hadn't mentioned they were that friendly. Or perhaps the man hugged all his potential clients?

Turning, Jordan smiled at the woman. "You, too, Margo. I was going to stop by the shop later this afternoon."

"You won't find me there," Margo drawled in a husky voice. "I'm taking the afternoon off to rest up for the big show tomorrow."

Jordan dredged up Maddie's notes. Margo was a tall brunette, who looked to be in her late thirties but was older. Her sundress was designer. Most importantly, she was Maddie's oldest client and supporter, so Jordan wanted very much to like her.

"I love the way you're wearing your hair." As Margo's eyes narrowed on her for a minute, Jordan felt her nerves dance again.

"It's a much more professional look than the braid. And it matches the sophisticated and feminine turn your latest designs have been taking. You should wear it that way to the show tomorrow."

Silently Jordan agreed, and she made a mental note to talk to her sister about a permanent change in her hairstyle.

Then Margo shifted her attention to Cash. "I hope you're going to introduce me to your friend."

"This is Cash Landry, my neighbor," Jordan said. She didn't like the way Margo was looking at Cash—as if she wanted a good-size taste of him.

"Margo Lawson," the brunette said as she took Cash's offered hand.

"Landry." Daniel sent him a nod, then turned to smile at Jordan. "This is delightful. I didn't expect to see you until the show tomorrow. You haven't forgotten that I'm taking you out to dinner afterward?"

Jordan thought fast. "I hope you don't mind if I bring Cash along. He's insisting on joining me in my booth at the show."

Annoyance flashed briefly into Daniel's eyes as he stepped closer to Jordan. "I'd planned on discussing business. You promised you'd have an answer for me about the ranch as soon as you put this show behind you."

Not about to let the grass grow under your feet, Jordan thought. As much as she might admire the move on a business level, she didn't like the fact that he was putting this kind of pressure on her sister.

Cash slipped a protective arm around Jordan's shoulders. "Someone broke into Maddie's studio this morning, and I plan on providing her with security until we find out who's responsible."

"Your new designs—did they steal them?" Margo's voice was laced with concern.

"No, thank heavens," Jordan said. "I keep them in a safe."

"They seemed more concerned with destroying the place than filling their pockets with jewelry or stones,"

Cash added. "I'll be staying at the ranch tonight and I'll drive her into Santa Fe for the show tomorrow."

Daniel was frowning now, but Jordan was pretty sure it wasn't the vandalism that was bothering him. She could read people well enough to know that he was a man who didn't like his plans changed. Trying to think how Maddie would handle the situation, she said, "Margo, why don't you join us for dinner tomorrow after the show and make it a foursome? That way you can amuse Cash while Daniel and I talk business?"

Margo kept her eyes on Cash. "I'd be delighted to amuse Cash. In fact, I'll look forward to it."

I'll just bet. There was no denying that it was jealousy she was feeling. But she could also feel Daniel Pearson relax.

"Great idea. Margo and I will see you tomorrow."

"Depend on it. I can't wait to see your latest collection."

With a brief nod to Cash, Daniel Pearson took Margo's arm and led her away down the sidewalk.

"I believe she's what they call a cougar," Cash murmured.

Jordan glanced at him and didn't like it a bit that he was still looking at Margo. "Cougar?"

His eyes when they met hers were brimming with laughter. "Isn't that what they call the older woman who's on the hunt for a younger man?"

"Cougar." She had to admit the term suited Margo Lawson. She had a feline grace and beneath it, Jordan sensed, a streak of ruthlessness. Plus, the woman hadn't done anything to hide the fact that she was interested in Cash. Jordan couldn't help being annoyed that she was still feeling jealous.

"And you're familiar with the term because you've had a lot of experience being 'hunted' by older women?"

He laughed and settled back into his chair. "You can

relax. I can handle Margo Lawson. I'm more worried about how you're going to handle Daniel Pearson."

With a frown, Jordan sat down. "*You* can relax on that score. Daniel Pearson's interest in Maddie isn't personal. He wants the ranch. And she has his number."

"Exactly." Cash's voice and eyes had turned hard. "But he thinks he's close to getting it."

Jordan's temper flared. "If you think Maddie's agreed to sell it to him, you're wrong. I'm positive she doesn't want to sell the place."

"It isn't a matter of what she wants. It may come down to necessity. And he seems pretty confident that he can close the deal." Cash fisted a hand on the table. "She's running fewer cattle, she's let all her hands go except for Mac McAuliffe. He hires on workers on a per diem basis when he needs them. I've been helping her out as much as I can. But your sister's proud. I don't know how much longer she'll continue to accept help from me. I *know* Maddie. She could very well let Pearson talk her into selling the ranch to make it easier on me."

Though she hadn't known her sister very long, Jordan found herself leaning toward his theory. "Not yet, she won't. Not for the next three weeks. Do you think that your prejudice against Daniel Pearson might be why you think he's behind the vandalism?"

Cash considered for a moment. "No. I believe he's a prime suspect. He knows she's in trouble, and a little vandalism here, a poisoned horse there, might be all it takes to have her signing on the dotted line."

Jordan thought for a minute. "If things are getting worse for Maddie, wouldn't he think it's just a matter of time before she agrees to let him sell the ranch? The look on his face when I said you'd be coming with me to dinner told me he had very high expectations for tomorrow night.

He thinks his plans are right on track. It doesn't mesh with hiring someone to kill her. Plus, he didn't look at all surprised to see me here."

"Perhaps it's Pearson's buyer who's getting desperate," Cash said. "He or she could be acting on their own."

"Why?" The question hung in the air between them for a few beats. Jordan tapped her fingers on the table. "Maddie's having trouble making ends meet, so why is someone so anxious to get their hands on the ranch?"

"Perhaps Shay's theory is correct and the attempt on your life is somehow connected to your mother's will?"

"Maybe. Could be I'm prejudiced against that idea because it would mean that someone in my family could be involved. And I just don't see it. Maybe I don't want to see it. In any case, I'm more anxious than ever to take that tour of the ranch you promised me."

Cash's brows shot up. "You think you'll find the answer there?"

"Maybe. Maddie's an artist. She's like my mother. I'm a business person. I see things from a very different angle. I wonder if my father were here—if he'd known what was going on—if he'd know what to do."

His smile was slow and easy. "I know one thing for sure. Mike Farrell would have liked you, Jordan Ware." Then he took her hand and drew her to her feet. "Why don't we go turn that expert businessperson's eye on Maddie's booth?"

CHAOS. That's what Jordan saw when she stepped into the hotel's cavernous exhibition room. Her first impression was that a huge movie set was being constructed. Saws buzzed and screeched through plywood. Carts rattled as they carried display cases, tables and chairs across the space. The smell of paint and woods chips mingled with the scent of flowers that were being placed around pillars and doorways.

Beside her, Cash was taking in the room as carefully as she was. She bet his mind was on the bodyguard thing. But right now, she had to concentrate on her job, which was to represent Maddie as well as she could.

From what she could make out, booths would eventually line the walls and run in several rows down the center of the room. That coincided with what she was used to. Thank heavens she'd had some experience with jewelry shows. Her mother had occasionally showcased her designs at the Jacob Javits Center in New York.

"My mother always hated these shows," she said.

"Maddie doesn't care for them much, either. She doesn't like the sales end of the business."

"It's an essential part. Without it, the pieces run the risk of spending their lives in display cases. My mother's jewelry is meant to be worn. Maddie's is, too. I'm coming to believe that two of them are a lot alike. It's such a shame that they never got to know each other."

For a moment Jordan felt a mix of emotions swamp her—regret, anger, frustration. Once again, her mind turned to the question of why her parents had cut themselves off from one of their daughters.

"It is a shame." Cash reached for her hand and gave it a squeeze. "You should have had the chance to know your father, too. At least, you'll get to know him a little better once you settle in at the ranch."

Jordan pushed the flood of feelings away. These were things she'd think about later, deal with later. It helped that Cash was there, and that he held her hand.

Turning, she studied him for a moment, absorbing once more the strong, lean face that her hands had explored so thoroughly before she'd even seen him. And she remembered the pleasure that came from merely touching him. Not just his face, but that long, hard body.

As if he sensed the direction her thoughts had taken, he turned to her, and the heat in his eyes had her breath stopping in her throat. Suddenly, they might have been alone in the room. Workmen stepped around them, voices chattered, saws buzzed, but to Jordan, the sounds came from a distance. All she could think, all she knew was that she wanted Cash to kiss her. All she felt was a pull that came not just from him, but from something edgy and needy inside of her.

All she had to do was move just a little closer and his mouth would cover hers. She would feel again that sharp, dazzling pleasure she'd felt when he'd kissed her on the side of the road. She took the step.

"If I kiss you, I might not be able to stop." His voice was low and rough. "Do you want me to see if I can get us a room?"

For a moment, Jordan was outrageously tempted. To spend the rest of the afternoon in a hotel room with Cash. To think only about the pleasure that they could bring one another. It would be wild and wonderful.

And completely impossible. Her sister was depending on her. "I can't."

Cash squeezed her hand and then released it. "Later, then. That's a promise, Jordan."

Her hand trembled as she took a catalog from a box. But scanning through it helped her gather her thoughts. "I want to see where they've put Maddie."

The catalog listed the names and photos of exhibitors, along with a booth number. And in another moment or so, she'd be able to focus on them. The pictures would help tomorrow, she thought. She was banking on the fact that buyers would introduce themselves to her or hand her a card. But over the years, Maddie had become acquainted with other designers, and the last thing Jordan wanted to do was snub them. Of course, Maddie had named and described them, but having a picture—well, it truly was worth a thousand words. Noting Maddie's booth number, she located it on the floor map of the exhibition hall and led the way.

"It's a good spot," she said when they reached it, pleased that her legs were working and her thoughts almost refocused. "Most people will take at least one complete tour of the room, but sometimes they skip the rows that run in the center."

She watched as the workmen—one white-haired with a grizzled beard and a muscular build, the other just barely out of his teens, unloaded a stainless-steel-and-glass case. She could see from a glance at adjacent spaces that each exhibitor was getting one. When the display case was centered in the space, she approached the older man and extended her hand.

"Hi, I'm Maddie Farrell. This will be my booth tomorrow. I'm supposed to be getting two display cases."

The white-haired man immediately frowned. "Not according to what I got here." He pulled a clipboard off his cart, flipped over a few pages, then angled it so she could see. "Booth one-twelve—one case."

As Jordan sighed and turned to Cash, she met his eyes and hoped that he would follow her lead. "It's Aunt Amy again. She assured me she'd arranged for the extra case. I asked her several times. I'm afraid she's getting more and more forgetful…"

Cash placed his hand on her shoulder. "You're going to have to think about letting her go."

"I'm not sure that I can. I'm the only family she has left, and she's worked all her life. I can't imagine her sitting home and taking up knitting." Then with an apologetic smile, she turned back to the man with the clipboard. "My aunt—who is my secretary—said she'd talked to the man in charge of the exhibits and arranged for me to have a second case. Is there any chance that you could hunt me up one? I know you're busy."

"Busy doesn't even begin to describe it, lady." But his frown was fading. "How old is your aunt?"

"Nearly eighty."

He studied her for a moment, then nodded. "You keep her on. My grandson and I will hunt you up a second case if we can."

Jordan beamed a smile at him. "Thank you so much."

"Nice job," Cash said in an undertone as the two men wheeled their cart away.

"Thanks for picking up on what I was trying to do."

"My pleasure."

She was about to turn back to the case when she spotted a pretty young woman in tribal Navajo dress hurrying toward her. Even as her mind raced, her stomach knotted.

"It's Lea Dashee," Cash murmured in a low tone.

Right. Lea Dashee had gone to college with Maddie. She was slender, with long black hair, and the white dress she wore, with its silver beading, looked stunning on her. Silver jewelry design had been a tradition with the women in Lea's family for hundreds of years.

"She's Pete Blackthorn's granddaughter. He's the turquoise prospector I told you about. She may know how we can contact him."

As Lea reached them, Jordan smiled. "Hello."

The young woman threw her arms around Jordan and gave her a hard hug. "So good to see you. It's a shame that we only get to see each other a couple of times a year at one of these things."

"Don't we say that all the time?"

"We do." Lea laughed. "But then we go back and bury ourselves in our studios." She drew back and gave Jordan a swift study. "Beautiful as always."

"Ditto."

Lea laughed again. "We always say that, too. And tomorrow we'll oooh and aaah over each other's designs." She took one of Jordan's hands and squeezed it. "You bring your appointment calendar with you. We're going to make a definite date. Have lunch and hit some galleries. I'm going to watch you write it in."

"It's a deal." Jordan made a mental note to hunt up an appointment calendar. It wouldn't do for her to use her BlackBerry.

Lea turned her attention to Cash. "Don't tell me you've suddenly developed an interest in jewelry?"

Cash tilted his head in Maddie's direction. "She dragged me here in case she needed some hauling and lifting."

"Good idea! I may ask a favor if you're coming back tomorrow?"

Cash nodded. "Sure thing. But I need a favor right now. Maddie's trying to get in touch with your grandfather. Do you know where we might find him?"

Lea thought for a minute. "He hasn't been back to his trailer for a few days. Usually when he camps out, it's in the hills to the southeast of Maddie's ranch." She glanced back at Jordan. "I'll bet if you take a ride out, you'll run into him there."

"Thanks," Jordan said.

Lea waved a hand as she hurried away. "Tomorrow."

Jordan turned to Cash. "I don't know what I'd do without you."

"My pleasure." And it was, Cash thought. His pleasure deepened as he watched her move closer to examine the beveled glass case in great detail. She was totally focused now, just as she had been at the small café when she'd been poring over Maddie's notes.

"If they get me that second case, we'll angle them into

a V." Then she circled to the back of the booth and studied the wall. It had been painted a sunny yellow.

"Not bad. The color should work with the turquoise. And I packed some swatches of silk in nearly the same color."

As she turned back to the display case, the wall behind her suddenly began to tilt forward. Moving on instinct, Cash shoved Jordan aside and braced both his palms against it.

For several seconds he struggled unsuccessfully against the downward momentum of the wall. He heard an ominous creak as the base slid an inch backward and the pressure against his arms built.

"Cash?"

"Stay away." Sweat beaded on his forehead. Fear arrowed through him. He wasn't going to win this battle.

8

TWO SETS OF HANDS suddenly joined Cash's on the wall of the booth. Working as a team, he and the two men who'd come to his aid managed to get it back into position. The moment it was upright and balanced, Cash turned to one of the workmen. "Thanks. What the hell happened?"

One of the men had already moved behind the wall and dropped to his knees. Cash joined him.

"Looks like someone didn't fasten the braces tight enough. Pretty careless. These things can do quite a bit of damage if they fall."

"Thanks." Cash noted that there was plenty of room for someone to fit behind the booth. Plus there was an exit doorway right behind the wall. He shoved through it, but the hallway was empty.

"There. That should hold it," said the man.

"Thanks." Cash stepped around the now secured wall and moved to Jordan's side. Pitching his voice low, he said, "Someone may have purposely unloosened the braces and then slipped out of the room."

Or perhaps they'd edged their way behind several of the other booths and joined the throng of people in the exhibition hall. He scanned the room. Everyone was busy. Carts were moving, workmen were hoisting walls. Hammers pounded, saws whirred. No one seemed out of place. Not one person glanced guiltily in their direction. And no one was making a beeline for the door. Frustration raged inside of him. He wanted badly to get his hands on someone.

"You think someone wanted that wall to fall on purpose?" Jordan asked.

She had turned to study it. He followed the direction of her gaze, and in his mind he pictured just how the wall might have fallen, trapping her against the display case on the floor. The glass would have shattered, and she could have been badly hurt. "I'm not willing to completely trust coincidence."

"But who would have known we're here?"

"Good question." And he didn't like the answers. "Pearson and your friend Margo knew we were headed for the exhibition room."

"But if something happens to me, Daniel won't get to list the ranch. He seemed very focused on talking me into that tomorrow night at dinner."

"Perhaps he only wanted to injure you, make you vulnerable to his offer." Cash ran a hand through his hair even as his gaze raked the room again. "Or maybe I'm getting paranoid." He met her eyes. "Do you have everything you need for now?"

"Yes."

"C'mon." Cash urged her toward the door. He wanted to get her someplace safe.

Jordan's cell rang the moment they stepped out of the exhibition room. Even as she pulled it out of her pocket, Cash nudged her against a wall between two potted plants. From their position, he could keep his eye on the lobby and the main door to the exhibition room.

"Maddie? What is it?"

Cash heard the fear in Jordan's voice. Neither had

expected Maddie to call again. It couldn't be good news. Moving closer, he leaned down, and Jordan tipped her cell so he could hear.

JORDAN SAT in the pickup next to Cash as they drove back to the ranch. Her head was still spinning from the news that Maddie and Jase had given them.

A professional hit woman had tried to shoot Maddie in Central Park.

Just thinking about it had fear tightening in her stomach. She'd nearly lost her sister.

When Cash had reported what they'd learned to Shay Alvarez and related what had happened at the exhibition hall, the detective suggested that they return to the ranch and provided them with a police escort home. The two men in the cruiser following them would stay, keep the ranch under surveillance and escort them back into Santa Fe for the jewelry show in the morning.

As they started up the hill where they'd nearly been driven off, Cash said, "You're too quiet. You have to be worried about Maddie. Talk to me."

She turned to study him. In profile, he looked tough and rugged. And he was. But he also had a streak of kindness that ran bone-deep.

"I can't seem to get my mind around it." She swallowed hard. "Someone tried to shoot my sister."

He flicked her a glance. "Someone tried to kill you, too, Jordan."

"I know. It's hard enough to accept that, but when I think of Maddie being in the sights of a professional sniper…I might never have gotten a chance to know her. And what if it happens again? What if the next shot hits its target?"

Now that she'd started talking, Jordan couldn't seem to

stop. "That's why I didn't tell her about the man trying to drive us off the road. I didn't want her to feel helpless and angry. More than anything, I want to go to her. I want us both to go to New York and help protect her. But because of the will, we can't. And we don't have a clue about who's behind all of this."

She could hear the rising hysteria in her voice, so she clamped her mouth shut.

"I think you were right not to tell her. Jase and she need to focus all their energy on figuring out who's trying to kill her. But it may be the same person who's trying to kill you."

Jordan stared at him. "You think?"

"Two professionals hired to take out two sisters on the same day?" Cash's tone was dry. "It's hard to think there isn't a connection."

He was right. She knew that. But she just hadn't wanted to think about it. A wave of disgust moved through her. "I'm being a coward."

Cash snorted. "A coward? You wouldn't know how to be one."

"Ever since the phone call, I've been wallowing in fear and self-pity. I don't do that. I deal with things."

He glanced at her again. "You don't have to deal with this alone, Jordan. And Maddie doesn't, either. Your friend Jase owns a security firm. He's got men he can call on for backup. And according to Maddie, he was the one who saved her life in Central Park."

His voice was as calm, as if he were trying to settle a skittish horse, but Jordan could see the tension in his jaw. When he reached over to cover her hand with his, she felt it in the tightness of his grip.

"You're worried that you don't have enough backup to protect me."

"Yeah. I'm worried. I'll feel better when Jase's brother, D.C., gets here," he said.

That was the one thing that Jase had insisted on—sending his brother to Santa Fe—and Cash hadn't objected.

"Have you ever met him?"

"Yes, back in the days when Jase and I were in college. He's a year younger than Jase and he went into the army right after he graduated. I didn't even know he was in New York."

"What's he like?"

"Jase used to tell me stories about the trouble they'd gotten into as kids. He claimed that D.C. was the brains behind most of their escapades. Even in college, he had a reputation for being a bit on the wild side. But I imagine a couple of tours of duty in Iraq have settled him down."

"He's in the military police, right?"

"Yes."

Cash glanced at his watch. "He's going to call when he lands in Santa Fe, but I don't imagine that will be until late tonight or early tomorrow morning."

Jordan turned to study him. "You worry too much. I'm used to taking care of myself."

"I'm beginning to understand that. I'm wondering why."

She could have given him an evasive answer. But he was always so forthright with her. "My mother was always focused on her jewelry design business, so I grew up trying to take care of the practical stuff. When I discovered early on that I didn't have her creative flair for jewelry design, I went to business school. I figured I could make my contribution that way."

"Your contribution to what?"

"Her dream."

"What about your dreams? Do you ever do anything just for Jordan?"

"Of course."

But when he said nothing more, she started to think. She'd done things for herself. She'd wanted to get her business degree. For as long as she could remember, she'd wanted to make a contribution to Eva Ware Designs. But had she ever done anything *only* for herself? Once more she turned to study Cash. Immediately, she felt the tingle of awareness, the heat of anticipation that he could ignite in her by simply being there. She wanted to touch him. And more.

"In your whole life, what have you done exclusively for yourself?" he asked.

"You. You're what I'm doing for me." She hadn't expected him—wasn't sure she was even ready for him. But if she hadn't ended up with him in Maddie's bed…if she'd had to go through life not knowing him, not knowing what they could bring to each other…she didn't even want to think about that.

"I have to confess I don't understand what's happening between us, but I'm sitting here right now wondering what would happen if I touched you."

He shot her a slow smile. "If that police cruiser weren't right on our tail, I could come up with a few ideas of exactly what we could do if you touched me. Have you ever made love in the back of a pickup?"

"No." But she was already starting to imagine what it might be like.

"We'll have to put it on our to-do list. Once we get back to the ranch, what do you have to do to get ready for the show tomorrow?"

"I want to take Maddie's jewelry out of the safe and experiment with some ways to display it. Then I'll review her notes again on the various buyers who might drop by.

There are also a couple of designers she's friends with besides Lea. Luckily I can look them up in the catalog and match names with photos."

He shot her a smile. "Sounds like a pretty full agenda. Before you dig in, why don't we take the horses out for a ride?"

The idea delighted her. "You mean it?"

"I don't say things I don't mean. I think we both need a break. It should be safe enough. It would be pretty tough for anyone to follow us—unless they were on horseback, too."

A careful man, she thought. And something inside of her warmed. She really wasn't used to someone looking out for her. Of course, Jase cared about her, but she'd never thought of him as her…what? Protector?

"We'll ride in the direction of the hills east of the ranch. There's a canyon there I want to show you. And it has the added attraction of being a place where Pete Blackthorn does a lot of his prospecting."

"Two birds with one stone?"

He shot her a grin. "Busted."

It occurred to her that the more she got to know Cash, the more she liked him. And she had a strong hunch that it was going to complicate their relationship. Big-time. He might not like to predict endings, but she did. So she couldn't let herself forget that whatever they discovered together would end in three weeks. But maybe they could enjoy each other and part as friends.

Something tightened around her heart. Perhaps if her parents had foreseen the inevitable ending, they wouldn't have been forced into difficult decisions.

AIR AS DRY as the land beneath them whipped past as they rode toward the hills jutting upward behind the ranch.

Once they'd exited the corral, they'd let the horses set the pace. Cash had chosen Lucifer, a black stallion he'd said had belonged to her father, and she was on Maddie's Brutus. Both horses were eager for a fast run, and they galloped side by side.

The only sound to mar the silence was the pounding of hooves. The hat she'd worn to shield her from the sun lay forgotten on the back of her neck as Jordan let her body familiarize itself with the movements of the horse beneath her. Gradually, her mind emptied.

Riding was something she loved. It had become an integral part of her life. Sports had never been her thing, and though her mother loved working out in a gym, Jordan just didn't see the point.

She'd made it a habit to get away at least twice a month to ride Julius Caesar, the horse she kept just north of the city. For her, the time she spent riding was better than going to a spa. It cleared her mind, toned her body and often provided her with a fresh perspective on some challenge she faced at work.

She spotted the fence coming up in the distance.

"You game?" Cash asked.

"You bet." She bent low over Brutus, using the stirrups to raise herself slightly as the horses sailed over in unison. She laughed and urged him on.

Usually, riding emptied her mind. But Cash kept sneaking in. Earlier, when they'd gotten back to the ranch, they'd showered separately as they had in the morning. Jordan had thought about joining Cash in the other bathroom, but her practical side had won out. If they indulged in shower games, they wouldn't have as much time for their ride. And after all, they'd have to shower again when they returned to the ranch…

While she'd selected clothes from Maddie's closet, she'd

heard Cash puttering in the kitchen. When she'd joined him, she found he'd filled canteens with water and packed them an early dinner in a saddlebag. The man thought ahead.

That's what she should be doing, too—thinking of Maddie's jewelry and playing some arrangements through her mind. But with the wind in her hair and the breathtaking scenery around her, she simply couldn't. Giving in to the moment, she simply let herself enjoy.

A short time later, they reached the spiky patches of grass at the foot of the hills and reined to a stop.

"Thank you," she said. "I needed that."

"Me, too. If you turn, you can get a different view of the ranch," Cash added.

Jordan glanced over her shoulder, then urged her horse around. The sun was lowering in the sky in front of those huge picture windows, and the back of the buildings were throwing off shadows. From this distance, the ranch, the stable, the bunkhouse and the white fences of the corrals all looked like a child's play set.

A memory flickered at the edge of her mind, and this time it pushed through. What she saw in front of her reminded her again of that toy ranch set that Santa had brought her all those years ago. Shifting the reins to one hand, she pressed fingers against her temple.

"What is it?" Cash asked.

"I had a toy ranch when I was small. There were buildings, fences that pulled apart, horses and cattle. I used to spend hours moving everything into different configurations. I thought about it earlier, but it didn't click."

She turned to him. "Maybe that's why I feel—I have felt from the moment I arrived—that I've come home. I thought maybe it was because I had some memory of this place. But that's ridiculous."

"Why? You have proof based on your birth certificates

that you and Maddie were both born here. This probably *was* your first home."

"But I was so little. How could I possibly remember?"

"Children remember love. I can tell you one thing. Your father—Mike Farrell—loved you. I saw the way he was with Maddie. He adored her. He taught her to ride. And when she showed an interest in jewelry design, he converted that building into a studio for her."

"He converted it? I assumed he built it for Maddie as a studio."

"No, it's been there as long as I can remember. When she was younger, it was her playhouse." He winced. "One time she asked me to come in and play with her dolls."

Jordan grinned. "Did you?"

"*Dolls?* Not on your life. I saved myself by persuading her to enjoy more manly things. I taught her how to rope a cow. Play poker. I'm probably personally responsible for turning her into a tomboy. Before she went to college, I even taught her some karate moves."

"Karate moves?"

"Just some basic stuff. They offered some classes in our high school, and Shay and I signed up for them. Maddie wanted to be able to defend herself. She's pretty good."

"Yes, she is." Jordan remembered the way Maddie had handled Adam right after the reading of the will. "I think I'm just beginning to know my sister." And that reminded her that she'd very nearly lost her sister.

Cash took her chin in his hand and turned her face toward his. "We're not going to think about Maddie's near miss right now. We're on a break, remember?"

"Okay."

"What you should know is that your sister was one of the most important things in Mike's life. He couldn't possibly have felt differently about a second daughter."

Jordan thought of the framed photo she'd discovered of Maddie sitting on Brutus and her father standing next to her. The love had been palpable.

"Then why…?"

"Why did they separate you? You may never find the answer to that."

"I know. I know."

"C'mon, I have something else to show you."

They eased the horses into a walk. Ahead of them, she saw a sharp break in the hills, and Cash turned into it. To her surprise, they were suddenly in a narrow canyon with the sheer sides of a cliff rising on either side. The ground beneath the horses' hooves was rough and rutted, and the trail twisted and turned through the mountain.

When a fork appeared, Cash led the way to the right. Before long, the trail opened into a small clearing. At one end, surrounded by tumbled rocks was a pond. The horses, sensing water, moved quickly toward it. As he dismounted and took the reins of both animals, Cash kept his eyes on Jordan's face. She knew how to guard her feelings when the occasion demanded. He'd seen her mask fear on that wild ride down the mountain. And she'd done a good job of hiding her nerves when she'd met Daniel Pearson and Margo Lawson.

But she wasn't doing that now. He saw surprise, wonder and pleasure race across her features. And he decided he'd made the right choice.

"It's like an oasis," she said.

"Your sister and your father called it paradise."

When she'd dismounted, he led the two horses closer to the edge of the water and let them drink. Thanks to the height of the cliffs surrounding them, the pond was half in shadow, and a cool breeze moved across the water.

Her eyes shifted to the cliffs, and there were still traces of awe on her face. "How?"

"Some kind of underground spring feeds it. Water is rare in these parts, so Mike Farrell kept this a well-guarded secret."

She glanced at him. "But he shared it with your family?"

"*After* I discovered it. The canyon is a shortcut between the two ranches. When I told him about it, Mike swore me to secrecy. He came from a long line of ranchers and he was very protective of his land. He didn't want to do anything to encourage tourists trespassing or to exploit the land that he'd inherited in a commercial way. He wanted very much to pass on his heritage the way it was handed down to him. My father was a lot like him. They were 'green' before they even invented the name for it."

"Then it's very important that Maddie hang on to the ranch—so that she can pass it down."

"Yes."

"If she's losing money, then I need to come up with a business plan that will allow her to start making some profit. Three weeks from now, if everything goes well, she'll have the money from my mother's will to invest. Of course, she'll sink some of it into her design business. But she'll also have enough to invest in the ranch. The problem will be not to throw good money after bad."

"What are you thinking of, Jordan?"

"You'll think I'm crazy. But it's one of the things I used to pretend when I was so fascinated playing with my ranch toy. I mean, what did I know about cattle ranching?"

"What did you pretend?"

"That I was operating a dude ranch. What else would a Yankee tenderfoot come up with? But why couldn't Maddie do both? She could protect her heritage, still keep it a running ranch, but open up a new business. She could add on to the bunkhouse or even build a new structure just beyond the stables to house guests. Offer comfortable accommodations, gourmet food, and give them a chance to get into the cowboy thing."

"Whoa. The cowboy thing?"

She waved a hand. "You'll have to help me with that. But I was thinking to start out very exclusive at first, offer guests the chance to really participate in ranch life, rounding up cattle, fixing fences. Just a ride through that canyon would be exciting. It's like a movie set."

Cash let her talk until she ran down. He led the horses over to a patch of grass and loosely fastened the reins to a tall shrub. Then he lifted off the saddlebag and the two canteens. When he walked back to her, she was still staring across the pond, seeing something that he didn't.

"I hate to rain on your parade, but how is Maddie going to run a dude ranch and still grow her design business?"

She turned to him. "Yes, that's the kicker, isn't it? Do you see anything wrong with the dude ranch idea besides that?"

"No. There are other dude ranches in the area, but you've got some unique ideas in terms of serving gourmet food and creating the 'cowboy' experience." Setting the saddlebag down, he took out two glasses and a bottle of wine. "I brought red because I figured white would be too warm."

She studied him for a moment. "You don't seem like the kind of man who'd be into wine."

"Your father got me interested in it. He has a good cellar."

She waited until he'd uncorked the bottle, handed her a glass and tipped wine into it. "You're not sounding very enthused about my idea."

"I'm thinking about it."

When he'd filled his own glass, she clicked hers against it before she sipped.

"Maddie has a lot on her plate right now, and she's very intent on her business. When she's in that studio, she loses track of everything. It's one of the reasons the ranch is suffering. When Mike was alive, he'd drag her out and insist she do other things. If I didn't come over and talk her into going riding or into a game of poker, I'm not sure she'd ever come out."

"Wow." Jordan found a flat rock and sat down. "She sounds exactly like my mother. I insisted that she and I have lunch together every Wednesday, and then we'd go to a matinee or shopping or to a gallery. I always had it planned out very carefully. Otherwise, she never would have taken a break."

For a moment, she sat in silence. Cash moved to sit on a rock facing hers. She'd turned away to stare out over the water again, and he could tell her mind was still focused entirely on the idea of a dude ranch. She wasn't a lot different than her mother and sister once she got her teeth into a business idea.

It was time to distract her. She'd taken the hairpiece off when she'd showered, and the wind had given a good toss to her hair. He reached out and touched just the ends.

She immediately turned to him. "I appreciate it that you're worried about Maddie. But I'm going to figure out a way. That's what a good business plan is for. And I won't hurt my sister. You can trust me on that."

He took the hand that wasn't holding the wineglass and raised it to his lips. "I do."

"Good." He released her hand and leaned back enough to stretch out his legs and cross them. He wanted very badly to touch her again. But not yet.

"Thanks for bringing me here. It's a good thinking place."

"I didn't bring you here just so you could think, Jordan."

"You wanted to share the beauty of the place."

"Partly. But I had another reason, too."

"What?"

"I brought you here to seduce you."

Jordan felt her throat go dry as dust. She sipped her wine. "You don't have to. I just have to look at you to want you." It was the simple, somewhat terrifying truth.

"I was considering earlier where I might bring you. Someplace private and safe where we could take our time. We haven't taken a lot of time."

"No." He hadn't made a move. All he'd done was sit there and talk to her in that slow, quiet drawl. But his eyes held such heat, such promise, that some of her wine spilled over the side of the glass. When she set it down carefully on the ground, she saw that her hand was trembling.

Seduction, she thought. It might not be such a bad idea. Rising, she sent him a smile. Then she lifted her hat off and tossed it on the rock behind her. Keeping her gaze locked on his, she toed her boots off next. Her knowledge of strippers was limited to the musical *Gypsy,* and it had been years since her mother had taken her to see it on Broadway. But if her memory served her, they always started with peripherals—gloves, hats, shoes.

She watched him as she undid her belt buckle. He hadn't moved. He was still sitting on the rock, his long legs stretched out in front and crossed at the ankles. On the surface, he appeared relaxed. The way his fingers gripped the wineglass told her he wasn't. He might speak slowly and move slowly, but there was always that energy she sensed below the surface. He kept it on a tight leash, and she wondered just what she could do to release it.

She took the belt off slowly. Since the buckle was one

of Maddie's, she rolled the leather around it for protection before she set it on the ground.

Still smiling, she slipped her fingers beneath her T-shirt, pulled it off and tossed it behind her.

"What are you doing, Jordan?"

Her brows rose at that. "I'm just getting into this seduction thing. Don't you like it?"

His gaze dropped to the lacy bra that still covered her breasts.

"Yeah, I do like it. A lot. But my idea was to seduce *you*."

"You still can. Later." She pulled open the snap of her jeans. In the silence, the sound was erotic. The horses stirred. So did something deep inside of her. Cash set his glass down and didn't notice when it tipped over.

Power pumped through her followed by arousal as she slowly lowered her zipper. She wanted to go to him then and drag off his clothes. Instead, she hooked her thumbs in the waistband of her jeans and slid them slowly down over her hips. When they dropped to the ground, she stepped out of them and sent him another smile. "Okay. Your turn."

9

HIS TURN? She was standing there in the sunlight, dressed in nothing but two wisps of lace that had been designed to make a man beg. With his body burning and his head spinning, Cash knew exactly how he wanted to take his turn. All of the time she'd been slipping out of her clothes, he'd been weaving a fantasy in his mind.

Three strides and he could turn her around, bend her over that rock she'd been sitting on. It would take only seconds to get rid of the barriers between them—his jeans and that froth of lace she was wearing. And he could be inside of her. Cash felt his mind spin, his thoughts blur. The pounding ride would be wild, wonderful—and it would relieve the aching desire she'd ignited inside of him.

Cash reined in his thoughts. It wasn't his plan to take her against a rock. Plus, he wasn't at all sure that if he stood up, his legs would support him.

But two could play at the game she'd just started. He'd never stripped for a woman before. But he knew how to take off his clothes. Focusing his attention on the job at hand, he took off his boots. Still seated, he met her eyes and smiled.

"More," she said.

"You got it."

His eyes never left hers as he pulled his shirt out of his jeans and then began work on the buttons.

"I could help with that," she said.

"I can handle it. Besides, turnabout's fair play, don't you think?"

"I can only think about wanting you. Now."

It occurred to Cash that she had a better handle on this seduction thing than he had. But he was a quick learner. Once he'd tossed the shirt aside, he had no choice but to stand up and test his legs. They held. The jeans came next. He had to bend over to free his feet. When he straightened, she was smiling at him, one arm outstretched, her finger crooked. Oh yeah, she definitely had an advantage in the seduction game.

"I want you. Now."

"Ditto." He moved quickly then. But when he reached her, he didn't turn her and bend her over the rock as he'd fantasized doing. Instead, he swept her into his arms and covered her mouth with his.

Then holding her close, he turned and leaped into the pond.

When Jordan surfaced, she was still locked in Cash's arms. Her mouth was still fused with his. And the fire that the kiss had ignited in her body more than blocked out the coolness of the water. When he pulled away, she nearly cried out in protest.

"Breathe," he said.

"Okay." Since she could feel her lungs burn when she did, it was good advice. She met his eyes. "I didn't see that coming."

"It was a last-minute decision, one of several alternatives I had in mind. I wanted to slow things down a bit."

"And you thought a little dip would do the trick?" She shifted suddenly, snaking her arms and legs around him, then wiggling down his body until the hard length of him was pressed against her just where she wanted him. Holding tight, she moved up and down his penis. Fire shot through her again, and she was almost certain she saw steam rise from the surface of the pond. "What do you want now?"

"You know what I want." Gripping her buttocks, Cash lifted her up so that her legs were around his waist.

She struggled for position, but his hands allowed no movement.

"You have some very dangerous moves." His voice was raw.

"My pleasure."

To her surprise, he chuckled and then rested his head for a moment against her forehead. "How about a truce? I want to take my time with you, Jordan. We've been on a real fast track—no detours. Let me try this my way."

She drew back, looked into his eyes. And she would have agreed to anything he wanted. "Okay."

He touched his mouth to hers, and though his impulse was to devour, he didn't. Instead, he used his tongue to trace the outline of her lips. Then he toyed with them—nibbling at the corners, nipping on her bottom lip.

Slipping his hands into her hair, he held her in place as he kissed her, slowly, thoroughly. There were flavors here he'd never lingered over. First he feasted on the initial tartness, then that incredible sweetness. It reminded him of the homemade lemonade his mother had fixed for him when he was a child. Addictive. He'd never been able to stop drinking it until the glass had been drained.

When he felt her body go lax and her legs slipped away from his waist, a simmering heat shot straight to his center. But he banked it down as he took his mouth on a lazy journey over her face, reacquainting himself with every angle and curve. Her breath caught and released, caught and released. Each time it did, his own pulse quickened.

Using his tongue, he traced her ear and whispered, "So far, what do you think?"

"I can't...I just...want..."

Cash drew back then and looked into her eyes. Confusion, need and arousal made an incredible aphrodisiac. But he didn't want to end it yet. When her head dropped back, he cupped it in one hand and began to explore her neck and shoulders. Even beneath the sheen of water, he could smell her scent, an exotic fragrance he suspected wasn't a perfume. It was subtle at her throat, stronger as he made his way to the valley between her breasts. She still wore the lacy bra, but through the sheer material he saw her nipple. When he closed his mouth over it and used teeth and tongue, she spoke his name in a strangled gasp.

There was so much heat, Jordan didn't think she could absorb any more. Any minute, she was going to turn into steam and vanish. But as he lifted her and took his mouth on a journey down to her stomach, she discovered she could. Her vision hazed. The world around her became dark. And oh, she could feel him. There was nothing but his mouth, his lips and the vivid sensations he was bringing her.

The water was cool on his skin, but she was so hot that his legs had begun to weaken again. His arms, too, he thought as he lowered her into the water. Time was running out. He shifted her, wrapping her legs around him once more.

"Jordan."

Her eyes opened and locked on his. They were still clouded with the pleasure he'd brought her.

"I'm going to take you now."

Her voice was thick when she spoke. "Let's take each other."

That simple sentence very nearly had his knees buckling. Gripping her hips, he slipped inside her. His heart nearly stopped when he felt her heat slip over him, surround him.

For a moment as her legs locked tightly around him, he swayed, stunned by the need that shot through him. If it hadn't been for the water, he would have raced hard to the finish. But he couldn't. Neither could she, though he could see she was trying.

Hampered by the water, the rhythm they created was slow, steady. As he looked into her eyes, he knew she was his. He was hers. And all the time, the pleasure built and built. When it was about to peak, he gripped her close against him and staggered with her to the edge of the pool. Kneeling, he settled her beneath him in the shallows and took her mouth with his.

Finally, they could both move the way they wanted to, had to. Faster and faster. His mouth was still pressed to hers when she tightened impossibly around him and cried out his name. His, he thought. He joined her in a shattering release.

AN HOUR LATER, Cash rode side by side with Jordan through the winding canyon. It was closing in on seven o'clock and he figured they had a couple of hours of daylight left. Still time enough to see if they could locate Pete. They'd lingered near the pond longer than they should have, but he'd been reluctant to leave. She'd been so carefree while they'd been there.

After they'd shared the sandwiches he'd packed, they'd taken a swim and then made love once more. But when they'd mounted up, Jordan had grown silent again. She was regrouping. And unless he was mistaken, she was building up a little wall of protection around herself.

From what little she'd said about her mother, he was coming to understand that Eva Ware had been totally focused on her work. He'd seen the same characteristic in

Maddie. But Maddie had grown up with a father who'd spent a lot of time with her. A father who'd enjoyed spending time with his daughter.

He was guessing that Jordan hadn't grown up with a parent like that. It had made her cautious. He figured with a little time, he could work his way around cautious. Problem was, all he had was a little time.

"Penny for your thoughts," he said.

She glanced at him. "We'll have to turn back soon, won't we?"

That hadn't been what she was thinking, but he let it pass. "I figure we can go another mile or so. If we don't locate Pete tonight, I'll send one of my men out tomorrow to make a thorough sweep of the canyon."

She nodded and turned her head to search the canyon walls. "There seem to be more caves in this section."

"Some of them are rumored to be old turquoise mines. That's why Pete frequents the place. Navajos were mining turquoise in New Mexico long before the Spaniards and the white man settled here."

When they turned the next corner of the canyon, they saw a horse, standing to one side.

Cash urged his own mount forward. "That's Pete's horse."

As they approached, the horse whinnied and pawed the ground. Cash scanned the cliffs. Without any direct sunlight, the walls on either side were deeply shadowed. It was Jordan who finally spotted something.

"Up there." She pointed a finger. "I see something red."

"Pete always wears a red neckerchief. It's his trademark." Cash dismounted and anchored his reins with a few rocks. "Stay with the horses. I'll climb up and see."

It took him only a few minutes to reach the ledge of rock where Pete lay. The old man was white as a sheet. His breathing was thready and ragged, but there was a steady pulse at his throat. Cash glanced behind him and called down to Jordan, "He's alive."

Then he glanced above. There was a ledge about fifty feet above him. From the looks of it, the old man had taken a fall.

He considered his options. He didn't know how badly Pete was hurt, and the cliff he'd just climbed up was tricky enough without carrying someone down on his shoulder.

He took out his cell. They were nearly at the point where the canyon passed onto Landry land. The satellite signal should be stronger here than it had been on the Farrell Ranch. He said a brief prayer and punched in a number.

It rang twice. On the third ring, Shay Alvarez picked up. Cash explained the situation. "I'm about a half mile from where the canyon empties onto Landry land. We don't have much daylight left."

"I'll have someone there as soon as I can. If you can build some kind of signal fire, it will help."

Turning, he yelled to Jordan. "Help is on the way."

"There's a blanket on the back of his horse," she called. "I'll bring it up."

It was while he was waiting for Jordan to join him that he noticed how battered and bloody Pete's hands were—as if someone had stomped on them. He glanced up at the face of the cliff above him. Not a fall, he thought.

When Jordan reached him, he showed her the damage to the old man's hands.

"It wasn't an accident," she said.

"Doesn't look like it." He tucked the blanket around Pete, then said, "Why don't you stay with him while I build a signal fire."

Saying nothing, she knelt and gently covered one of the man's battered hands with hers.

No panic. No questions. She was some woman, Cash thought as he climbed back down to the horses.

10

TWO HOURS LATER, Jordan paced in a waiting room. The medics had been fast and efficient, arriving on the scene in just over thirty minutes. Then she and Cash had had to ride the horses back to the ranch and drive into Santa Fe.

They were on the outskirts when her cell phone had rung. She'd thought it might be Maddie and wondered just how much she should tell her sister, but it had been Jase's brother D.C. His plane had landed. She'd filled him in on where they were headed and why, and he'd agreed to meet them at the hospital.

She wasn't alone in the room. Nearby, a woman sat patiently knitting, and there were groups scattered throughout the area, some engaged in hushed conversation, others silently drinking coffee. Occasionally a man or a woman in scrubs would enter the room and approach one of the groups.

In a corner, a TV offering a continuous and muted loop of news hung from a bracket. She glanced out the open archway to a nurse's station where she could see Cash attempting to charm information out of one of the aides.

Usually, pacing helped get her thoughts in order. But she was having trouble getting her mind around the series of events that had occurred since she'd first walked through the front door of her father's ranch.

Was the attack on Pete Blackthorn related to the vandalism that had been happening at the ranch? To the attacks on her? Or was it merely a coincidence that someone had shoved him off that cliff and then made sure that he couldn't climb up or down again?

She'd had time to study his hands before the helicopter had arrived to transport him. They were badly bruised, bloodied and swollen. One of them might have become that seriously injured in a fall, but not both.

Over and over again in her mind, she'd tried to figure out what might have happened. The ledge they'd found Pete on was about halfway up the cliffside. There was what looked to be a cave opening near the top. If he'd simply lost his balance, there were several ledges where he might have landed and gotten a handhold. Someone had made sure he'd fallen a second time.

He'd regained consciousness just as the medics were loading him into a stretcher. For just a second, she'd seen a light of recognition come into his eyes. And then he'd said her sister's name, the sound thready and faint. "Maddie?"

Moving to one of the windows, she stared out at the night. He was going to be all right. He had to be all right.

She nearly jumped when Cash put a hand on her shoulder. When she turned to face him, she saw that Shay Alvarez had joined him.

"Any news?" Jordan asked.

"They've stabilized Pete," Cash said. "But according to the nurse, he's still in line waiting for an MRI. The hospital's a bit backed up because of a tractor-trailer accident, and there are a couple of people with more serious injuries ahead of him. Shay here is the one with news."

"My men found evidence at the scene that backs up your theory that Pete's fall wasn't an accident," Shay said. "There are a string of caves that run along that section of the canyon wall, and in one of them, they discovered cig-

arette butts. Since Pete doesn't smoke, we think someone
else was up there, perhaps waiting for him."

Jordan glanced at Cash, then back at Alvarez. "Why?"

"That's the question," Shay said. "Lea Dashee and her
mother are Pete's next of kin. When I contacted Lea to tell
her about Pete's fall, she told me that he'd mentioned
something to her about six months ago. He'd said he had
a feeling that someone was following him. No proof. No
solid evidence. A few minutes ago, she called me back.
She'd stopped by his trailer on her way here to pick up
some things for him. The place had been trashed."

"Six months ago is just about the time that the vandalism started on Maddie's ranch," Cash said.

Shay nodded.

"There's a connection," Jordan insisted.

"Maybe. Maybe not," Shay said.

"Why? Why would someone do that to Pete?" Jordan
pressed her fingers to her temples. She was beginning to
feel like a parrot that only knew one word.

"Not for the turquoise he's been collecting," Shay said.
"He had several packets of them in his saddlebags. Whoever helped him off that cliff didn't rob him. The only
other possibility that occurs to me is the belief around here
that he has old maps of the turquoise mines that his ancestors once worked. Someone may have gotten the idea they
were valuable. That may have been why he was being followed. If indeed he was."

"Is there any way to figure out if the thief found any old
maps?" Jordan asked.

Shay smiled. "If I know Pete, they didn't find any. I
doubt he'd keep anything that valuable in his trailer, not
when he spent so much time away from it, or in his saddlebags. And if he felt he was being followed, he was
forewarned."

Over Shay's shoulder, Jordan saw a tall man using a cane step through the waiting room door. "D.C.," she said as she hurried forward, her arms outstretched.

"YOUR COMPETITION?" Shay asked.

Cash studied the tall man in the doorway. "D. C. Campbell, her roommate Jase's brother."

There was nothing in the friendly hug Jordan and D.C. exchanged that even hinted at a more passionate or intimate relationship. So why the hell did he have this coppery, bitter taste in his mouth? "He's on leave from Iraq where he's been serving as an MP, and he's flown out here at his brother's request to provide backup."

"Good idea."

Cash continued to watch as Jordan tucked her arm into D.C.'s and led him over. The cane and the slight limp didn't seem to bother D.C. much.

"Your leg," she said. "How bad is it?"

D.C. smiled at her. "Just a little collateral damage. The army sent me home for a few months to get it rebuilt." He tapped his thigh with one hand. "They replaced a lot of parts. I'm hoping some of them turn out to be bionic."

Jordan laughed. "Stop. I just got a mental image of you leaping over a tall building in a single bound."

"That's what I'm hoping," D.C. said.

Old friends, Cash thought, and something inside of him eased.

After Jordan made the introductions and they shook hands, Cash asked, "How are Jase and Maddie?"

D.C.'s eyes immediately sobered. "I checked in with Jase when I landed, and they were tucked up all safe and sound in a hotel. But there's been a development since I left New York. Earlier this evening, there was a second attempt on Maddie's life. Someone tried to run her down just outside her mother's apartment."

"That's where my mother was killed," Jordan said.

"Yes. The car—a cream-colored sedan—fits the description witnesses gave of the car that struck down Eva Ware. But this time they got a partial plate, and a taxi driver is sure it was a Mercedes."

Jordan stared at him. "That description could fit my mother's car."

"Yes. Jase has a friend at the NYPD who's working to track the car down even as we speak."

"But—" Jordan broke off when there was movement in the doorway and Lea Dashee and an older woman stepped into the room, and Jordan and Shay moved toward them.

"Pete Blackthorn's next of kin," Cash explained to D.C.

"He's the reason Jordan told me to meet you here, right? He's the old man who took a bad fall off a cliff."

"We're sure he was pushed."

"Ah." D.C. pulled a notebook and pen out of his pocket. Then he shot Cash an apologetic glance. "Sorry, old habit."

"No problem. Did Jordan fill you in on the fact that she's masquerading as Maddie while she's here?"

"No." He glanced at Cash. "That could put her in even more danger."

"She felt it was the best way to help her sister out at the big jewelry show tomorrow."

"It may also be helpful in our getting a handle on who's behind all this."

"You think the attacks on Maddie and Jordan are connected."

"Hard not to, but we'll see."

While Cash watched Jordan settle the two women on a couch, he filled D.C. in on what they knew about Pete

Blackthorn and his fall. After pouring coffee and serving the three women, Shay rejoined them.

"Let me see if I got everything," D.C. said. "Pete's been successfully prospecting the land around here as long as anyone can remember, and he reputedly has old maps of the mines his ancestors worked. Starting six months ago, he gets a 'sense' now and then that he's being followed. And today, you suspect someone was waiting for him in one of the caves and pushed him off the cliff."

"That's a good summary," Cash said.

Beyond D.C.'s shoulder, Cash watched Jordan take Lea's hands in hers. He wasn't at all sure how she was managing to hold up through everything. In one day, she'd learned her mother had been murdered, and then her sister's and her own life had each been threatened twice. And right now, her entire focus was on offering some comfort to Maddie's friend, Lea. He was beginning to understand that she'd had a lot of practice coping and taking care of others. Had anyone ever taken care of her?

He turned back to D.C. "Something else you need to know. It was six months ago that the incidents of vandalism began on Maddie's ranch. And six months since Daniel Pearson, our local wannabe real estate mogul, approached Maddie to list the ranch with him. Since then, the seriousness of the vandalism on the ranch has escalated. And this morning someone—we think a pro—tried to run Jordan and me off the road and over a drop-off. Later, there was an incident at the hotel's exhibition hall. The wall of a booth nearly fell on Jordan."

D.C. gave a low whistle as he met the eyes of Alvarez and then Cash. "You didn't mention either of those incidents to Jase."

"No," Cash said as Jordan rejoined them. "We figured he and Maddie had enough on their plates."

For a moment, D.C. glanced down at his notes. "Let's see if I can connect all of the dots here. We've got a man who's made a successful living collecting stones—mostly turquoise—from various abandoned and supposedly tapped-out mines in the area. Someone may have been keeping an eye on him for the last six months, and today this person may have helped him off a cliff. In the same time frame, Maddie is being urged to sell her ranch and there are some incidents perhaps designed to pressure her into doing just that."

"You've got the picture," Cash said.

D.C. scratched his head. "I may be taking a leap here, but what if Pete has at some point discovered a new vein or batch or whatever it's called of turquoise? One that hasn't been tapped out, and what if it's on Farrell land?"

"Not such a big leap," Shay said. "I think we can all make it even without a bionic leg."

D.C. shot him a grin. "Agreed."

"We ran into Pearson today," Cash said. "He seems confident that he's going to close the deal with Maddie tomorrow night over dinner. So why the attack on Pete?"

"Because if Pete gets wind of the fact that Maddie is selling the ranch, he might blab about the existence of a find of turquoise," Shay put in.

"And if she knew about the mine, Maddie wouldn't feel so pressured to sell," Jordan said.

"She wouldn't have to sell—especially if the turquoise is of the quality that Pete has been selling her for years," Cash said.

"The problem is if Pete was attacked so that Maddie would remain under pressure to list the ranch and sell it, why try to kill her? That won't get her signature on the dotted line."

"Good point," Shay said.

"And don't forget that someone's trying to kill Maddie in Manhattan," D.C. put in. "It isn't just one twin who's being threatened."

Shay rocked back on his heels. "The attempts to kill Maddie and Jordan could be unrelated to the sale of the ranch. They could very well have been triggered by the will. It's an open invitation to murder."

"Jase would agree with you on that," D.C. said. "There's a real possibility that there are two things going on here. We were having a similar discussion in my brother's office earlier today. On the surface, there seem to be two things going on in New York, too. Jase and his partner are trying to find the connection between Eva's death and a robbery that occurred at her store about a month ago. And then there are the attempts on Maddie's life."

"And Jordan's. What if it's one big picture, and we just haven't found a way to connect your dots yet?" Cash countered.

A man in a white coat with a stethoscope stuffed in his pocket stepped into the room. "Detective Alvarez?"

Shay moved toward him and guided him to where Lea and her mother were sitting. Jordan hurried to take a seat beside Lea and take her hand.

"He's a strong old man," the doctor began. "The MRI is clear. The X-ray showed no broken bones other than the ones in the hands. He has a good-size bump on his head, but there's no sign of a concussion. We've medicated him for pain and we're treating him for shock and exposure."

"He was unconscious when we first found him," Jordan said.

The doctor nodded. "The medics who brought him in said he was halfway down a cliff. Since his hands were pretty useless, there's no telling how long he might have been lying there before you discovered him. With no way down to his horse, no way to get water, it's not surprising that he was drifting in and out of consciousness. He might have died on that cliff."

Lea Dashee wrapped her arm around her mother's shoulders, then turned to Jordan. "You and Cash saved his life."

Although Jordan had suspected that on some level, hearing the doctor confirm it had her throat drying. What if they hadn't just ridden out? Their original plan had been to tour the ranch on the day after the jewelry show. Pete might not have lasted that long.

"He'll be all right?" Lea asked.

"We think so. We've given him pain medication and a sedative. If his vital signs remain strong overnight, an orthopedic surgeon will operate on his hands tomorrow morning."

"Can I talk to him?" Shay asked.

The doctor looked at Shay. "He's going to be out for a while, and he needs his rest for tomorrow."

"How about if I stop by before he goes into surgery? We believe he had some help falling off that cliff."

The doctor considered, then nodded as he rose. "Just as long as you don't upset him."

As Shay walked the doctor out, Jordan put her arms around Lea. "You're staying?"

"My mother and I will both stay."

"What about the jewelry show?" Jordan asked. "Can I help out in any way?"

Lea managed a smile. "Oh, I'll be there. My mother will stay with Pete. You should go back to the ranch now. Get some rest. I know you're going to wow them tomorrow."

Cash took Jordan's free hand and drew her to her feet. Quite suddenly, she was exhausted. They were halfway to the door when Lea said, "Maddie."

It took her a beat, and Lea called out the name a second time before Jordan turned.

"Thank you for saving my grandfather's life," Lea said. Then Jordan let Cash draw her out of the room.

HOURS LATER, Cash stood at the window in Maddie's bedroom and watched Jordan sleep. She was curled on her side, her hand tucked under her chin. Moments before he'd been lying next to her. The urge to touch her and wake her so that they could make love again was so strong that he'd forced himself to slide out of bed.

She was exhausted—emotionally, physically. He suspected that it wasn't normal for her. She hadn't had much sleep since she'd arrived in Santa Fe, and he was partly responsible for that. She'd dropped off on the drive to the ranch and had only roused slightly when he'd carried her into the house.

"What?' she'd asked. Her eyes had been glazed.

"We're home," he'd said. "Go back to sleep."

After laying her on Maddie's bed, he'd returned to the kitchen to talk briefly with D.C. Jase's brother had been making himself a sandwich.

"I'd say make yourself at home, but I see you're already doing that," he'd said.

"I usually do," D.C. had replied around a mouthful of food. "They don't feed you on airplanes anymore. Probably just as well."

"When you're done, turn left in the hall. You can take the room at the end."

"You'll be with Jordan, I take it."

Cash hooked his thumbs in the front pockets of his jeans. "You have any objection to that?"

D.C.'s eyes had been steady on his. "Just don't hurt her."

"I'm going to do my best not to. You can pass on the same warning to your big brother with regard to Maddie."

Two beats had gone by before D.C. had given him a brief nod. "Fair enough." Then he took another bite of sandwich. "Got any beer?"

"There's another refrigerator in the pantry."

"Thanks. You can go along to bed if you want. I may be up for a while unwinding. Plane trips rev me up for some reason."

As D.C. turned and made his way to the pantry, Cash said, "I don't like playing a waiting game. I'd like to figure out a way to take a more proactive role in this."

D.C. had turned and grinned at him. "You're a man after my own heart. You think this Pearson's behind the vandalism?"

"I do. And he might very well have attacked Pete."

"There might be a way to get him to reveal himself…I'll sleep on it."

"Me, too."

Then he'd left D.C. to his foraging.

Jordan stirred and then settled again. Cash hadn't slept on it yet, but he'd given it some thought. All he'd come up with was to get Pearson alone and beat the truth out of him. It was hard to think of anyone or anything but Jordan when she was in the same bed with him.

Even now she pulled at his thoughts. The hand resting on her thigh appeared delicate—even more so than Maddie's. But it wasn't. He'd seen the way she'd handled Brutus and felt the strength of those slender fingers on his skin.

He let his gaze drift to her face—that so familiar face. It too looked delicate, fragile, sensitive. It was all of those. *She* was all of those. But beneath all that, she had a strength of purpose and a generous heart. He'd watched her with Pete and with his family. If Lea and her mother hadn't said they were going to stay the night with the old man, Jordan would have insisted on keeping him company.

He'd nearly lost her. The thought frightened him, infuriated him. The impulse filled him again—to take her away somewhere safe. To lift her onto his horse and ride off into the sunset with her, just as if they were characters in one of those Western movies she was so fond of.

But they weren't. And they couldn't run away from reality—not while she was being stalked by a killer.

Without looking, he could tell the sky was beginning to lighten behind him. And he sensed deep in his gut that time was going to run out on them. He thought of Maddie in New York. The attacks on both the twins had escalated. He didn't have to be a security expert or a police detective or even an army MP to know that their would-be killer was getting desperate. And while desperate people could make mistakes, they also could get lucky.

Jordan stirred again, and this time her eyes opened. He watched her run one hand over the space in the bed where he'd been. "Cash?"

"Right here." He moved to the side of the bed.

"I thought you'd gone."

"I'm not going anywhere." He slid in beside her.

Her arms curled around him as she settled her body against his. "Is it time to get up?"

"Not yet." He pulled her closer. "Go back to sleep."

"Aren't you going to seduce me?"

"You need the sleep."

She began to nibble on his lips. "What about you?"

Cash knew what he needed, what he wanted. But everything was happening so fast. He needed time to convince her it was what she wanted, too.

"I want you to love me," she murmured against his mouth.
"I do."

Cash's mind began to reel. The words had slipped out of him, and as his heart tumbled into freefall, he realized that they were true. He did love her. When had it happened? How?

Even as he tried to recall, his body was slowly being seduced. Her lips, softened by sleep, were busy on his, teasing, tormenting. There was something familiar about her touch as her fingers grazed over his skin. And something new about her taste. When had it turned so dark, so addictive?

She brushed her mouth over his eyes, his face, his throat. There were so many things he wanted to tell her. So many questions he wanted the answers to. But now wasn't the time. With her name on his lips, he let himself sink into the sensations.

Using her mouth and hands, she began to work her way down his body, nipping one place, caressing another. Ribbons of fire skipped and skimmed along his nerve endings. Her tongue toyed with his nipples, then moved slowly lower, leaving a trail of ice and searing heat in its wake.

Cash tried to reach for her, but his arms were suddenly heavy. When she finally took the hard length of him into her hands, he felt his bones melt. And as her mouth closed around him, pleasure shot to a peak that bordered on agony.

Helpless. He couldn't move, could barely think. No woman had ever made him helpless before. The feeling streamed through his blood, slithered up his spine and steamed his brain. His world had narrowed to Jordan and the slow, steady movement of her mouth on him.

She'd set out to seduce him, to lose herself in him one more time before they had to face the realities of the day. But every time his breath caught or his skin trembled, her own pleasure shot to new heights. Each time he shuddered or moaned her name, her needs grew stronger. Should she have known that in making a man weak she would become as seduced as he was?

When he closed his hands around her shoulders, she still

didn't want to relinquish control. Moving quickly, she straddled him, then raised her hips and lowered herself onto him. They locked fingers and eyes, but for a moment neither of them moved. It was as if by mutual consent, they wanted to stretch out the moment.

When she finally began to move, she did so slowly, fighting against the urge to quicken the pace. Each time she lowered herself, she felt more of him fill her—more and more until she wasn't sure where she left off and he began. More than anything, she wanted to spin out the time for both of them.

When the first rays of sunshine streamed through the window, Cash gripped her hips and with one last hard thrust shattered both of them.

"I'M STUFFED," Jordan said, pressing a hand to her stomach when Cash emptied a fresh skillet of scrambled eggs onto the platter in front of her.

"I'll take some of those off your hands." D.C. dumped half of the eggs onto his plate, then offered the rest to Cash.

Jordan shifted her gaze to Cash as the platter was emptied. "I'd think that D.C.'s possibly bionic leg might be hollow, but you're eating as much as he is."

"It's the cowboy life," Cash said. "We load up when we can. Besides, there's no telling when we'll get a chance to eat anything again today."

Jordan tapped the open catalog in front of her. "The hotel is offering a free buffet lunch to exhibitors and attendees."

"According to your sister, jewelry shows aren't exactly known for their hearty buffet lunches," Cash said.

Because she knew from experience he was right, Jordan made no further comment as the two men made their way through a huge amount of food. She might have eaten more than the one slice of bacon and half a piece of toast if the nerves in her stomach hadn't objected.

"You're going to do a fine job of representing Maddie," Cash said before taking a last swallow of his coffee. "You've been practicing how you're going to display her designs for over an hour. I can tell you she never spent that much time figuring out a display in her life."

The phone rang and Jordan jumped. "Who would be calling now?" It was only shortly after seven. "Maddie?"

Cash slid off his stool and went to the phone. "Yes?"

In the silence that followed he mouthed the word *Shay,* and Jordan's stomach settled a bit. Of course it would be Shay. He had planned to speak to Pete Blackthorn before he went into surgery. She had to get a grip.

"And you're not going to arrest him?"

There was another stretch of silence, and as it lengthened, Cash's frown deepened.

"How's Pete?" she asked as soon as Cash had hung up.

"He's lucid and strong enough that his surgery's been scheduled for nine a.m. Shay got ten minutes with him before they wheeled him off for tests."

"Who isn't Detective Alvarez going to arrest yet?" D.C. asked.

Cash poured more coffee into all the mugs. "Pete didn't recognize the man who pushed him. His attacker shoved him from behind. Luckily, the first fall was short, and Pete grabbed a handhold on a ledge. The man followed, and that's when Pete got a look at him. The description he gave Shay could be Daniel Pearson. According to Shay, it could be someone else. But the diamond on the pusher's pinky finger narrows it some."

"Pearson was wearing a diamond on that finger yesterday," Jordan said.

"Yeah. He asked Pete why someone might have attacked him, but Pete was evasive. Shay thinks Jordan would have a better chance getting him to open up. And by the time Pete gets out of surgery and recovery, Shay hopes to have a DNA report from the lab on those cigarette butts."

"He left cigarette butts behind and let himself be seen by the vic?" D.C. shook his head sadly.

"Shay doesn't want to arrest Pearson or even alert him until he has all his evidentiary ducks in a row."

"I can't fault him there," D.C. said with a shrug. "You do want him to pay."

"I'd like to get my hands on him," Cash said.

There was an angry edge in his tone that had Jordan staring at him. It wasn't often that Cash let his laid-back facade crack.

"Do you think this Pearson will be at the jewelry show?" D.C. asked.

"He said he would stop by," Jordan said. "Margo may drag him along with her."

D.C. smiled at Cash. "That will give us some time to get a little proactive and see what else we can learn before Alvarez arrests him."

Cash's eyes narrowed. "You have a plan?"

D.C. spread his hands palms down on the table. "I have an idea. My leg kept waking me up, so while I waited to fall back asleep, I started thinking. One of the things we want to know is if Daniel Pearson has a specific client who wants to buy Maddie's ranch. I'm betting he does."

Cash nodded his agreement.

"A client who had knowledge of the turquoise mine we speculate might exist," D.C. continued. "Otherwise, why would Pearson develop and execute this elaborate plan of escalating vandalism to pressure Maddie into listing the ranch? Especially a ranch that was already struggling to keep afloat."

"That makes sense," Jordan said. "And as far as we know, Pete is the only person who might be able to confirm the existence of such an untapped mine."

"Exactly. While we're waiting for that, my plan is to put some pressure on Pearson. I'm wondering what he would do if he learned he had some competition—someone else who wanted to buy the ranch."

"Who?" Jordan asked.

"None other than one of my buddies during my last tour in Iraq. Greg Majors. His father is rolling in oil money. He's back home now and is always looking for some kind of investment or other."

Cash's eyes narrowed. "And Greg is going to go along with this?"

"Nah," D.C. said. "We're just going to pretend he is. I'll impersonate him, walk up to Jordan's booth, turn on my Texas charm and give her an outrageous offer for the ranch. We just want to spook Pearson. I'm betting if he's threatened or if he thinks there might be a bidding war on the ranch, he'll call his client ASAP. Then we steal his cell and get the number."

There was silence in the room for several seconds.

"It sounds crazy, but it might work," Cash said. "Who's going to lift the cell?"

D.C. grinned. "I think I can handle it. The cane gives me the perfect excuse to stumble up against him."

Jordan looked from one man to the other. "You two are serious."

D.C. turned to her. "It will give us something to do besides sit on our hands while we wait for Shay to get his evidence in order."

"I have plenty to do representing Maddie's jewelry," Jordan said.

"And you can still do it," Cash said. "It shouldn't interfere with the show at all. We'll work around you."

She wasn't going to talk them out of it. She could see it in their eyes. They reminded her of two boys planning some mischief on the playground. Except this was for real. And there was a killer out there.

Cash reached over and took her hand. "We're going to need to know who Pearson's client is. He or she may be the missing dots that we need to complete picture. And until we get that picture, yours and Maddie's lives are still in danger."

"Okay," Jordan said. "But I have a suggestion, something I'd like to modify about your scenario."

"What?" D.C. asked.

Leaning forward, she told them.

CASH STOOD at the back of Jordan's booth. From where he'd positioned himself, he could see anyone who approached her. He also had a good view of the entrance to the hotel's exhibition hall. The transformation that had taken place in the past twenty hours or so was nothing short of a miracle.

The chaos of yesterday had vanished. In its place were neat rows of booths, two running the length of the room, the others stationed at intervals along three sides. Jordan's occupied a central position along the back wall.

In a corner close to the entrance, overstuffed sofas and chairs were clustered and flanked by carved wooden tables. Diagonally across the huge hall from the seating area were tables covered in white linen and laden with trays of chilled fruit, water bottles and coffee. The necks of champagne bottles peeped invitingly out of huge silver buckets. In another corner of the room, a string quartet played something classical and muted.

Jordan stood a few feet away from him, totally focused on adding the final touches to her display. She'd gotten her request for two glass cases, and it had taken her a good ten minutes to arrange the silk scarves she'd brought. Now she was fiddling with the jewelry. She was being as meticulous with the display as her sister had been in designing the pieces.

Cash was willing to bet that even her outfit had been

chosen with the idea of marketing Maddie's pieces. The colors were muted, khaki and white, making the green turquoise dangling from her ears and around her throat stand out even more.

A man in a discreet suit walked by. His eyes never strayed to Jordan's display cases; they were scanning the room. Hotel security, Cash decided.

At the moment, D.C. had tucked himself behind the back wall and was doing some research on his laptop. He'd insisted on driving behind them into Santa Fe in his rental car. That way he could provide some extra protection in case anyone tried something along the road. From what Cash could tell, the man never seemed to take a break. He'd asked to be informed the instant Daniel Pearson appeared. Then he would slip out a back way and return through the main entrance as Greg Majors.

For his part, Cash was content to lean against the wall and just keep watch. It was five minutes until the show opened to the public. Exhibitors with catalogs in hand strolled by, greeted old friends and browsed the displays of newcomers.

Lea had come by earlier to report that her grandfather had been lucid and in good spirits when they'd wheeled him off to the OR. That Pete Blackthorn was alive was a miracle.

When Jordan straightened and backed away a step from the case, he moved to her. "Three minutes until show time."

"I'm ready."

He ran a finger down the bright slivers of turquoise dangling from her ear. "I never doubted it."

She glanced back at the glass cases. "Her designs are so lovely."

Cash studied the display. In each case, she'd clustered pieces in three areas. In one, a circle of earrings and a trio of bracelets were arranged at each end. In the other, a group of pins sat at one end while tie clips and hammered silver belt buckles filled the other. Center stage in each glass case was a necklace.

On his left sat a simple chain of hammered silver rings. The pendant hanging from it was a star studded with turquoise ranging in shades from green to bright blue. The other necklace was made of turquoise beads in varying shades, with an intricately designed silver pendant that made him think of a breastplate a female warrior might wear into battle. Feminine. Strong.

"She's so talented." Jordan's voice was laced with pride as she tapped her finger on the top of the case holding the warrior piece. "This one's my favorite."

"I like it, too."

When she turned back to him, he gave her earring a flick. "You're not a bit jealous of her, are you?"

She stared at him. "Why would I be?"

"Because she obviously inherited your mother's gift for design."

A frown formed on her forehead. "I'm happy for her. I just regret that she and my mother will never get a chance to meet. It's such a waste. All the while I was working on this display, I kept thinking my mother had a fifty-fifty chance of choosing Maddie when they split us up. But it didn't work out that way. I feel so bad for Maddie. For my mother, too."

It was his turn to frown. "What about you, Jordan? Don't you wish you'd grown up here in Santa Fe with your father?"

She thought for a minute. Cash could almost hear the wheels turning. Then she shook her head. "No. I wouldn't be who I am today if I hadn't grown up with my mother. I regret that I never knew Mike Farrell, but now that I know the ranch exists, I'll visit often."

Fear rushed through Cash in such a torrent that he very

nearly grabbed her. She spoke so calmly of returning to her life in New York. Couldn't she see that she belonged here in Santa Fe just as much as Maddie did? But at that moment, the doors opened and the first wave of customers poured through. Turning, he let her words echo in his mind.

I'll visit it often.

Could he be happy with that?

STRING MUSIC and ripples of conversation filled the exhibition hall as dealers wove their way from booth to booth. It was two hours into the show and Jordan was almost ready to relax. She'd collected several business cards, answered the same questions over and over and taken dozens of orders. Once she'd noted that the potential clients were especially interested in the jewelry pieces she wore, she'd started rotating other bracelets and earrings from the display cases. But she hadn't disturbed the necklaces. They were generating interest right where they were.

No one as yet had suspected she wasn't Maddie. More importantly, they loved her sister's designs. True, her smile was beginning to ache at the corners of her mouth, but thanks to Maddie's sensible taste in shoes, her feet were still fine.

Then she spotted a man coming toward her with a beaming smile on his face. Obviously, he knew Maddie but she was coming up blank. She shot a glance back at Cash. He'd helped her out before, but as the visitor moved toward her, Cash said softly, "Don't have a clue."

The man was small and round, with rimless glasses perched on his nose. He had kind eyes, and she saw in them the light of an old friendship. Who was he?

"Ms. Farrell." He extended his hand and she shook it.

"Maddie," she said automatically. "I'm so glad you came."

"Ah, there they are." Perhaps it was the slight Hispanic accent or maybe it was the way he leaned over to study the necklace centered in the first case, but the memory slipped into place. This had to be Joe Manuelo, the man who cut and polished Maddie's stones. Maddie had explained in her notes that when she got stones from a mine, she always took them to Manuelo, whose family had been in the business for years, and he often visited her shows.

"Beautiful," he murmured as he glanced up at her again. "Could I hold it?"

"Of course, Mr. Manuelo."

"Joe."

She beamed a smile at him as she opened the case and lifted it out. He took it carefully, then holding it in one hand, he removed his glasses and studied it more closely. "Are you happy with the way I cut the stones?"

"Thrilled. You did a marvelous job."

"Thank you." He handed her back the necklace. "I like to see what happens to the stones after they leave my shop. I admire the way you've mixed the various shades. But you have old Pete to thank for the quality of the stones. What you've been sending me lately—the hardness, the quality—are exceptional. It makes my work easy."

Of course, he would know Pete Blackthorn was her source, Jordan thought. "Pete's been hurt."

Joe Manuelo immediately frowned. "Hurt? How badly?"

Jordan told him what she knew.

"Someone pushed him off a cliff?" There was a mix of shock and anger on his face.

"That's what we think. The police are looking into it."

"They'd better find out who did it."

"Lea Dashee might know the latest on his condition."

"Thank you, Ms. Farrell. I had it in mind to look at some

of her designs. too." With a final nod, he hurried off in the direction of Lea's booth.

She felt Cash's hands on her shoulders. "Pete has a lot of friends," he said.

"And at least one enemy," she added.

An hour later, the crowds had thinned. Cash assumed the dealers would be taking advantage of the buffet lunch the hotel was providing for them. Then, according to Jordan, they'd be back for a final push. He studied her as she switched the necklace and earrings she was wearing for a new set from the cases.

Whatever nerves she might have had at the beginning of the show had faded. When she talked about Maddie's designs, there was an energy that emanated from her. She might not be a designer, but she knew how to talk the talk. And there wasn't a doubt in his mind that she was enjoying herself. No one watching her would ever suspect that her life and her sister's had been threatened more than once in the past twenty-four hours. By any standards, she was a remarkable woman.

He'd moved forward to tell her just that when he saw Daniel Pearson and Margo Lawson entering the exhibition hall. Margo had her nose in the catalog, and by the time she pointed in their direction, Daniel had already spotted them.

Cash backed up, slipped one hand behind him, and tapped lightly on the wall of the booth. "Showtime, D.C." Then he leaned back and prepared to enjoy himself.

Three hours of handling dealers and gawkers had brought color to Jordan's cheeks. She looked perfectly at ease as Margo and Pearson reached her booth. Margo sent him a look, but then she leaned over the case to study the collection. Clearly, she was focused on business before pleasure.

Pearson barely glanced at the display cases before he took one of Jordan's hands. The diamond on his pinky finger caught the light. "Lovely job. Our dinner reservations are for six-thirty here in the hotel. I thought after the show, you'd enjoy someplace close."

And the sooner he could get her signature on the dotted line, the better, Cash thought. He'd been working Maddie for months. Why the sudden rush? Perhaps the answer to that question lay in the little charade they were about to enact.

When he realized his hands had fisted, Cash relaxed them. Out of the corner of his eye, he saw D.C. making his way toward them. The only thing that Cash didn't like about the little scenario Jordan and D.C. had finally decided on was that his job wasn't a more active one. He was supposed to observe Pearson's reactions.

"I have to have this one." Margo pointed at the center piece in the second case. "You've never designed anything quite like it before."

"No sense in bringing the same old, same old to a show," Jordan said.

"You haven't sold it. Tell me you haven't."

Jordan beamed Margo a smile. "I've sold three of them, as a matter of fact."

Margo's face registered disappointment. "But then they won't be unique. My customers don't want to see themselves coming and going."

"But each one *will* be unique. The colors of the turquoise stones will vary. Look at the color variations in this other necklace." She gestured to the other case. "So will the color of the beads in the necklace. And the shape of the pendant will vary also. I've made some sketches. See."

Margo studied the sketches Jordan placed on the case. Then she turned her attention back to the necklace. Finally, she met Jordan's eyes. "Yes, I can see. Brilliant. When did you come up with that marketing strategy?"

Jordan shrugged. "When three different dealers asked for a unique necklace."

"Make that four."

Cash bet it was Jordan who'd come up with the strategy and not Maddie.

Pearson had begun to fan himself with his catalog. Bored to tears, Cash thought.

D.C. was closing in. Cash bet that Pearson wouldn't be fanning himself much longer.

"Ms. Farrell?"

The drawl was unmistakably Texas. The charm, Cash was beginning to suspect, was D. C. Campbell.

Jordan shook D.C.'s extended hand.

"I'm Greg Majors." D.C.'s grin was apologetic. "Of course, you don't know me from Adam, but I have a business card." He fished it out of a pocket and passed it to her. "I'm here representing Majors Limited. My daddy owns a bunch of oil wells in Texas, and he's always looking for ways to invest his excess cash flow."

Jordan looked a little confused. "Does he want to invest in my jewelry business?"

D.C. glanced down at the display cases. "I could certainly suggest that to him." Then he met Jordan's eyes. "But I'm here to talk to you about your ranch."

Every bone in Pearson's body stiffened. Good, Cash thought.

"Now wait just a minute," Pearson said.

D.C.'s good ol' boy charm didn't falter for a second. "And you are?"

"Daniel Pearson of Montgomery Real Estate."

D.C. nodded. "Good to meet you. Are you representing Ms. Farrell's interests here?"

"Yes."

D.C. pulled out his notebook, flipped it open. "I'm sorry. Has she listed her ranch with you? I don't see that in my notes."

"No. She hasn't. But—"

D.C. cut him off with a raised palm and turned back to Jordan. "Ms. Farrell, my daddy is interested in investing in a string of select properties and turning them into an elite group of vacation destinations. In your case, we're thinking of a dude ranch. It wouldn't interfere with the running of the ranch, nor would it change the landscape in any significant way. My daddy started out as a rancher, and that's where his heart still is. But if it hadn't been for the black gold that he discovered on his land...well, the Majors family wouldn't be where it is today. We've done our research on you."

And Pearson was doing research, too. His fingers were busy on the BlackBerry he'd pulled out of his pocket. Taking two easy steps forward, Cash was able to see that he'd pulled up the Majors Limited Web site. If Pearson decided to dig deeper, D.C.'s cover story would check out. He'd seen to it by contacting his old buddy on their way into town.

"You want to buy my ranch?" Jordan asked, doing her best to look confused.

"No, not at all. We want to invest in your ranch and in you."

As D.C. elaborated on his plan, Cash began to relax. Her modification of D.C.'s initial plan was working. Not only was it driving Pearson into panic mode, but what D.C. was describing to her were all her ideas. Cash was beginning to think that she was serious about turning the Farrell Ranch into a working dude ranch. One thing he was certain of. She and D.C. should be nominated for some award. The Daytime Emmys?

"We'll provide advice, financial support, advertising and

marketing help," D.C. was explaining. "We think that offering vacations on a working ranch will have great appeal."

Jordan pressed hands to her temples. "Wait. I get to keep the ranch, run cattle, do everything I'm doing now?"

D.C. beamed a smile at her. "That's the plan. And it will be just the attraction that draws your guests. Lots of dude ranches around. Very few offer a true ranch experience. Add quality accommodations and gourmet food…" He raised both hands and dropped them. "Daddy and I think it's a win-win idea. Good for a small rancher trying to make ends meet. Good for us."

"Maddie, we need to talk about this. You don't know this man." Pearson's knuckles had turned white where he was gripping his BlackBerry, and there was a thread of panic in his voice.

Jordan gave him a distracted glance. "Of course. But not now." Then she refocused her attention on D.C.

"My daddy and I have already opened a few. Our plan is to have a chain of them operating across the Southwest—Nevada, New Mexico, Colorado. But this isn't the place to go into details. How about we meet after the show is over—say around six or six-thirty? I have a suite on the top floor. We can grab a bite to eat."

Pearson nearly choked. "Maddie, *we* have dinner plans at six-thirty."

Jordan's eyes, her voice, were apologetic. "Daniel, I have to hear more about this. You know I don't want to have to sell the ranch. I have to see if this could be a possibility for me."

"Fine. But you're making a mistake." Pearson stalked away, and with an apologetic smile, Margo hurried after him. He was punching in numbers on his BlackBerry even as he detoured to the cluster of sofas at the far corner of the room.

Cash put some effort into staying right where he was. It would have been too bad to destroy their little charade now. But he'd been the only one looking at Pearson when Jordan had put their dinner meeting on hold. For one instant, the real estate broker's smooth facade had cracked. Cash had caught a glimpse of the fury and panic, and it hit home that they might have put Jordan in even more danger.

"I'll see you around six," D.C. said, staying in his role. Cash noted that there were a few dealers around who'd become interested once Pearson had raised his voice.

"I'll give you my suite number." After scribbling something on a card, he handed it to her.

When Cash stepped forward, he read the two words D.C. had written. *Be careful.* He met the other man's eyes for a moment and nodded. They were on the same page where Pearson was concerned. That was the problem with stirring up a hornet's nest, Cash thought. There was always a chance that you'd get more trouble than you wanted.

With a final nod, D.C. moved slowly toward the door as if slowed down by his cane. He timed it perfectly, reaching the exit and turning back just as Pearson bolted toward it. The collision looked perfect. A man with a cane was knocked on his backside. Pearson made a hurried apology and with Margo following, he left the exhibition hall.

Since several people, a few of them security, had clustered around D.C., Cash stayed where he was. A moment later, D.C. had settled himself on one of the sofas and appeared to be making a call on his cell.

"Hopefully, we'll have a clue." Cash spoke softly to Jordan. "It would be too bad to waste a performance like that."

Her eyes were on the display case, but her lips curved slightly. "I agree. In any case, I think I just canceled my date with Danny Boy Pearson."

"And he's furious," Cash commented. "What I saw in his

eyes was bordering on the irrational." He took her hand in his and squeezed. "He may try to take his temper out on you."

"Then we'll have to be very careful."

CASH SPENT the next half hour switching his attention between Jordan, whose business had once more picked up, and D.C., who spent the time alternating between his laptop and his cell phone.

At one point, shortly after he'd had his collision with Daniel Pearson, D.C. had signaled one of the guards and gestured to a space under one of the couches. The guard dutifully retrieved a BlackBerry and carried it out of the exhibition room. When Pearson missed it, Cash was betting he'd locate it in the hotel's Lost and Found.

Jordan was writing up yet another order when D.C. tucked his laptop under his arm, rose from the couch, and made his way back to the booth.

When he reached them, D.C. spoke in his Greg Majors voice. "Ms. Farrell, I know I said I'd wait until later, but I've got some preliminary figures for you."

Opening his laptop, he set it on one of the cases and angled it toward Jordan. Then he spoke in a voice that didn't carry. "Good news and bad news. The number Pearson called belongs to Rainbow Enterprises Limited. I even retrieved the extension number. But when I dialed it, all I got was a series of automated responses and invites to leave a message."

"So we still don't know who Pearson called or who his client might be?" Cash asked.

"Working on it," D.C. said. "I tried Jase and got his voice mail, but I was able to reach his partner, Dino Angelis. According to Dino, Jase and Maddie are currently out of cell-phone reach while they're tracking down a lead they picked up at Eva Ware Designs. Fortunately,

Dino knows just about as much as my brother does about hacking into records." He patted the laptop before tucking it back under his arm. "I'll be working on it, too. It's only a matter of time before we find out who's behind Rainbow Enterprises."

Cash put some effort into controlling his frustration as he watched D.C. walk away. What he couldn't entirely rid himself of was the feeling in his gut that time was running out on them.

12

IT WAS NEARLY SIX when Jordan and Cash stood outside
Pete Blackthorn's hospital room. Since the floor didn't
allow cell phones, D.C. had stayed outside the main
entrance to check in with Jase's partner again. They still
hadn't been able to find out who owned Rainbow Enterprises Limited. Jordan figured the position also gave him
a chance to see if anyone had followed them from the
hotel. They'd used two cars again, and the police cruiser
following them had made it a parade.

Lea had stepped out as soon as they'd arrived to announce the good news. "The surgery took a long time, but
his hands are going to be fine. You'll be able to see him as
soon as Detective Alvarez is through."

Jordan watched through the window of Pete's room as
Lea rejoined her grandfather. Shay was in the process of
showing Pete some photos, and the old man was studying
each one intently.

Now that the jewelry show was over, she should be
feeling relieved. During the closing rush, she'd rung up
several impressive sales, some with dealers who'd never
bought Maddie's designs before. And she'd taken at least
a dozen orders for each of the centerpiece necklaces.

She should want to celebrate. But the nerves in her
stomach were still jumping. She'd tried to contact Maddie
to tell her the good news, but all she'd gotten was voice mail.

Sensing her tension, Cash ran his hands down her arms, then up again to settle on her shoulders.

"You're just as worried as I am," she said.

"I'll relax once Pearson is behind bars. Whatever or whoever is driving him to take your ranch off your hands has pushed him pretty close to the edge."

"If Pete can identify Daniel's picture, will Shay be able to arrest him?"

"Hopefully. But I'm not sure that will get us all the answers we need."

A man in green scrubs stepped into Pete's room, and a moment later Shay joined them in the hall. His timing perfect, D.C. stepped out of the elevator and walked toward them.

"Time to powwow," he said. "I've got some news from the other coast."

"Are Maddie and Jase all right?" Jordan asked.

D.C. sent her a reassuring smile. "I got everything secondhand from his partner since Jase is currently in an emergency room. Nothing serious. And Maddie's fine." He glanced around. "Anyone mind if we continue this conversation in the hospital cafeteria? I'm starved."

No one objected.

FIFTEEN MINUTES LATER, the four of them were seated at an isolated table in the semicrowded cafeteria. A couple of potted trees blocked them from view on one side, and the scents of hot food and old coffee hung in the air.

Cash and Shay had procured loaded trays, offering a cornucopia of selections—everything from pizza to burgers and tacos. Jordan hadn't realized until she caught the scent of it that she, too, was starved. After she'd downed her pizza, she looked at Shay. "Was Pete able to identify Daniel Pearson?"

"He was."

"You're going to arrest him, then?"

"When I do, I want to be able to hold him. The man who tried to run you off the road yesterday still hasn't regained consciousness, but I've been able to trace his prints. Angelo Ricci. He's a professional from the East Coast—New York, New Jersey."

"I can have Campbell and Angelis Security check into it," D.C. offered. "Jase has a good friend in the NYPD, Detective Dave Stanton. Jase will give him your name."

"I'm obliged. In the meantime, I'm checking out Pearson's alibi for yesterday. Pete claims that he was attacked just as soon as he climbed up that cliff—maybe nine a.m. or so."

"We met up with Daniel Pearson and Margo Lawson in Santa Fe around noon. That would give him plenty of time," Jordan said.

"He didn't check in with Montgomery Real Estate until after that," Shay said around a mouthful of burger. "Still, he impresses me as a careful man. He may very well have established an alibi for himself. And he's socially well-connected. Either he or his lawyers are going to claim that Pete's a confused old man. The sun was probably in his eyes. While we're waiting for the DNA on those cigarette butts to come in, it'd be good if we could establish motive."

Setting his coffee down, Cash turned to D.C. "You got anything yet on that cell phone call he made?"

D.C.'s grin was wide as he pulled his notebook out of his pocket. "As a matter of fact, I do. Rainbow Enterprises Limited is one of many, many small companies owned or at least partially owned by Ware Bank."

"Ware Bank is run by my uncle Carleton," Jordan stated.

"Yep. And your Aunt Dorothy currently heads up Rainbow."

"Aunt Dorothy? As far as I know she's never been involved in Ware Bank—other than to host the annual Christmas party at Ware House."

"Pearson called her?" Cash asked.

"Whether or not he talked directly to her is a question. As far as I could tell, there's no human being on the other end of that line. But he definitely called a company she owns and he could have left a message."

"So Daniel Pearson might have a connection to my Aunt Dorothy?" Jordan asked.

D.C. nodded. "Which is very interesting when you consider that your Aunt Dorothy has just been arrested for killing your mother and attempting to kill Jase and Maddie."

Jordan reached for Cash's hand. "Aunt Dorothy killed my mother?"

"So she says," D.C. said. "She confessed to Maddie right after she took my brother out with a fireplace poker."

Jordan's throat constricted and Cash's grip on her hand tightened. "Jase and Maddie—are they—"

"They're fine. Jase is getting patched up in an emergency room. Maddie came out of their confrontation with Dorothy Ware unscathed."

"But why would Aunt Dorothy kill my mother?"

"Details are sketchy at this point. Both she and Adam Ware have been arrested and are still being questioned by the NYPD."

"Adam's been arrested, too? For what?"

"I can only give you a bare bones version. But about a month ago, Adam robbed Eva Ware Designs of one hundred thousand dollars' worth of jewels in order to cover some gambling debts. When your mother figured that out, she told your cousin that he had to leave Eva Ware Designs, and your aunt didn't believe that failure should be in the cards for a Ware."

"But that's insane." Jordan pressed her free hand to her temple as she watched D.C. and Shay exchange a look.

"I've come across worse excuses for murder," Shay murmured.

"What about Uncle Carleton?" Jordan asked.

"Adam and Dorothy both claim that he knew nothing about their activities," D.C. said.

"So Dorothy Ware killed Eva to protect the Ware name," Cash said. "But why in the world has she been in contact with a real estate agent in Santa Fe for the past six months? And what does she have to do with the attacks on Maddie's ranch and Jordan's life?"

"Ah," D.C. said. "That's the million-dollar question, isn't it?"

THROUGH THE WINDOW, Cash watched as Jordan went in to Pete Blackthorn's room. Lea had come while they were still in the cafeteria to tell Jordan that the old man wanted to speak to her alone. As soon as Jordan finished with Pete, he was going to take her back to the ranch.

D.C.'s news had been a lot to absorb. He imagined Maddie must be struggling with it, too. But Dorothy and Adam Ware were strangers to her. To Jordan, they'd been part of a family she'd known all her life. And because of the two of them, her mother was dead.

When they'd left the cafeteria, D.C. and Shay were making plans to return to his office and contact Jase's friend Detective Stanton directly for the latest update on the investigation there. And Shay intended to get an arrest warrant for Daniel Pearson.

Cash tucked his hands in his pockets and tried to relax. They were in the home stretch. As soon as Shay and D.C. nailed down a motive and a definite connection and between Dorothy Ware and Pearson, the threat to Jordan should be over.

Right?

According to D.C., Dorothy Ware had denied orchestrating the attempted hit on Maddie. Instead, she'd tried to run her down with the same car that she'd used to run down Eva Ware—a car that ironically belonged to Jordan's mother.

If Dorothy Ware preferred to handle things by herself, who had hired the man who'd tried to run them off the road yesterday? Or the sniper who'd taken a shot at Maddie?

Something—the same feeling that he often got on cattle drives when he sensed an unseen danger to his herd—told him that it wasn't time to relax his guard yet. Not until they had all the dots connected.

He watched Jordan pull up a chair to Pete Blackthorn's bedside. She was frightened. Cash had felt it in the way she'd gripped his hand on the ride up in the elevator. What that wild ride down the hill yesterday hadn't accomplished, a meeting with an old man had. And it wasn't merely that she was going to ask him about an untapped vein of turquoise. If he was up to answering, she was going to ask him what he knew about her parents' marriage and why they'd separated. And why they'd decided to separate their two daughters.

He wanted those answers, too, he realized. He glanced at the door to Pete's room, which was opened just a crack. He wasn't above eavesdropping to get them. He also wanted to know why Eva had decided to bring her two daughters together only after her own death. He thought he understood why she'd asked them to change places. It was a quick way to force them to get to know one another. And if she had the kind of tunnel vision Jordan had described when it came to her business, she would have wanted Maddie to experience what it would be like to work at Eva Ware Designs.

But had she given even one thought to the fact that she might be putting them in mortal danger with the terms of that will?

He moved closer to the door where he could still keep Jordan in view through the window. He wanted to go to her. He couldn't. All he could do was stand in the background and try to provide what support he could. Her shoulders were just as tense as they'd been when she'd been setting up the display of Maddie's jewelry earlier in the day. But she was just as ready to face what Pete might tell her as she'd been to meet the dealers at the show.

He thought of what she'd been through since she'd changed places with her sister. Jordan Ware was amazing.

PETE'S EYES were closed, so Jordan sat there in silence, not wanting to disturb him. His hands were bandaged and an IV was still attached to one of his arms. He looked even more fragile and vulnerable than he had when she'd sat beside him on that ledge.

Her head was still spinning from the news that D.C. had relayed to them in the cafeteria.

Aunt Dorothy had murdered her mother. And she'd tried twice to kill Maddie. Every time Jordan tried to reconcile those acts with the controlled and sophisticated society matron she'd known all of her life, she began to get a headache. Dorothy Ware was a woman who seemed to have everything she wanted. She was married to a very rich man. She led a prominent social life, one that frequently got her mentioned in the society pages. She served on prestigious cultural and charity boards, and she lived in a mansion.

If it was hard for her to imagine Dorothy as a killer, it was a lot less difficult for her to believe that her cousin, Adam, had developed a gambling problem and decided to turn to a loan shark for help. But that he'd actually had the guts to rob Eva Ware Designs to pay off his debts? That was a shocker.

Secrets, Jordan thought. They seemed to run in her family. Jordan wondered if she'd ever really known any of her relatives—including her mother.

When she saw Pete's eyes flutter open, nerves and excitement began to dance in her stomach. Maybe he would be able to expose some of them.

"Ah, you're here." His voice was surprisingly strong for a man who'd gone through what he had in the past two days. "Wondered if I'd ever get to see you again."

"You're going to be fine," Jordan hastened to say. "The doctors—"

"My granddaughter has filled me in on my prognosis," Pete interrupted. "Even though there's nothing wrong with my hearing. Dr. Salinas explained that with time I should recover eight-five percent use of both hands. I got it."

Jordan bit back a smile at the cranky tone.

"Need to tell you some things," he said. He jerked his head at the IV drip "—and there's no telling when the stuff they're pumping into me will have me falling asleep again."

"I'm listening," Jordan said. "And if you doze off, I'll wait right here until you wake up again."

"Good." Pete narrowed his eyes on her. "First, tell me where Maddie is."

Jordan had to work to keep her mouth from dropping open. What she read in his eyes sent any thought of continuing with her masquerade flying. "She's in Manhattan. How did you know I wasn't Maddie?"

A trace of a smile flickered briefly on his face. "Wish I could tell you I recognized you. But I stopped by the ranch a few days ago, and your sister left notes by the phone. Wanted to tell her something. Your name was there on a pad by the phone along with a reservation number for a flight to New York. When I came to on the cliff and noticed your hair was different, I figured you for Jordan."

Jordan felt her stomach take a little tumble. "You knew about me, then?"

"Held you in my arms when you were a baby. Your sister, too. Your grandfather and I were close friends. He let me prospect anywhere I wanted to on his land. When he passed on, your dad was in his twenties. I took to stopping by to see how he was doing. Not that he needed anyone to keep tabs on him. Mike Farrell was born to be a rancher. And occasionally, he could even beat me at chess."

"So you knew my mother?"

"Yes. Surprised me that she decided to put the two of you in contact after all these years."

Jordan moistened suddenly dry lips. "Why did they separate us? Do you know?"

He frowned then. "Your mother didn't tell you?"

Jordan shook her head. "She can't. She's dead." Then she gave Pete the *Reader's Digest* version of the terms of her mother's will and what had happened so far.

When she finished, he shook his head. "Hard on the two of you. I never did agree with what Mike did. Advised him against it. But he loved her. I'm not suggesting that she didn't love your father. She did. But to my way of thinking, he loved her more. And when he realized he had to let her go, you were the one gift he insisted on giving her."

"What?"

"He gave her you."

"I don't understand."

Pete shook his head sadly. "Neither did I. Eva was just out of college when she came out to Santa Fe. There was a job her family wanted her to take back on Long Island, but she didn't want it. What she wanted was for them to finance her so that she could start her own business as a jewelry designer. But when her brother and her father ganged up against her, she took what money she had and ran away to follow her dream. She came to Santa Fe because she wanted to study the Native American designers and work with turquoise. She and Mike met one day, and it was love at first sight. The kind you read about in books. You understand?"

Jordan nodded. A ripple of fear moved through her because she thought she did.

"Everything was fine—just like the fairy tales. Three weeks to the day after they met, they got married."

"Three weeks?"

"Twenty-one days. Mike crossed them off on a calendar. He'd wanted to tie the knot on day two, but she'd insisted they wait. In three weeks they'd be more certain of what they wanted. After the wedding, Mike built her a studio so that she could design jewelry to her heart's content. Then she got pregnant. Mike was ecstatic. She wasn't. Morning sickness kept her from her work. And when it passed, she buried herself in her studio as if she was racing against the clock."

Knowing her mother, Jordan thought she understood. "Eva was a very focused person. She was probably worried that becoming a mother would interfere with her goal of becoming a top designer."

"That's the way Mike explained it. But she withdrew from him, too."

"And after Maddie and I were born?"

"Whatever worries she had only grew. You were six months old when she told Mike she had to leave. She was going back to New York. He could have custody of the two of you. She wouldn't contest it. She wouldn't even ask for visitation rights."

"She wanted to leave us both here on the ranch?" For a moment, Jordan let herself wonder what that might have been like—to have grown up with a twin and a father and not her mother.

Pete nodded. "But Mike wouldn't agree. That's when he came up with the plan. He would give her the start-up money for her jewelry business, and he would let her go back to New York. But in return, she had to take one of you with her."

"Why?"

"Beats me. He tried to explain. He said he loved her and he wanted her to have someone in her life to care about besides her designs. He wanted her to have someone in her life who would love her."

Jordan swallowed away the lump in her throat. As difficult as it was, she thought she could understand her mother's panic. All her life Eva Ware been driven by a dream—to become a top designer. And for the first time since she'd come to the ranch, Jordan thought she might be coming to know her father. He was a man who was capable of great love—of his land and his heritage, of his daughters and of the woman he'd fallen in love with.

Her father had given her up so that Eva wouldn't be alone.

"I told him he was crazy—especially after she insisted that if she did take one of you, the other could never know about it. There was to be no contact."

"One child was enough," Jordan said, nodding.

"That's the way I saw it. She didn't want to be involved in visits or in dealing with trips when the two of you would want to be together. She wanted a clean break. I told your father he was a fool to agree. But he loved her."

"Very much, it seems." And she thought her mother, whatever she had accomplished in her life, had been a fool to turn away from that kind of love.

Unable to remain seated any longer, Jordan rose and

began to pace back and forth beneath the windows. But she turned when Cash entered the room, and when he crossed to her she simply stepped into his arms.

Safety, she thought as the warmth stole into her. And understanding. If this was what her mother had found with Mike Farrell, how had she ever been able to walk away?

"Your father didn't keep to the letter of the bargain," Pete said after a moment. "He sent letters and gifts and pictures of Maddie."

Jordan turned. "She never gave them to me." Suddenly she frowned. "But there were gifts sometimes, surprise presents."

"The toy ranch you talked about," Cash said.

"Yes. And she never objected when I became interested in riding and I wanted my own horse."

"Guilty conscience?" Drawing her with him, Cash moved toward the bed. "Thank you for telling her."

"'Bout time I told someone. Mike swore me to secrecy a long time ago. Your father, too. Shortly before he died, he gave me a sealed letter addressed to both of you. Made me promise I'd deliver it if you ever found each other. After Mike died, I thought long and hard about giving it to Maddie and telling her she had a sister. But a promise is a promise."

"Did anyone else know about the twins?" Cash asked. "Other than you and my parents?"

Pete frowned thoughtfully. "I don't think so." He shifted his gaze from Jordan to Cash. "Thanks for bringing me in here. I owe you one."

Cash smiled slowly. "I think I'll collect right now. Tell me about the fresh vein of turquoise you've been mining on Maddie's ranch."

Pete winced. "That's something Mike swore me to secrecy on, too. I discovered it years ago, right about the same time he met and married Eva. The deal was that I could work it for as long as I wanted. But I couldn't tell anyone where I was getting the stones."

"He never filed a claim?" Cash asked.

Pete shook his head. "Not Mike Farrell. He didn't want any of the big mining companies out at his ranch sniffing around. He didn't want the land harmed in any way."

"So part of Maddie's heritage is that she owns a turquoise mine?" Jordan asked.

"Yep. And it's a damn rich one, too."

13

IT WAS FULLY DARK when Cash turned his pickup down the road that led to the ranch. D.C. was about five minutes behind them in his rental car. He'd still been on the phone with Detective Stanton when they'd left him in Shay's office.

The NYPD was getting closer to wrapping up their cases against Adam and Dorothy Ware. Though both continued to deny having hired any hit people or having any connection to Rainbow Enterprises Limited, both had connections to John Kessler, Adam's loan shark, who could easily have put either of them in touch with a paid assassin. And to Cash's way of thinking, both Dorothy and Adam certainly had motive to kill Maddie and Jordan. If the twins were both eliminated, according to the terms of Eva's will, Dorothy, Adam and Carleton would each get an even bigger slice of the pie that was Eva Ware's estate.

Maddie and Jase were still out of cell-phone contact at the hospital, but Dino Angelis was using every resource he had at Campbell and Angelis Security to check into both Dorothy's and Adam's e-mail and phone records.

They'd left Shay questioning Daniel Pearson. The real estate man had lawyered up as soon as he'd been brought in. Faced with the DNA results on the cigarette butts, he admitted to having been in the area where Pete had been found, but he vehemently denied that he'd been there that morning. He had confessed that he did indeed have a buyer for the Farrell Ranch, but the only contact he'd had with his client was through a spokesperson for Rainbow Enterprises Limited.

Shay was having two of his men check Pearson's alibi. Since it promised to be a long night, Cash hadn't objected when Jordan had asked if they could return to the ranch.

She'd been dead on her feet. Little wonder. Still, she hadn't fallen asleep on the ride from Santa Fe. He suspected that she was just as wired as he was. He figured he wasn't going to get much shut-eye until he could be sure that the danger for Jordan was over.

And he wasn't sure that it was. He thought of D.C.'s analogy to a connect-the-dots puzzle. To his way of thinking, they still didn't have a clear picture. If it turned out that neither Dorothy Ware nor Adam had hired the hit woman in New York or the man who'd tried to drive them off the road yesterday, who had?

As they rounded a curve in the road, he glanced toward Jordan. "Penny for your thoughts."

"My mind keeps returning to the secrets everyone has been keeping. My aunt, my cousin, my mother. My father, too. All those years of hiding the existence of that turquoise mine. Preserving the integrity of the land and his heritage must have been very important to him."

She paused for a moment as he turned into the drive that led to the ranch house. "You knew him. Would he object to the idea of starting up a dude ranch as a side business? Would that go against what he would have wanted for his land?"

Reaching over, he linked his fingers with hers. "I think he'd go along with it if you believe it's a way that Maddie can make ends meet."

"I don't have it all thought through yet."

"I don't know about that. The way Greg Majors explained it to you at the jewelry show, it sounded pretty good."

She smiled at him. "It did, didn't it? I was really tempted to buy into it. But Maddie won't be able to take it on. I'll have to figure a solution to that."

Cash's heart took a hard thump. "Why not run it yourself, Jordan?"

There was a beat of silence. "I can't be in two places at once. I've thought about the fact that Maddie is now the most obvious choice to step into our mother's shoes as head designer at Eva Ware Designs. But that may not be what she wants. It could be that she'd like to remain independent. In that case, I'll be needed more than ever at my mother's company. We'll have to find a new designer, and I'll have to be there to negotiate the transition."

"And you seem to be equally committed to find a solution so that Maddie can keep the ranch."

"I am."

"Perhaps neither one of you are going to be able to return completely to your own lives. Maybe that's why your mother gave you twenty-one days."

"According to Pete, she needed that amount of time to be sure she was making the right decision in marrying my father. Clearly, it wasn't a magic number."

"Who's to say it wasn't?" Cash countered. "If Mike Farrell and Eva Ware had never married, neither you nor Maddie would be here. However much you may judge them for the decisions they made later, they both took a risk. And you were the result. Who's to say that it was wrong?"

For a couple of beats, Jordan said nothing, and something around Cash's heart tightened. Finally, she said, "We still have about nineteen days left to work out the details."

Cash had always thought he was a patient man, but to his way of thinking, nineteen days might be too long for him to wait. There were details that he wanted to nail down right away.

But it was the wrong time to push her. As he rounded the last curve in the drive, the shadowy outlines of the ranch buildings came into view. "That's odd."

"What?"

"The floodlights aren't on. They usually only go off during a power failure." He braked to a stop in front of the ranch house and they both climbed out.

Cash smelled it first. The faintest sting in the air. He glanced at Jordan and saw that she'd caught it, too.

"Smoke," he said as he scanned the outbuildings.

Nothing. In the starlight, it was hard to see.

Then a horse whinnied in the stables, and there was an explosion that blew windows at the near end of the stable out. Flames shot upward behind the broken glass. Then the night filled with the sounds of panic-stricken horses.

For a moment Jordan couldn't move. The horses. Brutus and Lucifer were in there. Cash had covered half the distance to the stables before she unfroze and tore after him. By the time she reached him, he had both palms pressed against the stable door. "It's hot. Stand back."

Once she had, he pulled the doors open, jumping back himself. Smoke and heat billowed out. Greedy flames began to lick their way up the frame as hooves crashed against stall doors. She recalled that Brutus was at this end, her father's horse at the other.

"I'll get Brutus," she said.

"No. Wait here. I can get them both."

The horses were shrieking now, and the flames had made their way to the top of the door frame. "There isn't time. I can handle Brutus."

"You'll have to take him out the far door. You'll never get him back through these flames."

"Go. We're wasting time."

He disappeared into the dark smoke that filled the building.

Jordan held her breath and kept her eyes straight ahead as she followed Cash. Out of the corner of her eye, she noted that the fire had taken hold in the stall to her left. Heat blasted at her as flames shot upward. When she had to take a breath, smoke stung her lungs. Just a few steps more. Brutus was in the next stall to her right.

"Brutus." She pitched her voice above the noise of the fire. "Brutus."

His only reply was to rear and shriek with fear.

Behind her, she could hear the fire growing, spreading, and a fit of coughing nearly overtook her. Wood splintered in the door of the stall. She felt her own panic; icy fingers of it clamped on her stomach like a vise. Ignoring it, she forced her mind to go cool. She had to act fast if she was going to save the horse.

Grabbing a blanket off a hook on the wall, she called Brutus's name again, then opened the door. He rushed past her, then reared in pure terror at the sight of the flames that now framed the doorway.

The second his hooves came down, she threw the blanket over his head and grabbed his halter rope. Screaming, he reared again. But the blanket stayed in place. When his hooves clattered to the floor a second time, she placed a hand on his neck and began to talk to him. A quick glance over her shoulder told her that the smoke had thickened. If she tried to lead him out the far end, the smoke could kill them before the fire could. Her best bet was to take Brutus out the way she'd come in.

She didn't let herself think about it anymore. Going on instinct, she moved her hand to where the tether rope circled his neck and half vaulted, half muscled her way onto Brutus's back. He reared again, but she held on. Then, holding tight to the rope and the ends of the blanket, she dug her heels into his flanks and sent up a prayer of thanks when he leaped forward.

For an instant, she knew what hell was like. The heat was intense, and fire reached out greedily on either side of them. Then they were out. Blanket and all, Brutus lunged forward. For the next few moments, she concentrated her attention on calming him. He ran blindly all the way to the ranch house before she was able to get him under control.

Still talking, she got the blanket off him and slid to the ground. Then she glanced back at the stables. The doorway she and Brutus had raced through was an inferno. Flames danced along the roof now, and an icy fear clawed through her. Had Cash gotten Lucifer out? Where were they?

CROUCHED LOW, Cash raced down the length of the stable. The fire wasn't as bad at this end, but the smoke surrounded him. It had his eyes burning and his throat stinging. But he was very much aware that the fire behind him had started to roar.

Jordan.

Fear clawed at his gut, freezing him in his tracks. But when he turned, all he could see was an impenetrable wall of blackness. How was she going to get through that? A fit of coughing overtook him. Then the sound of a stall door splintering and Lucifer's frightened shrieking had him whirling and running toward the sound. He'd get the horse out first, then circle around the barn to help Jordan. There would be time. There had to be time.

He ran to the stable doors first and opened them. Smoke whooshed past him and the straw in the stall to his right burst into bright flames.

Behind him he heard Lucifer's hooves crash against his

stall door again. Cash reached him just as he lunged free. Eyes watering, he grabbed for the tether rope, then held tight as the panic-stricken horse reared and reared. Cash pointed the horse in the direction of the open door and slapped his flank.

Lucifer raced forward, and Cash tore after him. He had to get to Jordan, make sure that she was out. He'd cleared the stable door and had just reached the corner of the building when the blow struck him from behind. He saw stars before the ground came up to meet him.

PUSHING DOWN her fear, Jordan kept her eyes on the far side of the stables as she tied Brutus's tether rope to the railing on the front porch of the ranch. The moment she'd secured it, a familiar voice said, "Hello, Jordan."

She whirled so fast that Brutus whinnied and pulled at the tether. Raising a hand automatically to soothe the horse, she stared at her uncle Carleton. He was standing in the doorway to the ranch house, and he had a gun pointed at her.

14

"UNCLE CARLETON, what are you doing here?" Jordan asked.

"Technically, I'm in Phoenix attending a conference for investment bankers. Several people attended the talk I gave this afternoon. Others will vouch for the fact that I ate dinner with them. But actually I'm here because of Dorothy."

"I don't understand." Behind her the fire was roaring now, but she couldn't seem to take her eyes off the gun in her uncle's hand.

"When your mother became a problem for Dorothy, she took care of it on her own. She didn't even consult *me*."

"You didn't know she killed Eva?"

"Heavens, no. Neither she nor Adam confided in me. We're not a particularly close family, and running Ware Bank takes all my time."

Her uncle's casual, careless tone had her blood chilling even further.

"However, Dorothy has inspired me to follow her example in this instance."

"You're the one who was working with Daniel Pearson. He was representing you?"

"No. He was representing Rainbow Limited, a charitable foundation that I established some time ago in Dorothy's name. I took care to make sure that he never dealt with me directly. They'll never trace him to me. Now, with the situation Dorothy is in, they'll probably be satisfied that she was pulling Pearson's strings. That part has worked out quite well."

"Why would Dorothy or you want the ranch?"

"For the turquoise mine, of course. It's worth a fortune. I learned about it years ago. Your mother let it slip once. Then she swore me to secrecy. Of course, I was already keeping a much bigger secret for her."

Jordan studied him. "You knew about Maddie all along. Did she tell you?"

"No." His voice took on an edge as he walked across the porch. Jordan had to keep herself from stepping back.

"I made it my business to find out exactly what my sister was doing when she deserted her duty to Ware Bank and ran away from home to pursue her frivolous dream. Keeping Maddie a secret gave me some real leverage over Eva for the first time. As long as I didn't say anything, Eva agreed to let me vote her stock at Ware Bank, make decisions on my own and live in Ware House. And that was only what was due me."

The edge in his voice had become angrier. Jordan had never seen her uncle express any kind of a heated emotion before.

"My father *should* have left the bank and the house to me." He gestured to his chest. "I was the oldest son. I was the one who shouldered the responsibility of running the bank. Eva ran away from all her rights to either of them when she went off to Santa Fe to study her *art*. Then when she returned, my father welcomed her like the prodigal son."

"But if you got everything you wanted by keeping my mother's secret, why do you need the turquoise mine?"

"Because Ware Bank is in trouble. Just temporary. A few unlucky calls on my part. All I need is a quick influx of cash to turn things around. I'd forgotten about the mine until Eva mentioned that Michael Farrell died. As I said, we weren't close but she seemed to need to tell someone, and I was the only option—fortunately for me. But Pearson was taking too long even after I offered a percentage of the future profits from the mine."

"So you hired someone to shoot at Maddie?"

"And to get rid of you."

His tone had calmed now and was almost sounding reasonable. It sent a new wave of chills through her.

"It all came to me while Fitzwalter was reading that will. Eva will never know how completely she solved all my problems. All I had to do was get rid of both of you, and the ranch would come to me as next of kin. Plus, I would have the added money that would come from the sale of Eva Ware Designs. My sister couldn't have played more completely into my hands."

"You won't be able to kill Maddie now. You'll be the prime suspect."

"Perhaps. But I would do anything to save Ware Bank. It's my duty, my responsibility. Eva would understand what I'm doing. She felt the same way about Eva Ware Designs."

Jordan doubted that her mother would have killed to preserve her life's work. But in an odd way, she thought her mother might understand her brother's absolute tunnel vision when it came to the family bank. Perhaps Mike Farrell would have understood it, too. Not the methods, but the intent.

Secrets. She'd thought before how good the Wares were at keeping them. Carleton, Dorothy and Adam had all been very good at hiding their true colors.

At least her parents, Mike and Eva, for all their faults, had never tried to hide what they were.

"Now, if you'll just come up and join me on the porch."

Brutus whinnied again and pulled at his tether. An answering whinny had Jordan turning to see Lucifer racing across the field beyond the stables.

Alone. There was no sign of Cash. Once more fear chilled her veins.

"If you're hoping that cowboy neighbor of Maddie's will rescue you, forget it. If he hasn't already, he'll die in the fire. One of my men will take care of that."

Jordan's heart nearly stopped. No, she wasn't going to let herself think about Cash right now. He could handle himself, and D.C. had only been minutes behind them in his car. He'd be here soon. Both men were smart and resourceful. So was she. And her job right now was to keep her uncle talking.

"Your men?"

"I brought two of them just to make sure. As you may have noticed, one of them is very skilled at setting fires. The other one is a pilot who flew us in on a small private plane. We'll be back in Phoenix in time for me to host a private party later tonight. Come now, Jordan. I don't like to be kept waiting."

Jordan stood her ground. "How did you know about Maddie's neighbor?"

"Pearson did manage to leave a rather detailed message about the guy sticking to you like glue, so we needed a distraction. And when he told me about another offer on the ranch, I knew I had to act fast. Now, it's really time for you to join me up here on the porch. I'm just going to knock you out until one of my men comes to take you to the barn. You and your neighbor are going to die tragically in the fire."

"No."

Carleton frowned at her. "Do as you're told, Jordan. Or I'll have to shoot you."

"You can't shoot me. I've met Detective Alvarez. He's a smart man and a friend of my *cowboy neighbor*. If I have a bullet in me, he'll know I didn't die accidentally. He'll track you down."

"If you don't come up here and join me, I'll shoot the horse."

Checkmate, Jordan thought. She stepped away from Brutus and began to walk toward her uncle. Once Brutus was safe, she was going to get that gun away from him.

THE PAIN in Cash's head was fierce. He welcomed it because as long as it was there, he was conscious. And his head wasn't the only pain he was experiencing. Someone had hold of his feet and was dragging him along the ground. Pebbles and stones bit into his back. He opened his eyes, blinked back tears and saw the blurred edge of the stable door, then the dark outline of the figure pulling him through it.

He closed his eyes and drew in a breath. His one advantage was that the air at ground level held more oxygen than the air at his opponent's level. Beyond his eyelids, he could see the brightness of the flames that had caught hold in the stall near the doorway. They weren't very far into the stables when the man dragging him began coughing and dropped his feet. Drawing back his foot, Cash gave him one hard clip to the kneecap.

The man fell like a tree, and Cash summoned all his strength, all his focus, to roll on top of him. Trying not to breathe, he grabbed the man's hair and smashed his face hard into the concrete floor of the stable. Once, then a second time. Afterwards, he rolled off and tried to stand. The flames were closer now, the smoke thicker. A fit of coughing overtook him.

"Need some help?"

Still crouching, Cash found the strength to swing a hand.

The man jumped back. "It's me. D.C. If you clip me in my good knee, neither one of us will get out of here."

"D.C.?"

"Yeah. If you can make it out on your own, I'll drag this guy."

They were both coughing as they staggered out of the stables. Once clear, D.C. dropped the body he'd been dragging next to another one.

"You've been…busy," Cash said.

"I knew the minute I saw the fire that something was up. So I ditched my car and climbed a few fences. Took your guy's pal out with my cane." D.C. retrieved it from the ground. "Are there any more?"

"Don't know. Have to help…Jordan. Left her…other end of the…stable."

"I saw her make it out on one of the horses."

Cash's relief was so intense his knees nearly buckled. "Got to…get to her."

Cash forced himself to take calm, even breaths. He wasn't going to be any good to anyone if he keeled over.

Together, they made their way along the stable wall. Cash spotted her first. She was standing near the front steps of the ranch house. The stars were bright enough that he saw the other figure, too—holding a gun.

His heart sank. There was absolutely no cover between the ranch house and the stables. If he and D.C. rushed the guy, he could easily shoot Jordan, then take them out like ducks in a shooting gallery.

"She's got his attention," D.C. said. "My brother claims she has a good head on her shoulders."

"She does." Remembering that helped Cash keep panic at bay. Brutus was tethered to the porch railing, and Jordan was standing close to him, her hand resting on his neck. They weren't close enough to hear what anyone was saying.

"How's your head?" D.C. asked.

"Fine. How's your leg?"

"Probably better than your head. If the man with the gun looks this way, we're right in his line of vision. So I figure our best bet is to angle our way to the bunkhouse. Then I'll circle around the far side of the ranch house and you take the shorter route to this side."

Cash pictured it in his mind. The trickiest part would be getting to the bunkhouse. But it was their best option. "And when we get to the house? He's got a gun. We don't."

D.C. shot him a grin. "I'll create a diversion and you take out the guy with the gun before he shoots me."

"How come you get the fun part?"

"See you in a few minutes." D.C. took off. Even with the limp, he was halfway to the bunkhouse before Cash started after him. He had to push the image of Jordan standing there facing a gun out of his mind. Instead, he concentrated on keeping his jog steady and his breathing even. Emotions would only slow him down. There'd be plenty of time for feeling later.

Once they were all safe.

By the time he reached the bunkhouse, D.C. had already started making his way to the far side of the ranch house.

Cash allowed himself the luxury of leaning against the wall for a moment. His mind cleared, and he didn't feel quite so breathless.

Still, he kept his jog slow. He couldn't risk another fit of coughing. When he reached his destination, he flattened his back against the wall and risked a quick look around the corner. Jordan had stepped away from Brutus and was talking calmly to a tall, distinguished gentleman in a business suit. Admiration mixed with fear as he watched her. There wasn't anything in her tone or demeanor to indicate that she was staring down the barrel of the gun.

Nor that the man holding it wasn't nearly as calm as she was.

Cash gauged his distance to the gunman. He'd need at least three, maybe four seconds to reach him. He prayed that D.C.'s diversion would last that long.

JORDAN STOPPED when she reached the foot of the porch steps. Out of the corner of her eye, she'd seen Cash look around the corner of the house.

He was safe. Relief mixed with fear because he was going to try to rush Uncle Carleton. She knew it. And heaven knew where the two men her uncle had hired were.

"One of my men should be here any minute."

He barely got the sentence out before there was a loud splintering sound and a section of the stable roof caved in.

"Bunglers." Carleton spit out the word in another sudden flash of fury. "I'm surrounded by idiots. They should have come to get you by now. You've got to be in that barn. Your death has to look like an accident." He descended a step. "I'm going to have to take care of this myself."

She had to calm him down. She wasn't sure the Uncle Carleton she'd always known was capable of using a gun. She was pretty sure the man pointing the gun at her right now was.

"Wait." Jordan raised a hand. "You haven't killed anyone yet, Uncle Carleton. Daniel Pearson acted on his own when he tried to kill Pete Blackthorn. Dorothy acted on her own to kill my mother. You could still walk away from all of this."

Okay, so he had hired professionals to do his killing for him. She wouldn't mention that.

"You don't understand," he said.

Jordan bit back a sigh of relief that the fury had faded a bit from his voice.

"I have to save Ware Bank. It was left in my care."

"I understand that. And Maddie and I can help with that. I can't believe my mother would have wanted the bank to fail."

"Your mother." He spat the words out. "She wouldn't have cared a fig if Ware Bank failed. And she wouldn't have lifted a finger to save it."

Jordan realized too late that she'd taken the wrong tack. She'd made him angry again.

"Enough. I'm through waiting. We're going to do this my way." He lunged down the steps toward her.

Even as she jumped back, Cash and D.C. raced around the corners of the house.

They both shouted something, and Carleton whirled in Cash's direction. He fired wildly once before Brutus neighed loudly and reared. It was the horse's descending hooves that knocked Carleton Ware to the ground.

Cash reached him first and kicked the gun away. Then Jordan rushed into his arms and held on tight.

"UNCLE CARLETON wanted to kill both of us." The shock and disbelief in Maddie's voice was a near perfect match to what Jordan was still feeling as she stood in the living room of the ranch with the phone pressed to her ear. The difference was that through the picture window, Jordan could see the spot where her uncle had stood on the porch the night before pointing the gun at her. She could also see the charred remains of the stables. And the lightning-fast images of Cash and D.C. rushing toward Carleton, of Brutus whinnying and rearing and knocking her uncle to the ground were still replaying themselves in her mind. If it hadn't been for Brutus, she might have lost Cash.

"But he didn't succeed." She turned and looked at Cash

and D.C., who were standing in the kitchen drinking coffee. They were safe. And so were Jase and Maddie now. The reality of that was slowly sinking in. Her uncle's injuries from his encounter with Brutus had been minor. He was refusing to talk, but Shay was confident that his accomplices would be more forthcoming.

Since it had been long after midnight by the time the detective had taken Carleton and his two henchmen into Santa Fe and Cash had arranged for Sweeney to transport the two horses to his ranch, she, Cash and D.C. had postponed calling New York with the latest news until morning. D.C. and Jase had spoken first. Then Cash had talked to Maddie. And now it was her turn to talk to her sister.

The sister she hadn't known existed until a week ago. Her knuckles white on the phone, Jordan shifted her gaze back to the window, to the land that stretched for miles until it gradually lifted into those hills, and something inside of her settled. A week ago, she hadn't known this place existed. She hadn't known Cash existed. So much had changed in her life so fast.

"He knew about us and the turquoise mine all these years," Maddie said. "And he never said a word."

"Keeping secrets seems to run in the Ware family," Jordan said.

"As far as secrets go," Maddie continued, "Mike Farrell was no slouch. Jase and I found a box in our mother's closet containing letters that he'd written to her over the years. She knew when I took my first step, when I cut my first tooth. He made sure she knew everything about me."

Jordan felt the rush of emotions, this time happy ones.

"And there was a letter to our father that she'd never mailed. It was dated just before he died. She wanted his permission to dissolve their bargain and bring us together.

Jase and I figure she found out that he'd passed, so she never mailed it. And she evidently couldn't find the courage to reunite us on her own. I'll bring everything once this twenty-one-day thing is over. And we'll search the ranch house. I'll bet our father has a box of photos stashed away somewhere, too."

When this twenty-one-day thing was over…

A little skip of fear moved up Jordan's spine. She glanced out to the kitchen again. Cash was standing, his hip against the counter, his long legs crossed at the ankles, his head tilted to one side as he listened intently to something D.C. was saying. Two days ago, she'd been so certain that when the three weeks were up, she'd be back in New York. So positive that her life, her responsibilities were there. Was she going to let herself be trapped by the same kind of tunnel vision and fear that her mother had?

Gripping the phone more tightly, she said, "I have news on this end, too. Pete Blackthorn knew about both of us all this time. He has a letter that our father addressed to both of us. He'll deliver it when you get here. And he told me why we were separated."

Jordan began to pace back and forth as she told her sister about the decision their parents had made all those years ago.

CASH WATCHED as Jordan paced, wishing he could do more to ease the burden of all she'd discovered in the past few days.

"She's a strong woman," D.C. said as he topped off Cash's mug and then refilled his own.

"So's Maddie," Cash said. "But they've got a lot on their plates. It's not only Eva Ware Designs and the ranch that they have to deal with. I'm betting they're going to have to take on Ware Bank's problems, too."

"Good thing they each have someone to lean on."

"Yes, they have each other."

"I was thinking of you and Jase."

Cash felt fear tighten in his belly. He'd nearly lost her twice yesterday. He didn't want to let himself think about the possibility that he might lose her again in eighteen days. "For now."

D.C. turned to him, studied him for a moment. "You don't impress me as a man who's slow off the mark."

"What?"

"Life's short. If I had a woman looking at me the way Jordan looks at you and I felt the same way, I wouldn't wait eighteen days to stake my claim. If you don't mind a bit of free advice, you could use the dude ranch thing as leverage—if you wanted to persuade her to stay here instead of returning to New York. She's really into it. I have half a mind to put her in touch with the real Greg Majors."

"Everything's happened so fast," Cash said.

"It's happened fast for Jase and Maddie, too. But I've seen the way my brother looks at her. And he's got that business background in common with Jordan. I'll bet he's already making plans—maybe to open a branch of his business out here in Santa Fe."

Cash looked back at Jordan. She was still talking to Maddie, and she'd paused in front of the window to look out at the land her father had sent her away from. He'd wanted to give her time, to give them both time, but she looked so right standing there.

Suddenly, all his nerves settled. They might come from different worlds, different backgrounds, but she was right for him, too. It was just that simple. Just that true. Now all he had to do was convince Jordan of that.

D.C. set his mug down on the counter. "Well, I think my work here is done. I'm going to pack up and get out of your hair. I'll stop on my way to the airport and get the latest update from your friend Alvarez."

Cash nodded absently, never once taking his gaze off of Jordan as D.C. left the room.

IT WAS LATE AFTERNOON when Jordan and Cash urged their horses up the last incline to the top of the bluff. Once D.C. had left, Cash had talked her into letting him complete that tour of the ranch he'd promised her—was it only two days ago? He'd driven her over to his place and had barely said a word. Then he'd given her a whirlwind tour of his home while Sweeney had saddled Brutus and Cash's horse, Mischief.

His housekeeper had packed them some food and they'd ridden off toward the canyon that joined the two ranches. The ride had been fast and hard, and it should have cleared her mind. But she'd felt wired from the moment that D.C. had driven off toward Santa Fe. It was as if a clock were ticking and time was slipping away from her.

At some point while talking to her sister, she'd come to a decision. Now all she had to do was share it with Cash. She'd made business presentations hundreds of times. She knew how to persuade people. So why was she ten times more nervous than she'd been representing Maddie's jewelry at that show yesterday?

When the horses reached a level piece of land, Cash turned Mischief around and Jordan followed suit.

"I brought you here because I wanted you to see this."

Jordan looked around and simply absorbed the view. The land fell away on either side of the hills, pristine and breathtaking in its beauty. In spite of the shimmering heat, she could make out the miniature buildings of the two ranches. With the exception of those structures, nothing marred the landscape.

"I see now why my father didn't want anyone to know about the turquoise mine. No matter how much money he could have made, it wouldn't have been worth it."

Cash smiled at her. At her count, it was the first one he'd given her all day, and something inside of her eased a bit.

"I'm sorry he didn't live to meet you."

Jordan felt her throat tighten. "Me, too. But you're showing me a lot about him. And I'll learn more." She shifted her gaze to the land again, knowing that it was an integral part of her father. "In the city, there aren't any places like this where I can get away and just breathe. Maddie told me that this place was special—that I would find something here."

And she had. She turned to Cash. It wasn't just the land. It was the man. They came from different worlds just as her parents had. Like her mother, she was a New Yorker. Like her father, he was a rancher who loved the wide-open spaces.

When he placed a hand over hers on the pommel of the saddle, she glanced down and saw the sharp contrast. His fingers were larger, his palm callused, and yet somehow they fit. She met his eyes. There were so many differences between them and yet she felt the pull—sure, steady and right. And she felt her heart drop just as fast and hard as if it had fallen off the ledge in front of them.

"I also brought you here for another reason, Jordan," Cash said.

"I figured. To seduce me." She tried a tentative smile, but he didn't return it.

"We'll get to that. But first I have something to say."

"Me, too." Ignoring the flutter of panic in her stomach, Jordan hurried on. "I was wrong."

For a moment his hand tightened on hers. "About what?"

"About us."

His eyes narrowed and the intensity of his gaze nearly had her throat drying up. She could do this. She had to do this. "I was wrong about the ground rules I set up at the very beginning of this…relationship. I thought I knew what I wanted—a mutually enjoyable time that we could both walk away from in twenty-one days. No harm, no foul. But I've changed my mind."

When he said nothing, she lifted her chin. "A woman has a right to do that."

"It depends. What have you changed it to?"

Without knowing exactly how, Jordan found her fingers had become linked with his. "I want more time."

"Why?" he asked again.

Panic fluttered again, but she shoved it down. "Because I need it. Because I think what we're discovering together deserves it. And I don't want to make the same mistake my mother did. I understand now that she walked away from my father and from Maddie because she was so focused on her goal of creating a successful jewelry empire that she couldn't see that she could have had that and more. When I thought that I had to go back to New York and make sure that her legacy lived on, I was being as blind as she was. I want more. I need more."

"Why?"

Jordan swallowed hard. "Because I really want to develop a business plan for the dude ranch, and I want to be here a lot of the time to run it. I can still oversee the business side of Eva Ware Designs. And I want to help Maddie, too. I don't want her to merely step into the job of head designer at Eva Ware Designs. She can do that if she wants, but she has her own reputation to build. I'm going to encourage her to do that. And then there's Ware Bank."

He gave her a brief nod. Whether it was approval or disapproval, she wasn't sure.

"There's no excuse for what my uncle did or tried to do, but I do understand his desire to keep a family business running. But I don't have to be in New York all the time to help out with that."

"You're nervous. You always talk a lot when you're nervous. So I don't think you've gotten yet to the real reason you want to change the ground rules. Give me the bottom line, Jordan. Why?"

She felt a sudden flare of anger and tamped down on it. Because he was right. And she was stalling. She studied him sitting there on his horse, and it wasn't some fantasy she saw. It was Cash Landry. And suddenly she knew.

Meeting his eyes steadily, she said, "I want to change the ground rules because I want more than twenty-one days with you. Because I love you."

He raised their joined hands to his lips in a gesture that had her heart tumbling again. "Same goes." He smiled that slow easy smile. "I know how much you like to map things out and see where you're headed. So how much more time are you thinking of?"

The mix of heat and amusement she saw in his eyes had her stomach settling. It reminded her of exactly what she'd seen that first morning she'd woken up in bed with him.

"I was thinking of a lifetime."

He pulled her close then, and when his mouth was only a breath away from hers, he murmured, "I hope you're open to negotiations. I brought you out here to convince you we'd need two lifetimes. Maybe more."

"Deal."

Then he kissed her.

Brutus whinnied, Mischief pawed the ground. But Jordan held on tight.

She'd come home.

Epilogue
_____

Eighteen days later

THE SUN had begun its descent behind the mountains southwest of the ranch as Cash stirred the coals in the barbecue
pit. They were just beginning to turn white at the edges.

"Let me know when you're ready for the steaks," Jase said.

Cash glanced over to the corral near the new stable.
Maddie and Jordan sat together on the top rung of the
fence watching Julius Caesar and Brutus take each other's
measure. Jordan had arranged for Julius Caesar to be
shipped across country, timing his arrival to coincide with
Jase's and Maddie's yesterday.

The women's heads were close, and in the slanting
sunlight they made a pretty picture. "I think the ladies will
let us know when they're hungry."

Jase followed the direction of Cash's gaze, then reached
into a cooler and pulled out two beers. "If we leave it
entirely up to them, we won't be eating those steaks until
breakfast."

Cash took a long swallow of the beer Jase handed him.
"They stayed up all night talking. You'd think they'd run
out of things to say."

Jase's brows arched upward. "I've never known Jordan
to be at a loss for words. And the two of them have a lifetime to catch up on."

"True." Cash smiled slowly. "With Jordan at the helm, they have another lifetime to plan."

Jase chuckled. "I see you're getting to know her. But I imagine Maddie will get her two cents' worth in. She went to bat for her cousin, Adam, and convinced Jordan that they shouldn't press charges for the robbery if Adam agreed to get help for his gambling problem. The D.A. was agreeable as long as Adam promised to testify against the loan shark he borrowed so much money from. I think Maddie felt sorry for him."

"And Jordan probably saw it as a good business decision because she believes him to be a talented designer. Without pressure from his mother, he might turn into an asset at Eva Ware Designs."

"They're going to make a good team." Jase turned to Cash. "By the way, I owe you one."

"What for?"

"Those karate moves you taught Maddie. One of them saved my life. Hers, too."

Cash smiled at him. "Then it was time well spent." He glanced at his coals. "Ten more minutes and we're going to have to round 'em up and bring 'em in. I'll open a bottle of chardonnay as bait and we'll take them a couple of glasses along with the letter Pete Blackthorn delivered while they were riding."

"Good plan."

"I've got another one. Tonight, I'm taking Jordan back to my place. That will give you and Maddie some privacy."

Jase studied Cash. "If you can pull that off, you're going to be my new best friend."

"Watch and learn. I know just what bait to use then, too. Making love in the back of my pickup is on our to-do list."

Jase raised his beer bottle in a toast. "I like your style."

"I'M STILL TRYING to get my mind around the other Wares," Maddie said. "I knew from the time I met them that there was something different about them."

"Different is way too mild a word. Carleton was absolutely nuts. I saw it in his eyes. I'm amazed he was able to hide it all these years."

Maddie shivered a little. "I saw it in Dorothy's eyes, too."

"At least Adam might be salvageable," Jordan mused. "I think you're right about him. He's a lot like our mother—focused on his career as a designer. I think she saw a lot of herself in him. That may be why she didn't want to prosecute him when she discovered he robbed the store. And the gambling may have been his way of acting out against his mother's constant derision and dissatisfaction."

"Our mother may have had some faults, but they were light years away from Dorothy Ware's." Maddie glanced at Jordan. "I have a question about Eva."

"Ask away."

"Are you angry with her for what she did? I mean, she didn't want either one of us, and then she was the one who insisted that we never know about each other."

Jordan shook her head. "I'm not angry at all. She may have been the cause of our separation, but in the end she brought us together." Jordan let her gaze sweep the landscape. "And in the end she opened up new worlds for me. Not just this place, but all the new business challenges I'm finding here."

"I feel the same way about New York and about working at Eva Ware Designs. I'm learning so much from helping Cho to finish her designs. I can't help but feel grateful to her."

Jordan glanced over her shoulder and saw the two men walking toward them. "If it hadn't been for the terms of our mother's will, I never would have found Cash."

"And I never would have found Jase. We owe her big-time."

"We come bearing gifts," Cash said as he reached them. Jase handed them each a glass of wine and Cash handed Jordan the letter. "Pete Blackthorn brought this while you were out riding."

Jordan looked down at the script—*Maddie and Jordan*—and she ran a finger over the writing.

"This is the letter you told me about," Maddie said. "Read it to us."

Jordan nodded as she broke the seal and held it so that Maddie could see.

Dear Maddie and Jordan,

If you're reading this, it means that you're together at last—something that I didn't live long enough to see. I'm also hoping it means that the gamble I took when I kept the daughter who even at six months loved to play with shiny stones and sent away the daughter who loved to ride with me on my horse has paid off and played some part in your finding one another.

Enjoy one another as I've enjoyed watching both of you grow up.

All my love,

Dad

Jordan reached for Maddie's hand and held on. "He mixed us up on purpose."

"Because he loved us and he hoped we'd be together one day."

"Hear! Hear!" Cash raised his glass in a toast. "To Mike Farrell."

"And to Eva Ware," Maddie said as she lifted her glass.

"To our parents," Jordan said.

And all four of them drank.

* * * * *

*After battling a hurricane of catastrophic proportions,
Jason needs some downtime badly! But there's no rest
for the heroic. During another deluge, Jason's saviour
skills are suddenly in demand by his hot friend Lizzy.
She's fiercely independent. But that doesn't keep them
from having incredible sex as they ride out the storm.*

Turn the page for a sneak preview of

Storm Watch
by
Jill Shalvis

Storm Watch
by
Jill Shalvis

JASON MAUER STAGGERED through the fifty-mile-an-hour winds and into the house with three things on his mind—food, sleep and sex.

Thanks to Uncle Sam and the National Guard, he hadn't been home for any real length of time in years, home being the small California beach town of Santa Rey. When he was in town, he shared a house with his brother, Dustin, and hoped to find the fridge stocked with at least sandwich makings and, please God, a beer or two.

As for the sleep…well, he had a bedroom. The question was could he shut down enough, push away the haunting memories long enough to actually get some shut-eye.

The jury was still out on that one.

Which left sex.

He needed a woman for that, at least the way he liked it, and seeing as he'd been working his ass off on his last military stint, spending some special quality time at every national disaster that had hit the news, plus a bunch that hadn't, he was fairly certain he was lucky just to be alive, much less naked with a woman.

With a bone-weary sigh, he dropped his gear and headed directly toward the refrigerator. He should call his brother, his sister and his mom, and let them know he was back a few days early…but they'd be all over him, wondering if he was really okay, if he'd recovered from his loss.

He hadn't.

So he didn't call, not yet. Instead, he looked out the windows into the growing dark, even though it was barely five o'clock in the afternoon in June. From the kitchen window, he watched the ocean pound the shore, the waves pushing fifteen feet minimum. The winds had stirred up some seriously ominous clouds, and he was surprised to see trees doubled over from the gusts.

He'd seen bad weather in his time—hello, hurricanes Rita and Katrina—but nothing here on the supposedly mild Central California coast.

His stomach growled, reminding him that it'd taken him all day and three flights to get here, bad storm or not, and he couldn't remember the last thing he'd eaten. Peanuts, given to him by a cute flight attendant? No, a candy bar grabbed at the airport.

And the damn fridge was empty.

Yeah. Pretty much how his life felt at the moment. Empty as hell. Matt would laugh at that and tell him to get over himself.

But Matt was dead, six weeks now.

Still shell-shocked, Jason's gut clenched hard at the thought of his best friend lying six feet under, and suddenly he was no longer hungry. Fuck it, he thought. Fuck thinking, he was going directly to bed, no passing Go. He kicked off his shoes, and so damn tired he practically staggered like a drunk, moved down the hallway. He was "in the tween" as his sister, Shelly, would say. In between military life, which was all he'd known since high school, and his old life, which no longer even seemed real.

Which world did he want?

The government wanted him back, of course. He was highly trained and valuable. That wasn't ego, but fact. He was a rescue expert who worked with nerves of steel. Or he had…

His family was hoping he'd stick here. His mother, living twenty miles north of Santa Rey in San Luis Obispo, wanted him to be safe and sound. His sister, who lived with her while going to Cal Poly, wanted him to date her friends. Dustin—here in Santa Rey—was his partner in their on-the-side renovation business, and wanted him home to be a more active presence.

As for what Jason wanted? No clue. None. Zero. Zip.

But he had a few weeks to figure it out. With a sigh, he looked around the empty house. Dustin lived with his fiancé, Cristina, most of the time these days, which left the place looking a bit neglected. It'd been just waiting for him to come back to help Dustin finish the upgrades, so they could sell it and move on to the next project. Dustin had redone the kitchen and both bathrooms. He'd pulled the carpet and refinished the original hardwood floors. And he'd done a good job, too. All that was left was a couple coats of paint and some tile in the entry, and this house could be flipped, something Dustin was eager to do.

As for himself, he was having a hard time caring. About anything—except his three simple needs.

Since there was no food and no willing woman, he'd get right to the sleeping portion of the evening. The room was furnished—as opposed to the last time he'd seen it, when it'd just had a mattress on the unfinished floor. Now there was oversize knotty pine furniture, complete with a king-size bed. It seemed hugely luxurious compared to what he was used to, and it hit him.

He really was back in the real world.

Physically, anyway. Mentally? Not yet. Not even close. He didn't even know if he could come back to his world and not be ready to protect and serve twenty-four/seven. Not be hard and cold and willing to do whatever it took…

Be normal.

With the wind continuing to batter the house, he stripped off his shirt and flicked on the small TV over the dresser.

No reception.

He pulled out his cell phone and searched for the weather, and discovered the reason. Apparently he'd walked into an unprecedented storm, with even heavier rain and wind expected. For an extra bonus, flash-floods warnings were in effect.

Wasn't that special. He hadn't dealt with a flood since six weeks ago, in the Midwest, where his unit had been called in to assist with SAR.

He and Matt had both gone in, but only Jason had come out.

Yeah. This was going to be a kick.

He headed straight for the bed and felt some of the tension leave him in anticipation of sleep. With a long sigh, he stripped out of his pants, then stretched out on the mattress with only his boxer briefs and dark thoughts.

Tired and edgy, and feeling old for his twenty-nine years, he let himself relax, hoping like hell he was too far gone into exhaustion to dream. As he drifted off to the wild winds pummeling the house, his stomach growled, and he promised it that even if a naked woman appeared at his side right then and there, *food*—not sex—was next on the list.

JASON AWOKE with a jerk and leaped to his feet to run for his gear. When he realized he wasn't on the line but back at home, he lay down again and swiped a hand over his face as the rain and wind continued to batter the house around him.

He didn't like to admit that he wasn't decompressing fast enough, or that his hand was trembling, but he'd deal with both. Because that's what he did—deal with things. That was his claim to fame, his skill, his MO.

Letting out another long, careful breath, he took in his surroundings and realized it was nearly dawn.

Which meant he'd slept straight through the night.

And then he realized something else. He'd been awoken by an assortment of brain-racking noises. The crazy wind. The steady drum of rain pounding on the roof and the windows.

Adding to the racket was the ringing of a phone, and then the click of a message machine.

"You know what to do at the beep," came Dustin's recorded voice from somewhere nearby.

And then a soft, female voice, crackling through static and hard to hear. "Dustin? Dustin, are you there?"

The male in Jason, the one who hadn't been with a woman in so long, took in the pretty voice and thought, *Go, Dustin,* but even through the incredibly bad connection, he recognized that she wasn't trying to be seductive and fun. No, she was filled with nerves. Something within Jason automatically reacted to that, the same something that had put him in the military in the first place, the thing that made it impossible for him to walk away from a fight or someone in trouble, and he lifted his head, searching the still dark room for the phone.

There wasn't one, not in here.

"I think I need help," she went on as Jason ran out of the bedroom to find the phone, wondering if she was Cristina, Dustin's fiancé. With the horrible connection, there was no way to tell for sure, but he doubted it. The Cristina he knew didn't ask for help.

He finally narrowed in on a blinking red light on the nightstand in Dustin's bedroom, and knew he'd found the machine. He reached for the phone connected to it, but the receiver wasn't in its cradle. *"Shit."*

"Dustin?" she said again, her voice breaking up with static.

Jason could hear the storm ravaging in the background, both through the phone and the windows, coming in with unexpected surround sound.

"I know you're not scheduled to work this weekend," she went on, "so I'm really hoping you're there."

"Hang on," Jason told the machine and slapped on the light, squinting into the sudden brightness as he searched for the on-the-loose phone. *Gotcha*, he thought triumphantly, eyeing the cordless handset lying on a dresser. He hit the talk button with his thumb and…nothing.

The battery was dead.

"Don't hang up," he yelled at the machine as if she could hear him, and once again went running, slamming his shoulder into the doorway. "Goddammit." In the living room, he looked around in the wan light for another phone.

There. On the small table beside the couch. Lunging for it, he barked *"Hello!"* into the receiver, just in time to hear the click.

He'd lost her.

He was getting good at that, losing people—and yeah, there it was, right on cue, the helplessness surging up into his chest, making it impossible to breathe without pain.

He rounded back toward the bedroom, holding his aching shoulder, going for his cell phone. Seemed he was on a mission after all—to first find Dustin and then, through him, hopefully the woman with the worry in her voice, the woman who needed help.

© Jill Shalvis 2009

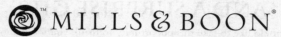

2 FREE BOOKS
AND A SURPRISE GIFT

We would like to take this opportunity to thank you for reading this Mills & Boon® book by offering you the chance to take TWO more specially selected titles from the Blaze® series absolutely FREE! We're also making this offer to introduce you to the benefits of the Mills & Boon® Book Club™—

- **FREE home delivery**
- **FREE gifts and competitions**
- **FREE monthly Newsletter**
- **Exclusive Mills & Boon Book Club offers**
- **Books available before they're in the shops**

Accepting these FREE books and gift places you under no obligation to buy, you may cancel at any time, even after receiving your free books. Simply complete your details below and return the entire page to the address below. You don't even need a stamp!

YES Please send me 2 free Blaze books and a surprise gift. I understand that unless you hear from me, I will receive 3 superb new books every month, including a 2-in-1 book priced at £4.99 and two single books priced at £3.19 each, postage and packing free. I am under no obligation to purchase any books and may cancel my subscription at any time. The free books and gift will be mine to keep in any case.

Ms/Mrs/Miss/Mr_____ Initials _____

Surname _____
Address _____

_____ Postcode _____
E-mail _____

Send this whole page to: Mills & Boon Book Club, Free Book Offer, FREEPOST NAT 10298, Richmond, TW9 1BR